Alex Gray was born and educated in Glasgow. She is the co-founder of the Bloody Scotland international crime writing festival, has been awarded the Scottish Association of Writers' Constable and Pitlochry trophies for her crime writing and is the Scottish Chapter convenor for the Crime Writers' Association. Married with a son and daughter, she writes full time.

Find out more at www.alex-gray.com.

ALSO BY ALEX GRAY

THE BIRD THAT DID NOT SING

Alex Gray

SPHERE

First published in Great Britain in 2014 by Sphere

Copyright © Alex Gray 2014

The moral right of the author has been asserted.

*All characters and events in this publication, other than those
clearly in the public domain, are fictitious and any resemblance
to real persons, living or dead, is purely coincidental.*

A CIP catalogue record for this book
is available from the British Library.

Hardback ISBN 978-1-84744-568-1
Trade Paperback ISBN 978-1-84744-567-4

Typeset in Caslon by M Rules
Printed and bound in Great Britain by
Clays Ltd, St Ives plc

Papers used by Sphere are from well-managed forests
and other responsible sources.

MIX
Paper from
responsible sources
FSC® C104740

This book is dedicated to Ann and Les, with my love.

This is the bird that never flew
This is the tree that never grew
This is the bell that never rang
This is the fish that never swam

Legend of the Glasgow coat of arms

AUTHOR'S NOTE

The *sgian dubh* (Gaelic for 'black dagger') is a sharp knife about six inches in length. Traditionally worn in the right kilt sock with the handle showing, it was once a blade concealed in the armpit out of sight of any potential enemy. The hilt was often embellished with a rare jewel, a practical means of carrying wealth secreted in a Highlander's apparel. The black (*dubh*) referred to the black bog oak from which the handle was usually made, as well as the blackness of evil intent.

Nowadays it is worn as part of a full Highland dress, often at Burns suppers, where it is used to cut open the traditional haggis.

Although the setting of this book is the Commonwealth Games, all the characters and events connected to them are fictional.

CHAPTER ONE

August 2013

The early-morning sun filtered through tall pine trees, warming patches of grass that were still green and lush, encouraging some rabbits to come out and feed. Cobwebs sparkled against the dark green bushes, momentarily transformed as their dewdrops were caught in rays of sunlight. Somewhere, hidden beneath the protective shrubbery, a moulting blackbird whistled quietly. It was not yet time to emerge; flight feathers were still to grow back and the bird sensed that it was easy meat for any predators wheeling high above the treetops.

Outside the perimeters of this wood the ground sloped away to a valley full of long tawny grasses and creamy meadowsweet, its scent wafting upwards as the night's dampness evaporated in a faint swirl of mist. A path that was regularly tramped by backpackers to test their stamina against the rigours of the West Highland Way wound around the edge of the field, disappearing into the darkening depths of the forest. But there was no human presence to be seen, no solitary figure beginning a hopeful route that would end in the Scottish Highlands.

As the sun rose higher, a trio of buzzards flew above the pines, catching the thermals, their mews faint in the still cold air. The rabbits beneath the trees cropped and hopped, heads down, ears twitching as clouds of midges began to dance against beams of light slanting between the trees. And, as though a clarion call to this new August morning was necessary, a robin opened his throat and trilled, a joyous song that resounded through the woodlands.

There was nothing to signify imminent disaster, no sudden silence presaging a momentous event.

The earth shook with a boom as the bomb exploded, splitting tree trunks and throwing every living creature skywards, a malevolent cloud billowing above the wood, casting debris hundreds of yards away.

The noise of the explosion was over in seconds, but the damage would last for decades. Fallen trees lay in shattered heaps, their pale flesh ripped open and exposed, while flames licked hungrily at any dry patches of foliage.

And tossed aside, its tiny beak still open, the robin lay motionless on the narrow pathway, all but one of its fires extinguished for ever.

CHAPTER TWO

Detective Superintendent William Lorimer woke with a start. For a few moments he was uncertain where he was: shouldn't the light be coming from the window beyond the foot of their bed? Realisation crept in as he blinked away the last dregs of sleep, turning his head to see the sun streaming in through the big window to his left: he was home again, back in Glasgow. The clock on Maggie's bedside table registered six thirty. This time tomorrow he would be back at work, preparing for the first meeting of the day, but for now he could bask in the knowledge that it was Sunday morning and the day was theirs to spend as they liked.

Lorimer slipped his hand on to the empty space beside him. It was still warm. No doubt Maggie had gone downstairs to feed Chancer, their ginger tomcat, and would return to snuggle in beside him soon. Closing his eyes again, he yawned, stretched, then turned on to his side, feeling the ache in his legs from that last climb up Ben Mhor.

It wasn't hard in this half-awake, half-asleep state to conjure up the memories of these last two weeks in Mull. They had sat often enough outside the cottage door on the old moss-covered bench, mugs of coffee clutched in their hands, staring out across Fishnish

Bay and the Sound of Mull to the mainland hills of Loch Aline, the scent of bog myrtle filling the air. A patch of brightness seemed to shine on those distant hills: shadows chasing sunlight, or a freshly cut wheat field glowing under the August skies. They'd watched countless yachts scudding up the Sound, racing towards the port of Tobermory, colourful spinnakers ballooning, catching the wind to speed them on their way.

Most days they had seen the buzzards, heard them mewing overhead, and Lorimer had listened to the melodies from the smaller birds, training his high-definition binoculars on the least little movement, too often foiled by the plentiful foliage. Reed warblers were there, he knew, and willow warblers too, but telling them apart took an expert eye. And of course there had been the sea eagles, Mull's celebrated birds of prey, that attracted twitchers and bird lovers from all parts of the world. They had been on their way to Calgary Bay when one had soared, skimming the treetops, causing them to stop the car and get out as quickly as they could to watch it. No need for binoculars that day; the huge bird was flying so low that Lorimer had felt he could almost reach out and touch it, the awesome silence so complete that he imagined the whispering wind ruffling its tail feathers.

'Cup of tea?'

Maggie was standing there by the bed, a tray in her hands with two mugs.

Lorimer sat up slowly. 'Thanks. Almost asleep again,' he murmured apologetically, reaching out for the tea and already regretting the wakefulness that dispelled his vision of green hills and quiet sandy bays where the blue waters stretched as far as the eye could see.

'Any thoughts on what you'd like to do today?' he asked as Maggie slid in beside him.

'Well I've just stuck on a load of washing and we'll need to get a pile of groceries, but that shouldn't take all day. What had you in mind?'

Lorimer opened his mouth to reply, but the peremptory ring of the telephone made him close it again in a thin line of disappointment as he reached for the handset at his side of the bed. Behind his back he heard Maggie's sigh of resignation. A phone call this early on a Sunday morning meant only one thing: chances were she'd be grocery shopping alone.

Anyone watching the detective superintendent at that moment would have seen the expression in his blue eyes harden, the knuckles clutching the handset whiten as he listened to the voice on the other end of the line.

'Why me?' he said at last, then stifled a sigh and nodded as the answer came.

'Right.' He rose from his sitting position on the edge of the bed, listened some more, nodding again before clicking the off button.

'No time for breakfast?' Maggie's voice held just a hint of wistfulness tempered by long years of being left alone at home while he rushed to the scene of some crime or other. 'What is it this time? A sudden death?'

Lorimer looked at her and opened his mouth as if to reveal the substance of the short conversation that had just taken place, then closed it again.

'Need to get a move on. Don't know when I'll be in.'

Maggie followed him with her eyes as he dressed hurriedly, pulling fresh linen from the chest of drawers and a clean shirt from his side of the wardrobe. This was something else she was used to: not being told what was going on, especially at the start of a new case. Later, perhaps much later when they were in bed once more, he might tell her what had happened. Or not. The details of his work could be guaranteed to rob sleep from the most innocent of minds, and Maggie also knew better than to ask idle questions.

In less than five minutes he was washed, dressed, out the door and heading towards the Lexus, a bottle of water clutched in his hand, leaving Maggie Lorimer to contemplate the day ahead.

The journey to Drymen was punctuated by several vain attempts to clear the fly-strewn windscreen, the wipers' blades leaving smears across Lorimer's vision. There were two options on the route to take: he could either drive straight down the Boulevard and through Balloch, or cut off at Clydebank and head past Milngavie, taking the twisting road across the moors. As the round-about approached, Lorimer turned the big car to face the uphill slope to Hardgate village. It would be the slower option, but, he reminded himself, this was still supposed to be his holiday, so he might as well enjoy the drive. Had it not been for the thought of what awaited him, it might have been a perfect morning.

As he left the city behind, Lorimer noticed the sheep grazing on the flanks of the hillsides. The lambs were bigger now, their mothers trimmer creatures since the annual shearing. For a moment he recalled the sound of hundreds of animals baaing, and the shepherd's high-pitched whistle as the sheepdogs rounded them up on the hillside above the cottage in Mull, white bodies running, running, running towards Corry Farm, where the sheep pens and the shearers awaited them.

When the car approached a distinctive stand of tall conifers, their graceful fronds arranged in scalloped skirts of green, Lorimer lifted his head in expectation. Queen's View, it was called, and as he turned the corner, the rolling landscape emerged in all its regal splendour. To his left, Stockiemuir was purple with heather, the bracken changing to the colour of a grouse's wing; ahead, the mountains peaked against a sky of perfect blue, stirring the desire to climb them once again. *One day soon*, he promised himself, nodding to the bens on his right as the car took the twisting slope through the glens and down towards the wooded dells below.

Even The Cobbler could be seen in the clear air, its anvil peak emerging for an instant between trees and hills as he drove on. It was on mornings like this that he asked himself just what he was doing. Why did he spend his life rushing to the aftermath of someone else's destruction? On such a morning he should be toting a rucksack and heading for one of the Munros that were still beckoning to be discovered, not speeding along at the beck and call of his paymasters. But a different sense of duty had been instilled into him long since, and Detective Superintendent Lorimer could only breathe a light sigh of regret as he passed the entrance to the village of Drymen and headed towards the scene of crime.

It was worse than he could ever have imagined.

Even from the roadside, where a line of police cars was parked, Lorimer could see the devastation. Plumes of smoke and flames still rose from the heaps of broken trees, and as he emerged from the Lexus, his skin was immediately touched by flakes of ash drifting in the air. The smell of burning wood was overpowering, and he could hear the occasional crackle and hiss of fire beneath the whooshing sound from the firemen's hoses as arcs of water were trained into the heart of the inferno. His eyes took in the gap in the hedge where the fire engines had broken through to reach the narrow walkers' path, and the tyre marks on the verge. It would be replanted, no doubt, but the burning trees would leave a scar that would take far longer to heal.

'Detective Superintendent Lorimer? Martin Pinder.' The

uniformed chief inspector was suddenly at his side, hand out-stretched. Lorimer took it, feeling the firm once up and down as the officer motioned them to turn away from the direction of the cinders. 'Sorry to call you out, but as I said, we needed someone to front this. And your name came up.'

'But isn't this a local matter?' Lorimer asked. 'We're in the district of Stirling, surely?'

Pinder shook his head. 'It's bigger than you might imagine,' he began. Walking Lorimer a few paces away from the line of cars, he dropped his voice. 'And there is intelligence to suggest that it may have a much wider remit.'

'Oh?' Lorimer was suddenly curious. The telephone call had mentioned an explosion, the immediate need for a senior officer from Police Scotland and a request to keep the lid on things, but nothing more.

'You said *intelligence*.' He frowned. 'You mean Special Branch?'

Pinder nodded. 'I've been charged with giving you this information, sir. And doubtless your counter terrorism unit will already be involved.' He licked his lips, hesitating, and Lorimer could see the anxiety in the man's grey eyes.

'We are given to believe that this is just a trial run.' Pinder motioned to the fire behind them.

'A trial run,' Lorimer said slowly. 'A trial run for what?'

Pinder gave a sigh and raised his eyebrows.

'The Glasgow Commonwealth Games.'

Lorimer looked at the man in disbelief, but Pinder's face was all seriousness.

'That's almost a year away. Why do they think . . . ?'

'Haven't been told that. Someone further up the chain of command will know.' Pinder shrugged. 'Perhaps you'll be told once you liaise with Counter Terrorism.'

Lorimer turned to take in the scene of the explosion once more, seeing for the first time the enormous area of burning countryside and trying to transfer it in his mind's eye to the newly built village and arenas in Glasgow's East End. He blinked suddenly at the very notion of carnage on such a vast scale.

'We can't let it happen,' Pinder said quietly, watching the tall man's face.

Lorimer gazed across the fields to the line of rounded hills that were the Campsies. Glasgow lay beyond, snug in the Clyde valley; on this Sunday morning its citizens remained oblivious to the danger posed by whatever fanatic had ruined this bit of tranquil landscape. He had asked why the local cops hadn't taken this one on, and now he understood: the threat to next year's Commonwealth Games was something too big for that. And since the various police forces in Scotland had merged into one national force, Detective Superintendent William Lorimer might be called to any part of the country.

'The press will want statements,' Pinder said, breaking into Lorimer's thoughts. 'It's still an ongoing investigation. Don't we just love that phrase!' He gave a short, hard laugh. 'And there is no loss of life, so we can try for a positive slant on that, at least.'

'They'll speculate,' Lorimer told him. 'You know that's what they do.'

Pinder touched the detective superintendent's arm, nodding towards the figures milling around on the fringes of the fire. 'Apart from you and me, there is not a single person here who has been told about the background to this event. So unless the press leap to that conclusion by dint of their own imagination, any leak can only come from us.'

When Lorimer turned to face him, the uniformed officer was struck by the taller man's penetrating blue gaze. For a long moment they stared at one another, until Pinder looked away, feeling a sense of discomfort mixed with the certainty that he would follow this man wherever he might lead.

Wouldn't like to be across the table from him in an interview room, he was to tell his wife later that day. But there on that lonely stretch of country road, Martin Pinder had an inkling why it was that the powers on high had called on Detective Superintendent William Lorimer to oversee this particular incident.

He was no stranger to the big hall in Pitt Street, once Strathclyde Police Headquarters; it was the place he had briefly hung his hat when heading up the former Serious Crime Squad. Nor was he unused to sitting at this very table, peering down at the crowd of newspaper reporters thronging the hall. It was scarcely midday, and yet here they all were, eager for a statement from the man whose face had often graced their broadsheets as they reported on the various crimes to blot their fair city.

The statement had been prepared by himself and Martin Pinder, sitting in the Lexus at the scene of the explosion. To minimise the incident would give rise to the notion that something was being hidden, and that was a path they didn't want any inquisitive journalist to go down. On the other hand, seeing a senior officer like Lorimer might rouse their curiosity further. In the end, they had decided to express outrage at the idiocy of whoever had planted the bomb and emphasise the sheer luck that nobody had been hurt.

'Ladies and gentlemen,' Lorimer began, pausing as the babble of voices hushed and every pair of eyes turned towards him. 'This morning around five a.m. there was a large explosion in a wood close to the village of Drymen. Firefighters were immediately called to the scene and have extinguished the ensuing blaze.'

He looked up, scanning the upturned faces, wondering at the thoughts buzzing inside their heads. 'We are grateful that, despite the proximity to the West Highland Way, there was no loss of life, but it is with regret that I have to announce that this section of the famous walk has been closed until the damage to the woodland has been cleared. There is an ongoing inquiry into the exact nature of the explosion, but at present we are working on the assumption that it was caused by some sort of home-made device.'

He stopped for a moment to let the murmuring break out. *Plant the idea of daft wee laddies messing about in the woods*, Pinder had suggested. *A prank that went wrong.* Lorimer had raised his eyebrows at that, but so far it seemed to be working.

'The main road should be accessible later today and diversion signs have been put in place until then. If you have been listening, you will know that the radio stations are issuing regular bulletins to that effect,' Lorimer told them, managing a smile.

He folded his hands and nodded, the signal for a forest of hands to be raised.

'Any sign that it's terrorist activity?'

Right off, the question he had expected.

Lorimer's smile broadened. 'It has all the hallmarks of a home-made bomb,' he reiterated. 'Something that anyone could get off the internet.'

'You think it was done by kids?' someone else demanded.

'There were no witnesses to whoever planted the explosive device,' Lorimer said, adopting a bored tone, as though he had explained this several times already. 'So we cannot rule out any particular age group.'

'But it might have been?' the same voice persisted.

'It would be entirely wrong for me to point a finger at the young people in the community,' Lorimer said blandly, knowing full well that they were scribbling down that very thing as he uttered the words, and mentally apologising to any computer-geeky schoolboys in Drymen.

'How much damage has been done?' one female reporter wanted to know. Lorimer told them, giving as many statistics as would satisfy a readership hungry for facts.

What he did not tell them was the way the clouds of ash had settled on his hair, the whiff of burning birds and animals discernible through the acrid smell carried on the morning breeze. Nor did he describe the scar on the hillside, a mass of blackened tree trunks instead of the once graceful outline of pines fringing pale skies to the west. And there was certainly no mention of any further threat to the good citizens of Stirlingshire or their near neighbours in the city of Glasgow.

CHAPTER THREE

The letter, when it came, had the typewritten address of the Stewart Street police office rather than his home on the south side of Glasgow. Lorimer picked up the long, bulky envelope, curious about the handwritten word *Personal* on the top left-hand corner. He tore it open with the sharp metal letter-opener given to him by an ex-SAS soldier turned crime writer, its twisted shaft crafted in the man's own workshop. Lorimer's face expressed resignation at what was probably just another missive full of political invective against the police in general: it was one of the several things that a detective superintendent with his public profile had to endure. But the envelope's thickness both intrigued him and made him cautious as he felt along its length for any device that it might contain.

The letterhead bore a familiar crest and Lorimer smiled to himself as he skimmed the covering letter, immediately banishing any suspicious thoughts. There were several pages, not clipped together, giving details of the other invitees, the hotel and a route map to get there, probably shoved into every invitation regardless of the recipient's proximity to the venue. Sitting back in his chair, Lorimer read the letter again. A school reunion. To take place next spring. Would he like to attend? The policeman's first instinct was to bin the whole lot. As if he'd have the time for something as inane as that! But as he continued to read to the end, a small frown appeared between his blue eyes.

Vivien Gilmartin. The surname was unfamiliar, but Vivien . . . ? Could it be the same person he had known all those years ago? Turning to the pages of names, Lorimer's eyes scanned the list. There it was, Vivien Gilmartin, née Fox!

For a moment he let the papers slip on to the desk, his eyes seeing beyond the four walls of the Stewart Street office to a place and time that seemed to rush back at him with an intensity that took his breath away.

Vivien. *Foxy*, they'd called her, not only because of the obvious surname but for her mass of glorious red hair.

He'd slipped his teenage fingers through those tresses in his first fumbling attempts at sex, believing himself to be in love. And tall, lanky William Lorimer and his red-haired girl had listened over and over to the words of cheesy pop songs and his mother's ancient collection of vinyl as though they had been penned just for them.

It had been the summer before his final year at Glenwood High school, a time of waiting for exam results, walking through the park on hot dusty days, dreaming about the future. He was going to become a famous art historian. Travel the world, maybe. Vivien would be somewhere in his plans, a vague figure but one he was sure of back then, in that idyllic time of carefree youth when everything was possible.

Her own plans had involved the theatre. That was something he could not fail to recall. And when she told him that RADA had accepted her and she was leaving Glasgow for faraway London, he had felt nothing short of betrayal. How could she abandon him? Why not take up the offer of a place at the Royal

14

Scottish Academy of Music and Drama, as it was then known? He was destined for Glasgow University; they could be together!

Alone in his bedroom he had indulged his sorrows in the words of an Incredible String Band song, wallowing in its poignancy. At the time it had seemed so apt. Now, many years on, he hardly remembered the lyrics; something about first love, *young love*: wasn't that right? What came after that? He had forgotten much of the rest except the lines referring to a girl's long red hair that had fallen on to the boy's face during their first kiss. Was that a real memory?

The telephone ringing on his desk brought Lorimer back to the present, and as he picked up the handset, the contents of the letter were pushed to one side.

Moments later he hung up again with a sigh. This was the day when the new alarm system was to be installed, and the engineer would require access to his office in half an hour. Minimum disruption, they'd all been told, but he doubted that. Still, the security of Police Scotland had to be maintained and upgraded to meet these new national standards.

Lorimer looked again at the papers lying on his desk, memories of the people he used to know swirling in his brain. He'd never kept up with the old gang, eschewing Friends Reunited and Facebook, preferring the caution of anonymity given his chosen profession. And now, as if the years had been peeled away, he had this burning curiosity to know what had become of them. *What has become of Foxy?* a little voice teased him.

It had all been so long ago, that summer he wanted to forget and the terrible months that had followed. He'd been in the art studio in late September when the head teacher had drawn him into the upstairs corridor with the news about his mother's death. A brain aneurysm, something sudden and unforeseen.

15

As the son of aged parents, Lorimer had never known his mother as a quick and graceful woman, the person so many of her friends had described at Helen Lorimer's funeral. Dad had died when he was just a wee lad, the sixty-a-day habit ruining his lungs, cutting off his life far too early, leaving his teacher wife to struggle on as best she could. And so, at eighteen, the tall young man who would become a detective in the city of Glasgow had grown up fast, leaving behind all his dreams, which included a red-haired girl and their cosmopolitan future together.

There was a slip at the foot of the page for current home address and dietary requirements, plus a box to tick if he decided to go to the reunion. It was the work of a minute to fill it in and stuff it into the ready-stamped envelope addressed to Mrs Vivien Gilmartin. For a moment he paused, the return letter in his hand. Then, with a careless flick, he sent it spinning to his out-tray, turning his attention to the report on the Drymen explosion.

He would likely hear nothing more about the bombing incident after today. Once the report was sent to Special Branch, his part in the sorry affair was over. And there were plenty of other crimes in this city to capture his attention, Lorimer told himself, tapping out the words on his keyboard.

Life would continue as before, the threat of a mad bomber something to be filed away under August 2013. The detective superintendent felt no undue premonition of disaster, neither to his city nor to himself.

What William Lorimer could not know on that August morning was that several malignant forces were already at work, insidiously preparing to wreak havoc in the very fabric of his life.

CHAPTER FOUR

Peter Alexander MacGregor scrolled down the page to read the final instructions. Everything seemed to be accounted for: the fares were paid, the passports up to date, accommodation taken care of. All he had to do was remember to get Joanne to pack his kilt carefully in layers of tissue paper and they would be off. He sat back, suddenly feeling every one of his sixty-eight years. Too much working in the garden yesterday, he told himself, knuckles kneading the base of his spine; he'd been overzealous clearing the winter debris from the paths after the gale that had swept up the coast. Peter heaved a sigh, looking round the old wood-panelled study. He'd be glad when the winter was over and he could sit in the garden enjoying a fine spring day, listening to the bell birds annoying his chooks. From the window he could see the wind blowing leaves high into the air, hear the rain rattling against the pane, a loud reminder that their Antipodean winter was reluctant to let go. He sighed again and closed his eyes, trying to imagine what it might be like in Scotland right now. It was seven p.m. here in Melbourne, so it was still early in the morning back there. And still summertime.

The trip was months away, but even now Peter felt a frisson of excitement at the thought of travelling through the old country.

To attend the MacGregor Gathering was one of his life's ambitions, but to do so in a year when the Scottish government was having a Homecoming, the city of Stirling celebrated seven hundred years since Bannockburn and Glasgow was hosting the Commonwealth Games . . . well, it all seemed too good to be true. He sat forward and blinked at the screen again, then scrolled back up, anxious not to have missed any small detail before he finalised the whole thing. That they had never met his host shouldn't matter; the man was another MacGregor after all, and the Scots were famous for their hospitality.

As his finger hovered above the send button that would signal his acceptance, Peter MacGregor felt a sudden sense of unease. What if something went wrong? What if either he or Joanne fell ill during the months away? What if his neighbour forgot to water the plants?

'Cup of coffee, darling?' Joanne was at his shoulder, smiling down on the page, her face lighting up when she saw what he was about to do.

He couldn't disappoint her, wouldn't wipe away that expression of delight for anything.

'Sure thing. Just be a minute.'

And as his finger pressed the send button, that small action sealed a fate that neither of them could possibly have imagined.

CHAPTER FIVE

April 2014

'"April is the cruellest month, breeding lilacs out of the dead land",' Maggie quoted. 'Why does T. S. Eliot say it is the cruellest month?' she asked the class of fourteen Sixth Years, who were all looking at her intently.

One hand shot up and Maggie struggled to hide a smile. Imogen Spinks reminded her so much of Hermione, the swotty character from *Harry Potter*, even down to the mass of mousy curls cascading down her back.

'Anyone?' Maggie offered, giving the rest of them time to answer.

'Yes, Imogen,' she said at last, to a quiet undertone of groans from some of the others. She swept a cross look at the class, as if to say *you had your chance too*.

'He thinks that the growth of lilacs is an irony after the carnage and death of the Great War,' Imogen said. 'Ironic things can be cruel,' the girl added thoughtfully.

'What is it with him and lilacs?' Jeremy Graham's grumble issued from the back of the classroom, making the other students turn round.

'How d'you mean?' Sarah Gillespie asked, flicking the black hair out of her heavily mascaraed eyes.

'Well he's always on about lilacs, isn't he? That wumman who had lilacs in her room, twisting them in her fingers?'

'Bet that made a right mess on the carpet,' Janice Gallagher suggested, provoking some mild laughter from the girls.

'Our lilac tree isn't usually out till May,' Kenny McAlpine said. 'So he's got that wrong, hasn't he?'

'The south of England is at least six weeks ahead of us,' Imogen said pointedly, giving the boy a withering look. 'And to suggest that anything Eliot wrote was wrong shows just how little you know about him!'

Maggie hushed the protests that followed the girl's remark. Imogen, who was the first of Maggie Lorimer's pupils to have been accepted for the University of Cambridge, could be a real pain in the neck, but she was very well read and certainly knew her stuff. *Just like Hermione*, a small voice teased, forcing the teacher to smile even as she tried to bring the lesson back to order.

'Eliot was an extremely well-educated man,' Maggie agreed. '*Erudite*, one might say.'

'Do we write that one down?' Sarah asked. 'And look it up?'

Maggie nodded, but already the pupils (with the exception of the already erudite Imogen) were consulting dictionaries and writing down the definition. It might be old-fashioned, but she had schooled them all to look up words they had never used before and write them in a notebook, insisting that a wider vocabulary was a huge asset to them all. It had taken a while since the beginning of the academic year, but now finding dictionary definitions and using new words had become second nature to them. And from the eager way they pored over the dictionaries, Maggie knew they actually enjoyed it.

Jeremy's hand was up first and the boy did not wait for Maggie to acknowledge him.

'"Having or showing knowledge or learning",' he quoted.

'Sounds like Imogen,' someone said, and sniggered. 'Specially the *showing* bit.'

Imogen's face reddened as Maggie glared at the giggling girls. That might be true, but there was no need to embarrass her in front of the class.

'Right, let's see how much knowledge and learning you lot are capable of,' she said. 'I want to be certain that you have all studied *The Wasteland* thoroughly by next term. I've set an exam question for you to work on over the holidays, so that's why we've spent time discussing this poem in class. Okay?'

Nods and sighs from the pupils were drowned out by the sharp drilling of the period bell, and Maggie watched as these fourteen young men and women shoved books and files back into their bags, rising to leave for their next class.

Imogen was the last to leave and she turned to speak to her English teacher.

'It doesn't bother me, you know,' she said. 'Once I'm at university, I probably won't see any of them ever again.' Then, with a rare smile that made the girl almost pretty, she shrugged and walked out of Maggie's classroom, closing the door behind her.

'Ah, the confidence of youth!' Maggie said quietly to herself. 'Best of luck when you get to Cambridge, Imogen.'

There was one period to go before the final bell of the day, which would signal the end of term, and Maggie had no class on her timetable. She had the option of packing up and leaving her classroom now, something that the head teacher had said was reasonable given the amount of work the staff took home anyway. But she would be spending long enough alone this evening as it was. Tonight was the night that Bill was going to this school reunion, something he had been a bit quiet about. Maggie guessed he wasn't really looking forward to seeing what had happened to mates from more than twenty years ago. She would sit here until school was over for the afternoon and wait for the car park to clear before heading off across the city. The evenings were so much lighter now and it was a pleasure being able to sit by the kitchen window and watch the birds feeding in their garden, Chancer the cat safely tucked on her lap.

Maggie drew the small blue poetry book towards her and opened its well-thumbed pages. *April is the cruellest month*, she read again. Then, looking out of the classroom window as a seagull soared past, she recalled what Imogen Spinks had said: *ironic things can be cruel.* Maggie shivered suddenly. She was married to a man whose life revolved around crimes where cruelties often occurred. But somehow she doubted he would ever voice such a thing at tonight's school reunion.

There were lilac trees blossoming in the gardens of the small market town that the lorry rattled through on its way back to the motorway. The stop outside this village, far from the prying eyes of any CCTV cameras, had been necessary, but the driver was glad to be back on the road again, his cargo safely stowed.

Don't think of them as human beings, the big man had scoffed. *See them in terms of the wad of cash you get every time you bring them in.* And he had tried to, he really had, thought Gerry. But the look in the young woman's eyes as he had bundled her back into that stifling narrow space had given him pause. It had been a look that had reminded him that she was more than mere cargo to be collected from the docks and delivered up to Scotland.

Gerry remembered the banging behind his cab, a faint sound

soon drowned out by the noise of the lorry's engine. He'd warned the girl during the toilet stop, taken her arm and clutched it so tightly that she had yelped in pain. He hadn't wanted to touch her, let alone hurt her, but the risk of discovery was too great a threat and so his fingers had left pale marks as he had released her black skin from his grasp. Then, that look. Those great solemn eyes had regarded him with an expression of utter fearfulness; no woman had ever looked at Gerry Collins like that before. He would be glad when the long journey north was over and he had delivered her to the big man.

The roof of the lorry brushed the trees overhanging the street, scattering the sweet-scented blossoms on to the pavement to be trodden underfoot or blown away in the chill April wind.

CHAPTER SIX

Everything was so much smaller than William Lorimer had remembered; even the playground where he had kicked a ball around every day with his mates seemed cramped, though perhaps that was due in part to the flat-roofed single-storey structure hemming in the space, a sorry-looking building that was clearly meant as temporary accommodation for the growing numbers of students. How many boots had kicked the wooden strip around that classroom door? Lorimer thought, looking at the patches of bare concrete exposed below the torn and battered fascia.

For a moment the tall detective hesitated, wondering if even now it wasn't too late to change his mind. Would it really matter if he turned back and left an empty place at the dining room table?

'My God! Big Bill Lorimer! How're you doing, pal?'

Lorimer blinked as the voice behind him became the figure of a short, thickset man whose suntanned face was beaming up at him. Someone who knew him, recognised him, and from whose expression it was evident that some recognition should be returned.

'It's me,' the man said. 'Stuart Clark! Don't tell me I've changed that much, big man?'

Lorimer took the outstretched hand, grasping it firmly, the

years falling away as his old school friend's face became familiar once more.

'Stu! Good grief! Hardly recognised you! Where have you been all this time?'

They fell into step and approached the main door together as Stuart's wide smile brought back memories of the class joker who had been everybody's mate.

'Emigrated after my first marriage broke up. Out in Brisbane now. Got my own business and doing quite well.' Stu grinned, his teeth white against the tanned skin. 'How about you?'

'Did you come back just for the reunion?' Lorimer replied, sidestepping the question.

'Yes and no.' Stuart's smile faded a little. 'Needed to see my daughter. We keep in touch fairly regularly but I only get over here once a year so thought I'd kill two birds with one stone.'

'Looks like we're being herded into the main hall first,' Lorimer said, pointing to an arrow beneath the printed sign CLASS REUNION as they stood outside what had once been the school office.

'Hey! Is that Stu Clark! My God! Long time no see, how are you?'

Both men turned at once.

'Eddie? Eddie Miller? Good Lord, you havenae changed a bit, not like some of us!' Stuart joked, patting his own ample stomach.

Lorimer shook hands with the new arrival and gave a perfunctory smile. If Eddie Miller hadn't changed much, then perhaps it was down to his athletic prowess. Miller the Miler, they used to call him, Lorimer recalled. The lean man who stood regarding them both quizzically had the look of someone who was uncomfortable wearing a shirt and tie, and Lorimer guessed that his normal garb was still some form of tracksuit.

25

'Let me guess,' Stuart said at once. 'You're a PE teacher.'

'Right first time,' Eddie murmured, though he looked less than happy to admit to the fact. 'I work here as a matter of fact,' he added reluctantly.

'No getting out of tonight's celebrations then, eh?' Stuart nudged the man with his elbow and laughed again.

They had reached a short flight of stairs at the end of a corridor, and as the three men approached an archway that led to the main school hall, the noise of raised voices told them that most of their fellow classmates had already arrived.

'Crikey, bit of a crowd! Didn't think that many would turn up!' Stuart exclaimed, rubbing his hands together as though ready and eager to join the fray. Below them in the centre of the hall several circular tables were set out for dinner, flanked by two long refectory-style tables laden with drinks, the laughter and loud voices suggesting that many old friends were already reuniting over a bottle or two.

'It's the whole year group,' Eddie explained. 'Not just our class. I'll leave you for a minute if you don't mind,' he apologised. 'Need to help behind the scenes.' He nodded at them and headed towards the far end of the hall. Lorimer's eyes followed him until he reached a red-haired woman holding a clipboard.

As Eddie spoke to her, she turned to look straight at them and Lorimer felt a strange sort of tug somewhere in his chest.

'Look who it is!' Stuart grinned, digging Lorimer in the ribs. 'Your old flame, Foxy Lady.' He looked up at him as if trying to gauge a reaction, but the years of maintaining a bland countenance in the interview room allowed the detective superintendent to conceal the turmoil of his feelings.

Instead he merely nodded and then turned to a board beside them displaying the seating plan for the evening.

26

'Let's see where we are, eh? Maybe they've put us together?'

But as they peered at the A4 sheets of printed names, Stuart Clark gave a snort of disappointment.

'Goodness' sake! All in alphabetical order. You'd think they'd have more imagination than that!'

It was true, thought Lorimer as he found his own place at table two, the G–L group. But the Vivien Fox he remembered had never lacked an imaginative spark, and he saw to his amusement that her name was at the top of the same list.

The next few minutes passed in a blur of handshakes and cries of 'Lorimer!' as he entered the hall and mingled with several men and women who seemed pleased to see him after a space of more than twenty years. Then, drinks in hand, they were called to attention by the clinking of a knife against the rim of a glass and all eyes turned to see Eddie Miller standing behind a lectern at the front of the hall.

'Friends, former classmates, distinguished guests or otherwise...' A small ripple of polite laughter followed his deliberate pause.

'Welcome back to Glenwood High School, though in truth some of us have hardly left the old place!'

There was a slight murmur amongst a few of the crowd, and Lorimer noticed a woman raising her eyebrows in surprise at something her neighbour was telling her as they looked at Eddie.

'As you may know, I am now principal teacher of PE at Glenwood, and it gives me immense pleasure to co-host this reunion and to see so many of you here tonight.'

Lorimer watched as Eddie nodded towards the slim red-haired woman, who acknowledged his words with the tiniest tilt of her head.

The rest of the speech was lost to him as Lorimer gazed at her, taking in the trim figure and the familiar flame-coloured hair, shorter now than it had been back then but just as luxuriant. In profile Vivien Gilmartin was even more striking looking than she had been as a teenager; the years had added some gravitas to her face. And were there other changes? Weren't those cheekbones sharper? And the fingers clasping the stem of her glass: weren't they just a little thinner than the ones that had clasped his own as they'd strolled hand in hand through the summer meadows?

Eddie's speech ended with a ripple of applause, the signal for everyone to take their places at the tables as dinner was about to be served. There were handshakes and exchanges of feigned surprise as men and women caught sight of their place cards and began talking to their neighbours. As far as he could make out, there were more women than men present, but someone had gone to the bother of trying to slot the guests into the conventional *man, woman, man, woman* arrangement. For some reason Lorimer felt irked by this. Why not just let friends sit where they liked? After all, the whole point of the evening was to reunite people, wasn't it? Then, as he looked at the name on the place setting beside his own, he began to wonder.

From the whispers around him and the glances of the women, Lorimer knew that Vivien was coming towards their table before he actually turned to see her.

'So you came,' a husky voice whispered in his ear. 'I wondered if you would.'

Lorimer rose from his seat to greet her, an innate courtesy that his late father had always said marked a man out as a gentleman, but the woman whose skirts swished as she sat down on his left waved this away.

For a moment they looked at one another, appraising the changes that had made the boy into a man, the girl into a very lovely woman. That wicked smile he remembered was more subtle now, the merest hint of mischief in those green eyes. And there was no denying that time had given Vivien Fox a dignity in her forties that had been lacking in the impetuous teenager. What did she see in him? Lorimer wondered as they spread napkins across their knees and made small talk with the people on their other side. Did she see the lines around his eyes, the way that years of chasing criminals had given a more sombre cast to his countenance? There were quite a few of the men at adjacent tables whose heads were either shaved or thinning on top; he'd been luckier, he thought, running a hand through his thick dark hair as he glanced over the platinum-blonde coiffure of the woman on his right. He had seen from the place card that her name was Janice, but try as he might he simply could not remember any girl from his schooldays in this matronly lady.

'You're looking well,' Vivien said, suddenly turning to him, a glass held aloft. 'Cheers,' she murmured, offering the rim. 'To us,' she said, glancing at him.

As he touched the wine glass with his own, Lorimer knew that her whispered words were just for him.

'To old times,' he replied, momentarily confused by the warmth of her glance.

'And what did *you* do after you left school?' Janice asked loudly, her face turned up to Lorimer's.

'University for a bit,' he replied. 'Then I joined the police.'

'*I* knew that!' a woman opposite said triumphantly, her bosom swelling inside a too tight black dress. 'I've seen your picture in the papers. And you've been on the telly. *Crimewatch*, wasn't it?'

He forced a smile and nodded, wondering if this had been a mistake after all. He could barely remember these women's names, let alone their faces.

'Weren't you involved in that football club?' someone else asked. 'The one where that referee got shot?'

'That's right.'

'And that woman—'

'I think William is here to see old friends, not to be quizzed on his night off,' Vivien said smoothly. She had not raised her voice in the slightest, but it held the sort of tone that made other people sit up a littler straighter, take notice of her words. It was, in short, a voice that contained authority, and Lorimer began to wonder just how Vivien Fox had spent the last twenty years.

He breathed a silent sigh of relief as the conversation turned to the other men and women around the table, their polite exchanges supplying nuggets of information that could be shared later with absent spouses.

'And what about you?' he asked softly. 'Did you ever achieve that dream of becoming an actress?'

There was a sadness in her eyes as she smiled at him, the slightest shake of her head signifying that no, that dream remained unfulfilled.

'But why?' His brow furrowed. 'You were so focused on the whole thing back then . . .'

One shoulder was raised in a shrug, but the red-haired woman seemed disinclined to offer any sort of explanation.

The frown remained. She'd been so adamant that the life of the stage was for her. And she had been so talented, good enough to be accepted by RADA, for goodness' sake. The notion that Vivien had abandoned him needlessly made Lorimer feel like that disappointed boy once more. She should have achieved fame and fortune, a tiny voice insisted. Hadn't she made a sacrifice to take up that course? Shouldn't they have stayed together?

For a moment it was as if a darkness had clouded his mind,

then she smiled again and Lorimer remembered who he was, and where: a senior police officer, a happily married police officer, at a simple school reunion.

The night drove on in a whirl of conversation and laughter. Several of the men and women became tipsy, some getting up to dance around the fringes of the tables as the disco got under way and the music changed from quiet background melodies to the more raucous sounds from their youth.

'Hard to talk above all of this noise,' Vivien said, leaning in towards him. 'Fancy a walk outside?'

Lorimer glanced around at the others on their table, clearly engrossed in different conversations. Their own exchanges had skirted around work and family life (no, she had never had children either, Vivien had told him), but there was a strange wistfulness in some of her glances. It was as if there was more to be said; things that she wanted to tell him privately. And his detective's curiosity was aroused.

As Lorimer hesitated, he saw her rise from her place at the table, one eyebrow arched in amusement at his indecision.

'Come on, then,' she said, and began to walk across the hall.

It was only polite to follow, Lorimer told himself. There was nothing wrong with her request to have a quiet chat, was there? And yet as he passed Stu Clark's table and saw the man's eyebrows raised and that mocking grin, he knew what his old friend must be thinking.

Vivien had stopped by a row of pegs that was their cloakroom for the evening and Lorimer watched as she pulled on a dark green coat, wrapping it around her slim body then flicking her hair out from the collar.

There were several people around the doorway, smokers who had left the hall behind for a cigarette, but none of them commented on the well-dressed woman and the tall policeman stepping out into the chill of the April night.

They walked on in silence, past the darkened windows of class-rooms and around a corner of the main building until they reached the playground. As they approached the scarred metal benches, Vivien looked back at him enquiringly.

'Remember ...?' she began, a small smile on her lips as she took her old place on the bench. And of course he did remember. All those hours after school when they had sat here putting the world to rights, the whole of the playground quiet at last except for the occasional cleaner passing by or the janitor who never seemed to notice them there at all.

She had crossed her legs and one foot was jigging up and down, Lorimer noticed, a sure sign of agitation.

Then he was sitting beside her, hands folded under his chin, wondering what it was that she wanted to tell him.

'Did you ever wonder about me at all?' Vivien began, staring out at the darkness beyond the school buildings, deliberately avoiding his glance. 'Ever think that first love was the sweetest?'

'Sometimes,' Lorimer admitted. 'But things changed after my mum died.' He shrugged. 'And there were lots of other things in my life.'

'Like your wife?' She looked his way for a moment and he nodded.

'Yes,' he said slowly. 'I've been lucky. And you?'

Vivien looked away again as she answered. 'Charles is marvel-lous,' she said. 'The sort of person you only meet once in a lifetime.'

Lorimer's brow furrowed for a moment. Was he imagining a tinge of bitterness in her voice? And was that sudden shivering simply from the cold night air?

Vivien drew out a packet of cigarettes from her handbag and

offered them to Lorimer, who shook his head. He watched as she lit a cigarette with a slim silver lighter then inhaled deeply, closing her eyes in a moment of relief as the nicotine hit her bloodstream. Neither of them had smoked back then, his father's early death having made the young William Lorimer determined not to acquire the habit. Watching as she flicked the ash from her cigarette, he saw a different Vivien, someone subtly sophisticated, a woman who was probably more at home in one of the many chichi bars and restaurants that London had to offer. With her husband, Charles.

'Charles Gilmartin,' Lorimer said suddenly. 'Of course! I didn't realise that's who you were married to! He's the famous theatre director, isn't he?'

Vivien smiled her familiar foxy smile.

'The very one,' she said. 'My husband, the famous director.'

'Then why...?' Lorimer frowned as the question came unbidden to his lips.

'Why aren't I an equally famous actress?' She shrugged. 'Didn't happen for me, did it?'

Lorimer shook his head.

'Too much competition,' she said lightly.

'But you still worked in the theatre?'

'As Charles's personal assistant.' Vivien turned her head away, blowing a pale line of smoke through the dark night air.

'And that was enough to satisfy you?' The words were out before he could stop them. It was none of his business, his wiser self reminded him. Yet once upon a time Foxy's career had been all he could think about.

'Charles has big plans,' Vivien said, turning to smile at him. 'There's a theatre group arriving from Africa this summer. Doing a UK tour. Taking in the Edinburgh Festival. He's bankrolling the whole thing,' she said.

Her speech was clipped, a hard edge to her voice as she spoke. Did she realise just how much he gleaned from the human voice? Or were her words meant to convey a sense of pride in her husband? Somehow he doubted that. Years of experience listening to people made the detective realise that there was something in Gilmartin's venture causing his wife some pain.

'Charles thinks he may be mentioned in the next Honours List,' Vivien added, a brittle smile on her face.

'A knighthood?'

She nodded and dropped her cigarette, grinding it beneath the toe of her black patent shoe. 'He's putting so much behind this whole thing.' She shrugged. 'Bound to be noticed in all the right places.'

Lorimer grinned back at her. 'That would make you Lady Gilmartin, then,' he chuckled. 'Lady Foxy,' he added, catching her eye.

For a long moment neither of them spoke.

Vivien lifted her hand and traced a finger down the left side of his face. Was this an invitation for him to bend across and kiss her?

Then she sighed, gave her head a slight shake and turned away to gather up her handbag.

'Better get back in,' she said softly. 'Smoking break is over.'

The hall was filled with flashing lights from the noisy disco, with dancers gyrating in the confined space making progress back to their table difficult and conversation impossible.

A quick glance at his watch told the detective that he had stayed long enough. Time to go home, he told himself, time to put this evening firmly in the past where it belonged.

'I'd better go,' he said, leaning over so that Vivien could hear him.

She nodded silently and there was an expression of sadness in her eyes as she looked up at him.

'If we do make the Edinburgh Festival, perhaps you would like to come,' she said. 'Bring your wife?'

'Of course,' he replied. 'Maggie loves the theatre as it happens.'

'Do you have a card? I could email you and let you know when the dates are all arranged.'

Lorimer fished out one of his business cards from the top pocket of his jacket and handed it to her.

'Detective Superintendent William Lorimer,' Vivien read. She looked up and smiled. 'Suits you,' she said. 'Well done.'

He smiled back, then reached down to flick a lock of her flame-coloured hair 'Bye bye, Lady Foxy.'

Once outside again, Lorimer gulped the chill night air as he headed for the taxi rank. It hadn't been too bad, he told himself. He had met up with a few old pals, shaken hands with men and women who were now complete strangers and whetted his curiosity over Foxy.

As the taxi took him the short journey home, the detective replayed their conversation in his head. She wasn't really happy, he told himself. London and all its glitz and glamour had been less of a dream than the young Vivien Fox had planned. And there was something else: the way she had spoken about her husband had made him wonder if she had found contentment in her marriage the way he had with Maggie.

As the lights of his house loomed closer, Lorimer experienced a rush of gratitude for the life he had. Inside, Maggie would be asleep, warm and waiting for him, Chancer curled up on his side of the bed, no doubt. He paid the driver and walked up the driveway, listening to the taxi's engine grow quieter as it passed out of the street and headed back towards the city. He thought of Stu

Clark and his Australian suntan, a daughter left behind in Scotland after a failed marriage; Eddie still at Glenwood; and Vivien, her fate wrapped up with the famous impresario.

If the school reunion had taught him anything at all, it was that he wouldn't change his life for any one of theirs, Lorimer told himself as the key turned in the lock.

CHAPTER SEVEN

London was full of little studios to rent, apartment complexes that catered for the traveller who was planning to do rather more than pass through the capital, but it had been much more difficult to find such a place in Glasgow. There was no lack of hotels and Charles had suggested several within the city, but his wife had shaken her head and smiled. There might not be anywhere here that Vivien Gilmartin could call home any more, she'd argued, but she baulked at the idea of staying in some impersonal hotel bedroom as if she were a total stranger to her own city.

Then she had found it: a quiet residential court with flats to let short term. The modern block looked out towards Glasgow Green, tipping its hat to the city across the river, its back door just minutes away from the Citizens Theatre and the once notorious Gorbals. It was perfect, Vivien had insisted, for all of their requirements. A short walk across a nearby bridge took them into the heart of the city, and it was less than fifteen minutes' taxi ride to her old school on the South Side. Charles could conduct his business with no interruptions from chambermaids or late-night guests while she completed the business of the school reunion, she'd argued. He had hesitated, and she had played her winning hand, offering to stock the rented kitchen with all his favourite food and drink, reminding him of the cost of room service. Charles might have money but he hated splashing it around unnecessarily. Vivien remembered this conversation quite distinctly as she waited for the lift to take her upstairs to the top floor, where Charles Gilmartin was ensconced in the little apartment, quite reconciled to being waited on by his wife rather than a nameless person in hotel livery.

Vivien leaned back against the wall of the lift and closed her eyes as it began to rise noiselessly upwards. The relief that the class reunion was behind her was tempered by a sense of anticlimax. Everything had gone according to plan and yet she was left with this irrational dissatisfaction. She had managed to isolate Bill Lorimer for a little while, marvelling to herself at how he had changed. There was something almost formidable about the man that had been lacking in the boy she remembered, strength of character as well as a physical presence that made him a person she could easily desire. Her chest heaved with a sigh.

Vivien opened her eyes as the lift came to a halt and the doors slid open, revealing a carpeted lobby with subdued lighting, a brown-painted door on either side. As far as she knew, the other flat remained unoccupied, something the letting agent had mentioned when he had shown her the apartment. She stood for a moment, listening, but there was no sound from the other side of the door. She felt in her coat pocket for the key, then, taking a deep breath, let herself into the darkened hallway.

A fumbled hand on the light switch illuminated the place, showing the narrow passage that led to the bedroom where Charles must be lying in bed. The flat felt stuffy after the chilly April night, yet she shivered, hugging her coat to her as she moved down the hall and entered the living room. There was no need for a lamp in here, Vivien thought, moving towards the huge windows that looked over the city. Lights glittered everywhere: blues and purples picking out the shapes of the bridges; the constantly moving headlights of cars as they crossed the Clyde; streaks of yellow from the riverside street lamps thrown across the dark waters.

Once this had been her city, but so much had changed, Vivien thought as she turned down the heating. She didn't belong here any more, and although London was the place that she called home, she knew that her hopes for the evening just past might have rekindled something she had lost.

With a sigh, she turned, her red hair glowing like a fox in the dark as she began heading towards the bedroom.

His hand reached out to grab the telephone as it shrilled in the darkness. It seemed only moments before that sleep had finally taken him into its deep embrace, and now Lorimer was awake, expecting a voice that would require his presence at a scene of crime.

'Foxy?' The word fell from his lips before he had time to think, his feet hitting the carpet beside the bed, taking him away from Maggie's side. This was something she should not, must not hear. The light from the side window shone across the hallway, throwing his shadow on to the wall.

'Slow down,' he commanded. 'Are you sure?'

'He's dead!' The voice on the other end of the line rose hysterically. 'Charles is dead! Oh God, please help me! I don't know what to do.'

'Call the police. Right now, d'you hear me?'

'I can't,' Vivien Gilmartin protested. 'I can't deal with strangers here, seeing him like this . . . Won't you . . . ?'

'Vivien, where exactly are you?'

Lorimer listened as the woman told him between sobs.

He stifled a sigh, glancing back at the open bedroom door beyond the upstairs landing. She was begging him to come, asking him *as a friend,* and something inside him weakened. He could contact the local division once he'd reached the flat, let them call out a doctor.

'Okay. I'll come, I promise,' he said. At once her crying ceased and he could hear her breathing hard.

'I'll be with you soon, all right?'

'Thank you,' Vivien said softly. 'I won't forget this, ever.'

Charles Gilmartin's body lay on the double bed, his arms flung out as though a bad dream had disturbed his sleep, his grizzled head turned to one side.

Vivien stood a little apart, wondering what it was she ought to be feeling right now. She was a widow, a grieving widow. Should she be keening like an animal in pain? Or stroking her dead husband's hand? Shock and numbness, she told herself. These were surely the initial sensations on discovering one's husband lying dead in his bed. She rubbed her hands together, realising that her fingers had become cold, wishing for some strange reason that she could put on her gloves again but thinking how odd that would seem, to be indoors wearing gloves. The notion seemed almost mad. But perhaps the thought was a good one, something outside this unreal situation to keep her sane, something that made her focus on the here and now. Like *Lear*, she thought; at the end the King's attention fixed on a small, insignificant detail that overwhelmed the enormity of dying. *Pray you, undo this button ...*

Lorimer rang the security buzzer outside, his breath smoking in the chill night air. The car had registered one degree above freezing. It was typical of Scotland's weather at this time of year: one day could be bright and sunny with nary a cloud in the sky, only to be followed by an unexpected snowfall. It felt cold enough for a frost at any rate, he thought, pressing the buzzer again, wondering why Vivien's voice hadn't broken through the ensuing silence.

'Lorimer?'

'Yes, it's me.'

'Top left.'

The door lock was released with a drilling sound, then Lorimer stepped into a dimly lit lobby with tired-looking pot plants in the alcoves by the inner door.

It was five floors up, the lift taking him there in seconds.

Vivien was waiting for him in the half-opened doorway and the detective saw she was still wearing her dark green coat, though it was unbuttoned, revealing her too slender figure in the smart black dress.

'Oh, Bill!'

She flung herself into his arms and began to sob, her words muffled against his jacket.

'Shh,' he whispered, stroking her hair as though comforting a child. 'Come on, better get inside. It's too cold out here for you.'

His eyes were on the corridor ahead, wondering which of the doors led to the body of Charles Gilmartin. Vivien snuffled into a handkerchief.

'You didn't expect this? I mean, he hasn't been ill or anything, has he?' Lorimer asked as Vivien led him into a square lounge with windows overlooking the Clyde and the glittering city lights beyond.

She shook her head, the lamplight catching her hair, making it a halo of fire.

'No. No, Charles was never ill.'

She put both hands over her mouth and he could see her throat move, swallowing her tears.

'I can't go back in there, Bill. I just can't bear to see him,' she whispered, her eyes large with fear as she looked up into his face. She pulled her coat tight around her, arms hugging her body, making Lorimer want to reach out and hold her again, take the horror away.

'Is that the kitchen?' he asked, pointing towards a door on the far side of the room.

She nodded.

'Okay, here's what we're going to do. You go and make us both a cup of tea, while I take a look at your husband. Right?'

She nodded again, a quick, shivery response.

'Then I'll call for some help,' he told her. 'There will be a few people here quite soon, I'm afraid, and you might find things a bit confusing. But I'll be here,' he said quietly, taking a step towards her and patting her shoulder. 'Which room . . . ?'

'The one across the corridor. Next to the bathroom.' Vivien blinked rapidly as though to prevent tears falling, and a tremulous smile crossed her face. 'Thank you,' she whispered, reaching up as though she were about to touch his arm. But then her hand fell to her side and she turned obediently towards the kitchen, head bowed.

You could be forgiven for imagining that the man was simply asleep. In death, Charles Gilmartin was still a big man, his grey hair flecked with white around the temples, mouth slightly open as though he was breathing deeply. But no breath would ever issue from those lips again, Lorimer knew as his gloved fingers felt for a pulse. The eyes were closed, so he must have been asleep at the moment of his death. Heart attack? Perhaps,

42

Lorimer thought, studying the man's profile, the hawk-like nose and the dark stubble shadowing his chin. A sudden death at any rate, something that would have to be reported to the Procurator Fiscal.

Poor Vivien, he thought. A post-mortem would be inevitable unless the man's medical history pointed to the likelihood of a sudden demise. But he was never ill, she'd said.

Lorimer walked slowly around the bed, looking for signs that might tell him something, knowing that a doctor was needed to determine just what had happened to cause the man's death. With a sigh he drew out his mobile phone and pressed a button, one small action that would set several necessary wheels in motion.

CHAPTER EIGHT

Further down the river, a large lorry was trundling across the Kingston Bridge, its cargo quiet now on this chilly April night.

Asa had never felt such cold before, a cold that had crept into her very bones. They had given her a thick grey coat and some woolly socks but the cold had seeped through the fibres long since, like an insidious creature invading every cell of her body. Sometimes during the long darkness she had tried to pray, but there had been no answer to her cries. Her head bowed, Asa began to wonder what she had done wrong to be so cast out from all that was dear to her. Eyes shut tight, she conjured up memories of morning sun across the veldt.

The weaver birds would be twittering above her little house, the long shadows of the acacia tree slanting across the hard cracked ground. She imagined the tethered goat flicking flies with its tail, and she wanted to draw a hand across her face almost as if she expected to brush them off herself. But there were no irritating insects here in this cold, cold place that shook and vibrated as the lorry drove on and on into endless night. At home Asa would be walking barefoot to the well as the sun rose steadily, warming her arms. The other girls might be chattering as they walked; if one of them began to sing, then all would raise their voices, joining in one of the ancient songs that girls always sang. And they would laugh together as they stepped out across the dusty landscape, happy in the way of innocent young women who were still unaware of what happiness was.

Asa had grown up so fast in the last three days, no longer a girl untouched by the world but brushed by experiences that were making her into a woman. Now she knew what happiness was. She had thought about this for hours, ever since she had been bundled roughly into the truck and taken to the airport.

Happiness was something you did not know you possessed until it was stolen from you. The simple joy of walking freely under the African sun, the certainty of every day arriving with its pattern of fetching water, cooking the mealie meal for breakfast, shaking her sleeping mat, then sweeping out the dust from her home: these had all been little acts of happiness.

The noise from the lorry's engine grew quieter as it sometimes did, but then the vibration stopped altogether and Asa heard the sound of the cab door being slammed up ahead. Had they arrived? Was this the promised destination? A flicker of hope entered her thoughts as the girl lay against the straps that confined her.

There had been barely enough space for her to squeeze between the hulking boxes piled up to the roof and the wooden ribs that fretted the metal side of the lorry. She had protested when the driver had pushed her to the floor, struggled to rise when he had buckled her arms to the rattling chains. At first she had yelled and screamed, kicking out at the hard boxes. But nobody would hear her over the engine's roar, she realised at last, and her toes had become sore and bruised.

Then the door swung open to reveal a cavernous place full of light so dazzling that Asa screwed up her eyes. When she opened them again she could see hands reaching out for her, hear the chains as they fell from her arms, feel the pain in her legs as she tried to stand.

'Grab a hold of her,' someone said, and Asa felt her body being lifted out of the narrow space. Then she was being carried, the rough cloth of a man's jacket against her cold cheek.

'Get her into the back,' a voice commanded.

Asa did not protest as she was bundled into a car and strapped into her seat belt, one man on either side of her.

She glanced at them by turn, wide-eyed, but neither man was looking at her face, just straight ahead as if she wasn't there at all.

CHAPTER NINE

'A sudden heart attack,' Dr Calder said at last, rising to his feet. 'Probably felt unwell and went early to bed. Looks like he died in his sleep, poor soul.' He stepped back, still looking closely at the man he had been summoned here to examine.

Lorimer nodded, following the doctor's gaze. Charles Gilmartin's eyes had been shut when the detective superintendent had first seen his body. He still looked quite peaceful, lying on the bed as though he had simply sighed one last time, drifting for an instant to the place between life and death.

'It's the way to go,' the doctor said brusquely. 'What *I'd* want. What everyone wants, eh?'

'I suppose so,' Lorimer agreed, though dying suddenly in his fifties like Gilmartin seemed a bleak prospect. And it would be of little comfort to Vivien to be told that her husband's death was, in the scheme of things, a good death.

'Any history of heart problems, d'you know?'

'She said there wasn't any,' Lorimer replied, his mouth tightening.

'Need to report it to the Fiscal, then,' Calder said, reaching into his case for an envelope containing an A4 form, something to be filled in as the necessary procedure began.

Lorimer nodded again. It had been as he'd suspected, a sudden death that might well require a post-mortem examination; somehow he would have to bring up that distinct possibility with the grieving woman across the passage.

Vivien was in the lounge of the small apartment, a uniformed female officer sitting beside her. A tray with mugs of tepid tea lay on a small oval table, abandoned by both women.

Vivien sat hunched over, arms clasped around her stomach as though she were in pain. And perhaps she was, thought Lorimer. Hadn't his psychologist friend, Solly Brightman, told him about the real physical pain that the bereaved could experience? A heartache that was more than a figure of speech. The detective stood by the doorway, wondering what he could say to make things better. He'd attended countless scenes of crime that had been far worse than this, an ordinary situation of an older man dying quietly in his sleep.

Yet seeing her bent head, its flame hair tousled where Vivien had raked it with those thin fingers, something shifted inside him that was more than pity. *If it had been Maggie* ... a little voice whispered. And at that moment he had an inkling of just how Vivien Gilmartin must be feeling.

'Vivien?'

She glanced up at him and for an instant it was like looking at a stranger, this woman whose green eyes were dulled, smudges of mascara making her look far more than her forty-one years.

'Is there anyone you can call? A girlfriend, perhaps?'

Lorimer heard himself asking the question, hating himself for wanting to be away from here, wishing that he were back in bed, Maggie's warm body against his own.

She shook her head, staring at him blankly.

'Surely ... someone from last night ... ?'

There had been so many people, lots of women that he'd seen her talking to, smiling with ... wasn't one of them a special friend? he thought helplessly.

'Mrs Gilmartin hasn't any family here, sir,' the female officer said, her face a mask of careful reproach.

'Your sister ... ?'

'She's in Canada,' the police officer answered for Vivien.

'Is there anywhere else you want to go to?' Lorimer tried again. 'A friend's place, maybe?'

Vivien shook her head. 'I don't think so,' she sniffed in a small voice. 'When will they take him away?' she asked, turning to the woman sitting beside her and catching hold of her hand.

'The doctor's called for an ambulance,' the officer said soothingly. 'They won't be long now.'

'There might have to be a post-mortem,' Lorimer said quietly, hunkering down beside her.

She nodded dumbly, her green eyes staring past him, making Lorimer wonder if she was taking in anything he was saying. He had seen the effect that shock produced often enough to make him realise that Vivien was maybe not hearing a thing that was being said to her. Instead she might well be replaying over and over the moment when she had found her husband's body, other people's words a mere blur of noise outside her head.

The female officer rose then, letting go of Vivien's hand, and left the room. He took her place, taking Vivien's hand in his, letting her body sag against him.

Outside he could hear the officer talking to the doctor. Then there was a knock on the door to the apartment and Vivien's body stiffened against his, her hand clasping his arm as if in sudden panic.

'It's all right, the paramedics will deal with things,' Lorimer soothed her blandly. He started as she looked wildly towards the lounge door. 'Do you want to go and see him before ...?'

The woman beside him shook her head fiercely, the edges of her hair caught like gold in the lamplight. She was biting her lower lip, controlling any sobs, though Lorimer guessed that a storm of weeping was not far away. The sounds of men's voices and heavy footsteps could be heard, then the door trembled as a draught of air entered the room. As the outer door closed at last, Lorimer felt rather than heard the long shuddering sigh from the woman by his side.

In the corridor the female officer was still talking to the doctor.

'... not nice to come back to,' she was saying. 'I could strip it and shove the lot in the kitchen. There's a washer dryer,' she was telling him.

Lorimer listened, realising that this officer wanted to be kind in a practical way.

'Not a problem,' the doctor was saying. 'Nothing I need there. Probably better for Mrs Gilmartin not to see the room like that again.' There were noises from the bedroom and then the officer was whisking through the lounge and he could hear the slam of the machine's door and its swish as the wash cycle began. Lorimer put his arm around Viven's shoulders. He understood what the police officer was thinking: it would be less horrid for Mrs Gilmartin to return to the flat to see a bare mattress, blank and impersonal, rather than the place where her husband had died. He watched through the open doorway as the woman gathered up Charles Gilmartin's clothes too, putting them carefully into the fitted wardrobe as neatly as she could.

'I can't sleep through there ...' Vivien broke off in a sob, gripping his hand as though she would never let him go, her eyes looking past him to the doorway and beyond.

Lorimer thought about the home he had left, the darkened corridor upstairs with its spare room where once he had given sanctuary to an injured, homeless boy. But Maggie had been far away then, overseas on that exchange project. How could he land Vivien on her in the middle of the night?

'Isn't there anyone . . . ?' he tried again.

'Only you,' Vivien said, smiling sadly. 'There was only ever you,' she whispered.

Lorimer hadn't blamed her for not wanting to see her husband's body taken away. Vivien appeared to be traumatised by the man's sudden death and now, sitting stiffly in the passenger seat of the Lexus as he drove through the city streets, she was silent, staring ahead, gloved hands clasped tightly together around the handle of an overnight bag she'd insisted on packing herself.

He'd called Maggie earlier, apologising for rousing her from sleep, telling her as briefly as he could what had happened to tear him from her side. She had been quiet, too, listening as he'd explained the situation, but *poor woman* and *that's terrible, of course she must come* had fallen from her lips as he had expected. Her natural sympathy and generosity was rushing out to this stranger coming to invade their home; no word of recrimination or anything about *your old girlfriend* mentioned at all. So why, Lorimer thought as the car sped along Pollokshaws Road on its way to the suburbs, did he feel so uneasy about the thought of Vivien Gilmartin spending time under his roof?

CHAPTER TEN

M aggie looked at the kitchen clock. It was twenty minutes to
five, no longer so dark outside, a pale drift of coral on the
eastern horizon heralding the new morning. She smiled as Chancer
awoke in his basket, stretching from slumber. He looked up at her
and gave a tentative miaow, as though questioning Maggie's presence at this early hour. Soon he was wrapping himself around her
legs and she bent down to tickle him behind his ears.

'Suppose you think this is breakfast time, eh?' The ginger cat
reared up against the hem of her fleecy dressing gown in reply,
evidently looking for more scratches on his furry head, and
Maggie complied, hunkering down, letting the cat leap on to her
waiting lap.

'Don't know what you'll make of her, Chancer,' Maggie murmured, caressing the cat, whose purrs had began to thrum though
her body as she stroked his fur. 'Don't know what I'll make of her
either, poor thing.' She sighed, leaning back against one of the
kitchen chairs. It was almost an hour since he'd called and in that
time she had made up the bed, putting fresh towels and a new
box of tissues in the spare room, wondering just what else might
be required for this unexpected house guest: Bill's old girlfriend.
A newly bereaved widow, she reminded herself. She was a woman

her own age with not a soul here in Glasgow to call family or friend. *But she'd called Bill*, a little voice insisted. And that same little voice had asked *why* more than once since that telephone call.

'It's because he's a policeman,' Maggie said aloud, trying to convince herself that this was true. But why had she not turned to another woman, a friend from her past? Vivien Gilmartin had arranged this entire school reunion thing, hadn't she? Surely the sort of person who did these things kept in touch with their pals over the years? Maggie frowned. There were only two or three women from her own school days that she would call good friends, and even then, their contact was more Facebook than face to face. It was something she regretted, though the demands of her teaching job seemed to take all of Maggie Lorimer's time and energy these days.

She heaved a sigh, the sudden movement making Chancer leap off her knee with a small cry.

'Better stick the kettle on,' Maggie murmured, getting to her feet. Tea, the balm for every difficulty, she thought. Why was it that in times of crisis people always made endless pots of tea? She filled the kettle at the sink, glancing out at the sky. The streaks of pink were suddenly brighter, dazzling her eyes, and she blinked, wondering if the fiery sky presaged rains to come. This was April, after all, a month when all sorts of weather could be flung at the poor Scots in the space of a single day.

The cruellest month, Maggie reminded herself, biting her lip. Would Vivien Gilmartin think of April like that for the rest of her life? Would she ever again feel that surge of joy from seeing the spring flowers and the blossom shaken from the cherry trees? Or would they become cruel tokens for the anniversary of her husband's death?

Maggie pulled her dressing gown tighter around her slim body, shivering at the thought. It was cold, she realised. Better switch on the central heating, warm the place up before they arrived. Vivien was in a state of shock, Bill had said, didn't seem to have taken in the enormity of what had happened. Soon the faint hum from the radiators had begun and Maggie was filling a hot-water bottle from the kettle. Tea could wait till they returned, and perhaps Vivien would want to go straight to bed anyway. Maggie hoped she would, saying a silent prayer that she and Bill could snuggle up together, catch up on their broken sleep for a few more hours. Thank goodness it was Saturday and there were no pressing cases to take her husband into the city today.

She took the hot-water bottle upstairs, looking out of the landing window at the street below, watching for the big silver car rounding the corner, but there was little life at this early hour, just a single blackbird flying silently over the garden. The bright dawn was already fading into a dusky lemon, the only trail of pink a jet scoring its way across the heavens. It was, Maggie fancied, as though the day was holding its breath, waiting for something momentous to happen.

Giving herself a shake, she opened the door to the spare room and pulled back the coverlet, sliding the hot-water bottle under the duvet.

'Poor woman,' she whispered aloud as she gazed at the bed. 'Poor, poor soul.'

When the car finally came to a halt, the man beside her unclipped her seat belt and took her arm, roughly pulling her out into the cold morning air. Asa looked around her, blinking.

Everything was grey.

Tall stone buildings flanked the drab grey streets, their rooftops as dark as the thunderclouds that soared over the veldt. There were rows and rows of doors at street level, many windows up above, staring out like blind eyes. The girl shivered, looking past them to the sky, where only a few stars pricked the icy blue heavens. A strange bleeping noise made her jump and she turned to see the car flashing twice, the driver pointing his keys towards it.

'Get a move on,' the man who held her arm grumbled, pushing Asa towards the pavement. 'In here,' he added as one of the other men opened a black-painted door set back into the stone building, and suddenly Asa was being marched into a narrow passage with white-glazed walls like a public toilet, and up several flights of stone stairs, their edges worn and broken.

Then another door opened and Asa could hear a woman's voice from somewhere inside as she was bundled along a corridor and into a square room with a bed and a dresser.

'Stay here and keep quiet. Okay?' the man commanded, staring at her. 'Understand? Comprende?' He frowned, lips twisting as he continued to stare at her. 'Shhh,' he whispered, putting a finger to his lips.

Asa nodded to show that she had understood his gesture if not the strange words he spoke. Then the door was closed and the girl listened to the unmistakable sound of a key being turned in the lock. She sat on the edge of the bed, her large dark eyes wide with fear. What was going to happen to her now? She took a deep breath, then wrinkled her nostrils. There was a bad smell in this room, a smell that Asa could not identify, both sour and pungent. It made her think of dead things.

She listened, straining to hear anything that might give a clue as to what was going on elsewhere in this house. Standing close to the locked door, the girl could make out the sound of human voices, but although it was impossible to know what they were saying, she felt a flicker of hope as a woman's voice was raised in laughter, the men joining in. Where there was laughter there was some sort of joy, and perhaps that would include a lonely girl from Nigeria shivering in her borrowed coat.

As she heard footsteps approach, Asa stumbled backwards to the edge of the bed and clutched the coat around her body, eyes fixed on the door.

'There you are.' A stout dark-skinned woman wearing a red flowered dress opened the door, her hands clutching a tray of food. 'Here, sit yourself down and eat.' She placed the tray at the foot of the bed, eyes watching the girl as she backed away.

'I won't hurt you, little one,' the woman said softly, stepping closer and brushing a hand over her hair. Asa looked into her brown eyes, recognising that age-old expression, the kindness of mothers. Then she was being hugged against the woman's ample bosom, swaying back and forth as the woman shushed her.

Asa began to weep, all her unnamed sorrows flooding out, her mind too full of tangled emotions to know just what she ought to feel.

'Would you like some breakfast?' Maggie asked hopefully. The woman sat rigidly in the rocking chair that had been Maggie's mother's, several embroidered cushions at her back.

Vivien Gilmartin looked up, giving a brittle smile. 'No thank you. I ... I couldn't eat anything ... ' She broke off, putting her hands over her face for a moment. 'Sorry,' she whispered, looking down at her lap. 'It's just ... '

'I've made the bed upstairs if you'd like to try and sleep,' Maggie said, biting her lip and looking questioningly at her husband over the woman's bowed head, the flame-coloured hair glistening like spun sugar in the lamplight. Lorimer raised his eyebrows in silent reply as if to say that he didn't know what to do either.

'Yes.' Vivien was nodding now, rising shakily to her feet. 'Perhaps that would be best.'

Maggie watched as her husband took Vivien's arm, leading her through the room towards the stairs. His tall figure bent over the red-haired woman, one arm supporting her tenderly as they disappeared from view. A pang of something like jealousy shot through Maggie, astonishing her with its ferocity.

'Stop it,' she whispered, fists clenched by her sides, listening as the footsteps ascended the stairs. 'He's just being kind,' she added. How many times had her husband assisted poor souls like this in the aftermath of personal tragedies? Maggie blinked, the thought comforting her suddenly. He was used to dealing with situations where people were in shock, their loved ones ripped from them in more horrific ways than this. So why, now that Vivien was under her roof, was she struggling to feel any sort of pity for this woman from her husband's past?

'Gilmartin,' Maggie yawned as she spoke the word. 'We saw one of his productions, d'you remember?'

A slight groan from his side of the bed was her husband's only reply. Was that a *no*? Or a *be quiet and let me sleep* sort of response? She rolled over, tucking the duvet around her body, trying to remember. It had been one of their few excursions to London's West End, a play about a crime of some sort. That was why they had gone. But as she drifted off into sleep, Maggie realised that she couldn't recall a single thing about it.

CHAPTER ELEVEN

COUNTDOWN TO THE COMMONWEALTH GAMES, the headline proclaimed. The blonde woman smiled as she read the article in the *Gazette*, recognising words and phrases that she had given the journalist only days before. They were all being sickenly positive about every aspect of the whole stramash.

Gayle Finnegan frowned and her fingers crumpled the edge of the paper she was still holding. Where on earth had that cynical thought appeared from? She uncrossed her legs, the memory of last night's rough sex a twinge of discomfort under the blue satin thong. Cam had rubbished her involvement in the Glasgow Commonwealth Games from the very beginning of their relationship, always seeking something negative to say about her colleagues, the government ministers (especially the government ministers) who had overseen the massive organisational operation and even the athletes themselves. When she had met and spoken to Sir Chris Hoy, Gayle had been full of enthusiasm. But Cam's putdown had withered all the joy that she had taken in meeting the great man himself at the velodrome that was named after him.

Why did she stay with him, then? What was it about Cameron Bloody Gregson that made her return to the flat night after night, in hope more than expectation? *Stramash* was Cam's word for the

Games, wasn't it? He demeaned the whole business as though it were something amusing, something for the masses who couldn't help themselves. Gayle's sigh was accompanied by the realisation that she had to finish this toxic relationship once and for all. Her own judgement was beginning to be affected by Cam's poisonous remarks and, she told herself, sitting up straight in her chair, this job was far more important to her than an affair that had overrun its course. She had her own place, a nice single-roomed flat in the Merchant City, a five-minute walk from Albion Street, headquarters of the Games, and tonight she would head home there, leaving Cameron to wonder if she was coming back or not.

The morning sun shone through the windows next to the young woman's desk, illuminating the figure of a cyclist that looked like an engraving on the glass door. Artist-designed, the figures depicting each of the sports were in fact simply stuck on to the glass. Once it was all over, the massive space over three floors and wrapped around this part of the old building would be taken apart and packed away, leaving the bright offices to be occupied by their next tenants. Everything had been thought of, Gayle had told Cam one evening early in their relationship, when he had still pretended to listen to her: the athletes' village would provide over six hundred homes for the city's East End, where the regeneration programme had been enthusiastically waved in front of its citizens. As one of the more senior members of the public relations team, Gayle would have no difficulty moving on from this job either; having Glasgow 2014 on her CV was like winning the lottery.

The coffee she had brought in from Berits & Brown was cold now but she sipped it anyway. The article was well written, Gayle told herself, skimming down the page again, the shadow of Cam's presence banished from her mind. And the journo had picked up on more than just the timeline for the arrival of the athletes at the village; he had written about the different ways that sportsmen and women from so many nations were preparing for this Scottish summer ahead, injecting a touch of wry humour about the probability of rainfall and the thousands of Games umbrellas already being sold around the city.

Gayle glanced out of the window again, remembering the feel of the early-morning sun on her skin and wishing hard that this summer might be warm and sunny day after day after day, unlike any Scottish summer she had known in her twenty-five years.

Peter MacGregor glanced across the aisle at Joanne. He had eased a bit more belt from the lap strap, aware of the curve of his stomach under the cashmere sweater. Where had that well-toned sportsman gone? He grinned ruefully, remembering the days of his youth when he and Jo had shared such a passion for athletics. She was still a trim woman, he thought, looking at his wife's slim legs in their designer jeans. *You could pass for forty*, he'd told her as they'd stood in the house that morning, making her blush and protest. *Well, fifty anyway*, he'd conceded, and he believed it. Joanne MacGregor, with that sleek bob of highlighted hair and her fine cheekbones, was often asked her age, officials raising their eyebrows to find that this lovely woman was indeed a senior of sixty-four. She had her eyes closed as she always did before take-off, hands clasped loosely on her lap. They had chosen aisle seats in preference to sitting side by side, the long-haul flight necessitating some decent leg room, but it was at moments like this that Peter regretted their choice, wishing that he could have held her hand, sharing the surge of joy he felt that their long-planned dream was actually beginning.

In his head Peter went over the itinerary that had been so carefully worked out for the coming six months. London first, with all its sights, then up to Scotland, where they were to hire a car to take them on a tour of the Western Isles. Then it was across to Inverness and the journey south through MacGregor country until they reached Gleneagles. He and Mrs MacGregor wanted to explore the old home country on their own, he had told his hosts. Once they were in Glasgow Peter suspected that the MacGregors there would happily take over all of his plans, and part of him wanted to resist being whisked hither and yon by a group of strangers, no matter how kind their intentions were. He blinked as the engine noise rose to a climax and the big plane began to move along the runway. They had been very thoughtful, though, hadn't they? They'd even reminded him not to bring his *sgian dubh*. One adorned with the clan crest would be awaiting him in Glasgow. But that was still several weeks away and Peter smiled at the thought of all the sights they would see during April and May, months when the weather was meant to be at its best in Scotland and the azaleas and rhododendrons gave their bonniest show. It would be a quiet prelude to the excitement of the Commonwealth Games, the Gathering and finally the Ryder Cup, back in Gleneagles. By October they would no doubt be ready to return to Australia and its summer months.

As the plane's nose tilted skywards, Peter MacGregor felt a childlike thrill of adventure. Melbourne lay below him, its familiar landmarks becoming smaller and smaller until they were swallowed up in cloud, leaving Peter with the drone of the engine ringing in his ears and a single thought in his head. He was on his way home!

Detective Superintendent Lorimer glanced back at the curve of the avenue as he turned the Lexus towards the main road. It was not yet six a.m., but there was a brightness in the sky that suggested another lovely day ahead. The drive into Glasgow was tinged with a sense of guilt that he was escaping somehow, leaving his poor wife to attend to Vivien Gilmartin's needs. Well at least the post-mortem could take place today, and after that she would surely be free to return south and prepare for whatever form of funeral her late husband might have expected. It had been a difficult weekend. Maggie had been overly solicitous to their guest, hardly giving her a moment to herself, and Lorimer suspected that both women would be relieved when the time came for Vivien to make her goodbyes. Several times Foxy had caught his eye and he'd seen the mute appeal there to be left in peace. She had feigned tiredness once or twice simply as a way of being on her own up in the spare room, Lorimer was sure.

'Can you not give her a bit of space?' he had begun during a Sunday that had been so unseasonably warm that Maggie had laid the table out in the garden for lunch.

'What d'you mean?' she had snapped back at him. 'I'm doing my best to be nice, aren't I?' And he had withdrawn, surprised at her tetchiness, wondering what tension had sprung up between the two women. *You're doing too much*, he wanted to say, but that would have been churlish. After all, it had been his decision to offer hospitality to his old friend and Maggie had seemed so sympathetic at first.

Vivien and he had not spoken much on their own over the last two days, Maggie always there with a pot of tea or the offer of a glass of something stronger. Then last night the red-haired woman had heaved a sigh that could only be relief when Maggie had left the room to go upstairs to bed, leaving the pair of them in front of the television, glasses of whisky still to be finished. They had watched an arts programme, something neutral to banish all talk of funerals and post-mortems from the conversation. Yet he had seen Vivien stiffen as a certain London-based playwright's name had been mentioned, her pale face more drawn than ever in the shadowy lamplight.

'Someone you know?' he'd asked, and she'd given a brittle little nod, eyes turned away from him as if to indicate that she preferred not to talk about the theatre world. She had been sitting on the big rocking chair, but now she rose quietly and slipped on to the sofa beside him, placing her whisky glass on the side table. Neither of them had spoken for a while, and Lorimer had sensed the woman next to him relaxing in a way he had not seen since the school reunion two nights before.

'Do you remember old Greeky?' she'd said suddenly, turning to him with a smile.

'Greeky Grierson? Classics teacher? He was mad, wasn't he?' Lorimer had laughed. 'Remember the time he took assembly and went on and on about some ancient old Greek long after the first bell? We were all holding our breath hoping he'd never stop so we would miss most of the first period.'

'Aristophanes,' Vivien replied.

'Eh?'

'It was Aristophanes. The old Greek.'

'Oh.' Lorimer had sipped his whisky, feeling a moment of confusion. 'How on earth could you remember that?'

'He was one of the most celebrated writers of his time. His plays are classics in more than one sense. They're still acted all over the world.' She'd turned to him, a curious expression on her face. 'Imagine being so famous after more than two thousand years. How could I *not* remember that name?' She'd asked the question lightly, but it had felt a little like a rebuke, and Lorimer wondered if even then their worlds had been too far apart.

The memory of their conversation came back to him clearly

now as he stopped at a red light. She'd enthused about the wispy-haired classics teacher, someone Lorimer had considered a bit of an eccentric, telling him about a theatre trip the teacher had arranged for them.

'It was to the Citizens,' she'd told him. 'To see *The Wasps*. I'll never forget that. It was like having my eyes properly opened for the first time.'

Lorimer had thought about her remark later. It had been an art teacher, a single older lady with massive enthusiasm for her subject, who had been responsible for giving the young William Lorimer his own passion for art. And hadn't Miss Sheridan taught him how to see the works of art that he had grown to love? Perhaps he and Foxy weren't so different after all, he mused, easing the car forward as the lights turned green, the touch of her lips on his cheek and the faint memory of her perfume lingering long after she had risen from the couch, leaving him to finish a contemplative whisky on his own.

CHAPTER TWELVE

Asa's body stiffened under the thin blanket at the sound of the knock on the door. Nobody had knocked before. Usually they simply unlocked the door and came straight into the room. Sometimes there would be one of them, usually the stout woman, but often two or more stood inside the room, staring at her then talking to one another while food was put down on the table. She had recognised some of the English words on her captors' lips. *Lorry* and *cargo* had been repeated several times, with glances in Asa's direction. Did these words mean 'girl'? Or even 'prisoner'? Asa shivered, watching the door, wondering when it would be opened. Since the night of her arrival no one had actually laid hands on her, but Asa sensed that any move to escape would result in physical violence.

It was daylight again, a weak sun hidden somewhere behind those forbidding grey buildings, so different from the glorious blaze that shone down on the earth back home.

Asa put her head in her hands, wanting to shed tears for the longing inside, the yearning to be where she belonged. But tears were a sign of weakness, and some instinct told the girl that she had to be strong for whatever lay ahead.

The sound of the key turning in the lock made her grit her

teeth, wide eyes staring. For a moment there was nothing, just a gap appearing as the door swung inwards.

'It's me.' The woman stood there grinning, a tray of food in both hands. 'Breakfast time,' she added.

Asa listened to her voice. *Breakfast* was a word she had heard before, and now she was sure it must mean 'food'. A meal.

There was a small table next to the bed where the woman set down the laden tray, and Asa's eyes roved hungrily over its contents. There were two bowls of cereal and a stack of toasted bread, the butter spread so thick that it slipped over the crusts, making the girl's mouth water. And two mugs of tea, its familiar fragrance making Asa look at the woman in surprise.

'Rooibos,' the woman said, smiling. 'You like that, eh? Here,' she added, picking up a mug and offering it to the girl.

Asa swung her legs out of the bed and perched on the edge, hands held out to receive the warm mug of tea. As she sipped, she saw that the woman had picked up the other mug and was drinking greedily. Two bowls, Asa told herself. *She means to have her own meal here with me*, she thought, surprised at how pleased it made her feel. They might share some sort of ethnic origin, but it had become evident that Asa's Yoruba tongue was completely foreign to the big lady, who now sat on the wooden chair, spooning corn-flakes into her mouth. Back home, English was the language of the city, of rich Nigeria, far from the village where Asa had lived for all of her fifteen summers. Yet if she was to survive, somehow she had to learn these strange new words and what they meant.

'Brek-fasst,' she tried, pointing to the other bowl of cereal.

The woman's grin showed that she had got it right. 'Aye, break-fast. Kellogg's cornflakes,' she added, nodding at the tray.

Asa picked up the second bowl shyly and began to eat, a small glow of satisfaction spreading through her. She had always been a clever one, her late father had said. She would marry well and have a husband who had many cattle. But then the sickness had come and Asa had been left alone, no husband willing to take her in case she too had the disease. Life had been hard for the children left behind, but there had still been enough food and the sun had shone down, warming the baked earth outside the tiny hut.

Asa blinked in surprise as she saw the empty bowl on her lap.

'Well done, little one!' The woman was clapping her hands and Asa smiled, wondering what was being said. Was it good to have finished the food? Or was it the custom here to clap once you had eaten? Just in case, the girl put her own hands together, giving a faint clap in return.

The woman's howl of laughter made Asa's cheeks burn with shame. Had she done something stupid? But the plate of toast was being pushed her way now, so perhaps whatever it was didn't matter.

The scent of warm toast and the fragrant tea made Asa relax. There were two pieces left on the plate and the woman's gestures indicated that they were both for Asa.

Wiping the crumbs carelessly from her dress on to the floor, the woman continued to talk, words flowing like water over the Nigerian girl's head. Then, in a pause, she tapped her breast and said, 'Shereen.'

She was watching Asa as she spoke; now, repeating both word and gesture, she pointed to the girl, a question in her eyes.

Asa tapped her own thin chest. 'Asa,' she said, surprised at the sound of her name being uttered in this cold little room.

'You are Asa?' The woman pointed at her again and Asa nodded. 'I am Shereen,' she said slowly. 'Sher-een.' The word was drawn out so that Asa knew she was meant to repeat it aloud.

'Sher-een,' she said obediently, as if she were a small child again learning new concepts from her elders.

'Good girl!' Shereen exclaimed, gathering up the empty crockery and placing it back on the tray. 'We'll have you ready in no time!'

Asa watched as the woman left the room, expecting the door to be swung shut as usual. But this time it remained open, letting in a draught of cold air from the darkened corridor outside.

Asa crept barefoot across the threshold, stopping to peer out at the hallway. She blinked, wondering if she had dreamt the night of her arrival; this seemed so different from her memory of a long narrow place where danger lurked at either end like hunting beasts. The corridor was shorter than she remembered, a few feet away from the front door on her right and about the same distance to the light shining from a room at the far end where she could hear the hum of a machine and the noise of music playing. Confused, she wondered whether she should return to the room, gather up the clothes she had been given and dress herself as quickly as possible. Had the woman made an error in leaving the door open? Would she be punished if she left the room and stepped into that lozenge of brightness?

Curiosity overcame the young girl's trepidation and she walked on silent feet towards the source of that warmth and brightness, lured as certainly as a moth to a candle. But there was no flame to scorch her fleecy Primark pyjamas, just a grin from Shereen, who had turned from whatever she was doing at the kitchen sink.

There were four high stools arranged around a length of table, and Asa slid silently on to one of them, watching Shereen, waiting to see if the woman would shoo her back to the room.

'More tea?' Shereen waved a teapot aloft, pointing at it with a friendly smile.

Asa nodded, understanding the gesture and sniffing the air to catch again the scent of the redbush tea leaves. *Moretea.* She held the word to her like a talisman, guessing incorrectly that this was the English word for rooibos. Staring at Shereen, she suddenly saw this fat, friendly woman as a possible route of escape. She would teach her English words, enough for Asa to tell someone out there that she had been captured, taken from her home and forced on that terrible journey. For, the girl reasoned, until she could speak the language, she was as effectively imprisoned in this land as if they had chained her to a wall and left her to rot.

Shereen waddled over to the table and placed a brown earthenware teapot between them.

'It takes time to brew,' she informed Asa, receiving only an uncomprehending stare.

'Tea,' Shereen said, pointing to the pot.

'Moretea,' Asa replied brightly as if batting back the single syllable with two of her own.

Shereen sighed and tried again. 'Tea,' she said. Lumbering off her stool, she opened a cupboard and took out a tin. 'Here,' she said, opening it and showing the contents to Asa. 'Tea.'

And so it was: dark leaves dried from the rooibos, their smoky fragrance rising as Shereen stirred them with one chubby finger.

'Tea,' Asa said.

'Cup,' Shereen continued, warming to her role as the girl's instructress as she touched the porcelain mug beside her.

'Cup,' Asa said, her eyes darting back to Shereen's to seek her approbation.

The woman grinned, then, as though something had come into her mind, stroked the line of her mouth with an index finger.

'Smile,' she said.

Asa touched her own mouth and repeated the word. But this time there was something wrong.

'Nah, not like that, girl. See, like this,' and Shereen swept her finger over her mouth in an exaggerated curve. 'Smile, see?'

Drawing closer to Asa, she touched the girl's lips, making the same shape so that Asa did smile, the moment of understanding a rare moment of joy between them.

'Smile, kid,' the man commanded, lowering the camera for a moment to jerk his head at Asa. The image would be transferred to a fake passport later, something the girl might never even see.

And she tried to smile, her face muscles obedient to the command, though in truth her heart fluttered with terror lest this man be taking part of her very soul away.

CHAPTER THIRTEEN

'Don't like it,' the white-coated woman murmured, shaking her head as she sat back from examining the tissue slide under the microscope. 'Don't like it at all,' she added, casting a quick glance at the toxicology report on her computer screen. Thanks to the new range of screening techniques, the samples had undergone rigorous examination, something that did not happen in every laboratory in the country. LC-QTOF was able to find multifarious substances, and now it seemed as though something highly unusual had turned up on their doorstep.

The samples had been hurried for testing as soon as the post-mortem had taken place, and now, as the afternoon sun slanted into the room, Dr Rosie Fergusson blinked against its rays, a frown of concern across her brow as she reread the words on the computer screen. *A home-made tincture of aconitum roots . . . several fatal deaths in China where highly concentrated forms of the tincture were sometimes prepared . . . No history of such incidents occurring in the UK.*

Lorimer had been adamant that Rosie should call him with the results as soon as humanly possible; now it puzzled the consultant pathologist why he was in such a tearing rush over this. Wanting to have the body released early was quite understandable, of course. But was there another reason why he had wanted Gilmartin's tox

71

results so quickly? Lorimer hadn't once hinted at anything sinister surrounding the sudden death of his friend's husband; had there been something that he had suspected and kept to himself? Rosie shook her head. No, they knew one another better than that. He would have said straight off if he had expected Rosie and her team to find any abnormalities.

'So maybe you won't like it much either,' Rosie muttered quietly, thinking of Lorimer as she looked at the telephone on her desk. 'Maybe not what you were expecting, hm?'

In a matter of minutes the test results were logged and an email with its attachment sent to her friend at A Division, whose insistence on prioritising this case had made Rosie Fergusson just a tad curious. Why was he being so pushy about getting the toxicology results back? There had been something edgy in Lorimer's voice when he had asked this favour. For some reason he had chosen not to share the story behind the case, but one thing she did know as she lifted the telephone: Charles Gilmartin, deceased, had not died of cardiac arrhythmia.

Lorimer read the email twice, blinking to make sure his eyes did not deceive him, then he swore softly under his breath, the unaccustomed oath repeated as his fist thumped the edge of his desk.

The tox reports showed a level of poison in Gilmartin's bloodstream that would have killed him in seconds. And its effects were exactly the same as if he really had died of a heart attack, Rosie had told him, her voice still ringing in his ears. *Just sent you an attachment*, she'd said. The pathologist had been adamant that the results were correct, and now, seeing them in black and white, Lorimer wondered what sort of conclusions Rosie had come to. She hadn't asked any probing questions, nor had he given any more information about Gilmartin. Yet his mind had immediately turned to the flat near the Gorbals. Was there anything there that he might have missed?

Lorimer sat back in his chair, head spinning. What the hell was he going to tell his old friend? Was there a possibility that Gilmartin had taken his own life? Had he been experiencing personal worries that might have tipped him over the edge? Or had he been suffering from depression? The policeman frowned. From what Vivien had told him, he knew that Charles Gilmartin had been full of plans for this forthcoming festival. The Scottish government had backed a number of enterprises to complement Glasgow 2014, many of them in the world of the arts. Maggie had signed up for several festivals, some with her senior pupils, others simply for her own interest.

Lorimer leaned forward, rereading the words on the screen. The other possibility didn't make sense either. Who could have entered that flat and administered a toxic substance to Vivien's husband while she was at the school reunion? The time of death had been calculated as around ten o'clock in the evening, when he and Vivien had been sitting side by side on that playground bench reminiscing about days gone by. She hadn't got back to the flat till well after one a.m.: those who arranged events were always required to stay till the bitter end.

A groan escaped from the detective super's lips at the irony of his thought. A bitter end right enough, both to the evening she had planned for so long and to Gilmartin's life. Lorimer had pushed for the tox results to come back quickly so that Vivien might have her husband's body released for his funeral. He had even hinted that he might have good news on that front today. But now ... how was he going to tell her that her husband might have deliberately taken his own life?

*

Maggie Lorimer's hand shook as she replaced the handset. No, she had insisted, she couldn't tell Vivien; he would have to come home and break that news to the woman herself. To be fair, he hadn't asked her to do it. But having this knowledge about the dead man while Vivien was still unaware of it filled Maggie with a kind of horror. He'd be home within the hour, he'd promised. But he couldn't stay long. There was a new case that was taking up his attention.

Maggie gritted her teeth. Wasn't it always the same? *Crime didn't take a rest*, one of her husband's colleagues had remarked ages ago, and it was true. Sometimes they'd had to cut short a holiday so that Lorimer could attend to something vital; other times she'd been left sitting at her own dining table apologising to guests for her husband's hasty departure. Maybe it was just as well that there had been no family. What would she have said to little children whenever their daddy had to leave them behind? Maggie gave herself a shake. Why on earth was she thinking these maudlin thoughts when that poor woman sitting in the garden was about to have her world turned upside down?

Vivien had her eyes closed. She was wearing sunglasses, but even so, the brightness of this April day was dazzling. She had applied her usual cream with its high sun factor, a necessity for a fair skin like hers, and now she was enjoying the sensation of warmth on her bare arms and legs. Lying back on the steamer chair, pillows thoughtfully provided by Lorimer's wife, Vivien allowed herself to drift into a mellow place between sleeping and waking. Somewhere a bird sang in the shrubbery, its sweet notes adding to the overall ambience of the day. There was no sign of the marmalade cat that made her stiffen with unreasonable fear every time it slunk past. It was, Vivien thought, letting her fancy wander, as if some unseen hand had set the stage: lighting bright on this side, music playing from the console at the back of the theatre and Vivien herself centre stage, caught in the moment, all eyes fixed on her recumbent form. She should concentrate on the moment, forget that Maggie was bustling around in the kitchen (she could discern noises though the open door) and listen instead to that inner voice that was telling her that all would be well.

'Hello? Maggie?' Lorimer closed the front door behind him and strode into the long room that combined study, lounge and dining kitchen, but there was no sign of either Vivien or Maggie. The sun streamed through the back door to the garden and he hesitated, listening for the sounds of voices.

Through the kitchen window he could see Vivien lying on the recliner, hands folded across her lap. Maggie was sitting opposite, a book in her hands, her sunglasses tilted forward on her nose. 'You are a good woman,' he whispered softly under his breath, looking at his wife. 'No wonder I love you,' he added with a sigh. For a moment he allowed the pair of them to remain quietly in the sun, undisturbed by the words he would soon utter that would destroy the peace of their day.

He stepped out of the shadow of the house into the sunlight, and as if he had called her name, Vivien sat up, her face turned towards him.

'What is it?'

As soon as she saw him, Maggie laid aside her book and came to stand by the woman's side.

Lorimer shook his head. 'Vivien, I'm really sorry but it's not good news.'

'Why? What's wrong?' She swung her legs to one side, grasping the edge of the wooden recliner with both hands. 'Tell me,' she said, her voice trembling with fear.

Lorimer hunkered down beside her. 'Charles did not die of a heart attack, Vivien. It was something else.'

The red-haired woman frowned. 'But the doctor said . . . '

'The doctor was quite correct to make the assumption. All of the signs seemed to indicate a heart attack. But that wasn't what happened, my dear.' He paused for a moment, trying to find the right words. 'A toxic substance has been found in his bloodstream.'

'Was it an accident?' she whispered.

Lorimer shook his head. There was no way of denying this sort of evidence.

'I'm sorry, but it appears that he may have deliberately taken his own life.'

Vivien's hand flew to her mouth and she shrank away, her back bowed as though the weight of this news had crushed her entire body.

'I'm so sorry,' Lorimer said again, looking at the woman's face, trying to see if she was beginning to weep. But it was impossible to make out her green eyes behind those sunglasses, and all he could see were twin reflections of his own image bending towards the woman he had once loved.

'What happens now?' Maggie spoke quietly as she waited for the kettle to boil. Vivien had disappeared upstairs to the bathroom, letting them have a few moments alone together.

'Further investigations,' Lorimer sighed. 'Up to the Fiscal, really. But there's no way she can have his body for burial right now.'

'What do you think she'll want to do?' Maggie asked, looking intently at her husband. *She can't stay here*, she wanted to say, but the words simply refused to be uttered.

'I don't know,' Lorimer replied truthfully. 'There are several things she might want to see to. Like what's happening about this theatrical enterprise.'

'Surely there will be someone else to take charge of that? Charles Gilmartin must have had other assistants for something as big as this.'

'I suppose so. Has Vivien spoken to you about any of that?'

'No,' Maggie admitted. She bit her lip. *Best to be honest*, she told herself. 'How do I go about asking her without sounding like we want her to leave?' she said at last.

'*Do* you want her to leave?' Lorimer was frowning.

Maggie hesitated. 'It's awkward . . . '

'She doesn't seem to have anywhere else to go, Mags. Surely we can help her out for a few more days?'

'Of course . . . ' Maggie broke off, hearing the creak of footsteps on the stairs. 'I'll make the tea, shall I?' She turned away, a surge of anger making her feel ashamed of herself for wanting rid of their house guest and irked that Bill might be thinking less of her for even hinting at such a thing.

Vivien stood across from them, her red hair a bright halo from the sunlight pouring in through the kitchen window. She held the sunglasses in her hand now and her eyes looked as though she had scrubbed them hard after a bout of weeping.

The very sight of her made Maggie feel a dreadful sense of guilt. *How would you feel if it was Bill who'd died?* a little voice asked.

'Come and sit down,' Lorimer said, already at his friend's side, guiding her to a chair.

Maggie busied herself with teacups and milk, glancing covertly towards the pair of them, listening intently.

'We're more than happy for you to stay here while you sort things out, Vivien,' he was saying, a kind hand on her arm. 'There's no way of telling how long this investigation might take. What do you want to do?'

Vivien looked up as if to catch Maggie's eye, but she had anticipated this and looked down, concentrating on pouring tea into the three cups, refusing to let herself be drawn into any discussion lest she give herself away.

'It's very kind of you ... really,' Vivien said in a small voice. 'Taking a stranger into your home ...'

'Hardly a stranger.' Lorimer gave a smile, covering her hand with his.

'Tea?' Maggie brought the tray to the little table and passed a cup to Vivien.

'Thanks, Maggie. You've been marvellous,' Vivien said sweetly, her green eyes meeting Maggie's own.

She was on the point of breaking down again, Maggie could see, the woman's voice husky with tears. Surely a few more days wouldn't matter? And how would she reply without sounding insincere?

As if sensing her hesitation, Lorimer came to his wife's rescue.

'Maggie always rises to the occasion,' he said. 'How she's put up with me all these years, goodness knows.' He grinned ruefully across at his wife, making Maggie feel at once reassured.

'I can believe it,' Vivien said slowly, looking from one to the other. 'You're a very special couple.'

'Meantime, perhaps there are people you need to contact? Folk from the theatre company?' Lorimer suggested.

Vivien nodded. 'Everyone is still down in London at the moment. It was only Charles ... Charles and I who came north to arrange the administration of things from this end.'

'But you have people you can call?'

She nodded. 'Martin Goodfellow. Charles's assistant. I already called him. He knows Charles died . . . ' She broke off, one hand flying to her mouth. 'Oh God, I suppose I have to tell him what's happened now, don't I?'

Maggie saw the colour drain from the woman's face.

'You can say that more tests are being done. Nothing of this needs to be made public just yet,' Lorimer reassured her.

'So the press . . . ?'

'Nobody will know anything until the Procurator Fiscal decides what steps to take,' he said firmly. 'I think it would be best if you could let this Goodfellow chap take over all the theatre management now, don't you?'

'But the project can't go on without Charles,' Vivien said suddenly. 'He was funding almost the entire thing by himself.'

'Wasn't it backed by the Scottish government?' Maggie asked.

Vivien shook her head. 'There was just a grant to pay for evaluating its effect on Scottish tourism. No core funding.' She gave a sigh. 'That was all going to be met from Charles's personal money.'

'So will the project not go ahead now?'

Vivien shook her head. 'Charles *was* the project,' she said vehemently. 'There's no way it can possibly carry on now he's gone.'

Lorimer hesitated. He had to detach himself, think like a policeman, but it was hard, seeing her face so racked with grief.

'I want you to give me the keys to your flat, Vivien,' he said. 'The Fiscal will probably want the police to have another look,' he added, making his tone as diffident as he could. 'Is there anything I can bring you back?'

'Shall I come with you?' Her face turned up to his, a flash of fear in her green eyes.

'No. You stay here with Maggie,' he replied firmly.

'Maybe some fresh clothes ...' Vivien looked down at her hands, then her whole body seemed to quiver with the sob that she could no longer contain.

Lorimer recalled Vivien's words as he drove back into town. It seemed that all the work on this ambitious project was for nothing now. Gilmartin had prepared so much, his widow had told them, arranging flights for the African actors, making bookings in Edinburgh for a prolonged stay during the Festival. It would all be cancelled now. She had already told Goodfellow he would have to see to that.

The detective frowned. It was the first time Vivien had mentioned the man's name, and yet she must have been in contact with him on her mobile since arriving back at their house during the wee small hours of Saturday morning. Odd, he told himself. Why hadn't she spoken about Gilmartin's business before now? They could have offered the use of their landline for anything she needed.

His fingers drummed against the steering wheel as he thought about it. He didn't really know this woman, did he? *Lady Foxy*, he'd called her, as though they had been pals for ever. But she had been Mrs Charles Gilmartin for much longer than the few years they had known one another as teenagers at school. Their lives had taken such different paths. Until now, when the sudden death of Charles Gilmartin had brought her glittering London theatrical world and that of a Glasgow detective very close indeed.

CHAPTER FOURTEEN

'That's the bend in the river, there's the athletes' village and there,' the end of a pencil tapped a small area on the map, 'is where the opening ceremony will take place.'

Several pairs of eyes looked at the man standing at the centre of the table. He was the sort of person who would pass unnoticed in any crowd – short and of slight build, his thinning hair making him look older than he really was; nonetheless he had command of this disparate group of men. His dark eyes roved around each one of the other five intently, seeking assurance that all present in the room were of one mind and one accord.

'You know our aim, *gentlemen*.' The last word was almost a sneer: several of the assembled group had been detained on more than one occasion at Her Majesty's pleasure. 'Maximum disruption. Getting our message across in the only way these idiots seem to understand!' He was glaring at them now, arms folded across his chest as though defying any sort of opposition.

'We had one hundred per cent success with the Drymen explosive and there has been absolutely no comeback from MI6. Right, Number Five?'

A black-haired man straightened his back as it became clear that the leader's question was directed towards him. No names were given in these clandestine meetings and at first some of them had sniggered over this, but that had been back at the start of the previous year. Now, each and every one of them understood the need for complete secrecy if they were to pose an effective threat to the success of the Glasgow 2014 Commonwealth Games.

'Right,' the dark-haired man agreed.

'They think it was some daft wee laddies out in the village,' added the explosives expert, the oldest man in the room.

A small ripple of laughter flowed around the table.

'All the better for us,' their leader replied. 'Now, listen carefully. This is what we are going to do.'

They all leaned forward more closely to look at the map of Glasgow laid out on the table, the afternoon sun slanting directly on to the creases where it had been folded and refolded, silvering the blue line of the River Clyde and the pencil point that was hovering above Parkhead Stadium.

As he explained the plan, the potential for damage and carnage was clear to even the dullest imagination. The man's words conjured up pictures of twisted metal, row upon row of seats upended by the blast and, best of all, the collapse of a regime that each of them detested so bitterly. They were fighters in a war, he reminded them, survivors of an ancient race. Their blood was purer than that of those upstart Hanoverians. It was time to let the world know that they would no longer tolerate being subordinate to such outdated rule.

Some time later each man left the building, singly and in different directions, avoiding the ever-present stares of CCTV cameras, buoyed up by their leader's rhetoric, surer than ever of the cause for which they were fighting.

Cameron Gregson strode along the city street, heart pounding. The expression on the leader's face might have been almost laughable had his words not had such deep intent. He was, Cameron had decided with each successive meeting, probably certifiable, but perhaps it took a madman to exert that sort of authority over the members of this group. *And* to effect the plan.

A thrill of excitement shivered the hairs on the back of the young man's neck. They could do this. It would happen just as they had planned.

His own contribution had been to gain inside knowledge from the ever-willing Gayle, though lately she had grumbled about his snide remarks. Cameron smiled to himself. He had taken the decision not to pretend too much. Better to be disparaging about the Games, let her protest how wonderful they were going to be as she tried to persuade him to come to the various functions that were happening on an almost weekly basis.

He crossed the road and slipped down a cobbled lane where the internet café door was open to the sunshine. Loads of students seemed to be out on this warm April afternoon, and as Cameron entered the café, he glanced around, hoping that there would be no familiar face there to distract him.

No emails, the leader had always insisted. No using computers to contact one another. Too easy for the spooks to follow a trail like that. So they used cheap mobile phones dedicated to this venture, their identities protected from any network and from each other.

But this afternoon Cameron Gregson was not intending to send an email from his identity as Number Six. The letter to Gayle was from his Hotmail account, one of several that he had set up.

As he ordered his latte, the young man was already composing the words in his head, sweet-talking the girl so that she would give him another chance.

It had been on a bright sunny day like this that he had met the leader. He had taken a pint out to the beer garden at the back of his favourite pub in Ashton Lane when the sound of bagpipes had started up, making the drinkers look up to see where the noise was coming from. Lots of the windows in Lilybank Gardens had been open to catch the warm breeze and it was from behind one of these that the lone piper was beginning his repertoire. After an initial wheeze and tentative notes of tuning, music began to spill: first a slow march, followed by some jigs and reels, then, hauntingly, the measured notes of 'The Dark Island'.

Cameron had not noticed the man coming to stand by his side then, so wrapped up was he in listening to the unseen piper whose music had captured his attention.

'That's the one that always gets me,' the man had said, looking past Cameron with a rapt expression on his face.

'Aye,' Cameron had responded. 'Know what you mean. Good piper, isn't he?'

The man had slid easily on to the bench next to Cameron, a polite discussion about the merits of various pipe bands ensuing before the conversation had taken a different turn.

It had been Cameron who had expressed his disgust with modern British politics, not caring to conceal his fervent hatred of the upper classes, especially the royals and all they stood for. It was easy to let your opinions flow with each successive pint when your companion was a stranger you would never set eyes on again. The man had concurred with Cameron's point of view, filling in historical gaps in the younger man's knowledge that had impressed the PhD student.

'What d'you do about it, though? That's the trouble,' Cameron had said, a note of bitterness in his tone. He recalled the faraway look in the other man's eyes, then the way he had turned and stared at Cameron for a long moment as though debating something within himself.

'There are things that can be done,' the man had said at last, his words spoken in a low voice so that only Cameron would hear them, 'for those who are brave enough to go through with them.'

Cameron sipped his latte, remembering the moment when their eyes had met. It was as if some kindred spirit had come to him that afternoon in the form of that ordinary-looking man. They had talked some more, then walked the length of Byres Road together, crossing over to the Botanic Gardens.

It was a war between the royalists and the people, the man had explained, and he had outlined the course of history so succinctly that Cameron felt that it answered all the years of frustration he had felt growing up in a Scotland that seemed ruled by outsiders.

'My name's ...' He had held out his hand, but the man had waved it away, insisting he didn't want to know. Knowing names was unsafe. If the young man really wanted to join the fight against the enemy, he would be given a number.

And so Cameron Gregson had become Number Six. A time and place to meet again had been arranged and the mobile phone duly handed over with strict instructions to use it only for operational purposes.

Each meeting with the group was arranged for a different house in a different part of the city. Sometimes it would be an upstairs flat in the heart of the university area; other times he travelled out to the suburbs to a bungalow or semi full of other people's belongings. Cameron was pretty sure that the properties did not belong to any of the other men, and suspected that the leader, despite his evident hatred of the upper classes and what they stood for, actually owned these places. He was always first to arrive and last to leave. Once, wishing to ask a final question, Cameron had turned back to see the man with a bunch of keys in his hand, ready to lock the front door of a lower cottage flat out in Knightswood.

That he might be making his living as a landlord intrigued Cameron Gregson. Was he a wealthy man, then? A disaffected member of the upper classes? His voice and manners were not of that ilk, though. He spoke with the Glasgow accent of an educated man, not one whose vowels were brayed out nasally like some of those public-school types Cameron had encountered at university. And he was always dressed simply, nothing fancy or expensive, just a navy anorak and a pair of Blue Harbour trousers from M&S. It was, Cameron had thought to himself, as though he wanted to merge into the crowd. As he had attended more and more meetings, his respect for the leader had risen, listening to how the plan could be achieved if they managed to infiltrate the various areas of Glasgow 2014 without really being noticed.

Cameron's mouth twisted in a moue of self-disgust. Becoming Gayle's boyfriend had brought him to the notice of several of her friends and colleagues. He was always careful not to bad-mouth the Games in front of them, of course, but somehow repressing his real thoughts had made him explode with fury in the private moments when they were together. If the others had any inkling what Number Six was saying to her, he'd be out on his ear, Cameron thought. Or worse.

They were a mixed lot, the soldiers in his small troop. Two of them had mentioned being in prison, though what crimes they had committed was never talked about. Number Two was a big brute of a man with fists like hams and shoulders that suggested he could have carried a beast off the hills. Sometimes Cameron imagined the man in full Highland dress as in the olden times, a plaid wrapped around his chest, a weapon in his hand. The impression was heightened by his muscular arms; they were covered in whorls of green and blue tattoos, Celtic runes that swirled and twisted right down to the backs of his enormous wrists. With his rust-red hair and full beard, Number Two looked well suited to his particular task: something to do with the Homecoming, one of the many events peripheral to the Commonwealth Games, though big in its own way. He was to accompany a party of overseas visitors to the opening ceremony, though just how that had been achieved, Cameron never found out.

It was best not to ask too many questions, he had discovered. The other ex-con had the privileged position of being Number Three, and Cameron was certain that he and the leader had been on first-name terms long before the group had been established, such was the rapport between the two men. Tall and thin, with lank black hair, he reminded Cameron of an emaciated spider that might scuttle swiftly towards its prey before a sudden kill. A look from Number Three was enough to silence any idle chatter from the members of the group, and Cameron had wondered more than once if this man had ever committed a capital crime, such was the sense of grim suppressed rage that emanated from him at times.

Of the other two, one was the white-haired explosives expert, an older man who always welcomed Cameron with a smile on his benign countenance. Grandad, as Cameron silently termed him, was evidently enjoying his part in the project, particularly in the wake of the Drymen bomb. 'Number Four blows up some more,' he'd joked quietly to Cameron, nudging him with his elbow as if the whole plan to destroy the Commonwealth Games was a huge schoolboy wheeze. Cameron had watched him during the meetings, his serene face turned to the leader, listening to every word yet giving the impression that he was still in an impregnable world of his own.

He assumed that each man had been given his number after joining the group, yet Number Five was the one man he felt could take over most easily from the leader if that ever became necessary.

In his late twenties, curly dark hair cut smartly, thick-soled shoes always polished, he was, Cameron had to admit, the most difficult member of the group to identify in any way. One day he might arrive briefcase in hand, like a city businessman, yet on others he would be wearing a thick parka, as if his day job entailed being out of doors. It was odd how they all deferred to him whenever he had something to suggest. His was the sort of authority that had made the younger man decide eventually that their mission was not some fly-by-night escapade but something much more serious.

Any failure would have devastating consequences for them all, this man had insisted more than once. And it was Number Five who seemed to know about the activities of MI6, though through what channels he received this information remained a mystery. Was he a government official of some kind?

Or – and this was a thought that had crossed Cameron's mind more than once – a senior member of Police Scotland?

The Anti Terrorist Unit consisted of four officers, whose domain was a small office upstairs in Stewart Street, though at eight o'clock on this April evening there was only one person still at work. Police Sergeant Patsy Clark smoothed back a loose strand of hair that had escaped from her bun, her fingers searching for a kirby grip to fasten it back. As the date of the Commonwealth Games approached, there were daily memos from the Home Office. Some of them were routine stuff, but there were a few that made the police officer's eyes gleam with anticipation.

That there were threats to the safety of the Games was not in any doubt. The security measures had been impressive, though, and Patsy's team had given wholehearted approval to everything carried out since the building work in the East End had commenced. Occasional notes would pass through the office concerning disaffected groups known to government sources. The general public had little inkling of the undercurrents of wrath and madness that went on beneath the surface. TV programmes about spies and films about world domination tapped into only a tiny part of what really went on; stuff that the Official Secrets Act made certain would never come to the consciousness of ordinary people.

Now there was a new memo for the officer to read, a note from someone on high to alert her squad to the possibility of a new group working in the Strathclyde area. Patsy had been commanded to stay in the office until it arrived, and the mounting anticipation had not been rewarded by anything special as far as she could see.

'Another lot of nutters,' she murmured, though the wording of the email was rather more stiff and official in describing this particular threat.

It has come to our notice … it began, making Patsy smile. Just how that had happened was something she longed to know. Being in this unit was the nearest she would probably come to the misty world of the Secret Services, yet that was a world she longed to be a part of, and she suspected that her fellow officers here in Glasgow no doubt nurtured similar dreams.

'Right,' she said aloud, though at this hour of the day there was no other officer in the room, 'here's one for you then, sir.'

She read the memo again, nodding in approval. Last year it was Detective Superintendent Lorimer who had been chosen to give a statement about the bomb near the West Highland Way out past Drymen. Now he had been suggested by someone further up the chain of command as the person to take charge of the Glasgow end of the investigation into what could prove to be a terrorist cell. Perhaps this time the team might be able to follow through on the information that came in these brief memos as though someone in the corridors of power were reluctant to let go of it.

89

CHAPTER FIFTEEN

The shopping mall was crowded with youngsters enjoying their last few days of freedom before the school term began again. Shereen steered the young black woman through the melee of chattering kids, pulling at her arm every time Asa stopped to stare at anything, which was often. She had tried to explain their destination as they had left the flat and got into the same car that had brought the girl to this part of the city, but Asa's terrified face as they were pushed into the back seat showed that the Nigerian girl had understood none of it.

Now, heading towards the entrance of Primark, Shereen hoped that the girl would relax long enough for her to be able to buy the things she needed. Leaving the men back in the underground car park had been her idea.

'Can't you see she's scared of you? It's taken me days to build up her confidence and I'm not having you pair of idiots ruin it!' Shereen had scolded them. She'd been aware of Asa listening to the heated exchange, their raised voices only making the girl shrink further into the corner of her seat. But the older woman had chivvied them into seeing things her way, and now she and Asa were together, her hand around the girl's waist as she steered her into the shop.

'Dress,' she said, pulling at a rack of summer clothes and then indicating her own cotton frock.

Asa looked at Shereen intently. 'Dress,' she parroted.

'Good girl, Asa.' Shereen smiled broadly and patted the girl's arm to show that she was pleased with her. 'Now let's find you some suitable things to wear.'

Asa's head was spinning after the walk through the marble-floored hall. Never in her young life had she seen so many white people together. There were, admittedly, a few Asian faces amongst them, and once, an African couple who had glanced her way before Shereen had tugged on her arm, making her walk faster. But it all looked so terribly strange, so *foreign*, that Asa's longing for home was stronger than ever. Now here she was in this enormous shop full of different sorts of clothing, some of it piled into towering stacks, and faceless white mannequins that made her shudder despite the clothes fitted on to their skinny frames.

Shereen's voice chattered on as the girl wandered further and further into this place full of colour and finery. Once, she had turned timidly to the older woman, hands outstretched as if to ask permission to feel the cloth of a particular blue dress, and Shereen had grinned widely, nodding her head. The girl's mouth was open in wonder as she touched the acrylic material, its soft folds slipping like water under her hands. After a quick rummage along the rail Shereen selected a small size and gave a grunt of satisfaction.

Quickly a pattern began to emerge. No sooner would Asa's fingers touch the silky fabric of one garment than Shereen had it whisked off the hanger and added to the growing pile over her arm.

'Come over here, time to try these on, Asa,' she said at last, pushing the girl towards the entrance of the changing rooms.

The girl drew back a little as she was faced with a row of white canvas curtains. What lay behind them? her frightened expression seemed to ask.

But just as she was resisting the pressure on her thin arm, a girl of about her own age emerged from one of the fitting rooms and twirled around. Asa gave a gasp and covered her mouth with her hand as she saw the same blue dress being shown off to a couple of other girls who were waiting outside.

The next half-hour passed in a dream, Asa trying on one dress after another, Shereen always there with an encouraging nod or a shake of her dark curly head if she didn't think the garment quite right for the girl.

Asa was in a daze as they left the fitting room behind. Shereen had selected four dresses, the blue and three others that Asa had chosen. Now the woman was heading towards a different area, where the girl saw baskets full of underwear and rows of matching panties and brassieres stretched over clear plastic hangers. Atop a high shelf a black figure reclined, another mannequin, clad only in the skimpiest pale pink bra and bikini pants. Asa's lips parted, the desire to ask questions burning inside her. Were these things for everyone, then?

Without a glance towards her companion, Shereen shoved several gossamer-thin sets of underwear, bright pink, turquoise and lime green, into the round shopping basket.

'Shoes,' she said, stopping suddenly. 'What size will you be, d'you think?'

Asa stared blankly, unable to understand what was being said.

'Shoes,' Shereen repeated, bending down and tapping her own footwear. 'Come on, we need to get you something you can walk in.'

And so it was that Asa found herself seated on a low stool,

several pairs of brightly coloured high heels scattered around the carpet as she tried on one pair after another, her slender feet slipping inside most of them. At last two pairs were deemed to be satisfactory and Shereen added leopardskin stilettos and navy blue slingbacks to the pile in her basket.

As Shereen led the way back through the mall towards the bank of elevators leading to the car park, Asa's grin faded along with the good feeling she had enjoyed in the huge shop. There were so many questions she longed to ask. Why had she been taken from her home? Why transported in that freezing truck then kept a virtual prisoner in the grey room? And why, oh why, was she now being given all these beautiful things, as though she were some sort of princess?

CHAPTER SIXTEEN

'It's time,' the man told her. 'You know what has to be done, right?'

Shereen swallowed back a pert retort, her eyes cast downwards. The last few days the woman had tried to forget that this day would come. The young girl, Asa, was different from the rest – more vulnerable, more childlike than the others had been – and knowing what lay ahead made the older woman fear for her.

Asa's head swam as she sat between the two men in the back of the car. There was a sickness in her stomach and she wanted to close her eyes and sleep, but the big man on her right kept nudging her awake, his elbow jabbing the soft flesh on her arm. Shereen had given her some pills with her breakfast and Asa had taken them, trusting the smile and the outstretched hand. Now the drugs had done their work and she was being taken somewhere, powerless to resist, only wanting this nausea to stop.

As if her unspoken wish had been heard, the car drew up against a pavement and Asa was helped out of the car. The relief of breathing in the fresh air was all too short as the men escorted her through a door and into a room with chairs around its white walls.

As she sat quietly, Asa looked at the place, wondering what it was. Two girls were standing beside a display of what seemed to be a bundle of shiny pictures attached to the wall, turning them over one after the other. Asa blinked, curiosity heightening her vision. Her brow puckered as she saw that they were examining sheet after sheet of black designs on white paper, their voices low and companionable. At last they seemed to come to an agreement and left the room, entering another door and closing it behind them.

There were windows to the front of the shop and Asa watched as people passed by, her drugged stupor making everything appear strange. They seemed so silent, these grey people, bowed down against the world, sometimes moving jerkily like puppets, and Asa began to wonder who they were and what their lives were like as she sat patiently between her captors.

Asa looked up as the man they called Okonjo nudged her side. Had she been sleeping? Okonjo was an African who reminded her of one of their neighbours back home. Although she had never heard him speak a single word of Yoruba – he always chose to converse in English – she suspected that he was Nigerian, like her. And now something was happening; the other one was on his feet, shaking hands with a white stranger, a grey-haired bearded man who stood there talking to her companion, the tone of his voice questioning, his glance shifting towards her face.

Asa looked up, surprised. Where had he come from and why was he staring at her? His high domed forehead gave him an intelligent appearance and those twinkling eyes seemed to be smiling right into her soul. Asa smiled back and he nodded.

'Nineteen? Okay. Hard to tell. Your girls always look so much younger,' the man said. 'Come on in.'

Asa felt her arm being taken firmly as she was led into the next room and seated in a black leather chair.

'Okay, you've decided that this is the design you would like?'

'She doesn't speak any English,' the big man said gruffly. 'Just get on with it, all right?'

Asa's eyes widened as the grey-haired man lifted her right leg gently and laid it across his lap. She held on to the edges of the chair, terrified, as he lifted her skirt and wiped her inner thigh with a swab. Once, long ago, Asa had visited a white doctor miles from home and she still remembered the line of weeping girls and the jab of a needle as they were vaccinated against that terrible disease. Was this a clinic, then? And was she being given something to protect her against some awful illness?

The man's fingers were soft, clad in pale protective gloves, as they touched her skin. He took the sterile needle carefully from its paper pack and placed it into a small metal machine. His voice spoke soothing words, making her body relax as a low buzzing noise began like some large insect hovering close by.

There was no white coat like that other doctor had worn, though, and Asa decided to close her eyes against whatever would happen next.

CHAPTER SEVENTEEN

It was a perfect morning, Samantha decided, as she entered the leafy wood. The sound of Badger's hooves was muffled by the carpet of soft pine needles and she fancied from the prick of his ears that the big cob enjoyed walking along this dusty brown path, a change from their usual route from the stables. Overhead patches of blue showed through a tracery of larch twigs, opening up to reveal a swathe of flawless skies, and as the horse stepped out from the trees, Samantha guided him towards what appeared to be a sheep track bordering the edge of the wood. Catching sight of a line of barbed wire that fenced off the land beyond the wood, she reined him in for a moment, trying to decide which way to proceed. Straight ahead the ground rose in a narrow series of hillocks that disappeared once more into the dark trees, but if she were to turn downhill then she might find a path that went around the marsh and back via the farm road.

Pulling the horse's head around, Samantha leaned back slightly to compensate for the gradient as Badger picked his way down, following the edge of the wood on one side, the wire fence on the other. The spring grass was lush here, fresh green and tempting to a big horse like Badger, but the animal kept plodding onwards, not once trying to snatch the reins from her hand and grab a quick mouthful as another less placid mount might have done. He was a big softie, Samantha thought to herself, relaxing into the horse's shambling gait as he stepped down her preferred path. Soon the hill gave way to a flatter area and Samantha caught sight of something glittering in the distance. That was surely the pond down by the marshes? She had been right to choose this way, hadn't she?

Suddenly the horse shied, moving sideways as a small bird flew out of a clump of reeds, and Samantha's grip was momentarily lost, jolting her in the saddle so that she had to grab a handful of mane to steady herself.

'Shh, boy, it's okay, just a stupid bird,' the girl soothed him, patting his neck and urging him forwards once more. The pond was a bright arc of shimmering light now, the path bordered by a low wooden fence instead of the barbed wire. Just below her eye level Samantha noticed a dragonfly hovering delicately before zooming off towards the water. She watched its translucent wings for a moment, then turned her attention to the path ahead.

It was just a glimpse, no more, but Samantha saw a familiar shape that made her rein the horse to a standstill.

The girl blinked, refusing to believe at first what it was that she was seeing.

It was right down there, at the very edge of the marshes, unseen perhaps by anyone on foot, the clumps of reeds thick against the path, but easily spotted from her vantage point on Badger's back.

Heart thumping, Samantha Lockhart closed her eyes as if somehow that would make this awful thing disappear. But when she opened them again there was still the unmistakable shape of a body lying face down, half hidden in the tall grasses fringing the pond.

*

'Black, late teens, has probably been here a good few days by the look of her,' the pathologist sighed. The ground around the marshy pond was teeming with human activity now; to one side was a police Range Rover, its doors open as yet another figure sat pulling on the regulation white forensic suit, several officers having already cordoned off the entire area. Detective Superintendent Lorimer sat back on his heels as the pathologist continued her examination of the body. Eyebrows might be raised at an officer of his rank appearing at the crime scene, but this was so close to the Cathkin Braes, one of the venues for the forthcoming Commonwealth Games, that he had made the decision to be there with the scene-of-crime officers and the pathologist.

It was Dr Rosie Fergusson, his friend and colleague, who was bent over the girl's body, examining her with a tenderness that never failed to move the senior officer. Each of them had been exposed to many horrors at scenes of crime, but on this lovely spring morning, with collared doves cooing innocently from a tree nearby, there was something especially horrific about this corpse.

There was no need to ask about the cause of death. Twin strands of stiff wire stood out from the back of her neck where someone had twisted them together, biting into the dark flesh. Lorimer had glimpsed her face then looked away, seeing the damage that many small creatures had already inflicted. A lesser stomach might have heaved at the sight, but Rosie kept on going, her voice quiet and firm as she described the wounds and a possible time of death.

'Several days ago,' she repeated, turning to catch Lorimer's eye. 'We can be more precise once she's in the mortuary.' She stood up, drawing closer so that only he could hear her. 'What's brought *you* here anyway?' she asked, brushing a gloved hand over her face as a small cloud of mayflies swooped and hovered.

'It's fairly close to the mountain biking route,' Lorimer explained. 'For the Games,' he added.

'Ah.' Rosie nodded, understanding. 'You think she's got something to do with that?'

'I hope not,' he said, blowing out a sigh. 'And I don't want the press knowing about this. We're all trying to keep Glasgow 2014 a trouble-free zone.'

'Young, slender, African ethnic origin ...' Rosie's eyebrows curved sardonically under the hooded suit. 'You don't think there's a connection?'

Lorimer sighed again. 'Oh God, I hope not. The murder of a foreign national involved in the Games is not what we need at this stage.' He stopped, biting his lip. Since the bomb explosion outside Drymen last summer there had been several alerts passing through his division, all of them continuing into the misty regions of Special Branch never to be heard of again. But a young dead woman, a young dead *black* woman, was most definitely going to be kept within Detective Superintendent Lorimer's own jurisdiction.

CHAPTER EIGHTEEN

Rosie Fergusson often thought that Glasgow City Mortuary sat at the juxtaposition of life, death, the universe and everything. The High Court was only a few paces from their back door, very useful whenever she had to hurry out after a PM to attend a case as an expert witness. And stretching out beyond a busy road that led into the heart of the city lay Glasgow Green, its swathes of grass a welcome respite from the bustle of city life. Often at twilight the pathologist had seen a fox trotting along the pavement then heading home across the parkland, unconcerned by the traffic rushing past.

The girl's corpse was still in its refrigerated cabinet but soon it would be time for the post-mortem to begin and the tray where she lay would be thrust into the room and placed on one of the surgical steel tables. It had been an odd thing to see the naked body out there in the open, and so many questions had coursed through the pathologist's mind even as she had examined the girl. Perhaps when the Fiscal arrived with Lorimer, the post-mortem would answer at least some of them.

Iain MacIntosh was a man with a reputation for fair-handedness, yet, as Fiscal, his were often hard decisions to make when dealing with matters of life and death. And much as Lorimer wished to talk to him about the fate of Charles Gilmartin, he knew that this was secondary to the reason they were standing together at the viewing window in Glasgow City Mortuary.

The girl's naked body was being examined closely by the pathologist, the scars and activities from small pond animals pointed out one by one under her careful scrutiny.

'Something that looks like a partial tattoo,' she had said, glancing up towards the viewing platform. 'Skin's been nibbled away from most of it. Fish predations,' she added. 'See these small oval and circular bite marks?'

The two men peered closer, trying to follow where the pathologist's scalpel was pointing.

'And here. You can see the traces of ink. And there is a raised piece of skin suggesting that an infection had set in. African skin is more prone to a keloid scar. A scar that continues to grow,' she explained, looking at the mark more closely. The blunt edge of a scalpel blade traced the mark, a small curve that had been tattooed on to her inner right thigh.

Lorimer strained his eyes but it was impossible to see more than a suggestion of a mark. Photographs would have to be taken then enhanced before they would know what they were looking at.

'She'd been there for more than three days,' Rosie told them. 'We will give you a more exact time once the insect infestation has been examined, but I think you can say that this girl was killed some time during last Friday night or the early hours of Saturday morning.'

Lorimer swallowed, a sudden bad taste in his mouth that was nothing to do with watching the post-mortem. On Friday night Charles Gilmartin had died. By his own hand? a little voice asked.

Or that of another? And he himself had been laughing and joking with people he hadn't seen in over twenty years, making small talk for the most part. The sudden memory of sitting next to Foxy out in the playground rushed back vividly and he shivered. The wire around the unknown black girl's throat might have been twisted cruelly even as he had been enjoying the company of a beautiful woman.

'Any missing persons fitting her description?' MacIntosh asked.

Lorimer shook his head, eyes still on Rosie bent over the cadaver on the steel table. 'No,' he replied. 'But that tattoo might help to identify her,' he added.

'And there was nothing in the vicinity of the pond to give any clues as to who she was or where she came from. Stark naked and dumped,' MacIntosh added in a tone of disgust. 'As if she was a bit of rubbish to be fly-tipped.'

Both men were accustomed to the cruelties that human beings could and did perpetrate on one another, but sometimes, as now, one of those atrocities gave each of them pause for thought.

'You think she was on the game?' Lorimer asked, raising his voice so that Rosie might hear his question through the intercom.

'The vaginal area is torn in several places. Tears are fairly new, I'd say, and there is a fair amount of scar tissue as well, so yes, I would guess that this girl has been used as a prostitute.'

Lorimer and MacIntosh exchanged glances.

'But that's not the only thing,' Rosie added, sliding a gloved hand across the abdominal area. 'If my guess is correct, she was in the early stages of pregnancy. A bit more work down here and we'll know for certain.'

'You say *girl*. How old do you think she was?' the Fiscal asked.

'Oh, less than eighteen,' Rosie replied. 'My estimate would be around fifteen or sixteen, no more.'

Lorimer and MacIntosh exchanged glances. She was a child, then, under their system of law.

The next stage in the post-mortem was to remove the girl's vital organs; they would be weighed on scales nearby, her fellow pathologist taking notes as Rosie talked them through every part of the procedure. The girl's body was soon open for all to see, the thoracic area having been cut through by Rosie's expert scalpel blade to reveal what lay within, and somehow this part of the examination depersonalised the victim, making her more of a case study than what had once been a living breathing human being.

The foetus, when it was removed later from the womb, could not have been more than fourteen weeks, but already it was a tiny human form curled in a bud of pale flesh, eyes forever closed against a forbidding world. Rosie handled it tenderly before replacing it in the mother's uterus.

Someone wanted this poor creature dead, she thought. Or did they? The girl was slender and the slight swelling on her abdomen could have been easily overlooked at this stage. Was the pathologist, after all, the first to know about the fleeting existence of these three inches of premature life? Rosie sighed, glancing at the men who stood above her. These were questions that they must ask themselves. Her role was merely to search for what could be seen and suggest possibilities; theirs was to find the truth.

'You can't do that!' The words were out of Martin Goodfellow's mouth before he could stop them. *It isn't what Charlie would have wanted*, he longed to add, but now his teeth had sunk into his bottom lip, forcing himself to keep calm, be more restrained. After all, wasn't Vivi in terrible shock?

'I can and I will.' The red-haired woman's voice was cold on the other end of the telephone. 'There is no way on earth that the project is going to take place now, Martin. I want you to begin dismantling it right away. Cancel everything,' she added, letting a tremor enter her words. '*Everything*. And that's an order.'

Martin Goodfellow heard the click and looked at the handset with a sense of disbelief. Only days ago he had been chatting happily to Charlie, discussing the various hotels that he had booked in Edinburgh. Gilmartin had sounded pleased with his suggestions. 'Money no object now, my boy,' he'd told Martin, and the assistant producer recalled that throaty chuckle.

He replaced the telephone, letting his hand drop limply to his side. It had all changed now, Vivi had told him. It wasn't just a case of a sudden heart attack after all. Charles had taken his own life.

Martin Goodfellow sank into the nearest chair by the desk where he had sat so often with the great man. The still air seemed redolent with their voices, the eager planning of this theatrical venture that had spun magical webs in this very room.

'Why?' he whispered aloud, looking towards the other side of the desk as though in expectation of an answer. 'What made you do it, Charlie?'

'May I have a cup of tea, please, Maggie?'

Vivien Gilmartin stumbled into the kitchen, grasping hold of the back of the rocking chair with both hands.

'Oh Vivien!' Maggie saw the white face, the woman's legs buckling beneath her, and rushed to her side, easing Vivien into the chair. 'Put your head down. Like this.' She motioned with both arms held forwards. 'That's right,' she added as Vivien dropped her head between her knees.

'I'll fetch you some water,' Maggie murmured, shaken by the other woman's sudden faint.

It had been too much for her to call that man in London, she thought angrily. Couldn't the police have done it instead? Surely voicing the news that your husband had killed himself would tip anyone over the edge?

'Here,' she said, hunkering down beside Vivien and handing her a glass of cold water. 'Take a few sips. It'll make you feel better.'

Maggie Lorimer was no stranger to young girls fainting at school, and although it was not always within her remit, she had sometimes taken the trouble to give them the immediate care that was required. A glass of water usually revived them long enough for someone to escort them to the school nurse.

A long exhalation of breath came from beneath that mass of red hair, then, slowly, the woman sat up again, sinking back against the cushions, still clutching the glass.

'Okay?'

Vivien nodded.

'Right.' Maggie rose to her feet, patting the other woman's arm. 'I'll make us some tea.' *And something to eat,* she told herself. Vivien had refused breakfast and her blood sugar was probably far too low. One of Maggie's home-made scones with butter and last year's plum jam should sort her out.

Soon they were sitting together, Maggie perched on the settee at right angles to her guest. The scones had disappeared, Vivien agreeing that she ought to eat something, and Maggie had poured them each a second cup of tea.

'Maggie,' Vivien began. 'What would you think if it was Bill?'

Maggie leaned back, surprised at the question. 'I don't know,' she replied slowly. 'I can't imagine that he would ever do anything like that.'

The red-haired woman nodded. 'That's exactly how I feel. There's no reason ... there *was* no reason ... for Charles to do it.'

She placed her mug carefully on a coaster. 'He had everything to live for,' she said quietly. 'No worries of any kind. Not that *I* know of anyway.'

Maggie Lorimer heard the tinge of bitterness in Vivien's voice. Had there been some distance between the couple, then? A lack of sharing?

As if reading her mind, Vivien went on. 'Here I was, too wrapped up in that blasted school reunion to notice if anything was wrong!'

'But you were together every day. And you had taken all that trouble to rent the apartment. You mustn't blame yourself, Vivien,' Maggie said, trying to find words of consolation.

The red hair was tossed back in a gesture of defiance. 'I must have missed something,' she growled in a throaty voice. 'Mustn't I?'

Maggie tried to catch her eye, but the woman was staring into the distance, her cheeks flushed faintly now. Even stricken with the worst kind of sorrow, Vivien Gilmartin was still quite lovely, Maggie thought, looking at her. And she could so easily understand the deep attraction that her husband had once felt.

The flats by the riverside were accessed by a wide gateway allowing traffic to enter at the stated speed of no more than twenty miles per hour. In addition there were speed bumps to slow down any vehicle attempting to rush into the complex. It was odd, Lorimer thought, that he had not remembered any of this during the dark hours when he had been hastened to the place by Vivien's hysterical phone call. Now, in daylight, he could see that the buildings that had seemed mere uniform blocks of pale brick were actually quite attractive, their bases softened by borders of shrubbery and clumps of yellow daffodils nodding in the afternoon breeze. It was largely privately owned, the factor had told him when he had called to enquire, but there were several landlords who had bought to let and the Gilmartins' flat was one of them.

He parked the Lexus in an empty bay and strode towards the main door. A memory of ushering Vivien out, his arm supporting her, flashed through his brain. She had been distraught to the point of collapse, thinking that her husband had suffered a sudden heart attack in his sleep. There had surely been a crumb of comfort thinking that Gilmartin had died quietly, peacefully. Now even that possibility had been torn away from her and he tried not to imagine what must be going through his friend's mind.

The hallway was cast in shadow, the sun favouring the far side of the building, as Lorimer waited for the lift. Looking around, he could see signs of care: potted geraniums, pink and scarlet, thrived at the doorways of the ground-floor flats, and there was a table where a pile of circulars had been neatly stacked. It was a decent-looking place, not one where he would expect to see murder rear its ugly head.

Soon he was rising upwards, his thoughts already on what he might find. The detective took a pair of latex gloves from his pocket, drawing them on before venturing into the flat, ever careful not to contaminate a crime scene, if indeed that was what it proved to be.

It felt cold as he entered the apartment, the heating probably on a timer. Vivien had told him that she and Charles had spent most of their waking hours away from the place, arranging the theatre project and the reunion, only using the flat as somewhere to sleep and eat breakfast. Still, it was a sharp contrast to the warm sunshine outside his own home where Lorimer had left his wife and former girlfriend.

He chose to go into Gilmartin's bedroom first, his eyes seeking out the bedside table next to where the man's body had lain. He stared at the plain, unvarnished cabinet for a moment, then peered closely to see if there were any marks on its surface, rings from a coffee mug, anything that might show what had been laid there. But there was nothing, only the thinnest layer of dust. He straightened up, pondering the facts before him, trying to recall what else that female officer might have done when she had elected to strip the bed. Had there really been no glass or cup lying by the dead man's bed?

As if retracing the other officer's steps, Lorimer walked through the lounge, where three half-empty mugs still sat on a tray, and into a galley kitchen. The bed linen was still inside the washer dryer and Lorimer left it there, his eyes turning to the cabinets fixed to the wall. His gloved hands opened them one after the other until he came to shelves containing glasses and crockery. With one finger he counted each stack of dishes and plates. As he'd expected, there was six of everything, plain white stuff that could easily be replaced if broken; three clean mugs plus the ones they had used for tea after Vivien's call. It was the same with the glasses; six of every size sat neatly side by side. Turning to look at the sink and the drainer beside it, Lorimer saw a plastic bowl on its side, a folded dishcloth laid on top, now dried by the sun shining through the window. There was nothing on the draining board, no single cup or mug from the last evening of Gilmartin's life. And this fact alone was creating a sense of disquiet in the detective's mind.

'There should have been an empty glass,' he said aloud.

And as though the spoken words had broken a spell, the detective superintendent turned on his heel and left the flat as quickly as he could.

'Tell me again,' he said, listening for a reply. He was in the Lexus now, heading back towards the mortuary.

'Aconitum,' Rosie replied. 'Sometimes called monkshood. It

was used in ancient times on an island called Ceos where they practised euthanasia. Anyone who wasn't essential to the state or was too old to be useful was given the poison and put to death.'

'And it should have produced vomiting and diarrhoea?'

'With muscular spasms, paralysis of the respiratory system, convulsions ...'

'But it didn't?'

'Well, there was quite a cocktail of stuff in the poor fellow's stomach. Anti-spasmodic drugs, for starters. Though the level of aconitum was enough to have killed him before convulsions began. All mixed up with ginger wine. Looks like he knew what he was doing all right.'

Lorimer listened, a grave expression on his face. If Charles Gilmartin had wanted to take his own life, the toxins that Rosie had found were easily sufficient to have acted swiftly and with no horrific side effects.

His mind flew back to the bedside table, where there had been no empty glass, no dregs for testing in the laboratory. *And the dark colour of ginger wine, with its sweet syrupy taste, would have disguised the tincture mixed into it.*

'He couldn't possibly have got up and washed the glass then put it away again?'

Rosie's snort of derision was all he needed to hear. 'No way. He'd have been dead in seconds. Perfect suicide,' she added.

Lorimer bit his lip. Unless he found that the female officer had washed up that glass and replaced it in the cupboard in a desire to be helpful, he would have to inform Iain MacIntosh that this was not a case of suicide at all.

'No, sir, I'm sure.' The woman's voice was firm. 'There was nothing at all on his bedside table. Actually,' she went on, 'I remember looking to see if there was an alarm clock. Thought it was a bit bleak, you know, being so bare.'

'And nothing in the kitchen. No glass, mug, anything he might have drunk from?'

'As I said,' the officer continued, her voice becoming increasingly frosty, 'nothing like that at all. I'm sure Dr Calder can confirm that. And no, I didn't wash anything up.'

'Thank you, PC Morgan. That is most helpful. And do bear in mind that you may be called on to testify to these facts in due course.'

There was a pause before she answered with a solemn 'Yes, sir.'

Lorimer exhaled a long breath as he considered the next stage in the investigation. He should hand this over to one of his fellow officers, but he felt uneasy at the thought of Vivien being grilled by a stranger. He was, he reminded himself, a potential witness should it transpire that Gilmartin had been murdered. And perhaps a conflict of interest might not go down well with a court of law. Sighing again, he resolved to wait and see what the Fiscal decided.

Meantime, there was still the huge task of finding out the identity of the black girl. DNA was being taken from her unborn child so at least there would be a slim chance of finding a paternal match. Otherwise, the girl's body might lie in the mortuary for months until it was decided no further investigation was possible. Then she would lie in an unmarked grave, a stranger deep within the green places of this city.

CHAPTER NINETEEN

It was hard to know what to say, Lorimer thought, closing the front door behind him. *Your husband was killed by person or persons unknown* was a bit brutal, though these were the words written on the report.

Iain MacIntosh had been unequivocal in his decision. The investigation would be carried out by another officer in Stewart Street due to Lorimer's personal involvement with the widow of the deceased. He had winced at that, but the Fiscal had not meant it unkindly and MacIntosh was not a man given to innuendo. It was what Lorimer had expected after all, and there was a sense of relief that he could no longer be in charge of this case while Vivien was staying with them. It meant, too, that he could concentrate on the death of the young girl.

She was Nigerian, Rosie had thought. The pathologist had travelled to Nigeria years ago and was familiar with the people there, though there were so many different ethnic groups on the great African continent that it was not possible to be completely accurate from the sight of a corpse alone.

'Hi.' Lorimer strode into the kitchen where his wife stood stirring something on the hob. Her face lit up when she turned to see him, giving Lorimer that momentary glow that he always felt on being home again. There was no sign of Vivien.

'Is she upstairs?' he whispered, eyes turned towards the ceiling.

Maggie nodded. 'Think she took something to make her sleep. Said she'd lain awake all of last night, poor thing.'

Lorimer exhaled a huge sigh of relief. All the way home he had been composing what to tell her, but nothing had seemed right except the unvarnished truth.

'What is it?' Maggie asked, laying down the wooden spoon and giving her husband all her attention.

'Doesn't appear to be suicide,' he told her, watching as her mouth opened in astonishment. 'The investigation will seek to find whoever murdered Charles Gilmartin.' He shrugged, as if actually saying it had released the weight of the burden he had been carrying.

'Someone broke into the flat while Vivien was at the school reunion?' Maggie's voice was a whisper of disbelief.

'There is no sign of a forced entry,' Lorimer replied. 'So it must be someone he knew or someone who had a key.'

'What will you tell her?' she asked, glancing upwards.

'Just that,' he replied simply. 'Oh, and that I won't be SIO on the case.'

Maggie nodded. She had been a policeman's wife long enough to know all the procedures that her husband had to follow.

'Right,' she said, then turned back to the soup pot on the hob, hand shaking as she picked up the ladle. 'Don't suppose you'll want any of this?' she asked doubtfully. 'It's one of your favourites: mulligatawny.'

Lorimer sighed and nodded. He wasn't hungry but she had gone to the trouble of cooking for him. 'Give me a minute to get washed. I'll be right back down.'

The fifth step on the staircase gave a creak as it always did, making Lorimer pause mid stride lest the sound awaken their house guest. He slipped into the bedroom and closed the door behind him, hoping that the noise of running water from their en suite bathroom would not disturb the woman sleeping across the corridor. A few minutes later he crept out again, careful to tread as quietly as he could.

'Bill? Is that you?' Her voice was sleepy and remote, more like the girl's voice he remembered from school days than the sophisticated woman whose original accent was barely discernible.

'Hi, how are you feeling?'

Vivien lay on the bed, the duvet swept to one side as though she had only just woken up. Was she unaware of the way her silky dress had ridden up, showing more of her thigh than was decent? Or did that not matter because it was William Lorimer standing there, looking at the figure of the woman he had once known so intimately? Her red hair spilled over the pillow making her look like a wanton creature from a Pre-Raphaelite painting, and for a moment Lorimer experienced a flare of desire.

'Hi yourself,' she replied sleepily, green eyes narrowing as she looked at him.

There was a silence between them as she studied his face as if looking for clues.

'Maggie's made some soup,' he told her at last, wanting to break the spell that threatened to draw him in. 'Coming downstairs?'

Vivien simply smiled and lifted one small white hand, gesturing for him to stay.

At that moment the telephone shrilled out.

'Better go. Come down when you're ready.' Then, without another glance at the woman lying on the bed, he turned and headed downstairs, listening for the sound of his wife's voice as the ringing stopped.

'It's for you. A Police Sergeant Clark?' Maggie passed over the handset as soon as Lorimer entered the room.

'Hello, Lorimer here.'

Maggie watched the changing expressions on her husband's face as he spoke to the officer from Stewart Street. Clark was not a name that Maggie Lorimer knew, so this was nothing to do with either Vivien's case or the one that had recently taken her husband to the mortuary. She could see the furrow on his brow deepen as he nodded, not speaking much, just asking an occasional question and listening to the reply, giving nothing away. At last he put down the telephone and turned back to his wife.

'I'd love some of that soup,' he said.

Maggie was putting the bowls into the dishwasher when she heard the woman's voice.

'Sorry. Must have fallen asleep again,' Vivien was saying.

'There's plenty of soup if you fancy some,' she offered.

Vivien was fully dressed now, dark tights cladding her shapely legs, a cashmere wrap slung artfully across her shoulders. She gave a delicate shudder. 'Sorry, couldn't face anything to eat. A cup of tea, though?'

Maggie nodded, turning to fill the kettle yet again. *I have measured out my life in teacups and spoons*, she said to herself, silently paraphrasing Eliot's famous poem. Yet she did feel a rush of sympathy towards the red-haired woman for the news that her husband was about to impart.

'Can't you get this cat off my chair?' Vivien was standing beside the rocking chair where Maggie's mother had sat so often,

Chancer purring loudly on her lap. She threw an angry look at Lorimer. 'You know I hate cats,' she said.

In three swift strides Maggie crossed the room, scooped up the ginger cat and walked back to the kitchen, cuddling her pet, heart beating with a fury that she could not voice. *My chair*, indeed! She had been here a few days and yet already Vivien was acting as though she owned the place! It was hard, Maggie thought, to feel sympathy for this woman, especially when, as now, she caught her smiling up at her husband in a manner that caused the school teacher a pang of dismay.

Soon have that wiped off your face, a bad little voice sounded in Maggie's ear, making her feel shocked and guilty in equal measure. This wasn't like her! What was happening to her normal kindly responses? She felt guilty tears spring to her eyes, and as she turned away to hide them, Chancer struggled out of her arms and fled into the garden. Maggie followed him into the dusky evening; she had no desire to witness the other woman's anguish.

'Vivien, sit down,' Lorimer said.

The red-haired woman's face paled even more as she sank into the rocking chair.

'It wasn't suicide,' Lorimer said bluntly. 'Charles did not take his own life.'

'But ...'

'There are several aspects of your husband's death that indicate he was poisoned. And not by his own hand.'

Vivien Gilmartin continued to stare at him, lips parting in a silent *oh* of disbelief.

'A good friend and colleague of mine has been appointed as Senior Investigating Officer. Chap called Alistair Wilson. You'll like him,' Lorimer continued. 'No-nonsense type of officer. Thorough.'

Traces of colour swam back into the woman's cheeks as he spoke. 'You won't ... ?'

'I won't be in charge of the case. Conflict of interest,' he said. 'After all, I might be cited as a witness to tell a jury where you were on the night of your husband's death.'

Vivien's mouth opened and closed again and Lorimer could see her hands shaking on her lap. Her green eyes widened. 'They don't think *I* had anything to do with it?' she gasped.

'Of course not. But you do see that my involvement with the case can't continue.'

They stared at one another for a moment, then Vivien let her glance fall. 'I'd hoped ... ' She bent forward, burying her face in her hands, shoulders heaving with silent sobs.

'Alistair will do a good job, don't you worry. He'll find out what happened to Charles,' Lorimer assured her.

But somehow the words that were intended to comfort only made the woman weep harder, a muffled sound of anguish escaping from behind her hands.

CHAPTER TWENTY

The image of the dead girl's tattoo had been thrown up on a screen in the incident room so that everyone could see its shape more clearly. The skin on her thigh had been torn or nibbled away, leaving a curled shape like the end of an old-fashioned coat hook, the sort that Lorimer remembered in the cloakroom of his primary school.

'It's been done in dark blue ink,' he told the assembled officers. 'Possibly some sort of Celtic symbol. Something for you to find out.' He nodded towards the youngest member of the team, a dark-haired girl whose blush of pleasure made Lorimer smile. PC Kirsty Wilson might be fresh out of Tulliallan, the Police Scotland training college, but he had managed to pull strings so that she could be with them in Stewart Street during some of her probationary period. Having dropped out of her course at Caledonian University after the investigation into her flatmate's murder, Kirsty was determined to make the police her career, following in her father's footsteps.

It had been a conscious decision on Lorimer's part to select Alistair Wilson as the SIO in the Gilmartin murder case. Kirsty's work should be kept strictly away from her dad's during her time here, the Assistant Chief Constable had told him when the detective superintendent had called in the favour. And Lorimer agreed. It would do Kirsty no good to have her father looking over her shoulder all the time, and putting her on this particular investigation meant that Lorimer could monitor her.

The detective superintendent continued to talk through the case of the unidentified body, giving all of the details that had emerged from the post-mortem, particularly the discovery that the unknown girl had been pregnant.

'DNA database might throw something up. Could be lucky,' he added with a shrug.

There were nods from some of the officers around the room. It was a great piece of technology to have in their possession nowadays, though the details kept on the records were only of those persons who had committed a crime. Records of non-convicted persons had to be destroyed. The strength of opinion from the human rights lobby that dictated this process was not something that all serving police officers shared, some being of the belief that a national database ought to be set up with every single citizen's DNA on permanent record.

The other actions were handed out; some officers were to trawl the known haunts of prostitutes to see if any Nigerian girl fitted the description of the deceased, others to search immigration records as well as the DNA database.

There were, thought Kirsty as she left the incident room, all sorts of ways of finding things out.

A Google search soon came up with tattoo designs that had their origin in Celtic and Pictish art. She trawled through several possibilities, but one particular motif made her pause for a closer look. It was a triple spiral, the three black hooks entwined, reminding the young officer of the Manx symbol, though the flowing lines of this were prettier, she decided, turning her attention

119

to the notes on one side of the page. *A triple spiral represents the three powers of maiden, mother and crone,* she read. *It is a sign of female power and especially power through transition and growth.*

'Didn't give you much power to protect yourself, did it, poor thing,' Kirsty whispered, recalling the photographic images of the girl's body taken at the scene and in the mortuary. She continued to read from the computer screen, one hand on the mouse, the other fishing for a piece of paper. There was something here that was worth noting down, she thought, just a few words but something she might want to remember even after printing off the whole page.

One meaning, she scribbled on a notepad. *Letting go, surrender, release.*

She sat back looking at her handwriting. Then, as though it really mattered, she drew the triple spiral as neatly as she could, shading in the lines. The words and phrases came in threes, Kirsty saw, and wasn't three a mystical number? 'A triple spiral,' she muttered to herself. 'Sounds like something one of those Commonwealth Games gymnasts would do.'

Pleased with her little bit of research, Kirsty went back to the screen and keyed in *tattoo artists, Glasgow.* Just to see, she told herself. Perhaps one of them specialised in designs like these. And if so, chances were they might remember a young black woman who had asked for a triple spiral tattoo to be inked on her right thigh.

'What d'you make of it?' Rosie asked her husband.

Professor Solomon Brightman paused, his arms full of the toys he had been clearing up from the lounge floor, to come and look at the paper Rosie was holding up.

'A triple spiral, hm,' he replied, his dark eyes bright behind their horn-rimmed spectacles.

'Not just that,' Rosie went on, following him as he bent to put a xylophone and a half-naked doll into the toybox. 'It's where the tattoo was located. I mean, who would choose to have something small and insignificant on their inner thigh? Who's going to see it there?'

Solly tried to close the lid of the white wooden box, but there were so many toys that it simply wouldn't budge any further. Abigail's bedroom too was testament to the generosity of family and friends, rows of rabbits and teddy bears ranged along the skirting board, except for special ones that were tucked up beside the little girl in her cot.

'Good question,' he replied. 'Has anyone actually thought to answer that yet?'

'There was the idea that she might have been on the game,' Rosie mused. 'Lorimer's team is investigating that angle.'

'It does make some kind of sense,' the psychologist agreed. 'Nobody is going to see the tattoo until she parts her legs, which does suggest ...'

'Yeah,' Rosie sighed. 'But why would you choose a wee Pictish symbol? Why not something from her own ethnic heritage? And in dark blue? You can hardly see it against her skin colour.'

Solly stood up, nodding his head sagely. 'That is a good question to ask. *Choose.* Did she, though? Choose the symbol for herself?'

'Maybe she just liked the design. Surely there are hundreds to select when you go into these places?'

'Or perhaps it was chosen for her?' Solly asked quietly, sitting on the arm of the settee.

'A tattoo artist would be able to give advice if the customer didn't have a clear idea of what they wanted.'

'A triple spiral. A dark blue pattern inked on to the skin of a young black woman.'

Rosie watched as Solly stroked his dark beard. There was that familiar faraway look in his eyes, a look that meant the psychologist's mind was beginning to formulate ideas and patterns. She slipped behind him and began to empty the toys out of the toybox on to the carpet, sorting them according to their shapes so that they could be replaced in some sort of order. She put in Abby's building blocks, the xylophone, cloth books and the various musical games, leaving enough space for the more awkward shapes like the plastic doll and several cuddly animals. Then, with a satisfied smile, she closed the lid and fastened the clasp.

Solly was still seated on the arm of the sofa, staring into space, oblivious to anything else in the room. He might not have anything to do with this strange case, Rosie knew, but it never did any harm to plant the seeds of a puzzle into the fascinating brain of Professor Solly Brightman.

'What does Maggie make of it, that's what I'd like to know.'

Betty Wilson placed the casserole dish on a heatproof mat on the dining room table, then lifted off the lid, her capable hands protected by thick oven gloves. A smell of herbs and cinnamon wafted up from the meaty dish, making Kirsty sigh with pleasure. Since joining the police, her visits home to West Kilbride had become rarer than ever. How on earth Dad managed that drive to Glasgow every day was beyond her, though coming back to Mum's home cooking was a big incentive, she realised, as her plate was heaped up with food. And now that he was acting detective inspector on this poisoning affair, the hours spent in Glasgow would be longer than ever.

'He hasn't said,' Alistair Wilson replied. 'But I got the impression Lorimer was mighty relieved when I took over the case.'

'It can't be easy having a stranger in your home. Especially one who's newly bereaved. I mean, what do you say to her?' Betty continued.

'Mrs Lorimer's nice,' Kirsty said, waving her fork in the air. 'She's just the sort of person you would want to be with when something bad happens. I'm sure Lorimer did the right thing in bringing the poor lady home.'

Betty Wilson shrugged. 'Can't say I'd be thrilled if your father brought one of his old flames back to stay.'

'Ooh, Dad, tell me, were you a right Lothario in your younger days, then?' Kirsty joked.

Alistair Wilson shook his head, affecting an air of innocence. 'Who, me? I only ever had eyes for your mum and well she knows it!'

Betty shook her head, but the dimpled smile showed that she was pleased enough with the compliment.

'Anyway, let's enjoy this dinner without all the shop talk, eh? There's more to life than the polis. What did *you* do today, love?' Alistair went on, turning to his wife.

Betty Wilson looked fondly at her husband. She knew fine that the pair of them would have been chatting about their respective cases all the way home. Hearing about her own job as a professional cook was tame stuff compared to that, but she was glad to turn the conversation away from the gory details of their work, especially at the dinner table.

'Is he always as late as this?' Vivien asked.

'Sometimes much later,' Maggie admitted. 'Depends on what sort of case he's involved in. Could be up through the night if need be, though I didn't have the impression he'd be that late tonight.'

The red-haired woman toyed with the food on her plate, a tasty bolognese sauce that had been simmering on Maggie Lorimer's hob for several hours.

'Do you cook a meal from scratch every day or are you just doing this to be nice to me?' Vivien said suddenly, looking at Maggie with a shrewd expression in her green eyes.

Maggie glanced down at her plate, avoiding the woman's penetrating stare. 'I like to cook,' she muttered. 'And Bill likes to come home to something freshly made.'

'My goodness,' Vivien countered, one eyebrow arched in mock surprise. 'Quite the little housewife, aren't you? I don't think poor Charles ever expected me to be any sort of domestic goddess,' she continued.

Maggie lifted her head at the woman's tone. Where was the grief that had flowed from her only a matter of hours ago? It was as if Charles Gilmartin had been dead and buried for years, the way Vivien was speaking. She looked again at those cat-like eyes, wondering. Were the pupils enlarged? Had Vivien been taking a bit too much of the doctor's medication? As a school teacher Maggie had encountered several episodes of substance abuse, mind-altering drugs that changed a person's behaviour. Had to be, she told herself. Such a sudden shift in her manner needed a logical explanation.

'Did you two meet at university?' Vivien asked, changing the subject, much to Maggie's relief.

As she related the tale of their meeting and the years of courtship after Bill had joined the force, Maggie saw that Vivien had begun to eat the supper, small forkfuls of pasta expertly twirled against a silver spoon.

'So how long is that? Twenty years?'

Maggie nodded. 'And you?'

Vivien smiled sadly. 'Oh, Charles swept me off my feet not long after I'd graduated. Saw me in a West End play and came back-stage afterwards. Sweet, really,' she sighed. 'We were married six weeks later.'

'Goodness,' Maggie replied. 'I mean, that was quite romantic,' she hastened to add.

'It would have been our twenty-first wedding anniversary this summer,' Vivien mused.

Once again Maggie was struck by the other woman's matter-of-fact manner.

'Were you planning anything special?' she asked.

'Oh, no, darling!' Vivien gave a short, brittle laugh. 'Charles was *far* too wrapped up in that African theatre group!'

Maggie glanced quickly at the woman's face. For a fleeting instant there was a shadow of intense fury, then it was gone as quickly as it had appeared, the flawless alabaster skin showing just a faint colour like the blush of pink on an almost white rose.

As the conversation continued, Vivien asked mundane questions about Maggie's own career as an English teacher, as though deliberately steering the talk away from Charles Gilmartin.

That small moment was one that Maggie Lorimer put to the back of her mind. But it was something that would be brought out again and examined, particularly in the days and weeks that were to follow.

CHAPTER TWENTY-ONE

'Nooooo!' The scream echoed through the darkness, making him sit bolt upright.

'Vivien,' Maggie murmured, rolling over to gaze at her husband.

'I'll go,' he whispered. 'You go back to sleep.'

She watched him take the dressing gown from its hook on the bedroom door, then he was gone, a shadow disappearing in the night, leaving her with a hollow feeling in the pit of her stomach.

He paused for a moment outside her room, wondering if the cry had been from a troubled dream. Was she awake? Then, hearing a whimpering from within, Lorimer pushed open the bedroom door. Moonlight filtering through a gap in the curtains cast a strange light across the bed where she lay, bedclothes up to her chin, hair tousled against the white pillow.

'Foxy,' he whispered. 'Are you all right?'

Her only answer was a loud sniff and a mumble into the duvet.

'Bad dream, eh?' He came closer to sit on the edge of the bed, Vivien automatically shifting to one side to make room for him.

'It was . . . horrible,' she said in a small voice. 'He was dead but coming towards me with this mask on his face ... It was ... ' She began to cry again, the words swallowed up in sobs.

'Here,' Lorimer put his arm around her shoulders, drawing her into his side. 'It was a nightmare. Nothing to be afraid of,' he soothed. 'It's over now. You're safe here with us.' He patted her back as though she were a frightened child.

'What if ... ' she hiccupped, 'what if it meant something?' Her eyes stared wildly into his and he could see the panic there, feel his arm clutched by a terrified hand. 'What if Charles is trying to tell me something?' she said breathlessly.

'You really believe that?' Lorimer smiled at her. 'Dreams are nothing to be afraid of, Foxy, even bad ones. They're just rubbish accumulated by your brain then all jumbled up inside, that's all.'

She drew closer to him and he could feel her body shivering through the thin silk nightdress.

'You shouldn't pay any heed to bad dreams,' he told her. 'Best to forget them and think of something nice instead,' he went on.

A sudden memory came back to him of another woman whose dreams had haunted her to the point where she had lost all sense of reason. Death and despair had been the result.

'Do you really think so?' she asked, her voice small and tremulous.

'Look, lass, you've been through a terrible few days. No wonder you're having nightmares. And that stuff the doctor prescribed. Could it be having an effect?'

'Don't know,' she replied, one arm coming across his chest as she snuggled into him.

'Listen,' he said gently, 'you're safe here. Nothing and nobody can harm you. Okay?'

As she looked up at him, Lorimer felt an ache of sadness for his old girlfriend. She tried to smile and he noticed that her cheeks were still wet with tears glimmering in the moonlight. He wiped them away with his finger.

'It isn't easy, I know.' He smiled at her. 'I remember something Maggie's mum used to say: *everything passes*. And she was right. It must hurt so badly now, but there'll come a time when this nightmare will all be over.'

'Nothing will ever be the same,' she whispered.

'No, that's true. But life is full of changes, Foxy. And we humans are pretty adaptable to even the worst of them.'

Vivien gave a huge sigh and Lorimer felt her head slip on to his shoulder.

Would she sleep again now? Drift into a dreamless sleep where no monsters chased her in that nameless place?

'Can I get you anything? Some warm milk, maybe?'

'No.' She yawned suddenly. 'Just stay with me. Please?'

He looked at the woman lying beside him, remembering the girl she had been: that long red hair falling in their faces as they had tumbled together, their lovemaking a joyous thing. He smoothed an unruly lock away from her face and bent to kiss her forehead. A subtle perfume filled his senses, something sophisticated, something that the young Vivien Fox would never have worn, and he drew back, seeing this woman for what she was to him now, a middle-aged stranger.

He rolled off the bed, tucking the duvet around her carefully, then went across to sit in a chair by the window.

'Go to sleep, Foxy. I'll be right here. Okay?'

She muttered something inaudible into the pillow, then turned on her side.

Lorimer raised his hand and pulled the curtains closed, shutting out the beam of moonlight, casting the room into a velvety darkness once more.

Time passed so strangely in the wee small hours that it may have been only minutes, but it felt like an age before he heard her breathing deeply and knew that she was asleep once more. Standing up slowly, afraid to make the least sound, Lorimer crept out of the room, leaving the door ajar, and tiptoed back along the corridor to his own bed.

Maggie was asleep, he guessed, as he turned back the covers and slipped into his side of the bed, feeling the sheet cold beneath his bare feet. With a sigh, the policeman closed his eyes, willing sleep to come.

But all he could see behind his eyelids was the dead face of Charles Gilmartin.

In another part of the city, a man lay staring at the darkened ceiling above his bed. One hand wiped at the sweat trickling down his chest. The dream that had disturbed his sleep had come yet again, showing Cameron Gregson that somewhere deep in his subconscious he still had some degree of empathy. Psychopaths were incapable of that, or so he had been told by those who read all that true crime stuff, and he certainly didn't consider himself in that light. The nightmare still had the power to make the postgraduate student stiffen in terror: the flames engulfing the people all around him, screams and yells of anguish, then the knowledge that he was trapped in the suffocating smoke and the press of heaving bodies trying to escape.

Cameron Gregson blew out a sigh, then turned to see Gayle slumbering softly by his side. It was just a dream, nothing more.

He would get out long before the bomb exploded, he had been told that often enough to believe it.

CHAPTER TWENTY-TWO

TERRY'S TATTOO STUDIO, the red words above the shop front proclaimed. Kirsty was waiting outside the studio for the other officer to arrive, as instructed. Being early was a fault she had acquired in her enthusiasm for this job, though to be fair, having her dad drop her off after last night at home had given her a head start too.

The weather had turned colder again and an easterly wind slanted the rain across Chisholm Street, rattling the metal shutters that covered the front door. Ten o'clock, the man had told her on the phone, and there was no sign of DC Lennox, the officer supposed to be leading this particular action. It was still ten minutes to the hour, and Kirsty could feel the rain beginning to soak into her uniform trousers, driving her from the tattoo studio to the deeply recessed doorway of the restaurant next door. The young officer shook her head, wishing she had taken the umbrella offered by her mother. Betty Wilson had been right earlier on, as she'd looked up into the sky. 'Too bright too early,' she'd proclaimed. 'Heavy rain coming in before long.'

Kirsty kept her gaze on the street, looking at every vehicle as it slowed down in case it was DC Lennox or the tattoo artist arriving for work. Across the road was the Tron Theatre, a side door leading to a café where her boyfriend, James, had taken her after they'd seen a play together. Glancing around, Kirsty could see that little had changed over the decades in this particular area; many of the buildings had been there since Victorian times, and her eyes picked out the architectural details of crow-step gabling and tiny turrets, though the shops at street level mostly reflected twenty-first-century preferences, like this tattoo studio. She had walked along Trongate, passing the old Panopticon Theatre and a double-fronted shop that had made her pause, mouth watering. Mrs Mitchell's Sweetie Shop was a modern take on the old-fashioned confectioners' shops of her granny's generation, something that was becoming more and more popular in these little pockets of the city. Maybe she'd buy a packet of soor plooms to give to Mum, a thank you for the great meal last night. Betty Wilson never bothered watching her figure and would enjoy these old-fashioned boiled sweets.

'You waiting for me?'

A grey-haired man stepped on to the pavement from his blue van, a younger girl hastening through the rain to open up the shop.

'PC Wilson?'

'Yes,' Kirsty said, coming out of the doorway. 'We spoke on the phone. Mr Wrigley?'

'Stuart.' He smiled, ushering Kirsty into the tattoo studio and out of the wind. 'Cup of tea? Coffee?'

'Aye, tea would be great, thanks,' Kirsty said, following the man as he led the way into a second room. This was obviously the tattoo studio proper, she thought, her eyes roving around the place. One mirrored wall reflected the cabinets and worktops opposite, pairs of black swivel chairs reminding her of a hair salon, though the cluttered surfaces suggested something far more

131

exotic. Her eyes fell on a bottle of dark green liquid containing what looked like a dead snake curled within, its opened fangs making Kirsty shudder. Beside it sat a pink glass paperweight, a sand-coloured scorpion trapped inside, and two other plastic shapes concealing a stag beetle and something strange that made her look more closely.

'A pig foetus,' Stuart said cheerfully, bearing two mugs of tea that he set down on the worktop beside them.

Kirsty managed a weak grin. 'Oh. Right,' she said. She bit her lip. 'I'm supposed to be accompanied by a more senior officer, but he hasn't turned up, so perhaps I can talk to you on my own?'

The grey-haired man's grin faded a little. 'You wanted to ask me about an unidentified person,' he began. 'Sad to say, it's something that crops up a fair bit these days.'

Kirsty nodded. He seemed a nice guy, this tattoo artist, and well spoken, too. She could imagine that a man like this would put a client at their ease without much difficulty. Stuart Wrigley's establishment was the oldest of its kind in Glasgow, founded way back in the 1950s by his late father, Terry, hence the name above the door. And given the popularity of tattoo art, the man sitting opposite her had often been visited by police officers for help in the identification of men and women whose lives had been cut short in some way or other.

Kirsty took out her notebook and showed him the drawing she had made.

'I think it might be like that,' she said, turning the page so that Stuart could see it.

He didn't say anything for a moment, looking at the curled spiral shape instead and nodding.

'Black girl?' he asked at last.

'Yes.' Kirsty drew in a sharp breath. 'How did you know?'

Stuart Wrigley turned his face to hers and she suddenly saw the furrowed brow and a look of intense sadness in his eyes.

'I think I may have done the tattoo for her.'

'When was this?'

Wrigley raised his eyebrows thoughtfully. 'Couple of days ago. Poor girl, what happened?'

Kirsty stared at him. 'But that's impossible,' she blurted out. 'She's been dead for . . . '

Wrigley shook his head. 'Definitely just two days ago. I remember her coming in with her uncles. Or at least that's who they said they were. Showed me her passport.'

Kirsty looked at him questioningly.

'Even if they come in off the street like these ones did, I need to have ID of some sort to verify the client's age.'

'Okay.' Kirsty nodded, intrigued. 'Go on.'

'They were quite specific about the design they wanted. A triple spiral on the lassie's upper thigh. Well I tried to put them off. Suggested placing it on her shoulder instead, but they said she wanted it somewhere discreet.'

'Why did you do that?'

'Tricky place for girls like that. Thinner skin there, you see, and black skin is more delicate than ours.' He shrugged. 'Told them the usual about keeping it clean, giving it time to heal, how it might be more prone to infection. But that's all we can do really. Unless they ever come back with a bad infection.'

'And she hasn't?'

'No. As I said, it was only two days ago. That's not the girl you're trying to find out about, is it?' Wrigley asked, his bright eyes shrewd with an intelligence that the young officer could not ignore.

'So you gave this girl a triple spiral tattoo? Do you have any details of her name and address?'

133

'Wait and I'll see.' He rummaged in one of the drawers opposite his workstation and drew out a sheaf of papers clipped together.

'Should be in this lot,' he said, leafing through the bundle.

Kirsty waited expectantly, her heart beating faster. Would she be returning triumphantly to Stewart Street with the information that Lorimer was seeking?

'Here we are,' Wrigley said, handing her an A5 sheet of paper with the heading: *Terry's Tattoo Studio. Our records are kept in the strictest confidence.* Underneath there was space for the usual name, address, contact number and email, followed by tick boxes for various illnesses like HIV, epilepsy and diabetes. Every box was ticked under 'No', and only a name and address had been filled in. The date of birth was given as 1 April 1995.

'I can tell you a bit about her if you like,' Wrigley continued. 'I thought the poor girl looked scared to death. Some of them get pretty nervous when they see the needle,' he explained. He frowned again, as if trying to remember something. 'She seemed a bit doolally,' he said at last. 'Thought she might have been not all there, know what I mean?'

'Or drugged up to the eyeballs?' Kirsty offered.

Wrigley's eyes widened. 'The two guys with her said she was their niece over on a six-month visa from Nigeria. Passport seemed to check out okay. Photo was definitely recent. Said the girl wanted something really Scottish to remember her visit.'

Kirsty looked hard at the man.

'And you're certain you never gave a similar tattoo to another black girl? Say within the last few months?'

Wrigley shook his head, his keen eyes staring into her own; he was either telling the truth or he was an exceptionally cool individual.

'And you didn't suggest the triple spiral?' Kirsty went on.

Wrigley tapped his beard thoughtfully. 'No. Like I said. Come to think of it, that was a bit strange. Two big black lads asking for a Pictish symbol for their lassie. One of them even had it on his iPad to show me exactly what they wanted.'

'And did they pay by credit card?' she asked, hoping that even more details might come to light.

'Cash only,' Wrigley said, pointing to a sign by the main door. 'Always has been. Saves us a lot of bother. So these are all the ID we keep, I'm afraid.'

Kirsty looked at the form. The address was in a street she had never heard of. But as she read the name above, *Asa*, no surname given, Kirsty began to wonder just where this might lead.

'Doesn't exist,' DC Patrick Lennox told her. 'Yoruba Street! They're havin' a laugh,' he snorted. 'That's one of the main Nigerian languages, Yoruba,' he explained.

Kirsty felt her face reddening. Okay, she'd found the source of one girl's tattoo. Surely that could lead somewhere?

'Even if it's true that Wrigley didn't do the tattoo for *our* black girl, the name and address are both probably false,' Lennox explained.

'If they were up to no good then they probably wouldn't use the same tattoo artist twice,' Kirsty mused.

'Still plenty for us to do, then, young Kirsty.' Lennox grinned. 'Let's see the list of all the tattoo artists in the area.'

DC Lennox had apologised profusely for his non-attendance at the tattoo studio; his mother-in-law had been rushed into hospital during the night and both he and his wife had overslept. 'Be grateful if you don't tell His Nibs,' he had whispered, his face pale with lack of sleep and the strain of waiting for hours in a hospital corridor. 'Don't want to blot my copybook.'

Kirsty had merely nodded, wondering if the information she had found was to be credited to Lennox or herself. There would be a meeting shortly where she would listen to Lennox reading from her report, though the email already distributed to other members of the team had come from her computer.

She had a lot to learn in this job, she realised, and not all of it had to do with catching criminals.

CHAPTER TWENTY-THREE

Asa woke with a dry feeling in her mouth. It was still dark outside and she had no idea of the time, though there was the sound of a pigeon cooing on the roof, so perhaps dawn was not too far off. It was good to hear some sounds at last.

Night after night the African girl had struggled to sleep, the traffic outside sometimes making strange high-pitched whines or pulsing notes that shrieked through the city. But it had been the long silences that had been hardest. Asa was accustomed to the texture of night noises, the small nocturnal creatures whose sounds lulled her to sleep, and she missed the gurgling croaks of frogs and the cicadas in the bush. This quietness made her stare into the shadows, an ache in her soul to be back where she belonged.

The girl rolled over on her side, then yelped aloud as the pain from her wound seared along her inner thigh.

He had not been a doctor after all. What had she expected from a man wearing jeans and a casual grey striped sweater? His voice had been kind, though, unlike the voices of the two Nigerian men who had persisted in speaking English. Asa had ventured a timid word or two in Yoruba only to be met with angry glares. They had understood her, she was certain of that, but they had refused to reply. The rest of the day had passed in a blur: memories of the car bringing her back from the tattoo studio to the tall grey building, of being huckled up each flight of cold stone stairs, then the relief of being able to sleep and sleep and sleep.

Asa's body tensed as she heard the creak of the door opening. Was it Shereen coming to bring an early breakfast?

'Shh!'

She sat up, the cry dying on her lips as she saw the bigger of the two Nigerians close the door behind him and approach her. There were tiny beads of sweat on his dark brow and he was breathing hard as he came to sit on the edge of her bed.

Suddenly he grasped the covers and with both meaty hands pulled them off, tossing them on the floor, hungry eyes boring into her own. Then, pulling up her nightshirt, he began to squeeze her small breasts, shifting his body so that he could lie beside her.

Asa closed her eyes, smelling the alcohol on his breath, feeling the hands coming down across her stomach, touching her in places that no man had ever touched before, her body rigid with fear.

Then, in one swift motion, he had pulled her thighs apart, making her cry out, and she could feel the weight of his body crushing the breath from her chest. There was a push and a stab and her whole body seemed to split and burn, the man groaning and roaring above her, waves of pain surging as he pressed himself again and again into her soft flesh.

Asa soon found that there was nothing to be gained from struggling beneath this terrible heaviness; her efforts to escape only seemed to redouble the big man's enjoyment.

At last, with a yelp that was more animal than human, he flopped across her body, a shuddering sensation deep inside her.

When he rolled away from her, Asa began to cry, but he took her by the shoulders and shook her until she felt her neck would snap.

138

'Shut it!' he commanded. 'You'll get more than this from our friends, so better get used to it!' he snarled.

The meaning of the words was lost to the girl but the sound of his voice was enough to make her cringe to the edge of the bed, fingers curled over the damp edges of her nightshirt.

CHAPTER TWENTY-FOUR

'Wrigley wasn't to know what was going on, though maybe being asked to place a tattoo on that part of the body could have told him something,' Lorimer said.

'He did say that the girl wanted it somewhere discreet. He'd got the impression that the folks back home might not be too pleased to see their daughter with a tattoo from Glasgow,' Kirsty answered.

Detective Superintendent Lorimer sighed. There was so little to go on. The tattoo artist's information had been helpful enough in its way, but everything seemed to point to something a lot more sinister than someone's niece (if that was what she really was) hiding a tattoo from her parents back in Nigeria. There was no doubt in his mind that these girls had been tattooed for a different reason altogether, the Pictish spiral more of a brand mark than mere decorative art. And Rosie's post-mortem had thrown up a suggestion of a different sort. Were these girls being trafficked as prostitutes? If so, perhaps they ought to be looking for this second girl, the one called Asa.

Most of the citizens of Glasgow did not regard their city as a hotbed of human trafficking, despite it being the fifth most popular place in the UK for such criminal activity. It was their Dear Green Place, the former City of Culture, *Glasgow's Miles Better* being a logo that had filled its folk with a pride in their couthy humour and welcoming manner to strangers. Now that the Commonwealth Games were coming ever closer, there was a sense of civic self-esteem amongst the populace, something that Detective Superintendent Lorimer had been told to consider. The girl's body lay in the mortuary, silent and still, her identity remaining a mystery that was not to be shared with anyone outside the investigation. No press release would be put out and every officer on the team had been strictly warned to keep the case completely secret.

Lorimer had now spoken to Stuart Wrigley at the tattoo studio, the quick visit to Chisholm Street necessary to keep the case under wraps. He'd liked the man on sight and trusted him to keep PC Wilson's visit to himself. Wrigley had nodded, understanding. It wasn't the first time he had helped with such a case, he'd reminded the detective superintendent.

DC Lennox and PC Wilson had received the sharp end of his tongue afterwards. Letting the probationer go there on her own was just not on, and despite the fact that Kirsty had coped well and obtained some salient information, she ought to have waited for Lennox or reported back to Stewart Street. Lorimer had hidden a smile as Kirsty and Lennox left his office. She wasn't used to seeing him stern like that, and her red face had made the senior officer realise just how raw she was to all of this.

Stuart Wrigley folded the form in two, along with a copy of the triple spiral designs, placed them in an envelope and dampened the edge, sealing it shut. His two daughters were completely unaware of what had taken place during these visits from the police officers, and he intended to keep it that way. Stuart's thoughts crept back to the young black girl whose skin had trembled under his touch. She hadn't been a willing client, had she? And his instinct ought to have told him that at the time. Asa, the man had called her, the name written on that form. He recalled the lift of her head, the response to her name. That hadn't been faked, he was sure. Fishing out the card from his wallet, Wrigley looked at the number beneath the detective superintendent's name. It might not be much, but perhaps even this little snippet could be helpful. *I think that was her real name*, he had written on the back of the form.

CHAPTER TWENTY-FIVE

The darkness outside made her feel safe, the street lamp's glow burnishing the pale green curtains of this bedroom, her haven for now. Memories of Charles lying on that other bed, his grizzled head against the pillow, still haunted her dreams, confused rags of nonsense that were no doubt partly induced by the medication the doctor had given her, as Lorimer had suggested.

Vivien listened, but there was no sound from the room along the corridor, no voices discussing what she ought to do next. On other nights she had heard Maggie's voice, low and murmuring, and she was certain the woman was trying to persuade her husband to ask her to leave. But he wouldn't do that, Vivien thought, a small smile curling on her lips. His sense of chivalry was the same as it had always been, something she had never forgotten, something that had been to the forefront of her mind even when his invitation had been posted.

William Lorimer was one of the good people in her life. And right now she needed him more than ever.

Maggie lay on her back, feet stretched out below the duvet, hands clasped loosely across her stomach. Beside her, Bill was snoring softly, a comforting sound, like Chancer when he purred himself to sleep. It was a gift, she thought, being able to close his eyes and drop off so quickly. Some nights were cut short by the demands of the job and so perhaps he had learned the secret of sleeping when he could.

Tonight Maggie Lorimer could not find that secret. There was little noise from outside; once a neighbour's car drew away from the avenue (Jill was on night shifts at the hospital), then all was silent apart from the deep breathing from the man whose back was turned towards her.

Since Vivien Gilmartin's sudden arrival, they had not made love once, Maggie reminded herself, the longing to be drawn into her husband's arms so acute that her body throbbed with an ache that demanded to be satisfied. It was no use, though. A night of passion would have to wait until the red-haired woman was gone for good. Was that why she had begun to resent her? Was it simply a physical frustration building up? Or was there something more to the antipathy that she felt for the widow?

Maggie lay staring at the ceiling, wondering what it was that she had begun to hate about herself. Mrs Lorimer was the teacher that all the girls came to for advice, her listening ear and box of Kleenex well-established facts in the school. *A soft touch*, her friend Sandie had told her more than once, but Maggie didn't mind. Nor did the guidance staff, who were overworked and knew that Mrs Lorimer would bring anything serious to their attention. Suddenly Maggie longed to be back at school, for the holiday to be over, and to immerse herself into the frantic weeks before exam time.

Perhaps Vivien would be gone by then. Things back to normal. The flat in Glasgow was rented out for another three months but Vivien had hinted that she was cancelling the lease. The landlord would understand. It wasn't every day a tenant died in your property, she had said with a hollow laugh that had raised Maggie's eyebrows. Such remarks touched with a world-weary cynicism had been spoken only to her, never when Bill was around to hear them, something that troubled the woman who gazed sleeplessly at the ceiling.

Gayle sighed, reaching down the side of the bed where her silk slip had been dropped on the floor. Cam was asleep already, his kisses and endearments still tingling on her body. It was no use, she thought. Despite her best intentions, she was still here, and if she was honest, that was what she wanted. Tonight had been different, though. Cam had been gentler, taking time to please her in ways that she had only dreamed of. The blindfold was still lying beside her, the sweet scent of the Elixir Sensual he had massaged on to her skin perfuming the air. And he hadn't said a single bad word about her job or the Games. Not one. Perhaps he was coming round to her way of thinking at last, the collective pride that seemed to grip this city having captured even Cameron Gregson.

Gayle had seen an expensive black dress in a shop window as she had strolled along past the Italian Centre, something that would look good at the opening ceremony. And if Cameron could be persuaded into the evening clothes she knew he possessed, then they would make a head-turning couple. He had been the recipient of many admiring female glances back in January at the Burns Supper. Cameron had the figure for a kilt, Gayle remembered with a smile. So, would he accept her invitation to the big event in the summer if she should be lucky enough to get the tickets she had applied for?

Shereen gripped the edge of the table with both hands as she listened to the girl's scream.

The big man had come earlier that evening, demanding to see Asa, the sight of his hulking figure making even the two Nigerian men shrink back in fear. One of them had taken the girl's virginity, she knew that. And not just because he was obeying orders, Shereen told herself with disgust. Randy old bastard! Now he was cowering with his pal in the room next door, waiting until the big man had finished with Asa.

Shereen sat down at the kitchen table, trembling. She was as guilty as any of them, wasn't she? The money promised had almost paid off her debts, and there would be more to come. Yet she was fearful of the man who was making the young girl cry out, fearful of his staring eyes and wild hair, fearful of those immense hands and those arms covered in slithering serpents, their red eyes and forked tongues entwined in curves and whorls inked on to his skin.

They had taken Asa to have her tattoo, a tiny thing really compared to the body art adorning the big man. And it had reminded Shereen of the other girl. She had disappeared one night and Shereen had never seen her again nor heard anything about her. It was not good to ask questions, she had been told right from the start. *Keep your mouth shut; it's better for your health*, the big man had told her, his eyes boring into her own, making Shereen nod frantically as he had jabbed her with his fat finger and walked away laughing.

CHAPTER TWENTY-SIX

Sometimes, Solly thought, life was almost perfect. He had left Morag, their capable nanny, brushing Abby's hair as she watched her *Toy Story* video for the umpteenth time, and now he and Rosie were walking through the park on their way to work. The daffodils were a swathe of yellow amid the swaying grasses on the bank above the river and above them the clouds scudded across a sky so blue that it was hard to remember that this was an April day in Scotland. He did not really have to be in his office in University Gardens as early as this, but walking there with Rosie by his side was one of life's small pleasures, the psychologist told himself, giving his wife's hand a squeeze. Rosie had her own office in the Department of Forensic Medicine, the entrance to which could just be seen from his bay window overlooking the curve of University Avenue. She was head of the department now, spending time there and at the city mortuary as well as attending numerous conferences and giving lectures. It had been a hard decision, he knew, for her to return to full-time work after her maternity leave, but he guessed from the spring in her step as they approached the place where their paths diverged that she did not regret that now.

'Any more news about the unidentified girl?' he asked as she let go of his hand to adjust her shoulder bag.

'Not so far. Lorimer was going to see if there was a DNA match from the foetus.' She shrugged. 'Maybe we'll never know.'

'Somebody does,' Solly said quietly, the thought robbing the day of some of its brightness as he waved his wife off, watching the wind toss her blonde curls as she walked swiftly down towards another day dealing with the aftermath of other people's violent behaviour.

The professor had not been asked to comment on this case, though he had been helpful to the police in the past as a profiler in cases of multiple murders, but Rosie's own involvement had piqued his interest. That the girl had been part of a people-trafficking organisation seemed fairly likely. Given his chosen profession, Solomon Brightman was conversant with the many vagaries of human nature, and only last night he had been reading around the subject of child trafficking with growing interest. It was, he now knew, one of the biggest types of organised crime in the UK, along with the illegal trades of drugs and weapons. Trouble was, it was hard to find reliable statistics. The belief that the level of crime was far greater than actual figures showed was shared by almost all the authorities that had investigated cases in the past.

Nobody wanted to tell of their plight. Many of the children lived in terror of deportation, the threats of repercussions to them-selves and their families keeping them silent about their continued abuse.

Was the murdered girl one of those unfortunate children? Rosie had estimated the girl's age at less than eighteen, the watershed between childhood and becoming an adult in this country. Solly had read that West Africa was one of the largest source regions for such children. As he looked around him at the students chattering as they crossed University Avenue on their way to classes, he wondered if they had any inkling of just how privileged their lives were. His thoughts turned to the little girl he had left sitting on her nanny's lap and his heart swelled with a longing to protect her from all the badness that her parents saw on a daily basis.

Maggie stood in the kitchen doorway watching as the red-haired woman approached the rocking chair where Chancer lay, curled asleep on the cushions. She paused, hidden from sight, the shadow from the open door concealing her presence, waiting to see what Vivien would do.

As soon as she noticed the cat upon the chair, Vivien stiffened and took a step backwards. Was hers an elemental fear of cats? Maggie wondered. Some people genuinely had a phobia about the creatures. Should she intervene, pick up her beloved pet and allow their visitor to sit on the rocking chair? For a long moment she did nothing, a vision of her mother coming back so suddenly that it took her breath away. Mum had sat there so often, Chancer snug on her lap. Then the memory was gone as quickly as it had arrived, Vivien still hovering uncertainly behind the chair.

'Come on, puss. Off you get,' Maggie said, stepping into the light and scooping up the cat in one easy movement.

'Oh!' Vivien gave a gasp. 'Thank you. I ... I don't know what it is about cats,' she faltered. 'Just can't abide them being near me.'

'That's okay,' Maggie replied, tipping Chancer out of the door unceremoniously and closing the door behind him. 'Can't have you feeling uncomfortable.' She shrugged.

Vivien stumbled around the chair, sinking into it as though she were about to faint. 'You've been so kind,' she began. 'It's not every woman who would take her husband's old girlfriend into her home,' she continued huskily.

'We could hardly leave you stranded.'

'It's just . . . well, William and I go back such a long way and he was so nice to me when we met up that evening . . .' Vivien choked back a sob and Maggie bit her lip, wondering why it was that she could not engage more with this woman. Was it simple female jealousy, seeing a beautiful woman making eyes at her husband? Or was there something deeper, an instinct that told her to hold back, not let her become emotionally tied to the woman whose husband had died in such strange circumstances?

'Cup of tea?' she said briskly, and, not waiting for an answer, turned towards the sink, ready to fill yet another kettle.

The mountains that had been shrouded in mist the day before now rose before them, craggy ridges etched against a pale blue sky. Peter MacGregor was sitting on the wooden bench at the edge of the loch, Joanne's hand clasped in his, each of them staring out across the water. There was no need for speech; they were used to the companionable silence after more than forty years of marriage, and any words would have been simply to echo one another's thoughts: how peaceful this was, how relaxed they both felt in this quiet, unspoiled part of Skye. Joanne squeezed his hand a little, and he caught her glance, a nod towards the water.

First it was only the suggestion of movement, then the unmistakable shape of a head broke the surface of the water. A sleek wet body curving into a dive. Then, with a splash, the otter was gone.

He heard Joanne's deep sigh of contentment as they continued to watch the ripples become fainter, the morning light dancing on the water. It had been worth coming down here early before breakfast. Their host had promised something special and at first they had thought she had meant the spectacular mountain range of the Cuillins against the morning sunrise. Now they knew what that twinkle in Mrs Macleod's eye had really meant. 'Oh, you'll see something a wee bit out of the ordinary,' she'd told them. 'Just you sit still and wait.' And they had.

Peter made to move, but Joanne pulled his hand back. 'Shh!' she said. 'Look!'

And there they were: two fully grown otters emerging from the water's edge on to a tangle of bladderwrack. The sun silvering their pelts made the creatures harder to see against the shining seaweed, but then, in a moment, they were playing together, bodies curving as they rolled and frisked along the water's edge, blissfully unaware of the elderly couple watching their antics. For perhaps ten minutes the two otters romped by the lochside, then, as if something had called them back, they slipped into the water, their sleek bodies disappearing beneath the surface.

'Whew!' Peter exhaled, his eyes still on the sun-dappled water. 'Don't think we'll see anything better than that on our trip, do you?'

'Not even the Games? Or the Gathering?' Joanne teased. 'What about the news you had last night from Glasgow?'

Peter smiled at her, the otters momentarily forgotten. 'I know. Fantastic, isn't it? Who would think that we would be invited to be so close to the royal family at the opening ceremony?'

'It's because we're Aussies *and* MacGregors,' Joanne reminded him. 'That's what the man said, wasn't it?'

Peter nodded. That was it, he thought. Yet why single out an ordinary chap like himself for such an honour? He smiled as he remembered the man's words. *You've been chosen to accompany the royal party*, he'd said. And he would make sure that Peter was properly dressed for the occasion, even bringing him the specially inscribed *sgian dubh* that he had promised.

As Peter MacGregor's gaze shifted back to the Cuillins and

their jagged tops, he was reminded of the small black-handled dagger he had been told to leave behind in Melbourne, and for a moment he shivered, a stray cloud passing over the sun and darkening the landscape.

CHAPTER TWENTY-SEVEN

It had been a while since he had visited this place, DS Wilson thought, as they rounded the corner of the avenue and parked outside the Lorimers' home. The house, like all the others on this curved street, was a post-war villa, built to last, the mature trees and shrubs providing a screen against prying eyes. Like so many others it had undergone changes in the decades since the first residents had moved into this leafy avenue. Several houses had been extended, dictated by the tastes of the owners and the demands of growing families. Conservatories had been added over the years and some of the original slate roofs had been replaced by different shades of terracotta tiles, giving the avenue a less uniform appearance.

Wilson looked up to his right, his eyes scanning the space between two of the houses. It was still there, he saw, and smiled. Cradled in the generous arms of an oak was an old tree house, its timbers weathered to a dull grey, half hidden amongst the leaves. He recalled the summer afternoon when he and Betty had brought Kirsty on a rare visit to the Lorimers' home, the banging of the hammer attracting their attention. 'A tree house!' Lorimer had exclaimed, and they had all wandered to the edge of the garden to peer at the activity nearby, two small boys yelling encouragement as their father sat astride one of the sturdy branches. Wilson remembered the expression on Lorimer's face as he turned to Maggie, her belly swollen with what was to have been their first child. 'We could have one of those!' he'd cried, eyes shining in anticipation of all the good things that fatherhood would bring.

But it was never to be, Wilson thought, a moment of sadness clouding his vision. The neighbours' two boys were long gone, grown men now, he supposed. And Maggie had never brought a live child into the world. Hopes of parenthood had faded over the years, her hysterectomy the final sign that they would remain a childless couple in a street full of families. Still, the old tree house had endured the passing years, its structure still visible behind the fresh new green of the emerging oak leaves.

DS Wilson cut the engine and sat for a moment ignoring the officer by his side and looking at the house that should have been home to the Lorimers' children. They had adapted it just for themselves, he knew, one of the big bedrooms upstairs now their main lounge, the lower floor all open-plan and airy, combining study, dining room and kitchen, with a bathroom at the back that a previous owner had added on. Maggie's mother had stayed with them briefly after suffering a stroke, Wilson recalled, Maggie ready to relinquish her career in order to care for her mother. But that had never happened.

Now there was this other woman, someone from the detective superintendent's past; an old friend, Lorimer had said, from his school days. Wilson sighed, reluctant to walk up that driveway and knock on the door. He'd never been good at having to face the bereaved, choosing whenever he could to delegate such tasks to a female officer, such was his dread of having to cope with the emotional aftermath of a murder. McEwan would make the tea and offer the paper hankies, he told himself. But he would ask the questions. He had been appointed SIO, was acting detective inspector now, a promotion that he had never expected to happen, and as he sat looking nervously towards the Lorimers' doorway, he wondered if he really wanted the responsibilities that came with this rank.

'Sir?' Detective Constable McEwan was looking at him quizzically.

'Okay, let's get on with it,' Wilson said, stepping out of the car and letting the younger woman follow him up the path.

The ring of the doorbell seemed to echo through the house, the two officers listening for footsteps within. The door was opened suddenly, however, as though the woman had been waiting for their arrival.

'Detective Sergeant Wilson. Detective Constable McEwan,' he said, nodding towards the red-haired woman who stood on the threshold.

'Come in,' she said, opening the door wider and standing to the side. *Just as though she were the lady of the house,* Wilson told himself, an irrational flash of annoyance making him frown; though to be fair to the woman, she had been expecting them, he reminded himself.

It was pretty much as Wilson remembered: the desk in the bay window to the front, the old rocking chair still with its plumped-up cushions to one side of the dining area, a breakfast bar the only structure to separate the kitchen from the rest of this long, bright room.

'Would you like to sit here?' Vivien Gilmartin asked, indicating the high-backed chairs around the square table. 'Easier to have tea,' she said, moving towards the kitchen, where Wilson spotted a tray already prepared with three of Maggie's best china teacups and saucers. He motioned McEwan to sit next to him while he regarded the widow with interest. She was smaller than Maggie, fine-boned and with the sort of pale complexion that redheads often had. Her black dress emphasised that slim figure, its full skirt sweeping just below knee length, elegant and understated as befitted a woman recently bereaved. Yet when Vivien Gilmartin returned with the tea tray in her hands, Wilson saw that beneath the pallor and the mourning clothes she was an exceptionally attractive woman.

'I am sorry to have to . . .'

Wilson bit his lip. Why was he apologising for doing his job?

Her tentative smile, these green eyes trembling with tears; they had to be ignored if he were to carry out this interview with any success.

'There are several things we need to ask you, Mrs Gilmartin,' Wilson continued more briskly.

Vivien nodded, a little sigh escaping from her lips. 'I understand. William told me what to expect.' She smiled at them both in turn, then lifted a silver teapot, one that Wilson had never seen before.

'Milk? Sugar?'

'We require information about your husband, Mrs Gilmartin,' Wilson began. 'Can you tell us exactly why he had come to Glasgow?'

'Work,' Vivien replied shortly, sitting at the table. 'Charles was setting up a project with an African theatre group. Part of the wider remit of the Commonwealth Games is to provide cultural experiences for all the visitors to Scotland,' she explained, looking at McEwan, who sat sipping her tea. 'We would have been bringing the show to several venues, notably the Edinburgh Festival.'

156

'Would have been? You mean it's being cancelled?'

'Oh yes.' Vivien nodded, eyes narrowing slightly. 'There is no way it can proceed without Charles.' Her glance fell and Wilson detected a tremor in her hand as she laid down her teacup.

'He has nobody to take his place, then?'

'No.' Vivien shook her head. 'It's quite impossible now. Charles was the driving force behind it all. Without him it is simply a non-starter.'

'Won't there be difficulties in cancelling it all?' McEwan asked hesitantly.

Vivien shrugged. 'The Africans weren't due to arrive for rehearsals until June. And the cultural programme for the Edinburgh Festival isn't out until then either.'

'That's a pity,' McEwan remarked. 'You must be disappointed after all the work that had gone in to make it happen.'

Vivien gave a short, dry laugh. 'Disappointed? I think that's the least of what I am feeling right now.'

'Who else was involved in the Scottish end of things?' Wilson asked.

'Oh, lots of people were involved, of course, but nobody we actually *knew*. At least, nobody in person. Various government agencies were behind it, of course. Masses of telephone calls. Lots of paperwork,' she said.

'So there wouldn't be anyone visiting you at the rented flat, somebody who had a key?'

Vivien shook her head. 'I can see what you're asking me,' she sighed. 'But it is as much of a mystery to me who was in the flat that night.'

Wilson watched as she sat back, clasping her hands together on her lap, no doubt digging her nails into the soft flesh to stop from weeping.

'Can you take me through the day of his death, Mrs Gilmartin? Tell me exactly what happened.'

Vivien looked up, eyeing the two detectives in turn. She swallowed hard before answering.

'I was out a lot of the day. Arranging the school reunion.' She paused as though collecting her thoughts. 'Charles went to the local theatre, the Citizens, where he was to put on a week of performances.'

'When did he go to the theatre?'

'Oh, late morning, early afternoon, I think. He was in the flat before that, on the phone to London mostly, making arrangements about the scenery, I think.' She shook her head. 'It was such a busy day,' she apologised. 'My head was full of the reunion and I was at the school all afternoon setting things up.'

'But you came back to get ready?' McEwan asked.

Wilson gave an imperceptible nod, approving the officer's question. A woman would ask that sort of thing, understanding the need to prepare for a special occasion.

'Yes.'

'And what time was that?' Wilson asked.

'About five o'clock, I suppose. I gave myself time to shower and change, then left again just after six. The taxi came to the back door of the building.'

'And how did your husband seem when you came back to the flat?' Wilson wanted to know.

Vivien's eyes widened. 'Oh,' she said. 'Didn't I tell anyone?' She looked from one to the other as though this was something that had never occurred to her. 'Charles wasn't there.'

Wilson tried to remain impassive, though in truth his mind was already creating a possible scenario.

'Did your husband expect to be returning with anyone from the theatre while you were out?'

Vivien frowned. 'I've really no idea. He certainly didn't tell me he had any plans like that.'

'Had anyone visited either of you at the flat?'

'No. Nobody.' She looked from one officer to the other, green eyes widening as the thought took hold. 'Do you think he brought his murderer back with him?' she whispered.

'It's the only explanation that makes any sense,' Wilson said as they drove away from the Lorimers' home. 'Gilmartin brings someone back when his wife is at her school thing. Goes to bed,' he turned to McEwan with a meaningful glance, 'then is given a lethal cocktail of some sort, already prepared by whoever it was who came back with him.'

'A woman?'

Wilson raised his eyebrows. 'Who knows? Some of these arty types swing both ways. Could've been a man. Could have been more than one person. And that,' he said firmly, 'is what we have to find out.'

Lorimer looked at the initial report. He'd been there, done nothing to stop that female officer from washing the bed linen. Had he been too preoccupied with Vivien sobbing on his shoulder to imagine that the flat could possibly be a crime scene? No, he reasoned. His instincts would have made him far more cautious had there been any grounds for suspicion. A heart attack, the doctor had said, and they'd taken his word for it. Never once had the thought of murder intruded into his thoughts that night. And now vital evidence was missing for good. Was there something else they might have found? Had Gilmartin been in bed with someone other than his wife? The thought came unbidden to the detective's mind just as it would in any case like this where so many possibilities had to be examined. Any traces in the bedclothes might have been tested for DNA and matched against the theatre people Gilmartin had known up here. Rosie had insisted that there was nothing like that on Gilmartin's body, however. So perhaps whoever had lured the man into bed had administered the drink before the promise of any sexual play. Lorimer shuddered. He was glad that Wilson was in charge of this case, but each step of the investigation still came back to him in the form of these reports. Vivien did not know that, and he wasn't going to let her know, though she must have suspected that he was keeping all further intelligence from her.

The detective superintendent thought back to the previous year when he had scribbled his signature at the foot of that letter of invitation to the reunion. It had been a capricious moment, the memory of his youthful dalliance encouraging him to see her once again, but it was now one that filled him with a deep regret.

CHAPTER TWENTY-EIGHT

The man in the corner of the coffee bar sat reading the *Gazette*, his face hidden from sight behind the opened paper, a deliberate ploy to remain unseen by the person he had come to watch.

As disguises went, his was fairly standard: false beard, a fashionable flat cap over his thinning hair and heavy spectacles that contained nothing more than ordinary plastic lenses. He had known this was the place that the couple frequented before Gayle Finnegan began her day's work at the Albion Street offices, for it was not the first time he had spied on the young man.

His newest recruit troubled him; that arrogant lift of his shoulders when he was asked to carry out a necessary action. As if he had done it all before.

None of them had, the man in the corner thought. This would be entirely without precedent. The bomb exploding at the opening of the Games at Parkhead Stadium would signal complete and utter contempt for the foreign regime that headed up his country. Every time the man thought of it happening he had a queer sensation in the pit of his stomach, the sort of excitement that anticipation for a promised treat had always brought him as a small boy.

As he waited for Cameron Gregson to arrive at the coffee shop, the man recalled the explosion in the Stirlingshire countryside the previous August. That had been a success, and according to his sources close to the security services, there was nothing to link any of them with the event. And there would be nothing to link them with the final explosion at Parkhead in July either. One of his team had served in Iraq, the bitter disillusion that followed making him a prime target for recruiting. But this was a different sort of war and his soldiers would remain anonymous. There would simply be a notice in the press about *why* their act of terror had been carried out. And it would be something that Scottish people would never forget, something to be written in the history books for all time.

He watched the young couple come into Berits & Brown together, their body language giving away more than they realised. Or perhaps, the man thought, they didn't care that their closeness and the way the young man pressed his thigh against the girl's was noticeable to anyone who cared to observe them. That was fine. Gregson (oh yes, he knew the fellow's identity all right) was doing just what he had been commanded to do: infiltrate the very heart of the enemy's territory, keep a close watch on all that was happening in the run-up to the Games.

Looking over the edge of the newspaper, he saw Gregson look his way and for a heartbeat he thought his cover had been blown. But no, the younger man had turned away again and was talking to the girl, telling her what sort of coffee he wanted. That was good, he told himself as they left the shop carrying small brown paper bags containing their breakfasts. She had less than five minutes before making it to work on time. Gregson must have kept her lingering in bed this morning, he thought, looking after them and seeing the smile on Gayle Finnegan's face as she cuddled closer to her boyfriend's side.

His own expression was quite impassive as he imagined the moment when the bomb exploded, that smile being wiped off the young woman's face for ever.

'You're sure you'll be all right?' Maggie asked, turning back to see Vivien standing at the kitchen sink, one hand already in the pocket of her silk dressing gown. *She'll be whipping out the fags as soon as I'm gone*, Maggie thought.

'I'll be fine. No need to worry,' Vivien replied with a brittle little smile. 'I don't mind being on my own.'

'Oh.' Maggie stopped and turned back for a moment, the heavy satchel weighing on her shoulder. 'You won't actually be on your own all day. Flynn's coming over this morning.'

'Flynn?' For a moment Vivien's brow creased in an anxious furrow.

'Our gardener. More of a friend, really. He'll come in and make his own coffee. Knows where everything is.'

In truth, Maggie had considered letting the young man know the circumstances behind the red-haired woman's presence, but Lorimer had cautioned against saying anything at all while the investigation proceeded.

Maggie closed the door behind her and set off for work. It had been a long Easter break, the red-haired woman's plight taking up all of her attention, and now that Charles Gilmartin's death was being considered as a murder investigation, goodness knows how long Vivien would be staying with them.

The school teacher drove off, a feeling of lightness in her spirits as she contemplated the term ahead. Despite the pressure of imminent exams, she was looking forward to being with her senior pupils again and preparing them as best she could. It was warmer today, another spell of sunny weather forecast after the changeable days they had endured throughout the holidays. Once the kids were on exam leave, heads down in a final effort to gain good passes, the weather would pick up. It was the law of natural cussedness, her friend Sandie often remarked, that term-time brought the best of the sunshine while the vacations were usually damp and miserable. Still, it hadn't all been a washout, Maggie thought. She'd managed a bit of gardening, tidying the borders before the time came to plant out the usual annuals. At least Flynn would see that she had made a bit of an effort.

Joseph Alexander Flynn had good reason to be whistling cheerfully as he drove the green van up the Lorimers' driveway. It was several years now since he had first stood at their door, a waif rescued from disaster by the tall detective, his feet set on a better path than the one he had followed before meeting William Lorimer. He grinned as he lifted down the mowing machine and trundled it around to the back of the house. The front garden was small and neat, easy enough for Maggie to manage, but the back was a different challenge. Here the lawn straggled over more than half their quarter-acre, the rest being given over to flower beds, shrubs and mature trees, a haven for Chancer the ginger cat, who came at that moment to greet him, tail erect, waiting for the gardener to tickle him behind his ears.

'Hello?'

Flynn stood up, surprised to hear a woman's voice coming from the kitchen doorway. Standing just outside on the step was an elegant red-haired lady, one hand cupping her elbow, the other languidly holding a cigarette.

This woman might have stepped straight out of a television

advert, she looked so perfect. The dark trousers emphasised her slim figure and under the pale grey shirt that was unbuttoned just low enough, Flynn could see the rise of her breasts. But it was the face that cast its spell; different from the ones plastered across all those beauty magazines in the newsagent's where he bought his daily paper, this face had character and experience, a knowingness in the green eyes that made the young man feel instantly aroused. She stood there letting him watch her, then smiled as though she could read his thoughts.

'You must be Flynn,' she said, and took a drag at her cigarette, blowing the smoke over her shoulder.

'That's right.'

'I'm Vivien,' she told him. 'Did Mrs Lorimer tell you that I'm staying with them for a while?'

Flynn shook his head, still gazing at this unexpected vision of loveliness, all too conscious of his own grubby dungarees and thick-soled boots.

'Don't let me keep you back,' she said. 'Just let me know when you'd like a break, won't you?' she added, smiling in a way that seemed to suggest she might be offering more than tea and biscuits.

Flynn continued to trundle the lawnmower towards the grassy areas, wondering who this woman was and what she was doing with the Lorimers.

Vivien Gilmartin stood at the kitchen window, watching as Flynn stooped to pull the cord on the mower, then, as the machine burst into life, her gaze followed him across the garden and her green eyes narrowed as an idea took root in her mind.

If Joseph Alexander Flynn was surprised to see the woman kneeling by a flower bed, hands safely protected by Maggie's gardening gloves, he did not show it. She didn't look the type to get her hands dirty, but appearances could be deceptive, as Flynn knew only too well. Besides, a little weeding would not go amiss, and perhaps this Vivien person wanted to be helpful to the Lorimers, he thought, concentrating on his own task as the red-haired woman bent over, the small gardening fork digging deep into the crumbly soil.

'Twenty thousand pounds,' Wilson said.

He was sitting in Lorimer's office, sun streaming through the slatted blinds, the detective superintendent leaning back in his seat behind his desk, fingers steepled against his lips.

'That's a lot of money. And the press release? When does it go out?'

'Tomorrow. With the mention of a substantial reward for information leading to an arrest and conviction. I can just see the headlines now,' Wilson sighed. '*Impresario poisoned in city flat.*' He shook his head. 'Poor chap. And he was in the running for a knighthood?'

'That's what Mrs Gilmartin told me.'

'She doesn't have to stay any longer,' Wilson said. 'The Fiscal reckons we can release Gilmartin's body for burial down south.'

'Burial. Not cremation?'

'Oh no.' Wilson smiled thinly. 'You never know when we might need it again.'

'I'll tell Mrs Gilmartin tonight,' Lorimer said.

Wilson nodded. Mrs Gilmartin. Not Vivien. The detective superintendent was saying and doing all the right things; his involvement was as a witness and a friend of the widow, yet there was no real warmth as he spoke, making Alistair Wilson wonder if his news came as something of a relief. He remembered the proprietary way that Vivien Gilmartin had ushered them into the

Lorimers' home, nothing that he could have put his finger on, simply a feeling that still rankled. He hid a grin as he left the office, pausing to throw one last remark over his shoulder.

'Bet Maggie will be glad to get the house back to just the two of you.'

'You'll be glad to see the back of me,' Vivien declared, turning to see Lorimer standing in the doorway of her bedroom. The bed was strewn with clothes and shoes, far more than she had arrived with on the night of her husband's death, Lorimer having made several trips since then to collect her possessions.

'Not at all,' he protested, attempting a sincerity that he did not feel. It would be a huge relief to have his visitor leave; the growing tension between Maggie and himself was becoming almost unbearable. Ever since the night when Vivien had woken from that nightmare, crying out his name, Lorimer had felt an unspoken resentment emanating from his long-suffering wife.

'You will come to Charles's funeral?' she asked him suddenly, looking down at a dark dress folded across her arms.

'Of course,' he told her. 'If I possibly can.'

'It would mean a lot, William,' she said, using the name that he had left behind at school.

Lorimer nodded. 'I'll be there. Just give me plenty of time to make arrangements.'

'Thank you,' Vivien whispered. 'I couldn't have made it through these last few weeks without you.'

'And Maggie,' he chided gently.

'And Maggie, of course,' she said lightly, though in a tone that made Lorimer wonder if there was something between the two women that he ought to know.

CHAPTER TWENTY-NINE

May 2014

There was something she ought to know, something she *wanted* to know, a feeling like a pain gnawing away at her insides that Shereen recognised as a guilty conscience. What had happened to the other girl? It was weeks ago now and she'd been told in no uncertain terms to keep her big fat mouth shut, or else.

Shereen still remembered the night when the girl they had called Celia had tried to escape from the flat, her tear-stained face turned to the older woman, eyes pleading for help. Then the door had banged shut, the footsteps receding until she could hear no more, only the distant sound of a car revving up on the street below.

Since then she had scanned every newspaper she could find, sitting for ages in the library or nursing a mug of coffee in Starbucks, but no report had ever appeared about the missing girl. Perhaps, Shereen thought, they had sent her back home; but she was only deluding herself with such hopes, she knew that. They had done something to Celia, something bad. She had seen the way the two men refused to meet her eyes later that night, a sure sign of their guilt.

'Just look after Asa,' one of them had told her gruffly when Shereen had dared to ask about the other Nigerian girl. 'You do your job and we'll do ours,' he'd said, his voice low so that the other man would not overhear him. 'Know what happens to a singing bird?' he said.

'What?' Shereen shook her head. What the hell was he talking about?

The man looked at her intently, fingers rolling a folded newspaper.

'A singing bird is never allowed to live. Everyone knows that,' he whispered, twisting the paper slowly until it began to tear at the edges.

Shereen had shivered, hands covering her throat in a protective gesture.

Soon afterwards Asa had appeared to take the other girl's place and Shereen recalled the way the young girl had smoothed the cover on the bed as though she had sensed someone had been there before her. Watching her grow in confidence had given the big woman a spurt of pleasure, enough to put Celia out of her mind, for now at least.

There had been a few clients climbing these tenement stairs now, Asa silently enduring their overtures; no doubt the pills she'd been given helped to put a veneer on these sexual encounters. Shereen had washed the bloodstained bedding after her first night, the girl's stolen virginity clear for anyone who cared to see. She'd had to do the same the morning after the big man had satisfied his lust in an attempt to purge the memory of whatever he had done. Asa's eyes had been dull as she'd sat fidgeting at the breakfast table and there had been no exchange of words between them. It was as if her spirit had been broken in some way, and the older woman had longed to take the girl into her arms, soothe her with false hopes. But she had done neither of those things. Shereen was a part of the young Nigerian girl's pain, powerless to prevent it happening, and she hated herself for it.

Professor Solomon Brightman turned the page of the book he was reading, then put his hand back against his chin, a thoughtful look on his face. Nobody had invited him to do this background research, no pay cheque would tumble through his letter box with a thank-you letter from the police, but nevertheless he had decided to look into what he could find about child trafficking. One author had suggested that the statistical rise in such activity coincided with major events in or around the cities where trafficking took place and Solly's interest had been piqued.

It was now May, and the Commonwealth Games were a matter of weeks away. Glasgow was filled with colourful signs. Everywhere he went there were posters and banners with the ubiquitous kilted mascot grinning from each and every one of them. At first the psychologist couldn't help but grin back; the whole city seemed to be filled to the brim with a sort of wondrous anticipation. *Don't knock us! We're as good as the rest of them!* these banners seemed to be saying, and it was true. The news filtering out from the 2014 committee was all good. The athletes' village had been completed to the highest of standards and would help in the regeneration of Glasgow's East End; figures were already suggesting that tourism to Scotland was expected to achieve an all-time high and the number of Games workers in paid employment just kept rising and rising.

It was hard, therefore, to imagine a darker undercurrent to this city he had grown to love, a seamier side where underage girls were groomed to satisfy the sexual lusts of those visitors who were looking for a good time in more ways than one. Solly had even

170

spoken to a psychologist friend who worked at the detention centre where illegal immigrants were placed prior to being repatriated to their homelands. His friend had some concern about a young African girl. Hints about an organisation had been given, no more than mere rumours, she had told him. Nothing substantial, no evidence that was worth taking to the authorities. But she was sure that something was happening, and Solly believed her.

Across the city Acting Detective Inspector Alistair Wilson stared at the latest report sheet on his laptop and swore under his breath. Nothing was coming right in this case, nothing at all.

'Evidence, we need some evidence,' he muttered darkly. But each time his team had come back empty-handed from the flat, the neighbours round about and the theatre where Gilmartin had spent his last afternoon. He had nourished hopes of a breakthrough when the tox report had mentioned the ginger wine.

'It's dark and sickly sweet,' he'd told his colleagues, 'a perfect base in which to mix a cocktail of drugs.' The fact that it was normally a seasonal drink, found in the shops for New Year's celebrations, had presented some difficulty, though when his wife, Betty, had reminded him that a cordial could be purchased to make the stuff at home, Wilson had become more positive. 'If we find the bottle, we can test for prints,' he'd told the team. But a careful search of the premises had produced absolutely nothing: no half-empty bottle, not even one that had been emptied then washed. Like many city flats, the one rented by the Gilmartins had a chute for rubbish, the large bins in the basement being collected on a weekly basis. Unluckily for the investigating team, the collection had taken place the Monday after Gilmartin's death, so there was nothing at all to show if a bottle had been disposed of in that way.

171

'Maybe they brought it and took it away again,' McEwan had suggested, after one discussion about whether there had been more than one person involved in the murder. Wilson had merely grunted and gone back to the laborious work of finding CCTV footage in the area round about.

But here again he had drawn a blank. No images of Charles Gilmartin in the company of other people appeared in the grainy videos, just one of the man entering the building alone at six minutes past six, the time duly noted in Wilson's report. He must just have missed his wife, as she had left round the back of the flats by taxi, though no CCTV footage covered that part of the complex. But Gilmartin couldn't have spent the rest of the evening on his own, Wilson thought, despite the fact that no other figures had been seen following him, none but the residents who lived there and, much later, Mrs Gilmartin herself. But by that time, he was dead, Wilson reasoned. There were no internal cameras to snoop along the corridors or the lift and so he'd had to think of other ways a killer might have entered the building. Or had he been there all along? Were they looking for another resident, perhaps? But a door-to-door trawl had come up with nothing, most of the residents having sound alibis for their whereabouts on a Friday night, while those who had been on their own, like the eighty-five-year-old lady downstairs, appeared from the further checks that had been carried out to have no reason to poison the impresario.

And despite the dangling carrot of a reward, the press release had only brought time-wasters into their orbit.

It was more than puzzling, Wilson had confessed to his wife; it was frustrating, especially as this was a case where he had been appointed SIO and solving it might lead to a late promotion, something he and his wife had dreamed about for long enough

172

now. The extra money in his pension would be a boost when he retired.

'What about the wife?' Betty had asked. 'Isn't poison supposed to be a woman's weapon?'

Wilson had shaken his head. They'd been sitting in front of the TV, Betty watching her favourite television adaptation of Agatha Christie's Miss Marple, when she had made the comment.

'She's got about a hundred alibis for the time of her husband's death,' he told her grumpily. 'Lorimer included.' And Betty had shrugged, said *oh well*, and continued to stare at the screen.

It was Kirsty who had posed the other question, one a cop would ask: *who benefits from his death, Dad?* And he'd told her. The sole beneficiary in Gilmartin's estate was his wife. No children, no previous marriage, nobody else who would inherit what was an astonishingly large amount of money. He remembered how Vivien Gilmartin had shrugged as though she were completely indifferent to such wealth. 'How can I enjoy it on my own?' she had asked him, her fingers reaching for another handkerchief from the box thoughtfully provided by Maggie Lorimer. And Wilson had nodded, silently thinking of how he would feel if it had been Betty. His world would be empty without her, and no material benefit could ever compensate for that kind of loss.

Now he was staring at his screen again, trying to work out who could have possibly entered the flat that night, a niggling voice telling him that this was one case that might remain unsolved due to lack of evidence. He'd be branded as a complete failure, but worse than that, he would be letting down the detective superintendent, a man he considered his friend as much as his colleague, and that rankled more than anything. Tomorrow he would be heading down to London in the hope that some of Gilmartin's theatrical colleagues might throw some light on to why this man had been killed. The thought of the long rail journey and nights spent in a cut-price hotel depressed him. This should be a job for someone more senior, he told himself, not for a DS who had begun to count the time until retirement.

CHAPTER THIRTY

'Why not?' Rosie asked her husband as she lifted a pile of Abby's clothes from the tumble dryer. 'Lorimer wouldn't mind, I'm sure of that.'

'But the Chief Constable might,' Solly murmured, thinking of the budgetary constraints of policing. Hiring a profiler for the case of one unidentified girl was very unlikely indeed.

'Well, you aren't looking for remuneration, are you?'

Solly smiled, his brown eyes twinkling through the horn-rimmed spectacles. 'No,' he said at last. 'I just want to let him have a few facts. Perhaps his team already knows about it, though. I might look a little foolish. As if I were teaching my grandmother how to suck eggs.'

'If I were that girl's mother, I'd want every single fact laid out before the police, no matter where it came from,' Rosie told him. She sighed. 'Poor wee soul. More than likely her parents sold her to buy basic essentials. We don't know how fortunate we are in this country,' she added, looking at all the little garments on her lap. Abigail Margaret Brightman was spoiled for choice when it came to wee dresses and cute outfits, partly because her god-mother, Maggie Lorimer, couldn't resist passing the window of the Monsoon children's department and often brought Abby a

175

new frock with matching tights or a patterned cardigan. Then again, Rosie herself liked to browse the internet for new clothes for her little daughter. For an instant she felt a pang of guilt; the amount of money this pile of clothing folded on her lap had cost would feed several African families for a year or more.

'All right. I'll do it,' Solly said. 'An email first, I think, just to give him an idea of what I have found so far. Anything else would be intrusive.'

Rosie watched her husband as he left the room. There was enough paperwork on his desk here and at the university to keep him occupied for weeks, but still Solly wanted to find time to help in this case. Had it been her fault that he had become involved? Probably. Talking about the girl after the post-mortem, Rosie had made some observations on the likelihood that the dead girl had been lured into prostitution. 'Maybe she was killed because she was pregnant,' she'd wondered aloud one evening. Then the discussion had begun and her husband had followed it up by reading around the subject then talking to his colleague at the detention centre.

In the study next door, the professor of psychology tapped out a message to his friend. Lorimer would take it the right way, wouldn't he?

They must know, Solly thought, pressing the send button. Surely they must know about such things going on in the city?

The sound of the door closing made Asa sigh with relief. The last one had gone and now she could have a shower before trying to sleep for what was left of the night. These acts of sex bothered her less nowadays, though sometimes one of the men would be rough and deliberately want to hurt her, the sound of her screams urging him on. Tonight it had been better than usual, just three men who had come into her room one after the other, speaking words she didn't understand, but with voices that sounded as though they meant her no real harm. The last one had called her by name; *Asa*, he'd said, stroking her face gently, as though he had known her from a previous life. She had pasted on the false smile, just as Shereen had instructed her, lain there in the flimsy undergarments waiting for it to take place, desperate for it to finish.

Shereen kept the door unlocked afterwards so that Asa could shower and freshen up, then the bolt would be slid shut and the girl would lie awake, wondering what had brought her to this place. But tonight would be different. She could hear the sound of voices coming from the television, recognising the background music to the programme that Shereen watched faithfully. And tonight she was alone. Neither of her two African jailers was in the flat. It was the perfect opportunity for the girl to creep out unnoticed.

She dressed hurriedly, stuffing spare underwear and socks into the pockets of the fleece jacket that Shereen had bought for her. Twice she stopped to listen, but the only sound she could hear was from the television in the far room.

It was safer to leave the bedroom light on, confuse the older woman for as long as she could, Asa told herself, slipping into the bathroom and reaching out to turn on the shower tap. The noise of the water cascading into the empty bath drowned out all sound along the corridor. She closed the bathroom door behind her, hoping Shereen would fall for the ruse.

Then, holding her breath, Asa crept along the hallway, opened the big door and slipped silently out into the night.

Should she close it? Risk the sound echoing through the flat? For a desperate moment the girl hesitated, then she pulled it shut behind her, shuddering as the noise reverberated in the stone landing. The stairs wound down and round, three landings with doors on either side that made Asa's eyes widen in fear lest someone should suddenly open one up and see her trying to escape. At last the bottom of the final flight of stairs approached, a space shrouded in darkness, shadows deepening in the corners, making her peer into the gloom in case someone was lurking out of sight. But there was nobody. And as Asa stopped to catch her breath, her throat constricted in a moment of sheer panic.

She had no idea where to go.

In front of her stood the big main door where her clients called for Shereen on the intercom, something the big woman had tried to explain to Asa in a charade of mimes. Beyond lay the kerb where she had been bundled several times into the car. If she could run fast along this grey street it would lead to the bigger road where Asa had seen shops and brightly lit buildings. On the last journey she had tried hard to take note of all the places between the flat and the city, though the signs that were written in English meant nothing to her.

The idea had come to her when they had passed two other vehicles; one was a black cab with the word TAXI emblazoned in yellow light, the other a big white car whose blue light flashed from its roof, POLICE written clearly on the paintwork. If she could find one of these, Asa reasoned, she might be taken to a place of safety.

Asa glanced behind her, noticing for the first time a narrow passageway that ended in a smaller door. Where did that lead? Should she make her escape a different way after all?

At that moment the sound of the buzzer made her jump.

Someone was at the door!

Heart thumping, Asa pressed her thin body against the wall, sliding into the shadows, feet taking her silently towards the back door of the close.

As the main door opened, she stood completely still, hardly daring to breathe. Would they see her hiding in the shadow of the stairs? She closed her eyes, willing the footsteps to pass her by, hearing the door swing shut again with a bang.

As the sound of the steps receded, Asa risked opening her eyes. He was gone!

Her hand felt all around the back door, seeking a lever or a handle, anything that would open it for her. Then her fingers closed around a hard, cold ring and she tugged, hoping to feel the door open. When nothing happened, she twisted it one way, then the other.

She let out a gasp as the door opened, cold air from the night streaming in, the faint glow of orange light from nearby street lamps illuminating the patch of grass that lay between this door and what looked like a high stone wall. She let the door close behind her, holding it carefully until she heard a dull click. Then she stood still, watching as her breath made faint ghosts in the night air.

It was wise to let her eyes become accustomed to the darkness. This was something the African girl had known all her life. Where she had come from, the stars lit up the sky, wheeling on their mystical courses. But here they were dimmed by that smouldering haze like a dust cloud hovering on the edge of the horizon.

At last shapes began to emerge and the girl could make out the barbed wire snaking across the top of the wall, a concrete shed containing dustbins placed at the far end of the path. There was no gate. No door leading from the back of the premises that she could see; just shrubs and trees straggling against the wall.

Asa crept on silent cat feet towards the shed, then stopped beside the wall where a tumble of ivy cascaded down to the ground. She blinked. There *was* a door. It had been hidden from her sight by the foliage, but now she could see the old wooden structure merging into the grey stones.

She pulled, but the door stood firm.

Once again she searched desperately for a latch, but her fingers found only an ancient keyhole set into the jamb of the door. With a sigh of despair she realised that the back gate must be locked from the outside.

Looking up, she saw that it, too, was covered in a curled strand of wire. No doubt the intention was to keep out intruders but, she realised with sinking heart, it also served to contain any prisoner trying to make an escape.

Suddenly she saw a light go on in the topmost flat and heard voices calling her name.

Shrinking back against the shed, Asa knew she had very little time to decide on a plan of action. Her feet found the lid of the first bin and she scrambled up, nails digging into the edge of the shed roof as she levered her body upwards.

Light shone from the back door.

'She's there!' a man's voice cried, and Asa saw a figure running towards her.

There was no time to think. No time to hesitate.

Biting back a cry as the barbs cut into her hands, she leapt over the wall and fell heavily to the stony path below.

CHAPTER THIRTY-ONE

Glasgow Royal Infirmary was a prime example of the city's split personality, the original hospital building with its domes and towers close to the ancient cathedral and the tourist attractions of St Mungo's Museum and Provand's Lordship on one side, and the modern concrete structures hugging the M8 motorway on the other, looking to the passing motorist as if a child had abandoned its building blocks, scattering them in careless heaps. Inside Accident and Emergency one might also see evidence of the city's diversity, people from several walks of life and from different ethnic groups all demanding the same level of care and attention from the overworked medical staff.

Asa sat wedged between the black man at her side and an Asian mother whose twin boys were running around the chairs, their whoops attracting glares from the other patients sitting opposite. The night outside made no difference to this place; with its wide-open spaces and bright lights it reminded Asa of one of the air terminals she had passed through on the long journey from her home. She was as weary now as she had been then, despair settling on her like a shroud.

They had brought her here afterwards, Shereen insisting that Asa's arm was broken and that they must take her to a doctor. As she sat beside her captor, the girl tried not to remember her scream of terror or the way the man had pulled her roughly to her feet, dragging her back up the stairs, hands bleeding, the pain searing through her arm. Instead she looked at the children running back and forth, their dark hair shining under the lights, patently ignoring their mother's pleas to be good. For although Asa did not know the language spoken by the harassed-looking woman, it was obvious from her tone that the children were testing her patience. And as she watched their grinning smiles and heard their laughter, Asa felt a different kind of pain, a regret for her lost childhood. She had not been unique amongst the village children; the illness that had taken so many adults had spread to several families and there were lots of orphaned children who had to fend for themselves. But they had stuck together, making the best of their meagre resources. And when the man had come with promises of work in the city and a better future, Asa had followed him willingly. Now another man sat beside her, proof that those promises had been a lie, a trick to lure her away to this cold, grey place.

It had been a shock when the man at her side had spoken to her in Yoruba. They had been in the flat, preparing to leave for the hospital, the cuts on her hands bathed and covered with a sweet-smelling white cream that did not sting.

'Keep quiet when we get there. I'll do the talking. And if anyone does ask, I'm your husband, got it?' he'd told her sternly, his voice low and hoarse as though it had been a long time since he had uttered any Yoruba and the words were rusty from lack of use. Shereen had produced a ring from somewhere, shoving it on Asa's finger with a look of admonishment. Then she had been bundled into the car and driven through the city to this huge place filled with artificial light.

It was not difficult for the girl to remain silent; the shock of the fall and the dreadful pain combined with the trauma of her capture had shaken Asa badly. What would they do with her now? That had been her only thought as she had been half pushed, half carried back into the flat, tears of agony coursing down her dark cheeks. And the thought that someone could have explained her plight from the start made things even worse.

Why had the man kept speaking only in English? Why had he refrained from giving her the slightest hint that he too was from West Africa? The questions buzzed around her brain like hornets caught in a glass jar. Did the others know he could speak Yoruba? Or was this some sort of secret that he kept from the big man with the tattoos and his white friends? She had looked at him as they had sat here on the padded hospital seats, a mute appeal in her eyes, but he had continued to ignore her as though she was a complete stranger.

A nurse in a pale blue uniform came out and called the Asian woman to follow her, the twins skipping at her side, one clutching at the spangled scarf that matched the woman's pink and beige sari. They were alone now, waiting their turn to see a medical person.

Asa felt the coat sliding from her shoulders where Shereen had slipped it on, and the man grabbed at it before it fell off the back of the chair.

'Remember to keep your mouth shut. I do all the talking,' he growled.

Asa nodded, torn between the thrill of hearing her native tongue spoken aloud and the feeling of hopelessness that she was still this man's captive. They would be next, he told her. Any funny business and she wouldn't live to see the dawn.

He'd looked at her then, eyes cold as ice, and Asa had shivered, knowing instinctively that this man had already taken somebody's life.

Maureen Lee pinned a stray lock of hair under her starched cap and glanced at the clock. Just three more hours and she'd be off, six whole days of freedom beckoning. There was a couple still in the waiting room, a man and his daughter by the looks of them. She'd seen them arrive, the girl clearly distressed and in pain. An accident in the home, the case notes said. Asa Okonjo, Maureen read, her eyebrows lifting as she continued. Wife of Mugendi Okonjo. She was wrong, then. Not his daughter after all. Maureen yawned. Suspected fracture, so they'd be shunted off to X-ray, then, all being well, the woman's arm would be plastered and they could be sent home.

Maureen made a face at the computer; she'd wanted to use it earlier that night when an Asian kid had been admitted, but the bloody thing wasn't working properly again. The engineer had been supposed to come to fix it and hadn't. It would be sorted on someone else's shift now. Story of my life, Maureen muttered under her breath. It just made everything so much more difficult. There was a program on the A&E computer that translated loads of foreign languages, making admissions smoother for both the staff and their patients. And now she couldn't make use of the darned thing.

As Nurse Lee stepped out of the corridor and into the waiting room, she saw that there was no overnight bag lying on the floor or an adjacent chair. *Hope it's not a multiple fracture, then,* she sighed to herself. *Or the poor bitch will be transferred to a ward where all she'll have is one of those washed-out hospital gowns.*

Asa lay on the narrow bed, the sheets of green paper below her, one arm laid out exactly as the radiographer had shown her. The machine whirred above her and the girl closed her eyes, pretending that she was somewhere else. But try as she might, no visions of her home came to comfort her; only the sounds in this room telling of the here and now: the woman's feet squeaking on the linoleum as she adjusted Asa's position, the clunks and clicks as the machinery began to photograph her damaged arm.

Then the tall white woman in the green jacket and matching trousers was helping her gently to her feet, one arm guiding her from the room and to another row of chairs where her 'husband' awaited her.

'A clean fracture, you'll be glad to know,' Maureen told them. 'You'll be plastered up and home in no time,' she added, smiling at Asa.

'She doesn't understand English,' the man explained. 'I'll tell her.'

Yet despite his assurances, no conversation began, the man seemingly eager to leave.

Maureen's smile drooped a little as she nodded. There was something not right here, she told herself, something about the way the young woman kept a distance from the husband. *If that's what he really is*, a little voice suggested. Maureen bit her lip. She could be home and in bed before Matt got up for work if she finished up here in time. And was the relationship between these two African people any business of hers anyway? She didn't know a lot about Nigerians. Maybe they married the girls off really young?

As if she had read the nurse's thoughts, Asa looked up, her large eyes filled not only with tears but with a mute appeal that Maureen Lee saw as a plea for help.

'Just take a wee look, will you?' Maureen urged. 'I'm not happy about that pair.'

The auburn-haired woman in the white coat sighed heavily. Night shifts were hell after a holiday spent in the Bermuda sunshine, and Dr Emily Bishop only wanted to finish and go home to her bed. But there was something earnest in Maureen Lee's expression and the psychologist recognised that, tired as she was, the nurse from A&E was genuinely bothered about this patient.

Emily sighed and pressed the save button before rising to her feet and following Maureen along the corridor to the lifts.

'She's in the plaster room just now,' Maureen whispered, though there was nobody else to overhear her words. 'He's waiting just outside. Looks shifty to me,' she added darkly.

Emily stifled a groan. Was Maureen's imagination playing tricks on her? Tiredness could do that to a person, make them see things that were not really there at all. But she would have a look all the same. There were procedures to follow, after all, agencies that recommended certain steps to be taken if a patient was deemed to be at risk of any sort. And Nurse Lee clearly thought there was something fishy about this girl and her companion.

The plaster room was halfway down a corridor. Emily could see an African man waiting on a chair outside the door, arms folded as though he had been kept waiting longer than he wished. He was, Emily supposed, around mid forties, fifty even, pretty old to be the husband of a young girl.

'Mr Okonjo? Dr Bishop.' Emily smiled and extended her hand, making the man jump suddenly.

'We wondered if you would like to have a chat about Mrs Okonjo?' she continued, watching him carefully.

The psychologist saw the man stiffening, hands now gripping the edges of his seat, shoulders raised in tension; all clear signs that he was afraid of something, afraid of *her*, no doubt.

'She nearly finished?' he asked, glancing nervously at the open

186

door to the plaster room. 'We need to get home. No time to talk to you people,' he said, his eyes darting at Emily and then to the nurse and back again to the woman in the white coat.

'There you are, Asa, all done,' a voice from the plaster room proclaimed.

At once the man was on his feet, grabbing the grey coat from the chair beside him.

Was this a solicitous gesture for his young wife? Or was he simply in a hurry to be off? Emily wondered, standing back a little and watching the African girl being escorted from the room by a nurse.

Even had she not seen the expression of abject fear in the girl's eyes as the man came towards her, the coat in his hands, Emily Bishop would have understood Asa's body language, something that overcame all the barriers of speech. The way that she slunk away from him, keeping as much distance as she dared, head bowed in complete resignation, made the psychologist give a nod in Nurse Lee's direction. Yes, she was saying silently. Make that telephone call. Report your misgivings. Someone will follow this up.

'A little word before you go?' Emily asked the man as he strode away from them. She had to quicken her pace as he hurried towards the exit.

But there was no answer from either the African man or the terrified girl by his side, and as she watched them disappear into the Glasgow night, Dr Emily Bishop hoped that whatever details were written on their case notes would be followed up by the proper authorities.

CHAPTER THIRTY-TWO

Police Sergeant Patsy Clark had been up since five, washing and setting her hair, putting her make-up on far more carefully than the usual slap of foundation and quick brush of mascara. Today merited the sort of attention to detail that Patsy had shown her reflection in the dressing table mirror. There was little she could do about the uniform, but that didn't matter: people who met you for the first time always looked at your face, and she wanted to be remembered by the man from MI6 as *Clark, that bright woman from Glasgow.*

She knocked on the detective superintendent's office door, glad that she was ready for this meeting, hoping that her eagerness would not show, like the lacy edge of a fancy slip peeping below her hemline. The image made the police officer frown for a moment, tugging at her skirt just in case.

'Ah, Sergeant Clark.' Lorimer rose from where he had been sitting next to his desk, a dark-suited man half turning to see who had entered the room. Then he too was on his feet, examining the new arrival with a smile that made his eyes crinkle at the corners.

'Connor Drummond,' the man said, extending his hand towards Patsy. It felt warm to her touch and strong, the sort of handshake she liked, but then he was back in his seat and Patsy was being ushered into the chair next to Lorimer.

Was that his real name? Patsy thought, wishing she could utter the question, fearful that to do something so inane would brand her as a complete idiot.

'We'll bring you up to speed, Sergeant Clark,' Lorimer was saying. 'Connor, why don't you give our colleague an outline of what you told me?' he offered.

'Sergeant Clark,' Drummond began.

'Patsy,' she blurted out suddenly, then blushed.

Drummond smiled at her and for a moment the woman was struck by the notion that he could read her mind, see the dreams she cherished of a life like his: secret, undercover, making the world a better place while the world slept on, unknowing.

'Well, Patsy,' he continued, and as he spoke about the cell that had been identified in Glasgow and the need for total discretion, she realised that Drummond's accent was Scottish. Perthshire maybe? An educated voice, clear and with overtones of the city about it, but a softness too, though not with the lilt of the Highlander or the measured tones of the Outer Isles.

'So you see,' Drummond said at last, 'we need to be aware of the potential for disaster on a massive scale. There is absolutely no doubt in our minds that the Games are their target,' he went on, though how that opinion had been reached Patsy would never be told. 'Our intelligence suggests that there are at least five of them working together. An explosives person, obviously, and at least one member of the Games personnel.'

'Really?' Patsy exclaimed. 'But surely Disclosure would have picked up any aberration there?'

Drummond's smile faded. 'You would hope so. But we are beginning to be of the opinion that one of the group has been recruited from the higher ranks of the Games committee.'

'But don't they all need to go through a vetting procedure?'

189

Lorimer shook his head. 'Not if they are someone already in the public domain,' he said quietly.

'That's right,' Drummond agreed. 'And in our business we have to make sure that each and every person who comes close to members of the royal family is checked out very, very carefully.'

'So will all the high heid yins go through this process?' Patsy asked.

Drummond smiled at her lapse into Glasgow slang. 'Yes.' He nodded. 'Everyone who is to be at the reception before the opening ceremony and the event itself will be carefully scrutinised. Background checks, the lot.'

'That includes all the military personnel,' Lorimer reminded her. 'And our own officers.'

Patsy nodded, understanding. Health and safety measures had rocketed in number ever since the attempted terrorist attack on Glasgow Airport, and though the public might moan a bit about the inconvenience of having to go through so many security procedures, they were all aware of the danger that such an attack presented.

'Lord Coe hardly had a wink of sleep throughout the Olympics,' Lorimer told her. 'On the surface he appeared calm, but I'm sure he must have been glad when it was all over without any incident.'

'And that's what we want for Glasgow,' Drummond went on smoothly. 'The public deserves to have an excellent summer of events with nothing to disrupt them. God knows the Games committee's worked hard enough to achieve a major success.' He looked from Patsy to Lorimer. 'And it is our job to make sure that nobody knows of any sort of threat that might take that away,' he warned them. 'We will find this group,' he went on. 'We already have one name and the identity of a second person to work on. So let's start with that, shall we?'

*

190

Lorimer blew out a sigh of relief. It had been a long morning, the empty coffee cups littered on his table testament to the hours of discussion with the man from MI6. Patsy Clark had been a tad intimidated by the idea of meeting the intelligence officer, but she, like Lorimer, had soon warmed to the young man with the sandy hair whose ready smile had put them both at ease.

Everything they'd discussed was written down in the notebook in front of Lorimer, not one word recorded on the usual office computer for added security. 'Never know who might hack into your system,' Drummond had said lightly, though the expression in the man's eyes belied his casual words.

A heavily tattooed man of large build and reddish hair, Lorimer had scribbled. Maybe involved in one of the heavier sports. *Weightlifter?* he had added, the question mark embellished with squiggles as he had listened to the intelligence officer. May have something to do with the Gathering of the Clans event out at Stirling. Battle re-enactment societies a possible source.

It was somewhere to start, anyway, plenty for police officers to follow even if they were not told any details of why they were investigating this particular individual.

The name should have given them a better way into the terrorist cell. But names could be stumbling blocks for those shape-shifting men and women whose true identities were often covered up by several aliases. And Drummond had not offered his opinion (or that of his Ministry) as to whether it was real or not.

Robert Bruce Petrie, Lorimer had written, each word underlined. He had hesitated to add a question mark this time. It would be easy enough to find someone of that name, tracing it through the databases at their disposal. And if he was anywhere to be found, they would seek him out.

CHAPTER THIRTY-THREE

The email from Solly had not gone unnoticed. Lorimer's frown had turned to a smile as he imagined the psychologist poring over the computer screen, anxious not to overstep the bounds of their friendship. *I hope you don't mind*, Solly had begun, showing a deference to Lorimer's authority that had not always manifested itself in the early days of their association. The detective superintendent read on with interest. A colleague of Solly's had some misgivings about a girl in the detention centre where she worked. *Think you ought to speak to her*, Solly had written. *Here's her number.* And Lorimer jotted it down on a page torn from the notebook he had been using earlier that day. It was the sort of detail that might or might not lead to something concrete, he mused, tapping his lips with the pencil.

Minutes later he was picking up his jacket from the back of the chair and heading out of the room. Yes, the psychologist at the detention centre had agreed, it would be better if he came down, though it was highly doubtful that the girl would talk to him. She was terrified of men.

As he drove away from Stewart Street, Lorimer felt his spirits lifting. It was one of those days in May when the morning clouds had cleared, the outlines of landmark buildings silhouetted against skies of perfect blue. Tonight he would be returning home to Maggie and it would be just the two of them now that Vivien had flown back to London, no other person there to disturb the peace of their suburban home. As he drove through the city streets, Lorimer imagined sitting out in the garden, Chancer curling around his legs, a glass of something tawny in his hand. It wasn't a bad life; he had a wife he loved, a house with no mortgage and the best job in the world. What more could he ask for?

A lopsided grin formed on the policeman's face. There were always going to be things he wanted, answers to all those difficult questions. Like this case now: who was the African girl who had been found out at Cathkin? And was there any significance in that Pictish shape tattooed on to her thigh? None of the missing persons enquiries had turned up a girl connected with the Commonwealth Games, but that did not mean that she had nothing to do with the events unfolding around this city. If Solly's idea about trafficking was correct, the body now lying in the mortuary might well be that of a girl brought into the country specifically to service the needs of men willing to pay for sexual gratification; men who would come to Glasgow for a while and leave again, their lusts for sport and sex equally satisfied.

'She won't see you,' Dr Jones warned him.

Lorimer nodded, stifling a sigh of exasperation. He was sitting in the psychologist's tiny office, no more than a glorified cupboard with one high barred window to let in the daylight. The window was shut fast, making the place stuffy, a desk fan moving slowly in a constant arc, the tiny breeze doing little to rob the room of its sultry atmosphere. Dr Jones was a thin woman of around fifty, he reckoned, short grey hair curled behind her ears, a pair of reading glasses perched on her nose, and a manner that brooked no nonsense from anyone in her domain whether he were a senior police officer or not.

'What can you tell me, then?'

Dr Jones thought for a moment before answering, reminding him suddenly of Solly Brightman, a man of many considered pauses in his speech.

'She spoke about a big man, a white man,' the woman began at last. 'With lots of hair on his face, red hair, she told me. And many shapes tattooed on his arms.' She swept her fingers across her sleeve as though to illustrate this point.

'What sort of shapes?' Lorimer asked.

'I asked her that after you called,' Dr Jones said. 'Curled shapes, like hissing snakes, she told me. But not snakes. Does that make any sense?'

'Perhaps,' Lorimer replied. 'Can you show her these.' He drew out a folded sheet of paper from his notebook and flattened it on the desk between them, turning it towards the woman so that she could see the designs that Wrigley had given them.

Dr Jones studied them carefully, one finger tracing the intricate whorls and curls.

'Pictish,' she said at last, looking up.

'You know about stuff like that?'

She smiled. 'It might surprise you, but many psychologists begin their careers with studies into anthropology. The fascination with the human condition,' she added, her grey eyes lighting up with an enthusiasm that Lorimer found infectious.

'Yes, I'll show her these, shall I?' The woman rose from her desk, taking the paper with her, and left him in the room, closing the door behind her.

Lorimer sat on the edge of his seat, the walls of the overheated office suddenly seeming to close in on him, a sure sign of the claustrophobia that had haunted him for most of his life. Hoping that he was not breaking any sort of rule, he stepped to the door and opened it wide.

The sounds of life were not from human voices but machines: a vacuum cleaner's drone, the shrill ring of a telephone somewhere down the corridor and the whirring of the electric fan on the psychologist's desk. What the hell must it be like to live in a place like this day after day? Adrift in a no-man's-land between the place you thought was safe and the threat of being deported back to wherever it was you'd fled from, waiting for the wheels of bureaucracy to turn. He could well understand why the young girl would not see him: he represented the very authority that posed such a threat. And more: he was a man and it was at the hands of men that girls like this had suffered.

At last Lorimer heard the woman's footsteps return along the corridor and he breathed a sigh of relief.

As she entered, the psychologist paused, one hand ready to close the door again, but one look at the tall man sitting back from her desk made her stop.

'You'd rather I kept this open a little?' she asked, settling her spectacles on to her nose again.

Lorimer nodded, too ashamed of his weakness to confess it to this woman, guessing that those shrewd grey eyes could see his discomfort anyway.

She settled herself behind the desk once more. 'Yes,' Dr Jones began briskly. 'It was indeed tattoos like that. Blue and green, she says. However, the man she describes did not have that one.' She turned the paper towards him, one finger on the triple spiral. 'Though she has seen it before.'

Lorimer suddenly wanted to tell this woman all about the black-skinned girl they had taken from the edge of that pond, tell her everything about the case. But it was impossible without breaching the same code of confidentiality that was imposed on the rest of the investigation team. She was looking at him, her clear eyes waiting for his response.

'There is a tattoo like this that interests us,' he began carefully. 'And not on the arm of a man.'

'Our detainee tells me that it was given to another girl, one she met before coming here. She won't say any more.' Dr Jones shook her head slightly. 'I am sorry.'

Lorimer thought about the bloated face back in the mortuary and the predations of the water creatures that had eaten away at her flesh. Who now would recognise the dead girl?

'It's important that we know where she met this other girl,' Lorimer insisted. 'Can you try to persuade her to tell you?'

Dr Jones smiled suddenly, a sad smile, then another regretful shake of the head. 'I can try, certainly, but I cannot guarantee that my question will be met with any degree of success.'

'It really is important,' Lorimer told her. 'Other girls may be harmed, like the one here. Tell her we only want to stop that happening, will you?'

'Look at this!' Kirsty exclaimed aloud so that several heads in the room turned her way.

'Sorry.' She blushed. 'Just found something . . .' Her voice fell to a mumble. She caught the expression of amusement on one female officer's face as she turned back to her own desk: *the rookie cop at it again, overenthusiastic.* And the blush deepened as she wondered what else they said about her. *Wilson's daughter, getting preferential treatment just because Lorimer's a family friend.* Was that strictly true, though? Kirsty had been given the same routine sort of jobs that any probationer would expect and Lorimer had never once shown her any special favours. His manner was completely professional whenever he was speaking to the team, concentrating their minds on the case in hand, explaining the reasons behind the need for each and every action. The occasional wry remark that would make them smile, a nod when an officer had achieved something worthwhile, and above all, the sense that he trusted them to do a good job; these were all attributes that PC Wilson was finding out about Detective Superintendent Lorimer here at Stewart Street. She had known him for most of her life and it was Lorimer, not her own father, who had inspired her to join the police after all, wasn't it?

Kirsty looked back at the email from the Royal Infirmary that had been forwarded to the team. No doubt everyone involved in the case had seen it by now, her exclamation of discovery quite redundant. The notes from the hospital were quite specific: the patient's birth date was given as 1 April and the address as Yoruba Street, a place Kirsty knew simply did not exist. The girl's name had been given as Asa Okonjo. Mrs.

Kirsty nodded. It all tallied with the same girl Stuart Wrigley had tattooed. Would he remember a wedding ring? she wondered.

There had been sufficient concern to alert the authorities, the email continued. The patient did not seem to be comfortable with the man who had brought her to the hospital and the nurse in A&E had suspected that he was not in fact her husband. Further suspicions arose when the psychologist had been called to have a look. She had seen the man's behaviour; was sure he was hiding something and in a very big hurry to leave. And there was more. Kirsty's eyes widened as she read on. The nurse in the plaster room had been embarrassed when the girl had lifted her skirt and pointed towards her inner thigh, the psychologist had written. But the nurse had remembered the tattoo all right. The three curled shapes revealed as the girl had taken her hand away.

'So we're looking for a black girl with a broken arm now,' Lorimer said.

The detective superintendent nodded at the officers assembled in the incident room. He had already reported back from his visit to the detention centre. 'We know the girl's identity tallies with that of the girl in Terry's Tattoo Studio. Same false address. We do, however, have a lead on the pair of them after they left the hospital. CCTV footage shows them getting into a car, and we have a partial on the rear number plate.'

What Lorimer did not tell them was that Professor Brightman had been instrumental in directing them to the detention centre, his concern that there was a ring of child traffickers at work in the city something that the police already shared. Nor did the detective superintendent dwell overlong on the big white man whose arms were covered in green and blue Pictish shapes. Lorimer had been sworn to secrecy over the matter of the terrorist cell. But it was too much of a coincidence that the description that Connor Drummond had given him tallied with the one from the girl in the detention centre.

And William Lorimer was not given to a strong belief in coincidences.

CHAPTER THIRTY-FOUR

Maggie opened the front door and bent down to retrieve the day's mail. The ginger cat appeared at her side, rubbing his flank against her leg, the purring a welcome-home sound that immediately lifted her spirits. She breathed out a sigh, feeling her body relax. It had been a hard day waiting for her seniors to finish their exam, having them come into her classroom afterwards eager to share what they had written, eyes hopeful that they had chosen the best questions to answer. But it was over now and there would be other teachers marking their scripts, those external examiners who determined the fate of so many young folk. The rest of the term was not so difficult: the seniors were on exam leave until June, when the new timetable would kick in, and Maggie's work-load would be diminished till after the holidays.

She sat on the old rocking chair, opening the mail, casting aside the flyers to be recycled in the bin outside the back door, putting the bills into a neat pile. There was one stiff envelope that looked like a card. Maggie's brow furrowed, puzzled for a moment. Neither she nor Bill had a birthday coming up, so what could this be?

She slit the envelope with her paper knife, a souvenir from one of their trips to Skye, the handle a slim greyish-green marble. The card portrayed a garden full of flowers, an empty deckchair in the centre, a discarded book on the grass.

Opening the card, Maggie's eyes immediately fell on the signature. *Vivien Gilmartin*. Not just *Vivien*. It was a thank-you letter, then, Maggie supposed. And so it was.

Dear William and Maggie,

Now that I am back in my own home, I realise what an awful imposition I placed upon you both. Taking a virtual stranger into your lovely home was indeed an act of true kindness and for that I will always be grateful.

Nothing will ever be the same. You understand that, of course. However, life goes on and I am already planning to travel later in the year, when I shall take myself away from London and all its memories of Charles for a while.

I do so hope to see you at the funeral next week.

Until then, be assured of my continuing gratitude and friendship.

Your friend,

Vivien Gilmartin

Maggie bit her lip. It was a gracious letter, so like the woman who had penned it, dignified and with just enough warmth to evoke genuine sincerity. And the card had been carefully chosen. A picture to reflect the times Vivien had spent in their garden, nursing her sorrow.

Why then, Maggie asked herself, did she feel that prickle of unease? A suspicion that all was not as it should be? Bill was intending to go down for the funeral on his own. Days off were only given to school teachers for the funerals of family members. Was it because of that? Was she worried that there was something still between the red-haired woman and her husband? Some flicker of romance? There had been nothing to suggest it when Vivien had stayed here, or had there? That night when she had cried out and Bill had gone to reassure her ... he had stayed in her room for such a long time ...

Maggie shook herself. Silly woman, she thought. Overactive imagination. It was the end of a long day and tiredness was making her irrational, that was all.

She sank back into the cushions, the motion of the rocker making her sleepy, a yawn compounding the need to close her eyes and rest awhile. In moments she was asleep, the card slipping from her fingers and dropping silently to the floor.

Lorimer stood watching her sleep. There had been no answer to his usual call, *I'm home*, and he had crept quietly into the big room, guessing that Maggie might have dropped off to sleep as she sometimes did. It had been a tough time for her, hosting a guest like Vivien as well as having to return to the strictures of work. Looking down at her pale face, Lorimer saw the dark shadows beneath her eyes, the faint lines he'd never noticed before. He sighed. Always so busy, always off investigating some case or other, had he been too caught up in the world of policing to see the years take their toll on the woman he loved?

His eyes fell on the pile of mail and he stooped to pick it up, curious to know who had sent that fancy card. In moments he had read the words, taken in the sentiments expressed and nodded. Was it really a thank-you letter? Or a subtle reminder to come down to London? His mouth twitched suddenly as he smiled. Always suspicious, he told himself. Goes with the job, he thought. Yes, he told her mentally, I'll be there at your husband's funeral. But I won't be coming alone.

*

Alistair Wilson stood at the counter, the black tie in his hands. Marks and Spencer had been the best bet, he thought. Any of those other fancy places would have cost a bomb down here. It had not been his intention to stay on for the funeral after his round of interviews with Gilmartin's friends and colleagues, but Lorimer had insisted.

'We'll travel back together and you can fill me in on whatever's come up,' he'd told the acting DI. Wilson had agreed, then telephoned Betty to explain why he would be staying in the capital for another day and night.

London was hot for May. More like real summertime weather, a bit humid and sticky by late afternoon, the temperature rising far above the normal for this time of year, and well above anything he would expect back home in Scotland. As Wilson stepped out into the hot street with its stop-go traffic inching along, he sighed longingly for a West Coast breeze. His eyes craned along the line of cars, looking out for a black cab. That was one thing about London: there were always plenty of taxis. In less than a minute he had spotted one with its orange light blazing, given the cabby his destination and settled down to unwrap the tie.

Odd time to have a funeral, he'd told Lorimer. Five o'clock in the afternoon? But his senior officer had not given any reply to that.

The funeral cars would wind their way up this path, thought Lorimer as he walked up the slope towards the burial ground. He had not attended the church service, a notice in *The Times* informing the public that it was for family members only. Reaching the brow of the hill, he turned and looked back at the church, its grey spire and dark slate roof beneath him. How many mourners had gathered to comfort Vivien Gilmartin? he wondered. Her sister and her family from Canada, perhaps? She had told him that both their parents, like his, were dead. But maybe there were Fox cousins somewhere and a number of Gilmartins setting off in cars to make their way up here to the open grave where Charles Gilmartin was to be laid to rest.

It was a peaceful place to end life's last journey, Lorimer decided, gazing around. There were no dark yews here, but a small copse of silver birches screened the back of the cemetery from the city beyond. Many of the graves were old and moss-covered, some leaning askew, battered by time and storms. In the distance he could see the gravediggers, one standing hand on his spade, the faint line of cigarette smoke barely discernible. The drone of a plane heading for one of the London airports made him look up; the silver-bodied craft shone like a strange fish in a sea of halcyon blue. It was still warm and Lorimer wished now that he had not worn this dark raincoat over his best suit. But it had been pouring when he had left the house early this morning and he had grabbed it on the way out, overnight bag in hand. Here, high above the city, the air was fresher than it had been as he had emerged from Euston, plunging into the traffic fumes and rancid smells of grease from the snack bars.

His gaze fell on a figure approaching, labouring a little as he climbed the steep path towards him. He smiled, recognising the man's familiar walk.

'Whew, thought I'd never make it up that hill,' Wilson said, puffing as he came to a halt. 'Shouldn't have paid the taxi off at the gates.'

'You're out of condition,' Lorimer teased. 'Need to send you out on foot patrol with that daughter of yours.'

'Aye, well. Maybe I need to think about losing a bit of weight. Too many of Betty's cakes,' groaned Wilson, patting the stomach that bulged above his belt.

'Nobody here yet, then,' he added, turning to look down the hill at the view where Lorimer had been gazing.

'Still in church,' Lorimer said. 'Oh, there's a car coming up now. Let's walk over a bit. Don't want to be hanging around too close to the action.'

The two men strolled away from the edge of the path, making for a spot near enough the grave to hear the service but not so close as to be mistaken for family friends.

The cars began to arrive, slowly snaking up the hill and parking in a crescent below this level of the burial ground. It did not surprise the detective superintendent to see such crowds of dark-clad men and women emerging into the sunlight; Charles Gilmartin had been a well-known figure in theatrical circles and there would be many here from that world to pay their last respects.

There were taxis too, disgorging the mourners one by one then heading back along the path and disappearing over the crest of the hill. Soon the grassy slopes were full of people standing around, casting their eyes towards the ribbon of pathway, waiting for the arrival of the hearse. Most people seemed to have gravitated towards friends or acquaintances, but there was one elderly lady standing on her own, clutching a large handbag with both hands, her felt hat jammed on top of tight white curls that looked newly permed. She appeared lost amongst the smartly dressed men and women, some of whose faces Lorimer recognised from television but whose names he had forgotten. As he watched, he could see her hand searching inside the cavernous bag to find a small, lace-trimmed handkerchief. After blowing her nose, the old lady wiped a hand across her eyes, the crumpled hanky stuffed into her coat pocket.

Nudging Wilson, Lorimer tilted his head, indicating the woman, and began to walk towards her.

'Couldn't help seeing you were on your own, ma'am,' he began. 'Do you mind if we stand with you?'

'Oh.' The woman looked up at him. 'You must be one of Mrs Gilly's friends from Scotland.'

'That's right,' Lorimer replied. 'We go way back,' he said, glancing at Wilson as though to include him in the reply.

'That's nice,' she said. 'Specially seeing that sister of hers didn't make it over from Canada after all. Not a lot of folks here from Mrs Gilly's side. Mind you,' she leaned in towards them, one hand against her mouth as though to impart a confidence, 's'pose I'm really from both sides, ain't I?' She stuck out one gloved hand. 'Mrs Porter, bin cleaning for the Gillys for years, I 'ave. How d'ye do?'

Lorimer and Wilson shook her hand in turn, murmuring their names but not their respective ranks within Police Scotland.

Just then a silence fell as everyone turned to see the big funeral cars arrive and park near the graveside. Lorimer stood beside the little cleaner, watching as she pulled another handkerchief from her bag to dab at her eyes. Then he held his breath as a slim figure emerged from the large silvery-grey Daimler.

Vivien was not alone, a younger man in a dark suit by her side, his hand slipped under the crook of her elbow, ushering her towards the grave, a priest following them at a respectful distance.

'That's Martin Goodfellow, Gilmartin's assistant,' Wilson whispered. 'Saw him yesterday. Tell you about it later,' he said quietly, a meaningful glance catching the detective superintendent's eyes.

As the pallbearers carried the coffin from the hearse, the crowd moved slowly forward, feet silent on the cropped turf, no jostling for position, most keeping a discreet distance from the edge of the open grave.

At first Lorimer heard the priest's words as a background

monotone, so intent was he on looking at Vivien Gilmartin. The widow's face was partly hidden beneath a black veil attached to her hat, red hair tamed into a simple knot, emphasising that long, slender neck. She stood, head bowed, as the priest intoned the familiar words: *ashes to ashes, dust to dust*. What was she thinking? Lorimer wondered. Was she remembering better times with her husband? Hoping that he was dwelling in the sort of afterlife that the man of God asserted was waiting for the deceased? Or was she simply numb, seeing the reality of death here in this place, the scent of newly mown grass and singing birds somehow at odds with the darkness engulfing her.

She was more of a stranger to him than ever, he realised. London was her home, her real home, this huge city with all these people around who were, he supposed, her friends. Was he here because of an earlier friendship? *First love was the sweetest*, she had told him that night as they had sat together on the playground bench. But Lorimer knew he would not have made the journey south just to give this woman moral support. He was here, he reminded himself, because the man being lowered into the ground had been murdered. And it was the job of his fellow officers to find out who had committed that crime.

'Can we get you a taxi, Mrs Porter?' Wilson asked.

'Oh, thanks, dearie. Will we travel all together then?' the old lady asked brightly. Now that the service was over and everyone was making their way back along the path, she seemed a lot less tearful.

Vivien had not spoken individually to the mourners; it fell to the priest to invite them back to a city hotel *for a refreshment*, as he put it. She had turned away, head bowed, acknowledging no one before slipping back into the big car.

The old lady tucked her hand into Lorimer's arm as the three made their way back down to the gates of the cemetery and the busy main road.

'Nice place, this,' she began. 'My Albert's buried just along there.' She pointed with one gloved finger at a row of gravestones curving on a lower terrace. 'Been dead and gone these twenty-eight years, 'e 'as,' she continued. 'Bad 'eart. Ran in the family.' She nodded. 'Lovely wake we had, best night in years. Pity 'e 'ad to miss it,' she chuckled.

Lorimer stifled a laugh. He had taken a sudden liking to this garrulous old lady.

'You don't still clean for Vivien, I suppose?'

'Mrs Gilly? Course I do, dearie! What would she do without old Porter, eh? And I can always do with the cash, can't I? Not so easy making do with the pension these days, eh?' She nudged him with her elbow. 'Always paid me, even when they were away. Got a lot done when they were up in Glasgow. Bad place, that!' she added with a scowl. 'Poor man, dying in his bed. Poisoned!' she added darkly. 'Did you know that, dearie?'

They were saved from replying by Wilson stepping out into the road, hand raised to hail a cab.

'Oh, that's better. Fair takes it out of these old legs of mine, that slope does. Always worse coming down than going up, don't you find?' Mrs Porter declared, settling back in her seat.

'Now then, tell me all about yourselves, dearies. Which part of Scotland do you both come from?'

Lorimer gave a discreet nod to Wilson, who launched into a glowing description of his home in West Kilbride and the views across the water. Mrs Porter nodded politely, and when Wilson paused, Lorimer broke in.

'What about yourself, Mrs Porter. Known the Gilmartins long, have you?'

'Oh yes.' The old lady smiled. 'Knew him when he was a boy, I did. Cleaned for his mother when they lived in that big house of theirs in Kensington.' Her face fell suddenly. 'Poor old soul. Was in a nursing home in her latter days, she was. Left everything to Charles, you know,' she confided, leaning towards the police officers as though to keep a secret. 'A fortune. Old man Gilmartin made millions in that cigarette factory of his back in the fifties. Course, everyone smoked then, didn't they? All lung cancer and outside the pubs nowadays, ain't it?'

'I suppose Mrs Gilmartin inherits his estate?' Lorimer asked, his tone as diffident as he could make it.

'Don't know about that, dearie. Charles had put a lot o' money into them theatricals, hadn't he? But yes, she'll get what's left over. Tidy bit, I shouldn't wonder, seeing as they had no kids.' She sniffed, then looked at the two policemen.

'You got kids, dearie?'

Once more Wilson came to Lorimer's rescue, giving an account of Kirsty's childhood and entry to the hospitality management course at university. He made no mention, however, of her dropping out of the course and joining Police Scotland.

'Good fer her!' Mrs Porter declared. 'Always stand a gel in good stead when she gets wed, eh?' She dropped a wink, then looked out of the window as the taxi slowed down and stopped outside the entrance to one of London's most famous hotels. 'Oh my, our Vivi's pushin' the boat out!' the old woman said, a smile of satisfaction on her plump face as she allowed a liveried doorman to help her out of the cab.

Lorimer followed Wilson and the old lady into the foyer of the hotel, casting his eyes around in appreciation. The expanse of marble floor might have given the place a feeling of chilliness, but that was offset by the magnificent gold and green drapes held back at each long window by tasselled cords, the sparkle of crystals from the many chandeliers above their heads and several enormous arrangements of flowers spilling exotic blooms over the lips of their urns. There had been a notice on a board in the hotel foyer discreetly informing visitors to the hotel (in gold lettering) where the Gilmartin wake would take place, but that really wasn't needed, thought Lorimer as they walked in behind a crowd of black-clad figures. Some of the women, he noticed, had opted for a clutch of feathers pinned artfully to their hair; others wore more conventional hats, but each of them appeared effortlessly stylish, apart from the homely little woman who now hovered uncertainly by his side.

'Never bin in this place afore, have you, dearie?' she asked.

Lorimer shook his head. 'My wife would like it, though,' he added.

'She young and good-lookin' like you, then?' Mrs Porter grinned.

Lorimer smiled. 'Maggie's lovely,' he said. 'She's a school teacher,' he added. 'All the kids love her.'

Mrs Porter nodded, satisfied to have drawn out a snippet of information from the tall man at her side who had remained so quiet on the taxi journey to the hotel.

There were waiters with an assortment of drinks as they passed into a high-ceilinged room, and young waitresses clad in dark green, offering glass-topped trays of canapés.

'None of your sandwiches and sausage rolls here, then,' Wilson whispered to his boss. 'Must be costing her a bomb.'

Lorimer nodded silently, looking around at the crowd of mourners and listening to the sound of voices rising as more and more people arrived. It was, he decided, more like a posh reception before a gala dinner than any wake he had ever attended.

'She done 'im proud, she 'as, I'll say that fer 'er,' Mrs Porter said grudgingly, one hand balancing a glass of bubbly, the other holding an empty cocktail stick, the large handbag now hooked across her arm. 'That's what they'll all remember, won't they? *Gave 'im a right good send-off*, they'll say.' She beamed with satisfaction as she picked up a concoction of something red and yellow from the tray of a passing waitress. 'Don't know what I'm eating, but it ain't half good!'

The old lady stopped and looked behind her as if some sound had caught her attention, but in truth it was simply the noise level decreasing as people stopped talking and heads turned to watch Vivien Gilmartin enter the room.

She was alone now, and both the funeral hat and the pinned-back hairstyle had been discarded, the flame-coloured hair catching the light as Vivien walked towards them.

'Mrs Porter, how kind of you to come.' She took the old lady's hands in hers as she bent to kiss her on each cheek. 'And I see you have already met my oldest and dearest friend,' she added, smiling at Lorimer for a brief moment. 'Don't go away too soon,' she whispered to him. 'I must do my widow's duties, but I want to talk to you.' There was a flash of something in her green eyes as she spoke, then she was moving away from them, reaching out to shake hands, murmuring *how kind* to other people, leaving Lorimer to wonder just what it was that she wanted to tell him.

By the time Vivien returned, most of the mourners had drifted away; even Mrs Porter, who had commandeered Wilson to find her a taxi.

'Thank God that's over!' Vivien gave a harsh little laugh as she sat down next to Lorimer.

'Were you dreading it?' he asked, looking at the woman's pale

210

face. Unusually, there were twin spots of colour marking those high cheekbones. The artifice of a make-up palette? Or a few drinks too many? he wondered.

'I am so glad you are still here, William,' she whispered, laying a slim hand on top of his, letting it linger there. 'I wanted to ask you something.'

He looked down at her, seeing the plea in those green eyes.

'Ask away, Foxy,' he said, his tone deliberately light.

She moved a little closer.

'Will you come back with me tonight? Stay with me?' she asked, her voice husky with emotion. 'I can't bear to be alone in that house ...' she added, her grip on his hand tightening as the fingers sought his own.

For a moment Lorimer wanted to take her chin and tilt it upwards, kiss away the tears that threatened to fall, but any comfort he could offer would be like the sort he gave to little Abby Brightman, he realised, not the kind of solace that this passionate woman was seeking.

'My train leaves tonight,' he told her, gently easing his hand from hers. 'Alistair and I are booked on the sleeper.'

'Oh.' Her eyes were wide with surprise. 'I thought we ...' She shook her head and looked down at her hands. 'Never mind. It was just a thought,' she added, smiling a brittle smile, then rising as a couple came towards them.

'Darlings,' she gushed. 'So good of you to be here for me. Give me a ring, Ruby. Next week?'

Then she was gone, no backward glance for the tall man who had risen to his feet. He watched as she left, linking her arm with that of another man, one more stranger to the Glasgow policeman, her slim figure disappearing out of sight.

*

Lorimer was relieved to see that they had the compartment to themselves. Darkness had fallen as the train pulled out of the station, the two policemen settling themselves down for the long night ahead.

'Right.' Wilson rubbed his hands together. 'Now I can fill you in on what's been happening down here. May as well give you the gen before I have to write the report.'

Lorimer nodded. He had been quiet on the taxi ride to the station, the memory of Vivien Gilmartin's proposition still warm in his ears. Had she really said that? Only hours after laying her husband to rest? Who was this woman, really? And what resemblance did she bear to the girl he'd once known and loved?

'It's been an interesting one,' Wilson went on. 'Saw a bit behind the scenes at a few of those theatres. Some of them are quite run-down and poky. Not like the auditoriums themselves, you know? All that fancy stuff, gold-painted and everything,' he continued. 'Reminded me of that saying: *all fur coat and nae knickers.*' He laughed.

'The recession has hit the arts especially badly.' Lorimer reminded him.

'Aye, they all told me that,' Wilson agreed. 'And that's why they were especially grateful for Gilmartin's money being poured into several of their productions.' He looked sideways at Lorimer, who merely nodded. 'Know what, though? They all said the same thing. Charles Gilmartin was dead keen on this African touring thing and none of them can understand why Mrs Gilmartin's pulled the plug on it.'

Lorimer shrugged. 'Maybe she felt it couldn't go on without him.'

'No, that's the odd thing,' Wilson said. 'The whole enterprise was ready to go. All the arrangements were in place, the London folk here like Goodfellow had it under control. At this stage Gilmartin was little more than a figurehead. *The money,* as one of them put it.'

'So why was he up in Scotland?'

Wilson's eyes narrowed. 'That was something Goodfellow wanted to know as well. Okay, Gilmartin was in talks with some of the Scottish theatres about the tour dates, and there was something about putting on a battle re-enactment in different parts of the country, but Goodfellow said all that sort of stuff could have been done by email or telephone.'

'What else did he tell you?'

Wilson took a deep breath as he looked his senior officer straight in the eye. 'Goodfellow reckons that the only reason they both went to Glasgow was because the wife wanted him to go with her. That school reunion thing you were at.' He continued to look at Lorimer as he went on. 'Seems that Gilmartin took a bit of persuading from his good lady an' all,' he said quietly. 'Any idea why he wasn't invited to the reunion?'

'It was only for former pupils, not partners,' Lorimer replied, remembering how Maggie had asked the same question.

'What about the possibility that Gilmartin invited someone back to their flat?' he asked.

'Seems unlikely that it was anyone he knew well, if he did,' Wilson said. 'According to his theatre friends down here, Gilmartin wasn't one to cross the border very often. And there were no close friends in Scotland that anyone had ever heard of. Mrs Gilmartin said just the same,' he added.

'What about his popularity? Rich folk aren't always best liked. Any jealousy? A reason of any sort for the man to be poisoned in his bed like that?' Lorimer's tone was terse, showing the first signs of the exasperation he felt.

Wilson shook his head. 'Mr Nice Guy,' he replied. 'Mind you, people don't like speaking ill of the dead. Especially superstitious types like those theatre folk.'

'But you didn't uncover any reason why someone would want him dead?'

Wilson shook his head again. 'It's a mystery, and that's saying something.'

There was a silence between them as the train gathered speed, lights from the city receding now as the countryside approached, plunging them into inky darkness.

Mr Nice Guy, Lorimer thought. The old cleaner had certainly been effusive in her affection for her late employer. *But not for Vivien*, a little voice reminded him.

Gilmartin's widow had been so eager to seek comfort from an old boyfriend. Was she in the habit of running into the arms of other men? Was her loyalty to her late husband something to be considered? The questions circled Lorimer's mind, probing into places that made him feel decidedly uncomfortable.

And for the first time, a chill settled into the detective's bones as he considered the woman who, it seemed, would benefit most from her husband's demise.

Three a.m. The death hour, some called it, Maggie thought, glancing at the red numbers on the digital clock. She felt deathly cold right enough, despite the sweat making her nightdress cling to her, the duvet thrown back as she'd tried restlessly to escape from whatever had been hunting her down. The nonsensical dream that had gripped her was fading but the fear it had engendered lingered on. She remembered that cry in the darkness again. The cry for help. But there was nobody here to comfort *her* in the darkness; Maggie Lorimer's husband was sleeping somewhere between

London and Glasgow, a train bearing him back to where he belonged.

Vivien Gilmartin wanted to keep him down there in London. She was certain of that, although no words had been spoken in Maggie's presence. But she had noticed signs of the other woman's predatory nature: the too-friendly glances directed towards her husband, the way she touched his arm whenever he did something kind or reassuring, the whispers meant only for him to hear. It had maddened Maggie, but what had upset her more was Bill's apparent inability to see what Vivien Gilmartin was doing, luring him into her web like some thin, seductive spider. What had happened at the funeral? Had she managed to corner him somehow?

Maggie felt the blood pulse through her ears as she shook her head.

What was wrong with her? Why was she having such terrible thoughts, such jealous notions? It was only her imagination working overtime, wasn't it?

She pulled up the covers, the cold air making her shiver. She would see her husband tonight, after work. Then everything would be back to normal.

Outside, the first signs of dawn had already arrived, with the birds singing in the garden, the clear skies presaging a fine morning, another working day ahead. Maggie had taken to sitting out of doors with her second-year classes, trying to instil something of the beauties of nature poetry into their heads. The school gardens were a poor substitute for the real countryside but they were better than nothing; at least there was grass, trees, a shrubbery and small beds of flowers, all lovingly tended by the janitor and his staff. Once she had taken them to the top of the science block, whispering that they must remain quiet, then allowing them to spend a few minutes staring out over the city skyline to the hills of the west.

Maggie's mind soared over the rooftops, longing for the term to end. She ached to be back in Mull, where they would rest and recover from all the stresses of their busy lives. She closed her eyes, a vision of Leiter Cottage and the Sound of Mull appearing, dark forests beyond the curve of the bay, the faraway hills of Morvern ... With a sigh, she rolled on to her side, all previous dreams banished, and in moments she was asleep once more.

CHAPTER THIRTY-FIVE

The girl had stopped crying at last.

Shereen sighed deeply, her back against the wall outside Asa's room. Since the night of her attempted escape, Okonjo, one of the Nigerian men, had been living in the flat, a suspicious look in his eye each time they had met in the kitchen or here in the hallway. Shereen had tried at first to avoid him, switching on her favourite soaps and quiz shows, but he had soon pulled the remote control out of her unresisting hand and changed the television channel to suit his own tastes: football, of course, and Formula One, the sound of cars racing around various circuits reminding the fat woman of a swarm of wasps zooming past. So Shereen had resorted to lingering beside Asa's locked door whenever she could, hoping to reassure the girl with a look or a smile. The man took little real interest in their prisoner; so long as Shereen laid food on the table the Nigerian seemed happy enough.

The big man had called once at the flat since that terrible night and Shereen had stood trembling in the kitchen, listening to Asa's weeping as the white man had yelled obscenities at her. Afterwards he had tossed a rolled-up bundle of notes on to the kitchen table, Shereen's wages for the previous month. She had tried not to snatch it up too eagerly, feigning a nonchalance that she did not feel.

It was one more step towards paying off the loan shark, one more step towards her own freedom, the woman told herself.

Asa lay on her side, teeth biting into her lower lip as she stared into the darkness. What had she done to deserve being here in this room with its lingering smells of human male sweat? The heavy plaster cast on her arm had not appeared to put off any of the customers seeking her young, pliant body. On the contrary, some of the men appeared to find something satisfying about making her cry out in pain as they rolled about on the bed, one even deliberately pulling at her arm so that the scream had brought Shereen running into the room.

The man had shouted at the dark-skinned woman, snarling monosyllables that Asa had often heard repeated over and over as a client brought himself to a shuddering climax.

She could not bring herself to look at Shereen now. *Trust no one*, a little voice whispered in Asa's ear at night. It was a voice that had once been her own, words spoken in the language she could hear only in her head. Except for that time in the hospital, before she had been brought back here. The memory of her surprise came back to Asa now as she lay thinking of the Nigerian man and how he had hustled her back into the car, speaking words she could understand; telling her in no uncertain terms what would happen if she tried to run away again.

And Asa remembered, too, the look in that nurse's eyes as she had lifted her skirt, the woman's disgust turning to astonishment as she had spotted the strange tattoo on her inner thigh.

Would it have meant anything to her? Or was it simply a strange happening that would be forgotten, the next patient putting that small incident out of the nurse's mind?

*

'Got it!' Kirsty Wilson put down the telephone, a smile of satisfaction on her face.

She and the CID officer had trawled each and every one of the tattoo studios around the city, not always able to speak to the proprietor, but always leaving word about what they were looking for. Now, it seemed, she had struck gold. Gathering up the jacket of her uniform from the back of her chair, she buttoned it up carefully, making sure that all her gear was properly in place. Then, grabbing her hat and jamming it on to her head, she walked purposefully across the big room to where DC Patrick Lennox sat hunched over his own laptop.

'Think I've found it,' she grinned. 'Place down by the river. Skin Art, it's called.'

'What did they tell you?' DC Lennox had swung into step with Kirsty and now they were heading downstairs and out into the foyer of the police station, past the curling posters and the row of plastic seating where a couple of young neds sat, legs stuck out, hands tucked into the pockets of their fleece jerkins. Kirsty ignored them, past experience telling her never to make eye contact with anyone waiting there; rude remarks had been thrown the way of the rookie cop before, making her blush.

'They specialise in Celtic stuff. Pictish too. And they remember a Nigerian girl having that triple spiral done,' Kirsty told him, unable to keep the sound of triumph from her voice.

'Well done you,' Lennox conceded. 'Let's see what they can tell us then, eh?'

It was a fine morning as the pair drove along the banks of the river in the direction of Glasgow Green, colourful 2014 banners flying on every side. Lennox parked the pool car and Kirsty emerged into sunlight, a tiny breeze catching dark wisps of hair already escaping from the chequered hat. Across from where they stood, the water sparkled, a bluish tint gilding the brown waters, the fast-flowing currents that could pull anything down and down into the depths.

Skin Art sounded grander than it was: a small shop with paint-work that had once been white but was now peeling and shabby, the sign ever so slightly askew as if a vagabond wind had knocked it off kilter and nobody had bothered to fix it again.

The door opened with the ping of a bell into a tiny anteroom, barely big enough to be called a reception area. Lennox strode ahead, knocking firmly on the frosted-glass door set into the middle of a partition wall. The entire panel appeared to shake as his fist drummed against it.

'Whaddyawant?' A gum-chewing woman stood at the crack of the door. 'Oh, it's youse. Harry!' she yelled, opening the door wider. 'It's the polis!'

Kirsty looked at the skinny woman in the doorway. Her mane of over-bleached hair was tied back, emphasising sunken cheeks and a sharp jaw, the look of a typical junkie, Kirsty thought, her eyes travelling down the woman's bare arms, noting old scars that were only partly hidden by the swirling tattoos.

'Oh aye?' A tall, thin man appeared and the woman seemed to melt into the background, such was the shock of Harry Temperland's appearance. Even as Lennox was taking the man's outstretched hand, Kirsty could not help but be fascinated by the tattooist's long white hair and piercing blue eyes, the blue circles curving over his cheek making him seem like a druid from ancient times. He wore a loose-fitting tunic over an embroidered shirt tied at the neck, and grey linen trousers, his bare feet thrust into a pair of well-worn Birkenstocks. Kirsty blinked. He seemed like a complete throwback to the sixties; a hippy whose style had weathered several decades of sartorial change. Could he be old enough to have lived through that era? she wondered, trying to calculate the man's age as they were ushered through the tattoo studio to a back room that doubled as office and print room. His skin was fresh and unwrinkled under the tattoos and he walked with the grace of a dancer; yet the hand that was offered to her at last was indeed that of a much older man, liver-spotted and gnarled.

'You wanted to see me about that black girl?' Temperland began. 'I've been away and only just got the message,' he explained, not offering any clue as to where he had been or why.

'You did her tattoo?' Lennox asked.

'Oh aye. That was my work.' The tattoo artist nodded. 'Quite a difficult part of the body to work on. Thin skin,' he explained. 'I do all the tricky ones. Marlene does the regular stuff.' He jerked his head towards the main tattoo studio, where they had passed the skinny woman seated at her workbench.

'Did the client come back for any reason?' Lennox wanted to know.

Temperland shook his head, sweeping back the wisps of hair falling across his face. 'Never. Are you thinking she should have?' The blue eyes regarded the two officers shrewdly.

'We have reason to believe that the tattoo became infected,' Lennox answered.

Temperland shrugged. 'Well they're all given the fact sheet about after-care. Part of health and safety regulations.'

'Who owns the studio?' Lennox said, suddenly changing tack.

Temperland's grey eyebrows rose in surprise and he hesitated for a moment. 'It's owned by a businessman in Glasgow,' he said at last.

'Not by you, then?'

Temperland shook his head, the brightness fading from his

face. 'I used to own it . . . ' he mumbled. Again no explanation was forthcoming, merely a shrug and a downward cast of those eyes.

'Does the owner carry out any of the art work?'

Temperland's smile reappeared. 'No way, man!' He gave a short laugh. 'We carry it out on *him*, though,' he said. Then he stopped, mouth still open as if he had said too much.

'We'd like the documentation from the girl's visit, please,' Lennox said crisply. 'And a full account of exactly what took place during her time at this studio.'

Clouds had obscured the morning sun by the time Lennox and Kirsty left the place, the river turning slate grey, a dampness in the air that presaged rain to come. As they walked along Clyde Street to the parked car, Kirsty wondered what Lennox was thinking. Perhaps, like her, he was silently processing the information that Temperland had given them. The details on the girl's form were fake. They'd already expected that, but it was still a shock to see *Yoruba Street* written in the space for an address. But now at least she had a name: Celia. Temperland had not remembered anything about the girl's personality, just that she had been very quiet. The black man with her had done all the talking. Her uncle? Could have been, Temperland had shrugged again, unable (or unwilling?) to remember such details. It had been a small but tricky job, he had told them. Needing a careful hand. Sometimes these little tattoos were harder than the big ones, especially on a place like an inner thigh. Was that a normal place for girls to ask for tattoos? Lennox had asked, and Temperland had pursed his thin lips. Not really, he'd agreed.

Kirsty pondered the meeting as they reached the car, easing herself into the passenger seat and fastening the seat belt over her bulky uniform.

'Well,' Lennox said at last, breaking the silence. 'What d'you make of him?'

'Bit of a weirdo,' Kirsty replied. 'But I thought he was telling us the truth about the girl. If she was being trafficked, then her minder wouldn't give anything away, would he?'

'And at least we've got a date when the work was done on her thigh,' Lennox said, putting the car into gear and heading off into the traffic.

Kirsty nodded, staring out of the window at the trees blossoming by the river walkway. She felt a sense of anticlimax now; they'd achieved so little from that visit, interesting though the tattoo artist had been. The people behind the human trafficking had not been stupid enough to return to the same studio, but why, she asked herself, had they asked for that same Pictish design?

Marlene shifted the wad of gum from one side of her mouth to the other. The folded newspaper was still in the back pocket of her jeans and the woman felt it every time she bent over to pick something up, a reminder of possibilities. Could she have followed those two coppers out of the shop? Spoken to them about the man she had seen? Charles Gilmartin's photograph was still there, a grainy image on the section of the paper that Marlene had cut out of the *Gazette*. She still didn't understand it; Harry kept her out here in the main studio, never in the back, especially when the big boss man was around. And the question was troubling her. Why had that nice, handsome-looking man spent time secreted in the back of the shop on the very day that he was supposed to have died?

CHAPTER THIRTY-SIX

'Why a triple spiral?' Solly asked, nodding his dark head as they walked along the path that bordered the river Kelvin.

Lorimer did not answer. He had barely slept on the train, his mind a fankle of questions that demanded answers; his first thought when arriving back in Glasgow was to seek out the one man who might possibly help untangle some of them at least.

'It's a female symbol,' Solly continued. '"Maiden, wife and crone",' he quoted. 'An odd sort of thing to have tattooed on girls who were little more than sex slaves.'

'Costing seventy quid a time,' Lorimer put in.

'Indeed.'

Solly stopped for a moment, turning to his friend. 'There is another symbolic meaning that we might wish to consider,' he said, sounding as though he were standing at a lectern delivering some sort of discourse to his students.

Lorimer merely raised his eyebrows in expectation. And waited. Solly's habit of creating lengthy pauses in his conversation might be irritating to some, but the detective superintendent was used to them.

'Freedom,' he declared at last. 'That is an alternative *translation*, if you like to put it that way. Hm, yes, could we see it as an ironic comment, I wonder?'

Lorimer watched the psychologist as he stroked the end of his beard. Solly's gaze was far away now and he was talking as much to himself as to the detective.

'They tattoo these girls who have no freedom. Why waste money on an irony? No.' He shook his head once more. 'These sorts of people are in the business of *making* money, not spending it without good reason. So,' he continued, shaking a finger to emphasise his point, 'there must be a good reason for giving them a tattoo, and not just any design. It brands them, of course, makes them identifiable as the property of their owner. Whoever he is,' he added darkly. 'But the freedom symbol is interesting. They tattoo it on girls who, after all, are merely commodities to them, right?' He looked at Lorimer as though he had become aware of his presence again.

'Right.'

'And it is not merely some scribble. These women are his property and he is defining himself by using that particular symbol.' The psychologist's eyes gleamed as he began to smile. 'I think that whoever has brought these poor unfortunates into the country has another agenda going on altogether. Perhaps nothing to do with his lucrative sex business,' he said, a note of eagerness creeping into his voice.

Lorimer cocked his head to one side, waiting for more.

'Could he be making a political statement of some sort?' Solly asked. 'Don't laugh,' he added quickly, 'but an image that keeps coming back to me is of those Highlanders in *Braveheart*. Remember? The blue tattoos and the battle cry of "Freedom"?'

'You're serious?'

Solly nodded. 'The symbol has to mean something to whoever gave the orders for it to be tattooed on to these girls. His property.'

'He brands them with a sign that is a sort of trademark, do you mean?'

'Exactly!' Solly beamed at the tall man at his side. 'Find the person who uses this symbol in a different context and you may well find your trafficker.'

'And the person who killed that girl,' Lorimer reminded the psychologist.

'Possibly one and the same, though I doubt it,' Solly said, his smile fading. 'Those sorts of people have others to do their bidding, do they not?'

'And yet he wouldn't be so stupid as to give away his secret sign, would he? I mean, we're hardly going to find it against a name on Wikipedia, are we?'

'No,' Solly agreed, 'but perhaps that is his weak spot. His vanity. Putting down his marker where he thinks no one will ever see it. But you did,' Solly spoke softly. 'And so did Rosie.'

Lorimer did not reply. Some of the skeins had begun to untangle themselves in his brain, but there was one particular thread that he was forbidden to share, even with the good man walking once more by his side.

Glasgow is a village, Lorimer reminded himself. It was something that people said all the time: people had so many links and there were so many overlapping circles that made nonsense of coincidences. The intelligence services were seeking out a man whose identity included being heavily tattooed, a man who was part of some militant group seeking to overthrow the British government. There had always been such people, disaffected types who wanted to expel others from their homeland. *Celtic lunatic fringe*, the intelligence officer had said during the meeting with Lorimer and Clark. But his tone had not been disparaging: they had to take these secret organisations with the utmost seriousness. *Might be mad as bats, but they can do one hell of a lot of damage,* Lorimer remembered the man telling them. Could Professor Brightman have suggested something that would help to trace this group? Was the man they sought also involved in a sex-trafficking business here in the city?

And why had the girl been murdered up in the wilderness of the Cathkin Braes? The cycle track for the Games was less than a mile from the marshy pond where her body had been discovered. Was there another sort of link? Did the man they sought have some legitimate presence within Glasgow 2014? Drummond had suggested this, but Lorimer was still disturbed by the thought.

The meeting was taking place in an upstairs flat in the Merchant City, less than five minutes' walk from the Commonwealth Games headquarters in Albion Street, a fact that had not escaped Cameron Gregson. *Isn't it a bit risky?* he wanted to demand, but the grim faces of the other five men made the words die on his lips.

'We have new intelligence that a senior police officer has been drafted in to find us,' their leader told them.

He was standing above them, his eyes glaring, hands spread on the table in front of him.

The other men exchanged glances, Number Five's eyes resting a fraction too long on his own for Cameron's liking.

'Detective Superintendent Lorimer,' the leader added. 'Anyone know him?'

Cameron looked at the faces of the other men but there was nothing. No recognition of any sort. So it came as a surprise when Number Five nodded.

'Aye,' he said. 'Works out of Stewart Street at the moment. Or so I'm informed.'

Cameron Gregson's eyes narrowed. Was this man a police officer himself, then, as he had suspected? Or did he have another inroad into organised crime?

'I'll keep an eye on him,' Number Five offered.

'Do it discreetly,' their leader said. 'We don't want to have to deselect you, do we?' He grinned. The others laughed and Cameron joined in, though he was uncertain just what the joke had meant. Deselect? What on earth was he talking about?

'Number Two, what new information have you to share with us?' the leader continued, turning his attention to the big ginger-haired man whose shirtsleeves were rolled up, showing the swirling patterns of tattoos.

'Meeting with the Aussie next week,' the man declared. 'I'll brief him on what he has to do. Not that he will be any the wiser, of course. He thinks it's a great honour to be part of the opening ceremony. Might even be his last thought!'

The laugh that went up was louder now, though for the first time since joining the group, Cameron Gregson experienced a sick feeling in his stomach at the idea of the immense explosion they were planning and the innocent lives that would be lost, including those of some elderly couple from Melbourne. While it had been about unnamed crowds of people he had felt nothing, but now, by personalising two of the victims, the young man felt a bit uneasy.

'Freedom!' Number Two raised his arm, fist clenched, and each man copied his action, the word resounding in this room with its locked door and windows closed to the street below.

CHAPTER THIRTY-SEVEN

H e was home.

Maggie breathed a sigh of relief as she heard the front
door open.

'Hi, gorgeous.'

And there he was, holding her around the waist, nuzzling her
cheek with a chin that had more than a day's stubble, making
Maggie pull back suddenly with a grimace.

'Sorry, need to shave, don't I?'

'It's okay.' She slid back into his arms, head against his shoulder, letting her body relax as he held her, breathing in the smell of
him: the faint hint of lemon drops he kept in the car and something else, a whiff that was acrid and sooty, as though the city still
clung to his clothes.

'Missed you,' he murmured, though whether he meant the
absence overnight or the long weeks when Vivien had intruded
into their home, Maggie wasn't certain.

'Missed you too,' she replied, knowing quite well what *she* was
trying to say. 'Hungry?'

Lorimer smiled and nodded. 'Starving. Quite a long day. Didn't
have time to eat much either,' he admitted.

'There's some lasagne in the fridge. Just needs heating up. And salad. That sound okay?'

'Wonderful. Shall I open a bottle of red?'

Maggie nodded. Was this homecoming different? Something to celebrate?

'Why not?' she answered lightly. Then, stepping closer to him, she saw the dark circles under his eyes, the sheer weariness of those slumped shoulders. 'You'll be asleep after one glass, though,' she warned.

While Maggie slid the dish of pasta into the microwave she could hear her husband as he busied himself with setting out place mats and cutlery.

'How was your day?' he asked.

'Oh, not so bad. A bit quieter still with the seniors off on exam leave. That all stops next week when we begin the new timetable, though. Hard to think it's almost June already.'

'Any good?' Lorimer reached into the wine rack to select a bottle of Italian red.

'Okay-ish. I've still got the Sixth Years, thank goodness, but there are some classes I'd rather not have been given, to tell you the truth. One Third Year lot that have been making their presence felt all through the school. And not in a good way,' she added gloomily.

'Here.' Lorimer uncorked the bottle of Chianti Classico and poured her a glass. 'This'll make you forget all about work for a while.'

As they sat together at the table, there were so many questions Maggie longed to ask. *How was Vivien?* seemed a little lame. And anything else would be making dull and unnecessary conversation, something simply to fill the silence.

At last her husband laid down his fork with a sigh and reached out to touch her fingertips.

'That was excellent. Thank you,' he said, looking at her intently. 'Don't deserve a wife like you,' he added quietly.

Maggie smiled. 'You're welcome,' she said, basking in the sudden warmth of his gaze.

Then he drew his fingers away, letting his eyes fall.

'She came on to me,' he said. 'Down there. At the *funeral*. Would you believe it?'

Maggie nodded. 'Yes,' she said simply. 'I would.'

There was a silence, then he looked at her again.

'What did you make of her, Mags? Really?'

Maggie Lorimer paused for a moment before replying. 'She didn't always seem consistent in her grief,' she said thoughtfully. 'Sometimes I wondered how much was real and how much was ...'

'... an act?' Lorimer finished her sentence for her.

'Yes. How did you know?'

'Did you really think I was completely taken in by her overtures?'

It was Maggie's turn to look away now and she took refuge in the Chianti, draining her wine glass then holding it out for a refill, wondering what to say without sounding like a jealous wife.

'She always was a bit of a drama queen,' Lorimer continued, pouring more wine into Maggie's glass. 'But that was to be expected, I suppose, when she wanted a stage career. Still,' he went on, 'she had every reason to be upset when her husband died like that.'

'I know,' Maggie sighed. 'I tried to be nice, I really did, but ...'

'She wasn't the easiest of house guests, was she?'

'Odd circumstances,' Maggie murmured. 'Having a stranger under your roof who just happens to be your husband's old girlfriend.'

'And whose husband has been murdered,' Lorimer added.

231

'Did Alistair find anything in London?'

Lorimer shook his head. 'No. And that troubles me more than a little. So far we've got nothing that resembles a motive for the man's murder. He was well thought of, happy in his profession, even expected a knighthood if the rumours are to be believed.'

'No skeletons in his closet, then?'

'None that we can find. And none that Vivien is admitting to either. They had the perfect marriage, so she said.'

'But not so perfect that she could try to tempt another woman's husband?'

'Exactly.' Lorimer tilted his head back as he finished his glass of wine. 'There may be more to Vivien Fox Gilmartin than meets the eye.'

'But she couldn't have killed her husband!' Maggie protested. 'She was at the reunion. With you. And all those other people.'

'I wonder,' Lorimer replied. 'Did she strike you as someone capable of taking another person's life?'

'No,' Maggie said firmly. 'Okay, I admit I didn't like her much. Don't get anyone who doesn't like cats,' she laughed. 'But she didn't seem like the murdering sort.'

'You'd be surprised,' Lorimer said darkly. 'Sometimes it's the quiet ones who harbour grudges, keep their emotions too well hidden, then lash out.'

'"Nursing her wrath to keep it warm",' Maggie said, quoting Robert Burns. 'Anyway, how could Vivien have killed her husband? It doesn't make sense.'

'Oh, nothing about it seems to make sense, Mags,' Lorimer sighed. 'But we have to explore every eventuality, even a crazy notion like Vivien hiring a hit man.'

'But he was poisoned!' Maggie protested. 'A hit man would have had a gun, surely?'

Lorimer shook his head, leaning back, twirling the empty wine glass by its stem. 'Don't mind me, I'm just playing with ideas. Possibilities.' He yawned suddenly. 'You're right, of course. Vivien couldn't have done something like that. Anyway, why would she? And why put up such a big reward?'

Maggie looked at her husband. He was slumped into his chair now, the fatigue that had shown earlier turning into exhaustion.

'Come on,' she said, rising to her feet and offering him her hand. 'Bed. To sleep,' she added sternly as Lorimer linked his fingers to hers, offering that familiar lazy smile.

'We've got another one coming in tonight,' the big man told her. 'See that you've got the spare room ready for her,' he added, flicking ash from his cigarette on to the saucer that lay on the table between them. He took the greasy paper that had held his pie supper and crumpled it in his hands, dropping it on the floor while he looked at Shereen through a haze of smoke, willing her to pick it up and bin it for him.

The woman rose to her feet, avoiding his eyes, which followed her every move, trying not to show the disgust she felt for this white man with the lank ginger hair and swirling tattoos that covered his brawny arms. There was something feral about him tonight, Shereen decided as she pushed the polystyrene container and the ball of paper into the pedal bin; she could almost smell the taint of animal desire from his body as she came back to sit on her chair.

'The girl busy tonight?' he asked, leaning forward with a leer that made Shereen want to shudder. But she remained still, willing her face not to give away the revulsion that the man across the table evoked in her.

'I think so.'

'You think so!' he exploded suddenly, thumping the tabletop so that the saucer jumped, scattering ash. 'You. Think. So,' he repeated slowly. 'You're paid to know what goes on in here and don't you forget it,' he snarled. 'Now, is she busy or is she not?'

'We're expecting some fellows quite soon,' Shereen said, eyes downcast lest he see her lie. 'Can't always be certain when they'll turn up.' She shrugged.

'Well, the car will be here around one o'clock. That's something you *can* be sure of,' he snapped. 'And I want this one kept away from the other girl. No speaking in their bloody Yoruba. Okay?'

He had risen to his feet now and picked up his leather jacket where he had flung it on to a chair. 'I'll be here to see when she arrives,' he added. 'And I don't want any more incidents. Understand?'

He leaned towards her so that Shereen could smell the vinegar that lingered on his lips.

'I understand,' she replied, daring to look him in the eyes.

He gave a grunt as he nodded, seemingly satisfied that the caretaker knew what to expect.

When the front door slammed, Shereen gave a great sigh, not realising that she had been holding her breath. Asa was safe from the brute for now, though the woman knew there was little she could do to protect the girl if the big man decided to have his way with her another night. If only . . .

The thought of going to the police, telling what she knew, was only briefly tempting. But Shereen had been told what would happen if she ever breathed a word of what went on in this place. Even if she managed to escape the consequences of such betrayal, the authorities would hold her partly responsible too. And prison was not a place that the fat woman wanted to be ever again.

*

'Kenneth McAlpin,' Lorimer said, savouring the words as he spoke them aloud. 'That's a name from the distant past.' He gave a faint grin as he looked from the paper in his hand to the man sitting beside his desk. Connor Drummond, the MI6 agent, had appeared without any appointment, slipping quietly into Lorimer's office as though he had simply come from an adjacent room. 'What do we know about this one?'

'Nothing bad about anyone of that name,' Drummond began. 'But we must assume it's not his real name. Any more than Robert Bruce Petrie is a name on the voters' roll.'

'Certainly smacks of the Celtic fringe,' Lorimer agreed. 'McAlpin was another Scottish king, wasn't he?'

'That's not what we think they have in common,' Drummond said. 'It's the surnames, McAlpin and Petrie. They're both linked to Clan MacGregor. The MacGregors are descendants of Kenneth McAlpin and the name Petrie is a sept of the MacGregor clan.'

'They were all outlawed, weren't they? Rob Roy and all of that lot?'

'Yes. And when that happened many of them changed their names or joined other clans, fearing they might be caught up in the persecution.'

'And who exactly is this McAlpin?' Lorimer wanted to know.

'There is a man of that name fitting the description we gave you,' Drummond said, crossing his ankles as he sat back in the chair. 'Big chap, tattooed, reddish hair. He is currently employed by the Clan MacGregor Society as their liaison officer. Also does battle re-enactments. But there's more, if you read on.' Drummond smiled and nodded at the paper in Lorimer's hand. 'He is on the payroll of Glasgow 2014. Quite legitimately, I might add, so you have nothing on him just yet.'

'What does he do?'

'Ah, that's the interesting bit,' Drummond said. 'McAlpin is one of the committee behind the opening ceremony. Big man. Former weightlifter. Won bronze at the European Championships in his time. Did a bit of chaperoning of the Scottish youth team. Well respected from all accounts. Seems to run a plumbing business now.'

'And just how did he come on to your radar?'

Drummond smiled at Lorimer and shook his head. There were some things that Police Scotland would never be told, the man's look seemed to say.

'So what do you want us to do about him?'

'Usual surveillance,' Drummond said. 'Nothing indiscreet. If he is one of the group, then he will be looking behind him every place he goes. So far we've put a tap on his phone but nothing's come of that. And his computer appears to be squeaky clean. They're not stupid, these people,' he added, uncrossing his legs and sitting up straighter. 'We must assume there is some sort of system whereby they communicate with one another: dedicated cell phones, no doubt, something that cannot be traced back to their normal server.'

'The Chief Constable . . .'

'. . . is quite aware of the need to deploy extra men on this job,' Drummond told him. 'Despite the huge amount of manpower already needed to cover the Games.' He smiled at Lorimer. 'We've been recruiting more personnel ourselves recently.' He gave the detective a quizzical look. 'Ever thought you might fancy a change of scene?'

Lorimer looked at the man from MI6. Was he serious?

'Think I'm a bit long in the tooth to make those sorts of changes,' he began.

'Hardly,' Drummond laughed. 'You're only forty-two. We sometimes bring in people much older than that. Think about it.'

He rose from his seat, gave the detective a quick but firm hand-shake and was out of the room with the door closed quietly behind him, leaving Lorimer with the sheet of paper in his hand and not a few thoughts in his mind.

The tall man stood up, biting his lip. One thing he had not shared with Drummond was the germ of an idea that this McAlpin might well be involved in a different enterprise altogether.

Freedom, Solly had said. And that was a battle cry that several disaffected Scots wanted to shout out loud. Could this be the same person who had paid for the girls to be tattooed with that black spiral? Perhaps. But until he could prove it, he was merely to keep an eye on a man who might be part of a terrorist cell, wondering all the while if he was the brains behind the human trafficking that was plaguing his city. And what if they found that McAlpin was indeed running African girls as prostitutes? There would be absolutely nothing they could do. The lives of hundreds of people, including members of the royal family, depended on finding this cell and smashing it before the opening ceremony, just seven weeks from now. Finding the African girl's killer and hunting out the people behind the child trafficking would have to take second place from now on. And that thought irked him more than somewhat.

CHAPTER THIRTY-EIGHT

June 2014

'The Centre for Social Justice is concerned about the possible increase in human trafficking during the Games,' the journalist said.

Gayle blinked as though she had been struck. The nerve of the woman! Coming in to Games HQ for a discussion, she'd said blithely over the phone. Pretending to want to talk about the influx of visitors to the city. Never once mentioning that amongst them might be men who wanted to pay for sex with underage girls!

'I really don't think—' Gayle began.

'Oh, but you *should* think,' the journalist retorted. 'Every eventuality must be covered, even ones you don't want to be bothered about,' she went on.

Gayle gritted her teeth. The woman sitting opposite had the sort of glossy dark looks that made Gayle feel washed out by comparison. Michaela Sadi was utterly beautiful: half Asian, possibly, with perfect coffee-coloured skin and kohl-ringed eyes that seemed to look right through her. *And* she was wearing that bright yellow dress Gayle had seen in the Italian Centre, the one

238

Cameron had laughed at when he'd seen the price tag. Gayle seethed inside, wishing she had made more of an effort before leaving for work.

'Our readers have the right to know what goes on in their city,' the journalist from the *Gazette* continued.

'Well, yes, of course, but . . . '

'Does the Games committee condone the increase of trafficking in Glasgow, then?'

Gayle narrowed her eyes. 'Where do you get your statistics from?' she asked. 'How does the *Gazette* know about an increase?'

The journalist smiled, showing perfect white teeth. 'Let's just say our sources are reliable,' she replied.

'Well I can give you our assurance that the 2014 Games committee is behind every action taken by the Centre for Social Justice,' Gayle said firmly, hoping that she sounded far more positive than she felt.

'And the police? Are they behind the CSJ reports?'

Gayle forced herself to smile sweetly. 'I couldn't possibly comment on Police Scotland's position,' she said. 'You will have to ask their press officer.'

'I'll do that.' The woman nodded. 'Thanks.'

Gayle took the journalist's security badge and handed it to the receptionist at the desk with a sigh. Sometimes this job had its difficult moments and this had been one of them. She had heard of the Centre for Social Justice, but only vaguely, never really connecting it with what was happening in Glasgow. And now this journalist had breezed in with the accusation that child trafficking was on the rise because of the Games! Foreign nationals would want the same level of services they found in other parts of the world, she'd said. 'Sex is sold everywhere there is a market for it.'

The statement had fallen from the woman's lips as if it were no big deal, despite her probing questions and the evident desire to write a big story about it. It shocked Gayle. To think that here, in her city ... It didn't bear thinking about. But the woman had made her think, and now Gayle wished that she could unburden herself of the facts that had been laid out coldly before her.

'You wouldn't believe what happened to me today,' Gayle had told him, rolling away from his arms after half an hour of very satisfactory sex.

She was asleep now, the baby-blonde hair fallen across her face, as Cameron lay on his back, thinking hard. Was this the sort of information that the group wanted? Was it something that could be used to discredit the police, perhaps? Bit by bit, anything that the girl told him was passed on to the five other men. Just in case. The leader had smiled encouragingly when Number Six had boasted about the possibility of being given tickets for the opening ceremony. It had been worth all the weeks of putting up with Gayle's gushing enthusiasm about the Games. Mind you, Cameron told himself, everyone seemed to have fallen under its spell. There were banners all over the Merchant City, and Clyde, that flaming mascot, its stupid thistle face grinning everywhere you looked. 'A sop for the plebs,' their leader had growled when the subject of the Games mascot had been mentioned. But Gayle loved it and even had a soft toy version sitting on the chair by her bed.

Quietly he slipped out of bed and pulled on his trousers. He'd risk a quick call on the group mobile while she was asleep. Moments later Cameron Gregson was pressing the button that would link him to the charismatic man who had recruited him into this adventure, hoping that the information he was about to give might be useful to the cause.

IT HAPPENS HERE

Michaela Sadi, Senior Reporter

Not somewhere else, but here. Yes, that is the message we want to give our readers as Glasgow gears itself up for the Twentieth Commonwealth Games next month. And for once we are not talking about the sports, but activities of a very different nature. Did you know that hosting the Commonwealth Games makes Glasgow a target for organised crime? No? Well, we have recently received a report from the Centre for Social Justice suggesting that the numbers of young women being trafficked for sex in our city is very much on the increase. And all because there is a lucrative market caused by the influx of visitors to the 2014 Commonwealth Games. I spoke recently to the marketing people at Games HQ and came away with the impression that they are blithely ignoring such facts. Sure, they claim to be behind the CSJ's initiatives, but are they really kept awake at night wondering what side effects the Games are having on the city?

And what about the people who are paid to fight organised crime? I spoke to representatives of Police Scotland, including Detective Superintendent William Lorimer, who said that 'the police services are doing everything in their power to ensure a smooth and safe running of the Games and to investigate any allegations of human trafficking'.

While that may be true, the CSJ has painted a dismal picture of police involvement in human trafficking up till now. The problem seems to be barely understood by forces throughout the UK and is often a low priority for the police as a whole. One serving police officer was quoted as saying that 'there is more incentive to investigate a shed burglar ... than there is a human trafficker'.

Given the rise of travellers from all parts of the Commonwealth it must be borne in mind that most young women and girls are trafficked from Europe, Nigeria and Vietnam, victims who are part of a lucrative crime wave to supply sex. And it is happening here, right on our own doorstep.

Lorimer threw down the paper in disgust. What rankled most was that it was probably true. And now that his hands were effectively being tied by an authority that exceeded their own, he and his fellow officers were being branded as people who did not care enough to take action against such organised crimes.

Drummond had been content for survelliance to begin on Kenneth McAlpin and there were now officers following the man from his home in the north of the city wherever he went. Oddly enough, his name had checked out as being real after all. Kenneth Gordon McAlpin had been born forty-eight years ago to another Kenneth McAlpin, suggesting that the name was used to being passed down the generations. His record was clean, too, though there had been some suggestion of trouble during a visit to Russia in his younger days: a fight in a bar that had been reported to the authorities but had gone no further. Sporting heroes were often guarded from the consequences of their misdemeanours, Lorimer thought. And McAlpin was perhaps lucky to have remained free from any taint of criminal activity. Till now.

The report on the man made interesting reading. He had been eager to leave school as soon as he could, joining the army for a spell where he had found moderate fame as a weightlifter. His army career was also unblemished, though he had eventually bought himself out. Lorimer's eyebrows rose. McAlpin senior's occupation was listed as bricklayer, and the mother had been a hospital cleaner; where, he wondered suddenly, had the money come from to gain their son an early discharge from the forces? *And* set himself up with his own plumbing business? Had his involvement with malcontents begun as early as that? He had worked with youth weightlifting teams, taking them to overseas events, not quite on the coaching staff but somewhere on the periphery. Then there had been the battle re-enactment stuff. Lorimer grinned. McAlpin actually had an Equity card and had been one of the extras for the film *Highlander.*

For a moment he thought about telling Maggie, then his smile fell. Nothing about this case could be uttered outside. Security was paramount. And as he thought about such a clandestine way of life, Lorimer knew that Drummond's offer was not one that he would want to take up. Sharing some of his working life with his wife was something that made it bearable at times; often cases would be too horrific to divulge to Maggie, but there were occasions when snippets could be passed on safely. She would listen, easing the darkness as they lay in bed, letting him talk about people he had met, places he had seen, the quirky, unexpected things that sometimes happened in the life of a policeman.

It was usually dark by the time she made the journey across the city, but tonight the twilight was a burnished sapphire, the air warm with the promise of another hot day to come. Shereen tugged at her raincoat then slipped it off; she'd only put it on out of habit, covering up the voluminous cotton dress. Her bare feet thrust into worn leather sandals made a soft flopping noise as she walked along, the rhythm of her pace soothing the woman, making her forget for a while why she was out and where she was heading. The envelope stuffed with money was in a bum bag. It bounced over Shereen's fat belly with each step she took towards the tenement flat in Dennistoun.

A fluttering movement made her look up and Shereen smiled to see yet another bright banner proclaiming the Glasgow 2014 Commonwealth Games. Hers might not be a long heritage here, but Shereen felt like a Glaswegian whenever she looked around at the flags and posters everywhere. It was odd, this sense of pride in a person whose parents had sailed from Jamaica last century, settling here in the UK, hopes of a better life foundering far too quickly. Shereen had never been back home, yet she'd yelled at the TV as loudly as any native-born Jamaican when Usain Bolt had won his medals in London.

A crack in the pavement made her stumble and for a moment Shereen gasped, expecting her large body to tilt forward and crash on to the stone slabs. But she righted herself in time, one arm flung out for balance. Heart beating wildly, she leaned against a wall and checked her watch. There was plenty of time before she needed to be there. She would catch her breath for a moment. The woman fingered the leather bag at her waist. She had been making this journey for many months now, paying off the loan shark with regular amounts. But business had been good lately, Asa's young body becoming more and more popular with the men who came to visit. And though it hurt her to see the girl's cowed demeanour every morning and the way she now avoided her glance, Shereen's purse had grown bigger from these visitors. The other flats would remain empty, however, the stream of girls that the big man had been promising cut off abruptly by that Englishman's death.

The light from the street lamps obscured any stars that might be overhead as the woman turned into the mouth of a close. She barely gave a glance at the buzzer as she pressed it, the familiar blank space against the topmost number giving nothing away. Anybody coming to make payments knew the person they were going to see; there was no need for a name.

Her breathing was laboured as she climbed the three flights of stairs, her leg muscles protesting under the weight of her huge body, left hand grasping the banister as she hauled herself upwards. She took a few moments to let the pain in her chest subside before knocking on the door.

There was a rattle as a chain was removed, then the door swung open to reveal a slightly built lad who stood aside to let her in. Angular jaws masticated the wad of gum in his mouth as he flicked his head to indicate that the woman should proceed along the dusty hallway.

Shereen did not give him a second glance, knowing that the youth would curl his lip at her, a disdainful sneer for yet another victim of his grandfather's moneylending.

When Shereen entered the room, the man was slumped in front of an enormous plasma television, cigarette in one hand, a cut-glass tumbler of whisky in the other, his eyes fixed on the screen, where figures in white and dark blue were chasing a yellow football around a grassy pitch.

She waited patiently, standing to one side so that he knew she was there, but not so close as to make a nuisance of herself. At last the thin sound of a whistle blew, a cheer arose from the unseen crowd, and the man stirred from his position on the leather couch.

'It's you,' he grunted, half turning to look at Shereen. 'Same as usual, I suppose,' he sighed, feeling down the side of the settee for the hardbacked notebook that he had jammed between the seat cushion and the arm.

'Actually, no,' Shereen began nervously.

'What?' The man started in surprise, half rising from the couch.

'Oh, I've got it all right,' Shereen assured him, unzipping the bag at her waist. 'I just wanted to pay it all off, though. Is that all right?' she asked anxiously, biting her lower lip.

'Hm, pay off the lot, eh? Well, it'll cost you,' the man told her, his eyes drawn to the book that was now balanced on his knees.

'How much?' she asked. And he told her, the glint from a gold tooth shining as he grinned.

Shereen nodded. It was more than she had calculated but she had it all here. Slowly she counted out the notes into his open palm, a sense of excitement growing in her breast.

'Right. That's it, then.' The man seemed slightly disappointed as he drew a line under the rows of figures. 'You can come back any time you need to, though. You know that, eh?' He leered at her. 'Good customer like you!' He laughed, then, to Shereen's surprise, thrust out a gnarled hand to shake her own.

'Thank you,' the woman said quietly. She rezipped the empty bag, and even before she had turned to leave, the man who had held her in such thrall was once more slumped in front of the television, grasping the remote control and turning up the sound.

She had intended taking a taxi back to the flat, but now, with no money left in her purse, Shereen resigned herself to the long walk home. Heaving the raincoat back on, she strode away from the grey stone tenement, a new feeling of lightness in her step. She was free! It was difficult to believe after all this time and all these visits to the man at the top of the stairs, but the Jamaican woman nodded to herself as she walked, lips moving as she repeated the word over and over.

As she turned a corner, Shereen caught sight of a white car parked at the kerb, its familiar livery letting her know what it was. Police Scotland. Two uniformed officers sat in the front, and as she passed the car she could see that they were holding papers full of fish suppers. Her step faltered as the thought came into her mind.

She was free now. Free as a bird. She could rap on the window, make them look her way. Then what? Tell them about Asa? The woman blinked for a moment, remembering that feature in today's *Gazette*. Didn't it say that the police weren't really interested? She looked more closely, hearing the laughter between the two cops, seeing one of them carelessly pop a chip into his open mouth. What would they see if she stopped? A big fat Jamaican woman wobbling as she leaned down beside their car?

Shereen carried on, a small sigh escaping from her mouth. And as she walked away, tears spilled down her cheeks, though she could not have said who it was that she was crying for.

CHAPTER THIRTY-NINE

He wouldn't be shedding any tears over the aftermath of his explosion. Doing the job well and having the desired outcome was all that mattered to Rob Worsley. Years of working with ex-military types hardened by their experiences had inured the explosives expert to any sort of empathy for the victims of his work. Mostly he had done jobs overseas, trained a few groups on the hillsides of Pakistan, set off bombs that had wiped out entire villages. But this would be a little different, he thought, looking at the blueprint of his plan. His name would never go down in the annals of history, but so what? In just a few short weeks he would have the satisfaction of knowing that he had undermined all that amazing and expensive security operation surrounding the Commonwealth Games to blow up the famous Parkhead Stadium.

Worsley grinned as he contemplated the outrage that would follow the explosion. How many of Glasgow's citizens would mourn the royals rather than their beloved Celtic football ground? He glanced at the mantelpiece. Placed neatly behind a silver carriage clock was the envelope containing his travel documents. His destination after one big job had been Spain, a nice warm bolthole to escape the British weather, but this time he was going much further afield. The mad fool who called himself their leader had no inkling that Worsley and McAlpin had planned their escape route together. Dubai first, then Jo'burg and on to Nigeria, where the ginger-haired man had all those contacts. After that? Well, Worsley had several ideas of where he would like to spend his retirement, all of them far, far away from this godforsaken country.

He smoothed out the drawings, eyes darting across the meticulously detailed pages. It was a work of art, he thought proudly. And he deserved to be paid well for his part in the scheme. Not all of them were in this because of their ideals. Freedom from oppression indeed! He chuckled. That student, Number Six, he was typical of the sort of nutters their leader attracted, carried away on a wave of nationalistic fervour. Worsley shook his head and sighed. He certainly wouldn't be hanging around to put his own mark upon the independence referendum. By the time the voters flocked to the polling stations he would be well away, hopefully on some sun-drenched beach.

Waiting was what they did best. Waiting in cars, watching windows and doors, looking at each and every person passing by. The man and woman seated in the front seats of the Vauxhall Corsa might have been weekend shoppers waiting for a friend to join them. There was nothing particular about their appearance that a passer-by would remember: Mr and Mrs Average, dressed in jeans and khaki raincoats, they stared out at the street with expressionless faces as though boredom had set in long since. In reality Kate MacDonald was an undercover officer of many years' experience, her ability to merge into a crowd one of her greatest assets. Joe Hammond, the bald-headed man sitting in the driver's seat, had been seconded from the Met. He had said little to the woman beside him after the briefing from Detective Superintendent Lorimer back at HQ. Joe knew how to take orders and follow them to the letter. The importance of the job had been impressed upon them, and both surveillance officers had been given some access to the intelligence that Drummond had supplied.

Last night other watchers had sat patiently outside McAlpin's home in Bishopbriggs, a featureless semi-detached villa like hundreds of others in the housing scheme, except that it sheltered a man who might possibly be a terrorist intent on targeting the 2014 Commonwealth Games. This morning MacDonald and Hammond had trailed their quarry across to the east side of the city to the tenement flat where McAlpin had parked his white transit van and disappeared inside a close, two bulky carrier bags in each hand. They had noted the moment when he had set the bags down, fished keys out of his jacket pocket and unlocked the heavy main door. It was a little bit of progress. What he was doing there and why he had brought the van was a matter of interest to these officers, their hidden camera recording each and every one of McAlpin's movements.

Asa looked out of the bedroom window. Her tattoo still felt sore from the activity of the previous night and even sitting in the hot water this morning hadn't made any difference. Shereen had insisted on it, leading her into the steamy bathroom, helping her over the edge of the bath. The caretaker had poured salts of some kind into the water, swirling it around with her fat fingers while Asa sat there naked, legs drawn up to hide her shame.

Now all the Nigerian girl wanted was to wrap her arms around her body, but the plaster cast inhibited this. Still, the fleecy dressing gown Shereen had given her helped to retain the lingering warmth from the bath as she stood staring down at the street below. Asa saw that the white man's van was there again. Surely he would not come into her room? Not so early? Her dark eyes took in the drab street; everything was so grey. Even that car across the street with a couple sitting in it was a dull metallic grey, the colour of guns. Asa had seen guns once, when the police had come to their village, big bulky things strapped to the officers' belts. They had made the policemen seem bigger and fiercer, strutting around the beaten earth with polished boots as they looked down at the cowed faces of the villagers.

Last night Asa had heard a girl crying. It was the familiar keening noise she had often heard back home, one that evoked death and grief. The sound had come from the room across the corridor, next to the bathroom, but there had been no noise this morning though Asa had listened intently once the water from the taps had finished flowing. Shereen had talked incessantly, words that meant nothing to the Nigerian girl, as she had strained her ears to hear.

She remembered how the big woman had wrapped the bath sheet around her, folding her into a hug, careful not to press the damaged arm. Asa had looked at her once, seeing tears in Shereen's eyes and something else: a look of regret, as if the woman was sorry for what had happened.

'He's on the move.' Joe Hammond put the car into gear and watched as the big man swung his body into the cab of the white van. In seconds they were driving along the quiet street, then out into the traffic of the main thoroughfare heading back into the city centre.

'What's the betting he just goes back home?' Kate said wearily.

Joe grinned. It was the same up here, then: surveillance teams everywhere probably put bets on their quarry's next move, anything to alleviate the tedium of hours spent waiting. 'A tenner says he's off to Albion Street,' he replied.

251

Kate looked at him through narrowed eyes. 'D'you know something, or is that a random guess?' she asked.

Joe laughed. 'Just a hunch,' he said.

'Okay, you're on,' she replied, watching the rear lights of the big van as it braked at a junction.

McAlpin heard the ringtone as he stopped at the traffic lights. He listened, waiting for the sixth note to die away before indicating left. There was never a good time to have one of these meetings; sometimes the leader notified them all a day or two in advance, but often as not the mobile would ring out, a signal for the six men to convene at the prearranged destination. The phone beeped, and McAlpin lifted it up to read the text message. It gave an address on the south side of the city, a good half an hour from where he was right now. Soon the plumber's van was heading across the Kingston Bridge, a small grey Corsa in its wake, each of the two surveillance officers curious to know just where they were heading, the ten-pound bet quite forgotten.

'Asa?' Shereen had slipped into the girl's room, locking the door behind her.

The Nigerian girl glanced up with dulled eyes then yawned and looked away again.

'How's the arm?' Shereen asked, tapping her own arm to signify what she was saying.

The girl looked away again, avoiding Shereen's stare.

'How would you like to come into the kitchen? *He* came by to drop off the groceries. Fancy having some tea?'

The girl turned to look at her, alerted by the familiar word.

'Tea? Come on.' Shereen beckoned towards the door and unlocked it. 'It's just the three of us today. You, me and our new girl. No bloody men to annoy us yet.' She grinned.

Asa stood up, her eyes on the hallway beyond the door. 'Toilet,' she said, practising a word she had come to use often.

'Okay,' Shereen agreed. 'Toilet first. Then you come through to the kitchen. His Nibs brought some cake with the groceries. God knows why. But let's enjoy it while we can, eh?'

Asa wrinkled her brow. 'Cake,' she said, savouring the word, then nodding.

'Aye, cake. Yum, yum,' Shereen said, rubbing her huge belly and laughing.

As she waited outside the bathroom for Asa to emerge, it was hard not to imagine the other girl in the room next door.

Shereen gnawed at her lip, wondering if she dared risk it. Then, 'Oh sod it,' she muttered. 'Why shouldn't the poor wee cow have a bit of cake and tea as well?' Taking a bunch of keys from her cardigan pocket, she opened the door next to the bathroom.

Shereen's scream of terror brought Asa running out of the toilet to the big woman's side.

She skidded to a halt, rigid with horror at the sight in the bedroom.

There, suspended from the light fitting on the ceiling, was the body of a thin dark girl, her neck twisted sideways, arms hanging lifelessly by her sides.

CHAPTER FORTY

The man with the golden tooth chuckled as he replaced the handset. They were all the same. Thought they could do without him, then something happened and they were running to his door once again. The big dark-skinned woman had sounded tearful, but then most of them tried that trick, employing emotion as though it could budge the moneylender from his usual rates of interest. 'Let one have a lower rate and they'll all want it,' he'd told that skinny wretch of a grandson who lived with him.

She would be round soon, she had said in breathless tones, as though she had been running. The man laughed out loud, the image of her overweight body swaying from side to side amusing him greatly.

Asa had never seen such fear in another person's eyes before.

She followed the woman around the flat, still dazed from the sight that was now behind a locked door, watching as Shereen took various items from the food cupboard and shoved them into a large carrier bag. She had already packed some of Asa's clothes and toiletries, talking and weeping as she pulled things out of drawers and cupboards, the Nigerian girl watching silently from

254

the doorway, one ear listening in case footsteps heralded the arrival of either of the men.

They were leaving. There was no doubt about that in Asa's mind. She might be unable to understand the torrent of words coming from the older woman's mouth, but she could hear the high-pitched anxiety in her tone and read the frantic way she bustled about, throwing things into bags, hardly sparing the girl a glance.

'Come. Now,' Shereen said at last. These at least were words with which Asa was familiar, and the girl followed her meekly along the corridor and out of the main door.

Her heart beat wildly as she headed downstairs after the Jamaican woman, eyes large with terror lest they be waylaid before they had effected their escape.

For escape it was, Asa was in no doubt about that. She had seen the way Shereen had slammed the door of that room shut, recoiling from it as though the corpse might climb down from its wire and catch hold of her. Okonjo at least was absent from the flat, though where he had gone was a mystery to Asa; he seemed to be around so much of the time.

A shiny black car was waiting at the kerb and Shereen bundled the girl in, pushing their bags on to the floor then rapping out instructions to the driver.

Asa looked back as the taxi drew away from the grey pavement, the tenement buildings growing smaller as the vehicle gathered speed. Then they were absorbed into a fast-moving line of traffic, the driver skilfully weaving his way in between other vehicles.

She glanced at her companion. Shereen was holding on to a handle by the window, knuckles pale against the brown skin, her back rigid as she perched on the edge of the leather seat.

Where were they going? Asa wanted to open her mouth to ask,

but there were no words for that question and she felt a well of frustration that their different languages created such a barrier between them. She was like a bird that did not sing, its silence making it vanish into the undergrowth, a lost thing prey to the dangerous creatures that sought to harm it.

He had never been slow to make decisions, but there were times when things needed a bit of thought before he handed out the tasks. And this was one of them. The surveillance report had come back about the flat in the East End and one part of him wanted to send a squad car over there. Now. Right now. He bit his lower lip as he mulled over the various consequences of this. McAlpin might be using that flat as a base where the terrorist cell hung out, but it was the first time they had seen him there, he reasoned. On the other hand, the bags of groceries might be for men who were holed up there.

'One wrong move and the entire operation will collapse,' Drummond had warned him. So should he send a car over there or leave well alone? Intelligence told him that McAlpin had been seen entering a detached house on the south side, an address not far from the detective's own home, something that had made Lorimer's eyebrows rise. Criminal activity was never somewhere else, he reminded himself; scratch the surface of any veneer of respectability and you'd find the same human weaknesses beneath.

He heaved a sigh. It was down to the surveillance team to watch and listen. He would let them keep an eye on the East End flat, but that was all he could do. His remit within Police Scotland included fighting organised crime but the man from MI6 had a greater say in this matter: the life of Her Majesty took precedence over any ongoing investigation that a mere

Glasgow cop was carrying out. It was almost midsummer now and there were signs everywhere counting down to the day of the opening ceremony. The detective super thought back to the previous year, when he and Maggie had been making tentative plans to join the melee of people heading towards Parkhead. And then the bomb near Drymen had exploded, destroying any ideas he might have had about being a mere spectator at the Commonwealth Games.

'He's on the move again,' Kate said, fastening her seat belt as Joe started up the Corsa once more.

The big ginger-haired man had emerged from the red-painted doorway of a 1950s bungalow overlooking Rouken Glen Park, one hand on the mobile phone pressed to his ear, the other holding the keys to his van. The video camera zoomed in on his face, capturing the expression of anxiety, the furrowed brow where beads of sweat made his pallid skin shine.

Something was up and neither officer needed to say a word to confirm this: the man's body language told it all.

McAlpin broke off the call with a curse then gazed round him as though searching for inspiration. The two officers exchanged a glance. If McAlpin made a move, someone needed to cover his steps, and it would be down to them.

'Grey Corsa,' the man remarked as he twitched the net curtains, watching the car move away from the kerb and follow McAlpin's big white van. Behind him nobody spoke.

He had anticipated something like this happening. But as the leader of the cell let his hand fall, he made sure his face showed no signs of the inner turmoil he was experiencing.

'Gentlemen,' he said, turning to address the four men around the old-fashioned walnut dining table. 'It seems we have to consider that one of our number has fallen.'

'He's in a tearing hurry,' Kate remarked as the van sped around the roundabout and headed back into the city.

'Nice to know what he's been called away for,' Joe replied.

'Or from?' Kate shrugged.

'Ach, it could be a genuine call-out. Blocked drain or something.'

Kate nodded. The old bungalow was in the name of a Mrs Soutar, a widow in her eighties. That much they had gleaned since McAlpin had entered the house, their colleagues back at base ready with as much information as they needed. Kate watched as the transit van gathered speed. Probably a blocked drain or something right enough, she told herself. Someone would check McAlpin's landline in any case, to see if anyone had telephoned for an emergency plumber.

Rob Worsley left the small white house and turned left. His own car was parked two streets away, hidden discreetly from any prying CCTV cameras. The explosives expert bit his lip. Having McAlpin deselected was a blow right enough, but as far as the cell was concerned the man had already done his bit. He would continue with the work, but from now on there was no way the big man could attend meetings.

Worsley cursed under his breath as he walked along the tree-lined avenue. McAlpin was just too bloody obvious: all those tattoos, and that thatch of red hair! How did he think he could have avoided detection? His thoughts turned to their leader, a mild-mannered fellow who would easily be lost in a crowd; just the sort that was needed for a game like this. Like Worsley himself, a harmless-looking white-haired pensioner. But this

258

particular pensioner had made arrangements with Kenneth Gordon McAlpin, arrangements that he had no intention of changing once the job was done.

Okonjo was standing in the hallway when the big man burst through the door.

'What the . . . ?' His oath was cut short as McAlpin followed the Nigerian's gaze.

'Bloody hell.' His voice dropped as he took a step into the room where the body dangled from the ceiling. 'Did you . . . '

'Knew nothing about it, boss,' Okonjo said, his hands spread in a gesture of innocence.

'Where's Shereen?' McAlpin spun round, seeing for the first time the open door across the corridor. 'Where's the girl?' He grabbed Okonjo by the shoulders, lifting the smaller man right off his feet.

'Don't know, boss!' the Nigerian squeaked, flapping his hands in terror. 'I had to go to the dentist. When I got back . . . ' He gave a cry as McAlpin thrust him heavily to the floor.

'They've gone?' McAlpin's mouth opened in astonishment as he realised the enormity of the situation. 'Where? Come on, Okonjo, think! Where could they go? Shereen doesn't have anyone in Glasgow, does she?'

'No, boss.' The man picked himself up and backed away. 'No. She only goes out to pay off her debts. Doesn't know anyone in the city,' he gabbled, shaking his head as he watched the big man's face darken with fury.

'Need to get rid of this,' McAlpin muttered, jerking his head towards the bedroom door. 'Cut it down and wrap it up in something.' He paced up and down the hallway, fists clenched as though ready for a fight. Then he stopped, a gleam in his eyes.

'There's a tarp in the van. Get it and bring it up here. Pronto!' he yelled, thrusting the keys into the black man's hands.

Alone in the flat, the red-haired man stood regarding the thin body of the dark-skinned girl with disgust. Sunlight from the bedroom window streamed in, reflecting on the dead girl's staring eyeballs, the flies on her body a shining mass of blue like spilled petrol.

It was approaching midsummer, a hellish time to have to dump a body. They would need to wait until well after darkness fell, and that was still hours away. Meantime there was the problem of a big Jamaican woman running around the city with the Nigerian girl in tow. McAlpin gritted his teeth. Though the Games were still a few weeks away, he had begun to make a tidy sum from these girls who had been lured to Glasgow.

And he was not going to let even one of them get away if he could help it.

'Could be doing another plumbing job,' Kate remarked as the black man took a folded tarpaulin from the back of the van. They watched as the back doors to the van were closed and locked and the plumber's mate (if that was what he was) hefted the bundle across his shoulders.

Joe did not reply, merely pursing his lips in consideration. 'Let's see which flat he's going into, eh?'

Kate grinned and slipped out of the passenger seat. What would she be today? Someone from the factor's office, perhaps? Or should she just be checking the voters' roll?

The policewoman caught up with the man just as the door was swinging shut.

'Thanks,' she grinned, one foot slipping between the step and the wooden door. 'Saved me ringing the buzzer,' she said, looking at the startled expression on the man's face. She pretended to stop and look into her shoulder bag, rummaging around in its contents as the black man climbed the stairs, struggling under the weight of the tarpaulin, one eye on his progress, listening for the footsteps coming to a halt.

She waited until he was out of sight before following him silently upstairs. Hidden on the landing below the top floor, Kate made a note of the man's destination. Top left. She smiled as she crept back down to the bottom of the stone staircase: she hadn't even needed to rap on every door to discover where he'd gone. At least now they could find out the owner of this property. And if it was let out to a tenant. All minor details in her line of work, but ones that had to be accounted for.

Cameron Gregson waited at the corner of the street; *mustn't be seen leaving together*, the leader had explained, so he was just out of sight from anyone watching the bungalow. Number Two had been deselected, a phrase that the young man now understood. The big man with the tattoos would not be coming to any further meetings. Someone had compromised him and it was no longer safe for him to be seen with any member of the cell. From now on, most of their communication would be by the dedicated mobile phone network, meetings kept to an absolute minimum.

It was a pity, the leader told them, because the plumber's van had given them some camouflage. Still, that could not be helped and everyone had to be extra vigilant as the date of the opening ceremony drew nearer. One by one he had dismissed them, until only Cameron remained behind.

'Stand around the corner,' the leader had told him. 'Wait five minutes and I'll pick you up. There's something I want you to do.'

Cameron had nodded, trying to glean something from the

man's expression, but he had already turned away as though dismissing him.

Now Number Six stood there, waiting and wondering just what task the leader had in mind.

CHAPTER FORTY-ONE

Strike up a conversation with any Glasgow taxi driver and he will begin to tell you his stories: stories about people who have travelled with him (dropping as many famous names as he can manage), stories about things that have happened to him, quirky or dangerous, but omitting the regular drudgery of cleaning vomit off his upholstery.

There was not much to say about the girl sitting in the back of his taxi today. She was young, had one arm in a sling and the usual expression of any teenager who'd fallen out with her mother. At least he supposed the big woman who had instructed him to wait was the mother. A quick glance via the rear-view mirror had produced nothing from the black girl, not a flicker of interest, no response to the winning smile he had darted towards her. She just sat there staring at the floor, a look on her face that he'd seen hundreds of times from his own girls. And yet ... it was a lovely face, the taxi driver told himself, taking more time to study the smooth dark skin, the perfect oval shape, those high cheekbones that gave her the air of an exotic princess.

She must have sensed his stare, for she looked up and he saw her eyes, huge dark pools observing him gravely. A man could lose himself in eyes like that, he told himself, the thought making him suddenly uncomfortable.

She was just a kid, his wiser self reminded him.

But as she looked away, he wondered if there was a story here after all. What was it the big mama had hissed at him as she'd slammed the taxi door shut?

Make sure she doesn't get out!

Lorimer listened to the officer's report as the evening sun shone through the slatted blinds. The second shift was still outside the flat, McAlpin's van right at the mouth of the close, and with each successive hour the likelihood that the ginger-haired man was upstairs on a plumbing job diminished. The name of the owner had been checked out: the flat was registered to an Asian landlord who had numerous properties all over the city, the current tenant being a Mrs Swanson, who paid her rent on time and was no trouble, according to the factor. So what was the big man with the tattoos doing in her flat with another man who looked vaguely Nigerian, as Hammond had put it?

Wait and see, the voice of reason whispered in his ear after he had finished the call. *Something will emerge in time.*

Lorimer stretched his arm out and pulled on the blind cord, letting the stream of brightness into the room, particles of dust dancing in the air. He was not good at sitting in the director's chair, waiting and wondering, planning the next move of a team who were only half aware of all that was transpiring in their city.

The tall man might have been telling that little voice to sod off as he gathered up his jacket and strode purposefully out of the room, leaving only a sense of the aerial motes being disturbed by his passing.

*

Asa stretched out on the bed, feeling the tingle in her bare toes. It was safe up here, high above the city, its traffic only a dim sound, like the rumble of thunder across the veldt. Shereen had brought a brown paper bag with some food: a hamburger in a roll with bits of slippery lettuce and a carton of thin chips that were already cold. But the girl had wolfed them down, realising that the pain gnawing in her belly was actually hunger.

'Food,' Shereen had said, waving the bags in the air as she entered the hotel room. Asa had grinned then, knowing that word. Food was after all a basic for all humankind, like water, the latter appearing in the form of a six-pack of Highland Spring, the label sporting the same logo that Asa had seen displayed as they had journeyed across the city.

She had pointed to the bottle and nudged the woman who sat beside her devouring her own burger.

'Thistle,' Shereen had told her. 'Thi-ssil. Okay?'

'Thiss-ill,' Asa repeated, looking at the green and purple emblem flowering on the top of the label.

Shereen squashed the empty carton and pushed it back into the paper carrier bag. Then she looked at Asa.

'Listen,' she told the girl. 'You're safe now, understand?'

'Safe?' Asa's puzzled face made the older woman give an exasperated sigh. Opening her arms and coming closer, she enveloped the girl gently in her arms, rocking her back and forth.

'Safe,' she murmured. 'Safe.'

For the first time in many weeks, Asa allowed her body to relax against the woman's warm bulk. The word had a gentle sibilant sound, like the trickle of a breeze through the thorn trees. It meant that they had escaped danger together. And that now she might finally trust one other person with her life.

*

When the detective superintendent eased himself into the back of the van, neither of the officers made any comment. It was for Lorimer to explain his unexpected presence, not for them to question why he was there. The night-time vehicle of choice was a dark burgundy van with an engine under its bonnet that did not match its ageing number plates. Anybody passing by would see a dilapidated-looking vehicle with an ancient roof rack. To outside eyes the van appeared empty. Several attempts to break into it had been made by opportunistic neds, but the sudden flashing lights caused by their efforts had always scared them off. Happily there had never been a need for either of the officers to leave their post and deal with the intruders.

Hidden in the back of the van, where they had a clear view of the outside world aided by an infrared camera lens, the two watchers sat quietly, well used to the strictures imposed by the job they had chosen to do.

'Any change?' Lorimer asked.

The man closest to him on the padded bench shook his head. 'Not much. A few other folk coming and going; one of the arrivals looked like another Nigerian. No lights on this side. Probably both gone to bed,' he said. Beside him, his partner had the camera trained on the top floor of the building, waiting, seeking, praying perhaps for some form of activity.

It was nearing midnight and the place was completely deserted apart from the white transit van, that glowed like a shabby ghost under the yellow street lamp, and their own vehicle, parked several metres along on the opposite side of the road.

It was a tiny movement, a small beam of light flittering like a moth along the ground, that made each of the men in the back of the surveillance van look towards the lane that ran between the houses. Then shadows loomed against the gable end of the building, followed by two black-skinned men carrying something between them. As they passed under the street lamp, there was a faint sheen from the rolled-up tarpaulin, the criss-crossed rope holding its contents securely.

The three watchers saw the men place their burden on the ground, heard the hinges of the van's rear door protest as the taller of the men pulled them open and the thud as the bundle hit the floor.

Just then a third figure emerged from the close, taller and heavier than the others.

'That's McAlpin,' one of the officers whispered as they watched him slip into the driver's side of the van.

The rear doors closed again with a grind and a screech, locks crying out for oil, then the Nigerians jumped into the van. The whirr of an engine starting up, a faint plume of white from the exhaust and the van glided away from the pavement.

In seconds Lorimer found himself seated behind the two officers, the panel between the back of the vehicle and its cabin open, eyes boring along the street where the plumber's van had disappeared.

It was going to be difficult to follow their quarry at this time of night, with so little traffic on the road, and so they kept a decent distance behind the white van as it travelled through the city towards the outskirts of Rutherglen. Several times their driver had to stop in a side street, out of sight, as McAlpin's van came to a set of traffic lights: to be sitting on their tail was a dead giveaway.

Lorimer listened as the officer in the front passenger seat gave their location to someone back at base, through Rutherglen Main Street, along and up past the stone villas of Cambuslang, their bay windows like closed eyelids against the little drama passing them by in the night. On and up they travelled, round bends and through recently built housing schemes until the road flattened out into a junction where four roads met at oblique angles.

The dark red van sat in the shadows, its engine ticking like a patient heartbeat as they waited to see which way McAlpin was headed.

'Cathkin Braes,' Lorimer said as he watched the tail lights disappear across the main road and head left. They followed slowly, their own lights now switched off for fear of alerting McAlpin to their presence. It was a necessary ploy, Lorimer realised as they turned off the narrow road and headed along a farm track. Several times their vehicle lurched and bumped as its wheels found unseen potholes. It was not absolutely dark; the night sky was a velvet blue studded with stars, no sodium glow from street lamps out here in this unspoiled part of the countryside. A stand of pine trees blotted out the view for a moment, then Lorimer saw that they were approaching what might be a little village.

The shapes of farm buildings and barns loomed large on their left, rows of neat cottages flanking their right. Somewhere a dog barked as they passed, and Lorimer looked up at the cottage windows to see if anyone was aware of their presence. But all the windows looked out with covered eyes, the residents slumbering safely within.

'He's heading for the nature reserve,' Lorimer said suddenly, remembering now where he was. The police had approached the low-lying pond from a different entrance, officers tramping across tussocky grass to reach the place where the African girl's body had been found.

The driver gave him a sharp look. 'How do you know?'

Lorimer shook his head. 'Recent crime scene,' he replied tersely. But despite the officer's intent stare, the detective superintendent was not ready to divulge just what the nature of that crime scene had been. MI6 might be looking at a potential terrorist, but Lorimer was beginning to believe that the men they followed along this narrow farm track were suspects in a murder investigation. And just how to extricate each of these tangled threads from the other was troubling his mind.

They came to a halt beside some scrubby bushes, well enough out of sight of the occupants of the white transit as it rolled over the track, its nose suddenly tilting forwards.

'They're stopping,' Lorimer said at last, seeing the beam from the headlights suddenly cut off. 'There's a pond down there,' he whispered, remembering the body that had been fished out just a few weeks before.

The surveillance officers glanced at one another before looking back at the transit, their high-definition binoculars trained on the yawning gap that was the opened rear doors, and the sudden activity of the two figures.

'Could be a body,' one of them suggested, as the bundle was lifted out of the van. 'Right sort of weight,' he murmured. 'What do you want to do, sir?'

Lorimer bit his lip. What he wanted to do was grab these men, uncover the heavy thing they were now carrying between them and haul them back to HQ for questioning. If McAlpin was compromised now, would it drive the rest of the terrorist group underground? Or could they use this event as something totally unrelated to their search for the cell? So far Lorimer had been unwilling to involve other police units as this was an MI6 operation, but the time for such considerations was clearly over.

'Call for back-up,' he said, leaning across and pointing towards the passenger door. 'I'm going after them. Don't let that van get away. Switch on a full beam as soon as I'm close enough.'

His feet made a soft thud on the long grass, then he was heading downhill, half crouching, half running, careful to keep to the shadows of the bushes, grateful that there was no traitor moon shining overhead. As he crept closer he could hear voices. Faint at first, then louder as one of them cursed and he saw the tarpaulin-covered bundle fall to the ground. More curses came, and then the massive figure of McAlpin swung a fist at one of the others, who cried out in pain.

Lorimer hunkered down behind a row of gorse bushes, their jagged branches digging into his side, the heady coconut scent of their yellow flowers sweetening the air, watching and waiting, listening and hoping for the sound of an approaching police car.

The three men had picked up the tarpaulin again, and now he could see them heading further downhill, heads bobbing out of sight as they approached the margin of the pond.

There was a splash as something heavy hit the water, then the place was flooded with light.

Lorimer stood up and began to run, aware of the footsteps coming behind him.

'Police! Stay where you are!' he called, his voice ringing out across the low-lying marshes.

For a moment the three men turned and he could see their faces illuminated in the full beam of headlights shining from the surveillance van.

One of the men slipped and slithered as he tried to regain the bank; another had jumped clear and was making for the transit, McAlpin himself seeming to hesitate for a moment.

Lorimer saw the big man's upraised arm, then heard a faint splash as something hit the water.

Whatever it was, the man now running towards the white van had wanted rid of it. He had caught up with the other African now, and Lorimer's mouth opened in astonishment as McAlpin struck out at the man, felling him to the ground.

Lorimer sped across the last few yards, intending to throw himself at the bulky figure. If he caught hold of his leg they would crash together to the ground, he thought, imagining the man's yell.

It happened so quickly. His quarry stopped and turned, so close now that he could see the naked hatred in those eyes.

Then, with an animal cry, McAlpin lashed out with both fists.

Lorimer heard the sickening blow to his head, felt a blinding pain. The last thing he saw were tufts of grass as the ground came up to hit him.

CHAPTER FORTY-TWO

He had two choices: to charge the Nigerians with disposing of the dead girl's body or to hold them as suspects in her murder. There was no possibility of questioning these men about a potential threat to Glasgow 2014. Whatever nefarious activities McAlpin had been up to in his spare time, Lorimer guessed they had nothing to do with his involvement in the terrorist plot.

His head still throbbed from the big man's blow. That he had let their chief suspect escape hurt more, though, despite the assurances from the surveillance officers that he had never stood a chance against the former weightlifter. They had seen his white van career across the parkland and out of sight, and now there were officers everywhere on the lookout for the fugitive.

Lorimer watched as the doctor took a swab from the Nigerian's mouth, noting the look of terror in the man's dark eyes. The other Nigerian was being questioned in an adjacent room, the whereabouts of McAlpin being only one of the things that the interviewing officers were keen to ascertain.

Now he could see that Okonjo was visibly trembling as he faced the tall policeman across the table. The duty solicitor sat tiredly by his side, a necessary figure in the small drama unfolding as the dawn came up on another Glasgow day.

'There is the body of a young girl of African origin in the city mortuary,' Lorimer began, shuffling the notes in front of him. 'This was found in the same pond where you and your colleagues dumped the body of another girl last night,' he continued, his voice deliberately flat as though he were reading out a shopping list. 'Cathkin Country Park has been kept under some scrutiny since we discovered Celia,' he went on, noting the alarm in the black man's face as he spoke the girl's name. It was a half-truth masked to let Okonjo believe that they had been spotted far from the city, not followed all the way from that tenement building in the East End.

Okonjo's eyes flickered, his back straightening a little. And was that a look of relief? Whom did he fear more, Lorimer wondered: the policeman sitting asking questions or the big man with the tattoos? Lorimer looked down, his own feeling of satisfaction at having successfully dissembled hidden behind the stack of papers that he held up in front of him for a moment. He tapped them on the tabletop then laid them down again, smoothing their surface as though he needed to have everything neat and tidy.

'Your client is being considered in relation to this other girl's murder,' he explained, looking past Okonjo to the lawyer. 'The cause of her death was thought by the consultant pathologist who carried out the post-mortem to be strangulation,' he continued. Nodding as though this was an everyday occurrence, not worthy of any great dramatic flourish. From the corner of his keen blue eye he could see Okonjo relax, Lorimer's voice lulling their suspect into a false sense of security.

'There have been several attempts to identify the victim,' Lorimer continued, 'and we are fairly certain that, like the girl who was thrown into the pond tonight by your client, she is of Nigerian origin.'

Okonjo looked at the man by his side as the lawyer gave an involuntary gasp. He clearly hadn't been expecting this. 'I would like to speak to my client alone,' he said, rising from his chair.

'All in good time, sir,' Lorimer replied smoothly. 'First we have to determine whether your client has a case to answer at all.' He looked at Okonjo through narrowed eyes.

'Where were you on the fourth of April, Mr Okonjo?' Lorimer spoke quietly. Diffident, that was the way he wanted to seem. He was good at disguising his real feelings, like an actor ... The thought brought him a sudden memory of Foxy, her sad eyes turned to his. But that had been real, hadn't it? He banished the image of her; it had no place here inside this interview room where so many criminals had sat trying to lie their way out of future imprisonment.

'I ... I can't re-remember,' the man stuttered.

'It was a Friday night,' Lorimer said helpfully, wondering if the man across the table was replaying a murder in his mind.

It was an evening he himself would never forget. That crowd of people in the old school hall, Foxy in her slim black dress, then the aftermath of it all when he had gone to her aid, Charles Gilmartin lying poisoned in his bed.

It might be a long shot, but by Rosie's reckoning that was one possible date for the Nigerian girl's death. And he had to begin somewhere.

'Ever seen this before, Mr Okonjo?'

Lorimer's voice was hard now, his blue eyes fixed on the man opposite as he slid the blown-up photograph of the triple spiral tattoo across the table.

Okonjo's reaction was immediate. He jerked backwards, hands sliding off the table as though the swirling pattern might actually burn his fingers.

'Is that an affirmative answer?'

Okonjo stared at him, then nodded slowly.

'Please speak for the tape.'

'Yes,' the Nigerian choked as if the word had been drawn out of his throat.

'Yes, you have seen this before,' Lorimer agreed. 'We have traced the tattoo artist who was commissioned to do this particular design and he remembers the girl who came into his salon. Celia, wasn't it? The girl you dumped in the pond on Friday, April the fourth.'

Okonjo stared at him, speechless, his lips parted.

'The tattoo artist remembers the girl who came into his salon. And the Nigerian *uncles* who accompanied her. Perhaps you can give us more details. Starting with her real name.'

Okonjo had lowered his eyes and was looking at his hands clasped on his lap instead.

'Don't know anything about it,' he mumbled.

'Oh, I think you do, Mr Okonjo,' Lorimer shot back. 'Right now we have several things in motion. A post-mortem to determine the nature of this second girl's death. Looks like the first victim's cause of death. Strangulation,' he added, nodding at the lawyer, whose mouth was hanging open like a fish out of water. 'And there will be test results back soon to see if any DNA from either girl's body matches the sample we took from you tonight.' *Soon* was probably pushing it, but the threat was real enough to make the Nigerian feel under pressure.

Lorimer looked from one man to the other. 'So in my opinion, gentlemen, you had better tell us the truth, because one way or another, facts are quickly emerging that place Mr Okonjo at both crime scenes.'

He pulled the photograph back and replaced it with one from

the post-mortem showing the Nigerian girl with her neck to one side, the wires cutting deeply into her dark throat.

He could feel the lawyer recoil as he glanced at the photo, but Okonjo stared at it, anger burning in his eyes as though he wanted to kill the dead girl all over again.

The detective superintendent put the original photo of the triple spiral back on top.

'The girl whose body you disposed of tonight has no such tattoo,' he went on. 'Which brings me to another question.' He looked long and hard at Okonjo, leaning forward so that the man had to meet his steely blue gaze.

'Where is Asa?'

It was the first night that the girl had slept on clean sheets and without the fear that some man would enter her room looking for sex. Asa had no inkling that the hotel was considered low-budget by Western standards. Nor had she questioned the Jamaican woman's choice as she had been bundled in from the taxi. Here in this quiet room, its curtains blocking out the city's light if not its constant noise, Asa felt something that she had thought to have lost: a sense of peace. It was like the stillness before dawn; before the birds in the bush began to sing, before the chattering weavers awoke to fill the trees with their constant twittering. Sometimes Asa would lie on her sleeping mat and think about the way her life had unfolded: the loss of her family, the hard grind of daily survival. But mostly she would look ahead to the demands of each day and what she needed to do in order to bring food and water to the village.

Now there was no way of knowing what lay ahead when the morning sun finally rose on this grey city with its heaps of buildings blotting out the yellow light. And yet she had escaped. Escaped the imprisonment of that terrible place, escaped the constant intrusion into her young body, and as she recalled the awful sight in that other room, there was no doubt in Asa's mind that she had escaped death.

The girl smiled as she heard the soft snores coming from the bed next to hers. Shereen was sleeping peacefully too. They had both escaped, though she wondered what the older woman had been escaping from. She had watched her at times, laughing and joking with the men in the kitchen, but seeing something like sadness in the big woman's face whenever she turned away. Shereen had worn a mask, Asa thought to herself, a thing to hide behind so that the men never guessed her real feelings.

But in the moment when she had come to the doorway, hearing Shereen's scream of terror, she had seen that mask slip for good.

'Four-thirty a.m. DI Grant entering the room,' Lorimer said aloud for the benefit of the tape.

Jo Grant motioned that he should come to the door, glancing meaningfully at the paper in her hand. There was an expression on her face that he recognised. *Gotcha*. And as Grant had been interviewing Boro, the other Nigerian, it looked as if that suspect had given the DI exactly what they wanted.

Lorimer looked at the signed statement. It was all there. The address where they had kept the girls as prostitutes, the identity of both dead girls, McAlpin's role as trafficker clearly outlined.

Now was the time when he could really be dramatic, Lorimer thought, walking back to the table, a swagger in his step. He sat down brandishing Boro's statement in his hand.

'Odunlami Okonjo, I am charging you with the murder of a minor known as Celia. You are also being charged with trafficking and imprisoning underage girls, helping to run a brothel and falsifying documents.'

He paused to look at the Nigerian, whose dark skin had taken on a sheen of sweat.

'It will be easier for you to admit this,' Lorimer said. 'No fuss with a trial. Shorter time inside.' He leaned back and folded his arms across his chest. 'Whenever you're ready, Mr Okonjo. I'm more than happy for you to talk to your solicitor meantime. Get your facts together.' He grinned at the pair opposite.

The duty solicitor's eyebrows were drawn up, waiting for Okonjo's response. Then the Nigerian nodded glumly.

'My client requires a few minutes to prepare his statement,' the solicitor sighed. It was a sigh of defeat, though in truth he had done little during the course of the interview to assist Okonjo, the revelations about the Nigerian's crimes coming as something of a shock to the man who had been summoned to Stewart Street during the wee small hours.

CHAPTER FORTY-THREE

It seemed to the young man standing on the street corner that something momentous was about to happen, and so it was with no little disappointment that he found himself being taken for a walk in the park.

'Thanks for hanging back,' the leader said, smiling politely, as if he was a different person from the one who had been mouthing all those clichés about freedom from tyranny and the need to rid the country of undesirable elements.

If he was being entirely honest, Cameron was beginning to find these meetings a little tedious, and the idea that such a disparate group of men could wreak their planned havoc on the enormity of the Commonwealth Games no longer appeared to be feasible. Perhaps it was the rhetoric: the constant affirmation of *why* they were plotting to blow up the stadium hosting the opening ceremony. Cameron had been as enthusiastic as the rest of them to begin with, brought up as he had been by parents fervent about the need for independence. And now this nondescript man was ambling by his side talking about how nice the weather had been for the time of year!

'Ever been on the boating pond?' the leader asked suddenly as they rounded a corner.

'Never been in this park before,' Cameron mumbled, kicking a stone in his path and watching it skitter along the edge of the little lake.

'Come on then.' The leader was grinning like any schoolboy off on a jaunt, and before he knew it, Cameron was sitting in the stern of a small rowing boat while the man heaved on the oars, slicing through the oily waters. As the shoreline receded, Cameron could see that they were quite alone on this circle of water, the rest of the flotilla of little boats bobbing together at the quayside.

They were nearing an island covered with thick shrubbery when the man drew in the oars and let the boat float along.

'I've never really introduced myself,' he began, holding out his hand. 'Robert Bruce Petrie,' he said. 'And *you* are Cameron Gregson.' He smiled warmly, as though this was the most natural thing in the world rather than a breach of what he had insisted was necessary security. 'Don't know about you, but I've always found given names a bit of a bore. Or maybe it was the expensive education.' He grinned sheepishly. 'Anyway, please just call me Petrie.'

Cameron felt the clamminess of the man's hand slip out of his own and then they were off again, oars cutting through the silky water as he ducked under an overhanging branch.

'How did you know my ...'

'Name? Oh, I know everything about you, my friend.' Petrie's smile never faltered. 'Did you think we met by sheer chance?' He gave a laugh that was pure merriment. 'Oh my goodness, you must have thought us a bunch of amateurs! No, Gregson, you were selected long before that day in the Botanic Gardens.'

Cameron blinked as though he had been struck, yet he was intrigued to hear more from the man who was pulling on these oars as though it was something he did every day of his life.

280

'We only took the best.' Petrie nodded, looking over his shoulder at the island, keeping a safe distance from the bank. 'Number Three and I,' he went on. 'I am not about to give you anyone else's name, though,' he warned, the smile fading a little.

'How did you know about the car following Number Two?' Cameron asked.

'We have our own ways of finding things out, just as they do,' Petrie replied enigmatically.

'They?'

'The police. MI6. The security forces are on high alert because they have wind of something.'

'You mean they know about us?' Cameron was horrified.

'Of course they don't know too many details. And,' his smile was warm once again, 'they certainly don't know about *you*. Which is why I am giving you this very special task.'

The rest of the boat trip passed in a blur as Cameron listened to what he had to do. It seemed at first that it was completely innocuous: taking care of a couple of elderly Australians and making sure that they enjoyed the Clan Gathering in Stirling before accompanying them to a Glasgow hotel and being their constant companion right up until the moment when they arrived at Parkhead Stadium for the opening ceremony of the 2014 Commonwealth Games. Then there was the matter of the *sgian dubh*.

He had been quite aware of the white-haired explosive expert's part in all of this, but until this moment Cameron Gregson had not known exactly what role the two Australians were to play in the attack. And as he listened to Petrie's instructions, he was uncertain whether the chill that ran through his blood was excitement or fear.

*

The journey back through Perthshire had exceeded all of their expectations, and now they were seated outside a country pub, enjoying a freshly made salad sandwich and a glass of the local beer. Peter MacGregor gave a sigh that summed up his feelings completely. It was indeed the trip of a lifetime and they had been extra lucky with the continuing fine weather. Almost every day on the Isle of Skye had allowed them to see the towering mountains, their view disappearing only once behind a bank of low-lying mist. But even that had its own romance, the swirling white clouds doing nothing to dampen their appreciation of the land-scape and the shifting patterns around the coastline. There had been sheep everywhere, this season's growing lambs baaing at their heels whenever the car slowed down to allow them to cross from one nibbled verge to the other.

The land had become gentler as Peter and Joanne had trav-elled south, though some of the places still held a fascination for the amateur historian: Sheriffmuir looked bleak even on a sunny day, the watery sound of curlews drifting over the fields as they had stopped at the roadside to gaze at a place where so much had happened in times gone by.

Peter stretched out a hand and gave his wife's fingers a friendly squeeze. 'Stirling tonight, girl,' he remarked. 'Plenty to see in that old town.'

Joanne smiled back. 'It's a city now, though,' she remarked. 'Says so in the travel guide.'

'That right?' Peter raised his bushy eyebrows, his eyes crink-ling up at the corners as he returned her smile. Then a familiar ringtone made him twist around.

'Wait up,' he said, shifting in his seat to pull out the phone from his trouser pocket. He raised the mobile to his ear and turned away from this village street where traffic lumbered slowly along.

Joanne watched as her husband nodded. There was no sign of recognition on his face, so the call was not from home. Nor was there a crease of anxiety between Peter's brows, nothing to cause her any alarm, simply a routine call of some sort.

'Okay. Pleased to speak to you, son,' MacGregor said, then paused to listen to the response. At last he clicked the phone shut and turned back to his wife.

'Change of plan,' he said, shrugging his shoulders. 'The guy who was to meet us has to go into hospital for an operation, poor sod. That was his replacement. Sounds a decent sort. Young.'

'Oh, that's a shame. Poor man.' Joanne paused for a moment. The fate of strangers was a passing thought, nothing for her to worry about. And if their host had been replaced by a different man so speedily, perhaps that showed how organised they were. 'What's his name, this new one. Is he a MacGregor too?'

'Well now. I'd have to say that he is, though not exactly by name. Same clan, different branch of the family.' Peter smiled as he looked at his wife. 'Our new host is a young man called Cameron Gregson.'

CHAPTER FORTY-FOUR

'I think she was hanged,' Rosie said at last. 'Though whether she did it herself or not is impossible to tell.'

Lorimer nodded. The post-mortem was certainly consistent with both Okonjo and Boro's statements. They had found the girl hanging from a light fitting in her bedroom. She had only arrived the previous night, Okonjo had insisted.

'No tattoo,' Rosie remarked, her gloved fingers indicating the smooth flesh on the inner thigh.

'If she had just come in, they wouldn't have had time to brand her,' Lorimer replied bitterly.

'Perhaps it's true. She did take her own life and they panicked?'

The detective superintendent made a face. That was certainly going to be the solicitor's defence for his client. They had found the girl dead in her room and needed to get rid of the corpse.

'And like a dog returning to its own vomit, they headed to the very place where they had dumped the previous body,' he declared.

It seemed days, not hours ago when he had been racing across the grass at that lumbering figure, certain he could bring him down in a rugby tackle. He closed his eyes for a moment, reliving the scene before the blow that had rendered him unconscious.

There had been that moment when McAlpin had raised his

hand and thrown something into the marshy depths of the pond. Something significant? Something to do with the terrorist cell? He sighed, weary from the lack of sleep as much as from the effort of thinking along parallel lines. Did they even have the resources to trawl that pond? And if they did, wouldn't it be a sheer waste of time, the layers of silt no doubt having swallowed up whatever small object had been hurled into them. Finding McAlpin himself was exhausting their manpower as it was.

'Why don't you go home?' Rosie said suddenly. 'You're as white as a ghost.'

Lorimer gripped the window ledge outside the viewing platform, feeling his body sway. She was right. He'd be no use to anyone like this, and a few hours' sleep alone in the house would make all the difference. Besides, he told himself, there was a team of Special Branch forensic officers already at the flat, picking over every little detail. He was to be permitted to take a look later on, once they had completed their task.

He had forgotten about it being Flynn's day to work on their garden, but as he drew into the driveway it was obvious that the young man was there, his dark green pick-up truck parked outside.

The detective superintendent could hear the sound of the mower coming from the back garden as he put the key into the lock; if he crept upstairs, closed the window and the curtains, then perhaps Flynn would not even realise that he was at home. Minutes later, his clothes laid on a chair next to the window, Lorimer slid naked between cool sheets, groaning in sheer relief as his head sank into the soft pillow. Despite the trundling mower outside, he was asleep in seconds.

*

Joseph Alexander Flynn whistled tunelessly as he strode up and down the lawn, the music from his earphones masking the noise of the petrol-driven mower. It was a good day to be doing this particular job: the sun shone overhead and there was just the hint of a breeze keeping the soaring temperature from burning his bare arms. A quick glance at the flower beds told him that there lay his next task. Weeds proliferated everywhere, and despite Maggie's best intentions, she rarely had time to devote herself to the garden except during school holidays. The soil would be dusty and dry, easy enough to manage, and any stubborn weeds would get a dose of the industrial-strength weedkiller that Flynn kept for his clients' gardens. As Lorimer slept on, the young man stopped from time to time, emptying the grass cuttings on to the compost heap before returning to his task.

Maggie had insisted that Flynn be given a key to the back door. 'You'll need to have a tea break,' she had told him way back when Flynn had first undertaken their gardening on a regular basis. 'Besides, what if you need the loo?' she'd added with a smile. And it was not as if Flynn did not know this house. It had been his home for a short time, a temporary refuge when he had been discharged from hospital, a homeless street lad taken in by the tall policeman after the accident that had almost cost Flynn his life. They had forged a strange friendship back then, one that had been nurtured by Maggie on her return from that exchange programme in the US and, Flynn recalled with a sad expression on his face, by Maggie's late mum. He still missed the older woman's bossiness and the cartons of home-made soup that she had always put aside for him.

As he trundled the mower back out on to the pavement, he spotted the silver Lexus. A swift glance upwards took in the curtains drawn against the bright sunlight. He nodded to himself, glad that the rest of his work would be quiet. He would leave the strimming for another day, concentrating on the weeds instead to allow the man upstairs time to sleep. God alone knew what sort of case the tall policeman was working on, but Flynn was savvy enough about Lorimer's life to understand the long hours that were sometimes demanded.

Maybe he would have a cold drink first, he decided, heaving the machine back into the truck. Wiping his hands on the greasy sides of his trousers, he headed back around the side of the house and let himself into the kitchen.

'Hello, you!' He bent down to the orange cat that was stretching itself beside his basket and tickled it behind one ear. 'Sleeping off a night's hunting, eh?' The cat rubbed its flank against the young man's leg, then strolled through the open door and out into the brightness of the day.

Flynn opened the fridge and selected a carton of cranberry juice. His eyes fell on a half-finished lemon cheesecake with a Post-it note attached. *Help yourself*, Maggie had written, and Flynn grinned as he drew out the plate. It was his favourite and Maggie knew it.

Outside, Chancer the cat stopped at the patch of earth between two purple and yellow plants. There was just enough room to squat and do his business. His fastidious habit satisfied, the cat sniffed the earth then scraped hard, his back paws making deep gouges in the dry soil. He was completely unaware of the tinkling sound behind him or of the light catching the slim glass phials as they rolled on to the path. His green eyes had spied a butterfly hovering above a shrub straight ahead and Chancer crouched down low, belly to the ground as he began to stalk the creature.

Flynn pushed the silver foil plate into a triangle before shoving it into the pedal bin. With a sigh of satisfaction, he stepped out of the shady kitchen and into the sunlight once more. Pulling on a cotton hat to protect his head, he walked up to the flower bed nearest to the back door.

The gardener tilted his head to one side, screwing up his eyes. What was that glittering on the path? And why hadn't he spotted them before? He hunkered down, noticing the soil scraped away from the border. Chancer had been there. And his strong paws had dug something up. Flynn put out a finger and touched the three thin tubes of glass lying on the path. As he did so, he saw that there was something inside them, like dark stains clouding the glass.

Thought you might want to take a closer look at them, the note said.

Lorimer rolled the three tiny phials in his fingers, his eyes trying to focus, his mind still blurred from the hours of sleep. Call me, the note had concluded. Flynn's mobile number was scribbled below, although Lorimer had it on his own phone. *Found these in the garden.*

It was as if a clammy hand was clutching his heart, such was the feeling he had of imminent trouble. His policeman's sixth sense? A forewarning of some sort? That chilling sensation that folk described as a goose walking over their grave. Lorimer gripped the telephone tightly, steeling himself for what was to come.

'Hi, big man, sorry to have to bother ye. It wis these funny wee glass things . . . ' Flynn's Glasgow accent was laced with a note of contrition.

'I saw them,' Lorimer said. 'Where did you find them exactly?'

'Aye, well . . . ' Flynn hesitated, and Lorimer could imagine the young man's awkward expression as he sought to find the right words to tell the policeman what he was beginning to guess.

'See yon wee red-haired wumman that stayed wi' youse?'

'Mrs Gilmartin?'

'Aye. Her. Well, wan day she wis oot doin' stuff in the gairden an' I seen her diggin' a wee hole jist aboot where ah foon these glass thingmies.'

'Are you saying you saw her bury them, Flynn?' Lorimer's voice was quiet.

'Well, no' exactly. Kind've. Like, she must've, eh? Ah mean, she didnae spend awfie long doin' the weeds in that border, jist kneeled there an' did a wee bit diggin'.'

There was a silence for several moments as Lorimer digested the information.

'Did you or did you not see her burying those glass phials?'

'Och, no' exactly. Like ah said, I saw her diggin', but didnae see the wee glass ... whatdye call them.'

'Thanks, Flynn. Listen, son. Keep this to yourself for now, but it might come to the bit that I need you to make a statement.'

'Whit? How?' Flynn sounded wary. 'Me? Give a statement?'

'Only if it becomes necessary, Flynn,' Lorimer soothed. 'It may turn out to be nothing at all,' he consoled the lad. But as he turned the three glass phials in his hand, the detective experienced the stomach-churning certainty that what Flynn had found was going to bring Vivien Gilmartin back up to Glasgow very soon indeed.

'Are you sure?' There had been the customary pause after Lorimer had spilled out the story to the psychologist, then that damning question.

'Of course I'm not sure,' he retorted. 'If I was *sure* then I'd be going straight to Alistair Wilson and telling him to arrest her.'

Lorimer was standing at the large bay window in the professor's room, gnawing at a raggle on his fingernail. Outside the day was bright, clouds scudding across the azure sky, a mild wind turning the silvery leaves of the trees along University Gardens. Rain would set in by tonight, he thought idly. And had it rained earlier today, perhaps Flynn would not have made the discovery that had prompted the policeman to come here to seek guidance from his friend.

A few students were hurrying along the avenue, no doubt thankful that the end of term was in sight, exams all but over for this academic year. How long ago had that been William Lorimer in their place? That year spent here, at one of the country's oldest universities, had been happy, hadn't it? In truth there was little he could recall about the day-to-day business of studying History of Art, but the general feeling he always had when walking through the cloisters, or even here in Solly's department, was one of satisfaction that he had made a good choice. It had been youthful enthusiasm, much like his relationship with Foxy, that had led him to follow an academic path for a while.

Yet there was no regret in Lorimer's mind at having spent time here as a student; on the contrary, this was where he had met his future wife. Some things were just meant, his mother-in-law used to say, fondly.

And perhaps the gardener's discovery was one of those things.

'Motive, means and opportunity,' Solly said suddenly, making the detective turn away from the window. 'Isn't that what you try to look for in a case like this?'

Lorimer blew out a sigh. 'Usually, yes, but this is what makes it so difficult. The only motive anyone could come up with right now would be that she inherits his estate. His *considerable* estate,' he added grimly. 'As for means, well, the residue in those phials is being tested right now. If they should match the contents of Gilmartin's stomach, well ... ' He gave a meaningful shrug. 'It's the opportunity that baffles me, though. I was with Vivien

Gilmartin for several hours that night and there were witnesses who could testify that she spent the best part of the day and the entire evening at the school.'

'She came back to the flat to change her clothes?'

'According to her statement.'

'And the time of death is reckoned to be around nine or ten in the evening?'

Lorimer nodded.

'I don't normally turn in at that time on a Friday, do you?' Solly asked, his bushy eyebrows rising as he posed the question.

'No, but there was no reason why the man might not have felt tired ...' Lorimer tilted his head to one side, trying to see where Solly was going with this.

'But sometimes, after Abby is asleep, we might go to bed ...' Solly's eyes twinkled and his shy smile ended with a laugh. 'You know ...'

'You think Gilmartin had bedded someone mid evening? While Vivien was out at the school reunion?'

'Or had he gone to bed with his wife earlier? When she had come home to change her clothes? She would be taking off her day clothes, having a shower perhaps, then going back into that bedroom to slip into her good frock,' Solly said, nodding as his eyes took on a distant look.

Lorimer listened to his friend, knowing that he was imagining the events in his mind as they might have unfolded.

'And Gilmartin takes her to bed before she dresses, stays there after she's gone.'

'Vivien says he was out when she returned to the flat,' Lorimer said slowly.

'And the CCTV images from the nearest camera tell you that nobody walked away from the area around the flats.'

'There is a back door. He could have left that way. Vivien says she went out that door to meet her taxi.'

'Why would he use the back door?' Solly shrugged. 'It's a short walk to the Citizens Theatre and back. No need for a cab. As far as we know, there is no reason for Gilmartin being clandestine about his movements. She may be lying about her husband being out when she returned to get changed.'

'But if he were expecting someone that he didn't want his wife to know about, *they* might arrive around the back of the building,' Lorimer mused.

There was a silence as each man considered the possible scenario.

'Why did she bury those bottles in your garden?' Solly asked suddenly, fixing Lorimer with a stare.

'You really think Vivien killed her own husband?' Lorimer shook his head. 'But it's impossible. I was with her all through the evening.'

'That seems to be the case,' Solly replied slowly. 'But nothing is ever as it seems when it comes to the taking of another person's life. Pity about the bedclothes.'

'What?'

'The bedclothes,' Solly repeated. 'If that well-meaning policewoman hadn't shoved them into the washer, then there might have been some trace evidence to show if Gilmartin had had sex that evening. And with whom. He wasn't wearing pyjamas, was he?'

Lorimer shook his head. 'Not everyone does,' he demurred. '*I* don't.'

'Ah, you hardy Scot!' Solly joked. 'I wonder if you would find any nightwear for Mr Gilmartin in among his belongings. Too late now, I suppose?'

'Yes,' Lorimer said slowly. 'Everything was packed away and taken back down to London.' He blinked, remembering the funeral and the crowd of people on that hilltop overlooking the city. 'But I could still find out,' he said.

'By asking his wife?' Solly's eyebrows rose above his horn-rimmed spectacles.

'No, actually. I was thinking of someone else,' Lorimer replied. 'Someone who would know about things like that.'

Alistair Wilson leaned across the desk. 'Are you seriously thinking that your old girlfriend might have murdered her own husband?'

'Apart from the impossibility of her actually administering the poison at the time when he was supposed to have died, yes, I have been considering that.'

'Why would she?' Wilson asked. 'Didn't she seem grief-stricken to you?'

Lorimer did not reply. That word again. *Seem*. How had she seemed? So many times they had seen outpourings of anguish in the wake of a domestic dispute that had ended in tragedy. Often the emotion was regret for a crime committed during a moment of passion or drunkenness; sometimes the tears expressed self-pity at being found out and charged with a capital offence. Had Foxy's tears been real?

'Perhaps,' he said at last. 'She is a trained actress, remember.'

Wilson nodded, then heaved a sigh.

'What now?' he asked at last.

'Here's what I want you to do,' Lorimer told him.

CHAPTER FORTY-FIVE

Odunlami Okonjo had expected to be taken from the cell in Stewart Street by van to some place like Her Majesty's Barlinnie Prison, not bundled into the back of a sleek Mercedes with blacked-out windows. None of the men sitting beside him or up front had spoken a single word to him since the moment the cell doors had swung open and a uniformed officer had stood aside to let him leave. It had been done in the dark of night with nobody to see him being led away, hands still cuffed, out of the rear of the building where the car was waiting, its engine note barely discernible, a cat purring into the cold air.

It had been hours now since the car had taken the road south, and the miles of motorway had slipped easily under its tyres. The silence was beginning to unnerve the Nigerian, something that he guessed was designed to do just that. Still, he resisted the temptation to utter any words aloud. Let *them* tell him what was going on, he had snarled in his mind, flexing his strong hands as though reminding the muscles of what they were capable, given the chance.

This was not about McAlpin's flats in Glasgow where he had set up several illegal immigrant girls. Nor was it about the bodies he and Boro had dumped out in that marshy pond at Cathkin.

The Nigerian cursed McAlpin for choosing that particular place. He should have known better than to let his two different worlds collide; the big man had boasted about his legitimate involvement with the 2014 Games allowing him to see all the venues around the country, including the remote mountain-biking trail and the hidden valley with its nature reserve tucked out of sight. It was the perfect place to dispose of the bodies, he had told them.

Of course the police would have been keeping an eye on the area after finding that bitch Celia! But how the hell could anyone have known they'd found her body? McAlpin had assured them that there had been nothing in the papers about it so that Okonjo had felt totally safe taking the new girl's body there.

For a moment he saw the corpse hanging in that room again and cursed her silently. The sight must have freaked Shereen and the caretaker had fled, taking Asa with her. Well, that lucrative part of their lives was over now, he thought gloomily.

No, he decided, being here with these silent men was not about the trafficking of girls. It had to be something else, something that the big tattooed man had kept hidden even from the two Nigerians.

'We've got a match for you!' Rosie Fergusson's eyes glinted in triumph as the detective superintendent entered her office. The Department of Forensic Medicine was tucked away between the end of the Western Infirmary and the lane that led on to University Avenue. Rosie's office did not appear to be very special, certainly not a place that held the mysteries of life and death, mysteries that sometimes revealed secrets about the way a person had been dispatched into the hereafter.

'Yes?'

'The DNA from the swab you took from the Nigerian, Okonjo, matches the foetus from the African girl,' Rosie told him.

'You're kidding?'

'Nope. Clear as day.' She bent her head and gave him a quizzical look. 'Something you're not telling me?'

Lorimer looked back at his friend, her open countenance waiting for his reply. Rosie was as accustomed to the machinations of the human condition as any of his professional colleagues, and he longed to be able to tell her about why this man had been released into the custody of the MI6 officers.

'It's complicated,' he began, then bit his lip, considering what to say. 'There is a question of national security involved,' he went on. 'Nothing to do with the dead girls,' he added, raising his hand as Rosie was about to break in. 'At least not as far as we know.'

'Are you trying to tell me you haven't apprehended a suspect in the girl's murder?'

Lorimer sighed. 'No. I mean, yes, there is a suspect. Hell! You've got his DNA!' He banged the table with his fist. 'Oh Rosie, I wish I could tell you what was happening, but I can't.'

'A matter of national security.' Rosie nodded. 'The spooks are involved, then, I suppose. Does this mean that they're taking over the investigation into human trafficking?' Her voice was bitter. 'Find them and deport them, I suppose?'

'It's not like that, Rosie.' Lorimer leaned across the table. 'And I'm still determined to find out all about the trafficking if I possibly can. This is much bigger. *Much* bigger.' He leaned back, shaking his head. 'Hopefully I'll be able to tell you all about it one day. Make it into a story for wee Abby.' He gave the ghost of a smile.

'And meantime? What do we do about these girls' bodies?'

Lorimer shook his head. 'That's a matter for the Fiscal,' he said. 'But I think even Iain MacIntosh is taking orders from higher up the chain of command these days.'

Asa watched the buses passing by on the street below. Sometimes they stopped to allow passengers to get on and off and she craned her neck to follow the alighting figures to see what they looked like, wondering where they were heading in this city with all its noise and glamour. They were people with lives full of purpose, Asa had decided, people with places to go, other folk to meet. Sometimes a woman struggled off with a baby buggy; often a fellow passenger would stop to lend a hand, then go their own way, a small kindness freely given. Once she had watched as a tall black woman had strolled away from the bus stop, her slim figure swaying gracefully as though she carried a burden on top of her elegant head. The pain of longing for home had swept through the girl then, a pain that was worse than the ache in her broken arm under the weight of its plaster.

Shereen was afraid, she could tell. The older woman had hardly smiled once since they had taken refuge here in this pleasant room with its comfortable beds and pictures of gardens on the pale pink walls. Asa was not to leave; it had been made very clear to her in both words and gestures that it was not safe outside the hotel. Someone might be looking for them. To her credit, Shereen was trying hard to increase the paltry stock of English words and phrases that the Nigerian girl had amassed. And Asa was grateful for the lessons; it helped to pass the time here, waiting and wondering where they would go next. She had tried to ask that very question but had been met by a shrug that had made her shiver.

For the caretaker to be at a loss was not good. She was safe with Shereen, she had learned to trust her again, but there was a new

297

anxiety gnawing at Asa's heart when she realised that the big
woman did not have all the answers to her many questions.

'Where is the castle?' Joanne asked the young man who was striding across the street beside her husband, making it hard for her to
keep up. The cobbled stones on this road were difficult to nego-
tiate and the Australian was glad that she had worn a comfortable
pair of sneakers this morning.

'That's it right above us,' he replied as they ascended the steep
incline and turned a corner.

Joanne MacGregor peered past a high wall flanking the buildings to their left, and then there it was: Stirling Castle, its ancient
stones rearing high above them. A flag near the entrance fluttered
in the wind and Joanne pulled up her shirt collar against the
sudden stream of cold air.

'I've got your tickets,' the young man assured them, patting his
top pocket. The fleece jacket with its Commonwealth Games
logo looked brand new, like the blue lanyard slung around his
neck. But then Mr Gregson had been brought in to replace their
original host, Joanne reminded herself. He looked so young, she
thought; probably a student, one of the many volunteers involved
in this year's Games. And yet as she listened to him telling them
of the castle's history and Scotland's bloody past, she heard an
enthusiasm that endeared him to her. There was a glint in his eye
as he spoke that surely showed a passionate love for his country.
Joanne watched him intently as he retold the story of Scotland's
rise and fall against their English neighbours.

Of course this was the year of the famous referendum, she
remembered; by the time they were ready to set off for home,
Scotland might well have voted to become an independent nation
once more. She gave a silent shrug. It was no skin off their noses

whatever happened, but she would be sorry if it meant they were no longer a sovereign nation. She liked the royal family, especially the Queen. And to think that they might be sitting close to Her Majesty at the opening ceremony!

The young man's words were lost to her as Joanne daydreamed about the big event to come, never once guessing just what part she and her husband were meant to play in the disaster that was planned, nor that one of its architects was standing only feet away, the morning sun shining on his eager face.

The flat was situated in the East End of the city, on a quiet street that ran parallel to Alexandra Parade. It was, Lorimer estimated, only a five-minute drive away from HM Barlinnie Prison, home to some of the more notorious criminals that he had helped put away during his time on the force. Until today, the detective superintendent had been unable to gain access to the upper flat, the SOCOs having been hand-picked by Drummond and his cohorts. It had been a definite case of *stay away until we're finished our job*, something Lorimer found irksome, to say the least. And yet if they had been searching for something to do with the terrorist cell, who could blame them? But so far nothing had turned up, and the latest from Drummond was that Boro and Okonjo had still not said anything about McAlpin's part in a plot to disrupt the Games.

Now, at least, the detective superintendent could begin to piece together what had taken place in this flat since the body of the first Nigerian girl had been discovered. They knew about the missing girl who had been given a tattoo – Asa, the one who had attended the Royal Infirmary to have her broken arm set – and the third girl who had only just arrived in Glasgow was in the city mortuary, hanged by her own volition, according to Boro and Okonjo.

Neither of the men knew how he had watched them as they left this flat, carrying the bundle that contained the body of the young girl. The surveillance that was meant to shadow McAlpin for his possible part in a terrorist plot had produced something quite different in the end. A coincidence, they would no doubt tell him later, once the operation was complete and the Games had ended. Possibly, but then the criminal mind was a fertile source for all sorts of activities, and it was not really a surprise to find that the big ginger-haired man with the garish tattoos all over his body was responsible for human trafficking in the city. It was rife, Professor Brightman had told him solemnly. Solly's psychiatrist friend in the detention centre had hinted at the rumours: gang masters running brothels full of foreign girls, Vietnamese and Nigerian. And some of these gang masters were from foreign parts themselves, she had heard, Albanians amongst them. Their discovery was only the tip of the iceberg, Solly had said with a sigh when Lorimer had revealed the latest activity out at Cathkin Country Park.

Lorimer turned the key in the door of the flat, wondering about the people who had been living here. There was no echo of the despairing cries that the imprisoned girls might have uttered, nor did he hear a sepulchral moan from any dark ghost lingering in this place. And yet his imagination could recreate some of what had happened here as he entered the flat and stood in the long hallway. The carpet was slightly rucked, possibly from the girl's body being dragged along in that tarpaulin sheet.

His gloved hand pushed open a door to his right. This was where the girl had been found suspended from the ceiling. Or so the two Nigerians had insisted. Lorimer stood on the threshold, taking in the room. It was small and poorly lit, overshadowed by tenements in the neighbouring street. There was a single bed, a dresser, and a small chest of drawers, but as he opened and closed each one,

Lorimer could see that they were empty. A clothes rail stood against one wall; had they meant to bring her some things to wear? There was no sign whatsoever that anyone had prepared for the African girl's arrival. It was as if she had simply been thrust into this room and left alone without so much as a spare pair of knickers.

Looking up, he saw the end of an electric flex, cut close to the ceiling. The lampshade still lay on its side, rolled across the floor. She must have stood here on this dresser, Lorimer thought, imagining the girl's bare feet on its empty surface, tying the flex around her neck, willing herself to make that leap into the darkness. How had she felt? The utter despair that had led the unnamed African girl to take her own life rather than be subjected to the horrors of a ravished body was something he tried to contemplate. But all he could think about was the complete blackness in her mind.

She would have felt that it was the only way to gain her freedom, Solly had suggested. And perhaps he was right. But the very idea was so grim that the tall man standing alone in the room wanted to weep.

The kitchen and the other two bedrooms were a shambles: cupboards still open, their contents ransacked. The SOCOs were not responsible for that, he had been assured; this was how they had found the flat and they had at least endeavoured to leave it the way it had been on the night of Okonjo and Boro's arrest. Someone had left in a hurry, that was plain, Lorimer thought as he wandered from room to room. Across from the bathroom was a small room with locks on the outside of the door, like the one where the girl had been hanged. But whoever had been imprisoned here had been luckier. The opened drawers revealed some skimpy nighties and several flimsy pairs of underwear in garish colours: tarts' knickers, purchased no doubt as a turn-on for the girl's numerous clients.

In the corner of the room was a narrow cupboard, its door ajar. And there, suspended from its rail, was a pretty blue dress, its ruffled neckline reminding him suddenly of the sort of frocks Maggie would buy for Abigail Brightman, his little goddaughter.

This had been Asa's room, Lorimer told himself. A young girl, scared to death by what she had seen, fearful that her own life was in danger. And somewhere in this city she was hiding from the men who had brought her here.

She had tried to explain it to the girl, really she had, but her words had been met only by a blank, uncomprehending stare.

'I am the bird who cannot sing,' Shereen sighed, flopping back on to the bed at last.

'Bird.' Asa smiled, making her hand flap like the wings of one of the sparrows she saw from the window.

'I wish we were as free as the birds, girl,' Shereen said. 'Then we could fly away and never come back.' She bent towards the girl lying on the bed next to her own. 'They told me they'd kill me if I let on. And they'll kill you too, little one,' she said sadly, looking at Asa. The girl had started to smile, but her lips closed as she caught the older woman's tone.

'Stool pigeons, that's what they'd call us. Grasses.' Shereen shook her head. 'You don't know what on earth I'm talking about, do you, darling?' she said softly, stretching out a podgy hand to pat the girl's good arm. 'It's a bad old world they've brought you into, Asa, and I don't know how I'm going to get you out of it.'

CHAPTER FORTY-SIX

Mrs Porter folded the clothes that were still warm from the tumble dryer. The skimpy silk panties and matching bras that Vivi kept buying were ranged along the clothes horse to dry: no way would the cleaner risk that lady's wrath by shrinking her expensive undies! She heaved the laundry basket on to her hip and left the utility room. The towels were to be stacked in the airing cupboard, then she could begin to put away the rest of Vivi's things. Ironing next, she told herself with a sigh. There would be no more of Mr Gilly's shirts to smooth under her caring steam iron, she thought sadly. Vivi had packed the whole lot up and sent them to a charity shop already.

Funny that that nice tall man from Scotland should turn out to be a copper, Mrs Porter mused as she opened the door to the linen cupboard. And what an odd question to ask her! Did Mr Gilmartin wear pyjamas in bed? She shook her head, baffled by the ways of policemen. No doubt there was something significant to be had from her answer. 'No,' she'd told him tartly, 'Mr Gilly never wore night things; always in the buff he was. Gave me a shock more'n once, I c'n tell you!' The old lady smiled, remembering the silence on the other end of the telephone, then that discreet cough. Well, that Mr Lorimer had seemed happy enough at what she'd told him. And she'd been able to let on about Vivi's sudden trip to the South of France an' all.

'Lovely time of year,' she'd told her cleaning lady. 'The lavender will be a mass of purple all over the fields in Provence.'

Then she'd upped and went, hadn't she? Place was always safe with Old Porter to see to things, that was for certain. And she'd given her a nice fat envelope.

No, she didn't 'ave any address for Mrs Gilly over there. And she hadn't said 'ow long she'd be gone, neither.

The detective superintendent sat looking out of the window of his room. Southern France in June. The hills would be a hazy blue stretching all the way to the Mediterranean, a sight he and Maggie had enjoyed from the plateau of Les Baux-de-Provence with its ancient instruments of war. And they'd enjoyed a memorable al fresco dinner in that exclusive restaurant that had cost as much as their entire holiday. Would Vivien Gilmartin make herself known in that sort of place? Or would she be holed up somewhere in a tiny French village where life rolled by ever so slowly, the locals minding their own business even when a ravishing red-haired actress appeared amongst them? Had she gone to France at all? Lorimer wondered. It was a bit rich, he thought, taking off like that while her husband's murder was still being investigated. Hadn't she been told to stay put? Well, the passport control office would soon be able to let them know if she had left the country. But after that? Was Vivien Gilmartin already out of his reach?

His ringing telephone broke into his reverie.

'Lorimer.'

The furrows on his brow cleared as he heard the psychiatrist's voice.

'Dr Jones, what can I do for you?'

Lorimer listened as the woman explained the reason for her call. Leila, the Nigerian girl at the detention centre, had been having strange dreams, dreams that involved the tattooed man, and she had begged the psychiatrist to use her magic to make them go away.

'Sadly there is no magic to do that,' Dr Jones told him. 'But I listened to her and suggested that she let you come here. Can you do that? She seems to want to unburden herself of whatever has been haunting her. You don't have a lot of time, I'm afraid. She's due to leave here within the next week or so.'

'I can come over later this afternoon,' Lorimer told the psychiatrist. 'And I might even be able to help her feel better. We've arrested two men for human trafficking,' he added.

'Good,' she replied. But there was a congratulatory note in that single syllable that made him feel absurdly pleased. Dr Jones had struck him as a person who did not waste her words in lavish praise.

'See you later then,' he told her, and rang off.

A knock on his door made him look up.

'Alistair,' he said, nodding at the entrance of his colleague. 'What news?'

DS Wilson sat down opposite the detective superintendent without waiting to be asked; old friends, they only stood on formalities if one of the top brass was present. He ran a hand across his thinning hair, the dark widow's peak that had once been so prominent now threaded with grey.

'The phials contained the poison all right,' he began. 'No doubt about that. Same as the substance found in the tox report. But no sign anywhere of a bottle that may have held the ginger wine.' He gave a half-hearted grin. 'Don't suppose you checked your recycling bin?'

305

Lorimer gave a hollow laugh. 'It was put out while Mrs Gilmartin was there,' he replied. 'And if she did have a bottle of ginger wine in her possession, I never saw it.' He shrugged. 'She could have put it in our bin easy enough, I guess.'

'You don't have one of those cleaning guys who come around and wash your bins, do you?' Wilson asked. 'Betty always has to put money in a wee plastic bag at the door for our man.'

'No.' Lorimer sat up a little straighter. 'Maybe we ought to have someone take our blue bin away for testing? See if any residue from a bottle of ginger wine happened to leak out?'

'Aye, I'll arrange for that to be done,' Wilson said. 'But even if we do find that, it wouldn't be conclusive evidence.'

'No?'

Wilson shook his head. 'A prosecuting counsel might suggest you'd put the bottle there yourself,' he said, looking his friend in the eye. 'The former lover helping his old flame to destroy the evidence.'

'You're not serious?'

'Why did she make such a stramash about having to stay with you and Maggie?'

'She said there was nobody else.'

'Bollocks!' Wilson retorted. 'My guess is that she had it planned all along. The class reunion, the chance to reel you in again ... I'm betting that Mrs Vivien Gilmartin had things nicely worked out.'

'But she couldn't have murdered her husband ... '

'Because she had the perfect alibi? Detective Superintendent William Lorimer?' Wilson nodded. 'That's the one thing we've still to work out. It's all there except for the timescale.' He frowned. 'But Flynn seeing her bent over that patch in the garden where he found the poison phials ... well, there is so much circumstantial evidence here that we mustn't rule her out. Plus,' he nodded grimly, 'the fact that the lady stands to inherit more than three million pounds of his estate. And,' he wagged a finger in the air, 'we've found that Gilmartin had planned to sink a huge amount of that capital into the African project. Bringing those people over and putting on a tour like that was going to cost him a fortune.'

'And Vivien was less than keen that it should go ahead,' Lorimer sighed, remembering the woman's insistence that the entire project be cancelled.

He looked past the man who was senior investigating officer in the hunt to find Charles Gilmartin's killer. They had to locate his widow. And she had to tell them the truth.

'We need to find the Nigerian girl,' Lorimer told the assembled officers. 'We believe she is still in the city and is probably terrified out of her wits. She may be accompanied by a Jamaican woman by the name of Shereen Swanson.' He held up a blown-up picture. 'This is Swanson. She has been on the Met's radar but hasn't blotted her copybook up here till now. Was involved with a Jamaican gang master in South Shields. We need to find out where they are.'

'Sir, what will happen to Asa when she's brought in?'

Several heads turned to look at the rookie cop who was regarding the detective superintendent earnestly. Young Kirsty Wilson was asking the question that any soft-hearted person might want to ask. One officer gave a cynical smile as he turned back, shaking his head as if to say that Wilson's girl would need to toughen up if she wanted to be as good a cop as her father.

'That's not up to us, Kirsty.' Lorimer gave her a kindly smile. 'If Asa is found she will be the responsibility of the immigration authorities. Poor girl might well want to go back home,' he added, raising his eyebrows. 'We have enough from Okonjo's statement to know about this particular flat, but it seems there may well be others dotted around the city, a far bigger network of trafficking than we can imagine. And we want to nail it,' he said firmly.

It was all very well telling them this, Lorimer thought as he headed out of Stewart Street, but finding people like McAlpin was far from simple. They had been lucky, that was all. McAlpin had been under close surveillance and they had found one of his nests over in the East End; how on earth were they supposed to find every last brothel in Glasgow where underage girls were being held against their will?

Would Shereen Swanson be able to tell them more if they located her? That had been his unspoken hope as he'd pinned the Jamaican woman's picture on the whiteboard at the meeting. No other tattoo artists had come back with reports of the triple spiral being given to any young woman in their studios. So perhaps Okonjo's story that he had brought over only three Nigerian girls had been true. Lorimer's expression was set as he started the big car and drove out of Stewart Street car park, wondering just what awaited him at the detention centre.

While Cameron Gregson was doing a reasonable impression of tour guide to the Australian visitors in the city of Stirling, two men were approaching an upper cottage flat in Croftfoot.

'We're not meant to arrive together,' the white-haired man reminded his companion.

'Couldn't help it this time,' Number Five replied with an easy shrug. 'Had to get petrol and there was a queue like an execution.'

'*He* won't like it,' the explosives expert pointed out, nodding towards the house.

'Too many things he doesn't like, if you ask me.'

'You still take his money, though, don't you?'

The other man laughed. 'Why not? He's rolling in it. Who d'you think owns all these houses we've been meeting in? He's one of the biggest buy-to-let merchants in this godforsaken city.' He pushed open the small metal gate, then turned to Worsley. 'Our little capitalist wants to start his own private army once this is over. Did you know that?' He gave the older man a keen look.

'No,' Worsley replied. 'An' how come *you* know so much about him, eh?'

The other man stopped for a moment and tapped the side of his nose.

'Part of my profession, isn't it? Finding things out about people.'

Rob Worsley gave the ghost of a smile as he took in his colleague's words. They had all been selected for their varied attributes and he had long suspected that Number Five had some inside knowledge that involved the security services or the police. Maybe even both.

The six men knew little of one another outside the group, or so it had appeared. Worsley had been recruited by McAlpin early on, their association having been forged by a mutual understanding over time spent in the forces. But he had only been able to guess at the background of the other men in the group. His plans to skip the country as soon as the stadium was blown to kingdom come had changed with the disappearance of McAlpin. The big tattooed man had given him assurances that he would be safe in Nigeria. He knew people, he'd told Worsley. He'd arrange everything.

Well, McAlpin was out of the picture now, though why he had not answered his personal call Worsley did not know, and the older man chewed his lip anxiously as they ascended the inner staircase to the room where two men already sat waiting for them.

'Sit down, gentlemen,' the leader commanded, staring hard at Worsley and Number Five as they entered the room.

It was, Worsley realised, typical of so many of the rooms where they had met before. The decor was bland and the furniture old-fashioned, as though it had come from a saleroom. Why it had never dawned on him before, he did not know, but he could see now that this was exactly the sort of place that would be rented out. The more modern flats in the city had confused him; they had all looked so much the same and now he knew why: they'd probably been kitted out from the same IKEA job lots.

'There are some serious developments to discuss, gentlemen,' the leader began, fixing them in turn with his gimlet stare, bringing Worsley's attention back to the meeting.

He paused for effect before leaning forward and proclaiming, 'We have lost one of our number.'

There ought to have been a gasp of alarm, the explosives expert thought. That was what the wee man wanted, after all. But there was a stubborn silence as they waited for the leader to continue.

'The police tried to apprehend our friend,' he began. 'But happily they have failed. However, two of his colleagues have been arrested and they are being questioned by . . . ?'

The man who had walked in by Worsley's side took up the thread. 'Spooks have got them,' he said shortly. 'According to my sources, the Nigerians were taken from Stewart Street during the night. That's as much as they could tell me.' He shrugged. 'But they haven't been taken to any Scottish prison.'

'How do you know that?' Worsley blurted out suddenly.

'Got the ear of the folk who arrange transportation, haven't I?' He grinned.

'We do not need to ask such questions.' The leader glared at

Worsley, who spread his hands in mute apology. 'What we need to determine now is how much Number Two may have told his Nigerian friends.'

'He wouldn't ...' Number Three, the thin man who sat nervously beside the leader, raked his hair with one hand.

'One never can tell,' the leader said darkly. 'And it may be a problem for us now that our deselected member has disappeared so effectively.'

'Number Two can take care of himself,' Worsley declared, already tired of the histrionic note that was creeping into the meeting. This was a serious matter, not the stuff of a schoolboy's fantasy, though it did occur to him to wonder what sort of things the leader dreamed about at night. 'We've got a job to do and we need to decide how we're going to carry it out if the original plan has to be scrapped,' he declared firmly. '*I* have to know,' he added, as if they needed any reminding that the explosives expert was key to the entire plot.

'Yes,' the leader agreed, nodding. 'And this is what I have to propose to you. Number Six has taken over the duties concerning the two Australians. He will be told to accompany them to the opening ceremony and stay with them until he is given the signal.'

There was a faint smile on the man's face, a shark's smile; white teeth showing between thin lips.

'But there will be no signal.'

'You're going to let him be blown up?' Number Three looked incredulous and Worsley saw him glance at the man who had come in with him to gauge his reaction. But Number Five remained impassive, making Worsley wonder if he had known already what was coming. He seemed to know quite a lot else.

'He's expendable,' the leader said, nodding. 'Besides, he's getting far too cosy with that girl for my liking. And,' he looked at each of them in turn, 'I think he may have begun to develop what he would call a conscience.'

Gayle turned the key in the door, her heart beating faster. She had raced up the stairs, eager to break the news to him. Letting the bunch of keys drop on to the side table by the telephone, she took her handbag into the bedroom and flopped down on the bed. Her smile broadened as she unzipped the front pocket and drew out the two tickets. It was like winning the lottery, she told herself, holding the tickets out and staring at them. To be selected as guests at the opening ceremony was an honour that the young woman had never dreamed of. Okay, so she had applied for the tickets; they all had. And just today she had been given two! 'One for your young man,' the senior committee member had murmured. 'He's been quite supportive of you, hasn't he?'

Gazing at the tickets, Gayle had to agree that Cameron Gregson had indeed been supportive of late. Something had changed in his manner, too. He was softer, less abrasive, more solicitous towards her. And for Gayle, that meant only one thing: Cam was in love with her!

It was then that she remembered. He was going to be in late. Something to do with a meeting. She stood up, finding it hard to settle, wanting her boyfriend to walk in the door *now*, not later on once he had done whatever he had to do up in ... where was it? Stirling. That was it. She recalled his words now. *University stuff*, he'd said vaguely.

The young woman opened the windows of the bedroom, letting in the noise of the city, breathing in the air. She was restless and wanted Cam here. Wanted to have him in bed beside her, murmuring endearments. Wanted to show him the tickets with a grin of triumph. *Wait till you see what I've got for you*, she longed to tell him.

She could always text him, but that wasn't the same as seeing his expression when she had her ta-da moment. She tucked the tickets carefully back into her handbag, wondering if she ought to tidy the place up a bit before Cam came back. His side of the bed was cluttered with books and bits of paper. An odd sock lay half hidden under the bed and the wire for his iPhone adapter snaked out from behind the bedside cabinet. She had begun to pick things up, a desultory attempt at making the place a little smarter, when she saw it.

The mobile phone was a cheap red thing, not like the expensive white iPhone her boyfriend carried everywhere. She had joked that he had to be surgically removed from it; he was always checking for messages, sending texts or googling something or other. Turning the mobile over, the girl was surprised to see a small sticker on the back placed neatly over the battery compartment. And on it, in red ink, the number 6. Did this belong to Cam? Or had someone left it here? She bit her lip, imagining another woman here in her flat. He wouldn't ... would he?

Several times lately she had woken to hear him muttering in his sleep, a restlessness that he had laughed off as bad dreams. But what if he had been cheating on her and these nocturnal ramblings were the result of a guilty conscience?

There was one way of finding out, wasn't there?

A few minutes later Gayle replaced the mobile phone where she had found it beneath the pile of papers, no wiser as to the owner of the device, knowing only that there were four other numbers listed under the headings 1, 3, 4 and 5.

'Something to do with uni,' she said aloud, not really believing her own hollow-sounding words, but refusing to contemplate any alternative that might have to do with Cameron Gregson seeing four other women. And trying to suppress the idea that she might only be number two in his life.

CHAPTER FORTY-SEVEN

Lorimer sat opposite the young Nigerian girl, watching as she turned the box of sweets over and over in her hands.

'They're for you.' He smiled. 'A present.'

She looked at him warily, then laid the box on her knees, still unopened.

'Thank you,' she said.

'You like sweets?'

She looked away then and murmured something that he did not catch.

'Leila's never been given a present like this before without having to give something in return,' the psychiatrist explained.

Lorimer nodded, saddened that his gesture might have been misinterpreted. And yet in a way, Dr Jones was right. He did want something from this young girl, though it was unlike any of the sexual favours that she had been forced to yield to a host of men willing to pay for them.

'I was hoping you could tell me things that will help me to find a lost girl,' he began, leaning forward so that he was not towering over her. 'Her name is Asa and we are anxious for her safety,' he continued, watching as Leila turned her large liquid eyes on him, eyes that were wary still.

'I do not know anyone called Asa,' she replied at last.

'She is Nigerian, like you,' Lorimer told her. 'And she has been badly treated by some bad men. We have caught two of them and they are in prison.'

The girl sat up at that, her expression less fearful.

'These are pictures of the men,' Lorimer added, taking the photographs of Abezola Boro and Odunlami Okonjo from his pocketbook and laying them on top of the box of sweets.

Leila's recoil was instant and the photographs dropped to the floor as she let out an eerie wail of anguish.

'It's all right,' the psychiatrist soothed. 'Mr Lorimer here has put them in prison. They can't hurt you any more.'

'Are there any other men with tattoos like this, Leila?' the detective superintendent asked, taking out a photograph of McAlpin.

The girl shook her dark head and Lorimer could see that both hands were clutched around the box of sweets, not because she wanted the gift but rather for something to hold on to in her anxiety.

'Was that the man who hurt you, Leila?' Dr Jones asked, putting a kindly hand on the girl's arm.

A nod of the head was answer enough.

'Where did she come from?' Lorimer turned to ask the psychiatrist quietly.

'She was found by a *Big Issue* seller wandering around the streets one night,' Dr Jones told him. 'She was brought to me by the man and his lady friend,' the grey-haired woman added.

'Here?' Lorimer frowned, puzzled.

'To my home,' Dr Jones said shortly. 'These people happen to be patients of mine,' she continued. 'I don't wish to give you their names,' she added with a thin smile.

'Patient confidentiality,' Lorimer agreed. 'That's okay.' He

315

turned to the girl once again. 'Leila, can I tell you how you might be able to help us find this girl?'

'I don't know anyone called Asa,' Leila said again. 'But I did have another friend. She was called Celia.' She looked hopefully from Dr Jones to the tall man, who was bending down to meet her gaze. 'They gave her a tattoo. The one you showed me,' she said, turning to the psychiatrist. 'Do you know where she is?'

Rosie clicked CLOSE and the report on the girl disappeared into the ether. Was she ever to have closure on this case? The tiny form that had been taken from the dead girl's womb had saddened her more than she had expected. To have been carrying another human life only to have her own snuffed out so cruelly made the whole thing much worse. And yet what sort of life could a baby like that have enjoyed? The mother entrapped in a life of prostitution, the father imprisoned somewhere ... Rosie sighed. Lorimer would tell her about it some day. He had promised that at least. For now she had to leave the victim's body where it lay in its refrigerated cabinet. She had already attached a label with the name Celia, the only name they had for the dead girl; her unborn child would remain forever nameless.

The meeting with Dr Jones and the Nigerian girl had given Lorimer much to think about, not least the fact that Leila was to be deported back to Nigeria within the next ten days, something that had raised the young girl's spirits, according to the psychiatrist. There had been no means of contacting family members: the village where Leila came from was remote and without the modern means of communication that Westerners took for granted. However, a member of the British consulate had undertaken to meet the girl and arrange for her transportation back home.

The detective inspector closed his eyes tightly, resting his head against clasped hands. There were too many things vying for his attention right now. Asa, Foxy, Drummond's latest missive about the Glasgow cell ... For a moment he found himself wondering what life would have been like had he followed his original dream of becoming an art historian. Would he have liked the life of academia? Or would that too have brought the stresses and strains he was feeling right now?

Recently he had addressed Rosie's students at one of the weekly meetings that comprised the course in forensic medical science. 'I've got the best job in the world,' he'd told them towards the end of his lecture, after outlining some of the more celebrated cases where he had been senior investigating officer. And it was true. Though the case that demanded most of his attention right now was one that would never reach the ears of any of those students.

Both Okonjo and Boro had denied any knowledge of a man called Robert Bruce Petrie, but Drummond persisted in his belief that Petrie and McAlpin were the men behind the plot. And it was Detective Superintendent Lorimer's task to hunt them down before the date of the opening of the Commonwealth Games, a date that was edging closer with every passing day.

It was now midsummer, June soon drawing to a close. Next week Maggie would be on holiday from school and then the countdown to the Games would gather momentum.

The twenty-third of July was a date etched on the detective superintendent's brain. He had just over a month to track down the members of this terrorist group and take them into custody. Finding McAlpin's nest had been almost too easy, and he wondered just where the big bearded man had gone in the wake of the Nigerians' arrests. Would that have scared them off? Would they have abandoned their deadly scheme? Or had they cast McAlpin adrift and changed tack somehow?

Alistair Wilson was in charge of the Gilmartin case and Lorimer knew that he had to stop himself thinking about the flame-haired woman and the way she had beguiled him so long ago. *And* the way Maggie still looked sideways at him as if trying to read his thoughts. There had been a distinct coolness from his wife lately that gnawed at the edges of his conscience, something he would have to put right when he had the time.

There were officers combing the city for Asa and Swanson, every hotel and boarding house being looked into as the tireless search went on. For a moment Lorimer wished that he could be one of those foot soldiers again, a copper like young Kirsty Wilson, not a senior officer who had to delegate so much to others.

Rooting out the terrorists was one thing that he could not delegate, however. The man from MI6 had made that very clear indeed.

'Not go to Mull?' Maggie put down the salad bowl that she had been drying and looked at her husband. 'Oh.'

A muscle twitched in Lorimer's jaw. It had been another long day, and breaking the news about cancelling their holiday seemed insignificant against the dangers lurking within the city.

'It's difficult,' he told her. 'To do with the Commonwealth Games.'

'Something you can't tell me?' Maggie gave a wintry smile. 'Security stuff?'

Lorimer sighed. 'One day I might be able to,' he said at last. 'Oh Mags, come here.' He buried his face in her shoulder as she stepped into his arms. 'You must get sick of my job at times.' There was no reply, just a tightening of her grasp around his waist, reminding Lorimer that he was one of the lucky ones to have such an understanding wife.

'All off,' the big man grunted, glaring at the reflection of the man in the mirror.

The tattoo artist nodded. The man seated before him, a hasty towel wrapped around his neck, was the boss and anything he demanded had to be satisfied. Harry Temperland picked up the thin-bladed scissors and began to snip, his eyes trained on the face of the owner of the tattoo studio rather than the locks of red-gold hair that were falling to the floor at his feet.

McAlpin would have preferred to flee the city, knowing that he was a wanted man, but he had decided instead to call in favours from those who owed him big time, Temperland included. The ageing hippy had been lucky to keep this place on, his gift as an artist his one saving grace. The Celtic designs adorning McAlpin's body were proof enough of the man's consummate skills.

McAlpin had turned up last night on Worsley's doorstep, the older man's face turning as white as his hair as he'd bundled his friend inside.

'You know they've deselected you?' he had said as McAlpin had headed into the main lounge, one hand on the blind cord to shut out any prying eyes.

A grunt was all the big man had been able to muster as way of reply.

'Want a drink?' Worsley had already opened a cocktail cabinet full of bottles and lifted out a bottle of Glengoyne. 'Whisky?'

McAlpin's glare and nod as he'd slumped into the squashy arm-chair were answer enough.

'That young guy, Number Six, he's been given your job with the Aussies,' Worsley had told him as he'd poured generous measures into two plain glass tumblers. 'Straight or with water?' he'd asked.

'Wee drop water,' McAlpin had said shortly, remembering how his eyes had followed the old man as he'd disappeared into the adjacent kitchen to fill a little brown jug.

'Say when,' Worsley had murmured, handing the big man his glass and carefully pouring a trickle of water into it.

'Nuff!' McAlpin had exclaimed, taking the glass and downing the dram in one greedy gulp.

'Another?'

'Just bring me the bottle,' he'd told him.

Now, as he watched the hair being shorn from his head, then the foam applied to his beard, McAlpin wondered if Worsley would be as good as his word. He had promised to find the best forger in the East End, someone who would take a new photo and make it look old, give the big man a new identity. It was just a pity about the tattoos, Worsley had said, as the Glengoyne was emptied for the last time; looking at his heavily tattooed arms in the mirror, Kenneth Gordon McAlpin knew he was going to be hard pushed to conceal these intricate blue and green patterns from sight.

'Goes without saying I've never been here,' he said, catching Temperland's eye.

'Sure, boss.' Harry Temperland nodded, the razor in one hand. 'Never saw you today or any other day,' he agreed as the blade cut through the first springy curls of the big man's beard.

CHAPTER FORTY-EIGHT

Had anyone noticed the two men walking by the pond in Queen's Park, they might have been forgiven for assuming that they were Mormons discussing their next missionary visit. Both men were dressed smartly in suits and ties, document cases tucked under their arms, but a closer look would have shown their expressions to be less joyous than the perpetual smiles fixed to the faces of those latter-day saints.

'It's serious,' Petrie told the tall, thin man walking by his side, a man known only to the rest of the group as Number Three. 'That bloody detective's determined to ferret us out.'

'We could call it off,' his companion suggested.

'Never!' Petrie wheeled around, catching the man's sleeve. 'I don't believe you really mean that, Frank,' he said.

Frank Petrie made a face. He had been recruited by his cousin a long time ago, perhaps even as a child, listening to Robbie's fervent stories about Scottish heroes and how they had been deprived of all their land by these foreign incomers. Now the plans they had made to take back what belonged to them seemed to be unravelling and Frank was beginning to wonder if they should admit defeat before the police and security services closed a net around them.

'Maybe—'

'Maybe I should have left you to rot in that stinking jail instead of spending thousands on the best lawyer money could buy!'

The thin man shrugged his shoulders and walked slowly on. It always ended with the same old argument. Robbie had saved him from that hellish stretch. And he owed him. It was as simple as that.

'There's something we can do to make it all right,' Robbie said, catching up with the taller man and flinging an arm over his shoulder.

'Oh aye? What's that?'

Petrie's eyes glittered with the fanatical gleam that the other men in the cell had grown to recognise.

'Get rid of Lorimer,' he said simply.

The telephone rang in Lorimer's office and he picked it up, giving his name as usual. It was a normal enough call, one from the Stirling office, a routine call about the initial explosion.

There it was again. Faint but just discernible, a tiny noise on the line when the officer paused for breath.

Had it been there before that engineer's visit? Lorimer thought hard about it. No, he didn't think so. Should he be concerned?

Since Drummond's arrival into his life, the detective superintendent had noticed how he had begun to question every little detail in a case; it seemed natural that having to work with the man from MI6 had heightened his suspicious nature. Should he make enquiries into these noises? Was someone infiltrating his telephone extension? He sat back for a moment, steepling his fingers as he considered what to do. Would their internal security people call him neurotic? He was under enough stress from these cases to make them believe that.

Then, thinking of Drummond and what he would advise, Lorimer took a sheet of paper and began to write a note, not trusting either to email or telephone in delivering his message.

He looked at his shoes, then gave them one more rub with the cloth, nodding in satisfaction at the shine on the leather. Everything mattered, he told himself. Looking smart had been dinned into him from childhood by his father, a man who had made a success of bending the rules while appearing to be perfect in so many other ways. Malcolm Black had inherited the old man's name and dark good looks, as well as his knack of making money from other people's ignorance. Nobody had ever caught the police constable who took backhanders from the shadier folk who passed his front door. Had any whiff of suspicion come to rest on him, it would have been treated with derision: *not Malcolm Black!*

The younger Malcolm looked at the photograph of his father that sat in pride of place on the sideboard. Smiling down on him, the man in full Highland dress was still capable of making his son feel the sense of pride that had been part of their shared heritage.

'"Royal is my race",' he'd often said, quoting the MacGregor motto before reminding the young boy of his duties. 'We need to take it back again, son,' he'd told him countless times, going over that dreadful time when the foreign incomers had stripped the clan of every vestige of decency. These English king's men had branded their women, stripped them naked and whipped them through the streets, taken away the children to be sold into slavery, executed the men. And even after these atrocities had stopped, the remnant of the clan had been persecuted by the denial of their human rights. It was not only their names that had been outlawed. They were forbidden to meet in groups of more than two persons, and there was no giving food, water or shelter to a MacGregor for fear of reprisals. Even the Church was ordered to shut them out, denying the clan the holy sacraments of baptism, marriage, Holy Communion and the last rites. 'We were like rats,' his father had told him fiercely, 'hunted down by dogs and bounty-hunters whose humanity had disappeared in the lust for the king's gold.'

Malcolm Black stood up and brushed invisible flecks from his well-pressed trousers. He was a trusted employee of Folkfirst Securities, a firm whose reputation had earned them several big contracts in recent years, including Police Scotland and the 2014 Commonwealth Games. That their duties included updating telephone services had been most fortuitous.

It was during a conference on security that he had encountered the man whose identity badge had borne the name John MacGregor. Meeting the man whose vision held the key to the restoration of the MacGregor lands and fortunes had been a pivotal point in Black's life. And given his own extensive knowledge of security systems, he had found it possible after much searching to locate the leader's true identity. Not John MacGregor, but Robert Bruce Petrie, a man of wealth and privilege who had recruited several like-minded men to his cause. Petrie paid them well, but for Black the reward was not the money being amassed in his bank account but the thought of a Scotland freed from the tyrannies of its absentee landlords. Once the bomb had exploded there would be a sense of outrage from the public, and it was their aim to turn that outrage against their foreign masters and rally good honest Scots to the cause. To others the Proscription might be ancient history, but to Malcolm Black it was as if the last four hundred years had nourished resentment in every one of his ancestors, culminating in his own fierce desire for change. *Wait for the referendum*, some might have told him. But the time for waiting was over as far as he was concerned. The time for action was now.

Petrie had insisted that getting rid of Detective Superintendent Lorimer was of paramount importance, and Black smiled as he recalled how his own part in that was being played out. They had infiltrated the heart of the man's working environment, although bugging the offices in Stewart Street had taken months of painstaking work, Black posing as a telecommunications engineer on several occasions. Now it was up to him to reach into Lorimer's domestic life too. Like most policemen, Lorimer was aware of the need for a home alarm, and today Mr Black from Folkfirst Securities would be at his property on Glasgow's Southside to check that everything was in working order. By the time he left, there would be eyes and ears secreted in the Lorimers' house, devices planted to help them bring down one of the people who seemed to stand in the way of their success.

CHAPTER FORTY-NINE

*H*ide in full sight, Worsley had suggested, and McAlpin had nodded his grudging agreement. No one would be looking for a short-haired, clean-shaven man whose shirtsleeves and double cuffs hid his snaking tattoos, the former weightlifter told himself. He'd hail a taxi in Gordon Street outside Glasgow Central Station, he decided, crossing the road along with other pedestrians. A quick trip to that place in Dennistoun should help pick up Shereen and Asa's trail. He'd find the pair of them, and when he did, there would be two less bitches on the loose to make trouble for him.

McAlpin sat in the back of the cab, silently looking out at the city he knew like the back of his pale, freckled hand. George Square was awash with banners and flags now, the melee of tourists everywhere adding to the growing excitement of the approaching Games. They were still on for 23 July, Worsley had told him. And it gave the big man looking out at the grand City Chambers no little satisfaction to imagine the shock and horror that would follow the explosion out at Parkhead. Pity for the footie fans, of course, but some insurance company would take care of that little problem, he thought as the cab's meter ticked on.

In minutes McAlpin was thrusting some notes into the cabby's hand and striding away towards the close mouth of the tenement building where the moneylender lived.

He listened for a reply from the insistent buzzer, stepping back a little to catch a glimpse of the twitching curtain high above the street before a familiar thickly accented voice asked, 'Who is it?'

'It's me, Stefan. You know fine who I am,' McAlpin growled. 'Probably smelt me coming, you old bugger.'

He heard the chuckle, then the door was released and McAlpin stepped into the gloom of the close and headed swiftly up the stairs to the top of the building.

It was the grandson who waited at the open door, and McAlpin thrust past him, deliberately knocking the boy's skinny shoulder, making him gasp.

'Right, Stefan, where are they?' McAlpin grabbed the old man by his arms and lifted him bodily from the chair where he had been sitting in front of the television.

Stefan Kovary opened his mouth to scream, his gold front tooth gleaming in the light, but no sound came, the breath knocked out of him as he was slammed against a wall.

'Where are they?' McAlpin repeated, his hands around the old man's throat. 'Swanson and the girl. They must have come to you for money!'

He released the moneylender long enough for the old man to choke out a reply.

'She came, yes, she did.' He nodded, eyes bulging as he saw the big man's hands looming over him. He would shake him like a dog shakes a rat before it kills, and the Hungarian knew this, blind terror making him stutter out the words. 'J-just the fat woman, n-nobody else.'

McAlpin let him go and the old Hungarian slumped to the floor.

'How much did you give her?'

'Three hundred, no more than that, I swear!' Stefan squeaked, eyes darting to the open doorway, but there was no slim figure hovering there to effect his rescue, his grandson having made himself scarce.

'Address?'

'She said she was staying at your place,' Stefan whined in an injured tone that was soon drowned out in a stream of invective from the red-haired man towering above him.

'What about her first payment?'

'Tomorrow,' Stefan replied quickly.

Their eyes met, and in that moment it was clear to Stefan Kovary that he would never recover the roll of notes that he had lent to the Jamaican woman. If McAlpin was seeking her, she would know better than to turn up here.

And as he dropped his gaze, the Hungarian was certain of one thing more: the big man whose facial appearance had changed so dramatically was not only desperate to find these women but was also scared for his own life.

'You never saw me here,' McAlpin growled, reaching out a hand to raise the old man to his feet.

'No worries, no worries,' Kovary agreed, relief that he was still alive making him prattle on. 'Never saw you in my life, never did any business with you.'

'Make sure you keep it that way,' McAlpin told him, giving the old man a final push that sent him back into the armchair. 'Healthier if you do,' he added, before striding out of the flat and slamming the door behind him.

'Grandfather?' a timid voice enquired. 'Are you all right?'

'Get away,' Kovary spat at him. 'Follow that *fattyú* wherever he goes and let me know. Understand? Nobody comes in here and treats us like that,' he added, spittle coming from his mouth as gnarled fingers felt the place on his throat where the big man had grabbed him. 'Nobody!'

'You need to get that taken off,' Shereen told the girl, looking at the angry red rash that was seeping from under the plaster. 'Cut off. Snip, snip,' she added, making scissors of her fingers and cutting motions all along the cast.

'We'll go back to that hospital,' she said, then sat down on the edge of the bed next to Asa. 'Or maybe not.'

There would be people at the Royal Infirmary who might remember Asa and alert the authorities, take the girl away from her to some hellhole of a detention centre. Perhaps it would be better to cross the city and find a different hospital altogether. Claim that the girl was visiting and needed her plaster removed. Yes, that was a better idea.

Shereen searched in her handbag and counted out the money that remained. She had to be careful what she spent, and paying for a taxi to take them to the Southern General and back would eat into her meagre resources.

'Come on, Asa,' she decided. 'We're going out.'

The young girl's eyes lit up. Asa had learned several English words now, and the woman could see from her expression that *out* had a magical ring to it. *Out* meant away from the room where she could see Asa beginning to feel so confined and into the busy street where there were lots of people. Shereen had taught her more than new words, however, warning the girl that danger lurked everywhere, even in a crowded street.

Buchanan Street bus station was a magnet for druggies who needed a fix, their eyes watching each and every passer-by as they held out their polystyrene cups, begging for change. They had come to this pass somehow, demeaning themselves publicly before their fellow men, yet persisting in their task, the need to put fire into their veins overwhelming any sense of shame. Asa paused, the look in those pale blue eyes something she recognised. The boy sitting under the grey blanket was just like her, a waif, a stray desperate to be shown some kindness.

'Come on.' Shereen pulled the girl away. 'Haven't time to stop and stare,' she added.

Asa nodded, more at the gesture than the woman's words. In truth, the young girl wanted to stare at everything, including the strange sculpture of legs running under a clock face. Were those legs trying to escape from the inevitable progress of life? Or was it something to do with catching a bus? Asa had been on a bus back home, a trip to the medical centre in a nearby village. The authorities had sent the dilapidated vehicle to take them there and she could recall being hustled on board for the return journey. 'Come on, it's time to go,' the driver had shouted to the youngsters. Perhaps the legs were hurrying to catch a bus. Though to Asa's eyes they appeared to be running away from the bus station. It was very puzzling.

Once inside the glass-walled building, the Jamaican woman seemed to relax and took Asa's hand, guiding the girl into a small queue that was forming. The big red bus stood empty outside and the girl looked at Shereen then pointed at it.

'Yes.' The woman nodded. 'That's ours. Need to wait for the driver, and when it's time to go we'll get on.'

Asa caught a word or two, the *yes* and the nod sufficient to let her understand that they were to remain standing until a driver came to start up the bus that would take them to the hospital.

Afterwards, Asa wanted to talk to Shereen, to tell her how she had felt as the big bus trundled out of the square and into the city's traffic. *Like everyone else*, she might have said, in an effort to express the way she had envisaged herself, a passenger on that seat, face up against the window, looking out. There was a sort of kinship with the other people on the bus, her fellow travellers, as well as those on different buses stopping at the pavement to disgorge their human cargo and let more come on. For a time the girl was mesmerised by the flow of figures arriving and departing, people who chatted together or were silent, eyes fixed on their destinations. It was, she might have said, a peaceful interlude in her tempestuous young life, that bus journey from Glasgow's busy heart out to the district of Govan.

The voices around her were like a song, the shapes of the words a joyous wave of camaraderie, the accents rising and falling in a rhythm that reminded her of home. And occasionally those words made sense. The old women directly in front of her spoke about the hospital; were they going there too? Asa's glance fell on them from time to time: one with dyed black hair and many wrinkles on her orange skin, the other a bleached blonde whose ponytail allowed the girl to see the large silver hoops dangling from her earlobes and the smudges of mascara around her watery blue eyes. And when Shereen nudged her to stand up, the bus slowing to a halt, the two women did indeed shuffle out from the aisle and into the warm day, their feet also taking them to the entrance where a huge sign proclaimed their arrival at the Southern General Hospital.

What the Nigerian girl did not see was the broad-shouldered man, face half hidden by a baseball cap, skulking along the city streets, hands in his pockets.

Kenneth Gordon McAlpin (or simply Kenneth Gordon, as the

passport in his pocket now read) had alighted from the taxi and was now heading up Renfield Street as a line of buses came to a halt at the traffic lights. His eyes scanned the street for any dark face in the crowd. The anger that had risen against the Hungarian had not yet abated and McAlpin clenched his fists tightly, imagining how it would feel to grip the girl around her skinny throat till she choked.

It was a moment he would never forget. He blinked, hands falling loosely to his sides as he saw her. They might have passed one another by had he been slouching along, eyes to the ground. It was, he told himself, a miracle, seeing the girl's dark face gazing out, blithely unaware of his presence.

In that moment all of the big man's senses seemed to be heightened: the fresh breeze touching his naked chin, the sound of the bus as it drove away, the smell of its exhaust fumes lingering.

As long as Asa was blithely unaware of how easily her tormentor could have jumped on to that bus and grabbed her, he had a chance to do just that. But here in this busy city centre, with cameras tracking his every move, that was not such a great idea. If only he hadn't had to ditch the van ...

The orange lights of an approaching cab were like a beacon of hope to the big man, and in moments he was seated once again in the back of a black taxi, its destination as yet unknown.

CHAPTER FIFTY

'Last one for the day, Mrs Lorimer.' The man in the navy rain jacket smiled cheerfully at Maggie as she signed the two spaces on the form headed Folkfirst Securities.

'Glad you were able to be in at this time of the day. Not bad being a school teacher in this weather,' he continued, nodding towards the back door that was lying open to let in the afternoon sun.

'No,' Maggie murmured. Had she mentioned being a teacher? She hadn't thought so, but perhaps the engineer remembered her from a previous visit, though she could not recall his face. Malcolm Black was a handsome young fellow, well groomed and with just the right amount of charm to make a tedious visit from the alarm company that little bit more pleasurable.

'Nice to have the long holidays to look forward to,' Black continued. 'The wife's a primary teacher. Can't wait to get away to Spain for our two weeks,' he lied. There was no Mrs Black, though for working purposes he wore a wedding ring. It made the married ladies feel safer, he had joked to his colleagues. The comment about Spain was half true, though, a package holiday having been planned to coincide with the date of the opening ceremony so that the man known to some as Number Five would be free and clear when the mayhem began.

As she shut the front door, Maggie could hear the engineer whistling as he walked towards his bright blue van, but the sound that gave a lift to her spirits was one of triumph for the man who had so recently placed bugging devices inside the detective superintendent's home.

Getting rid of Lorimer was a priority, but it would be easy now that they could track his movements. *Make it look like an accident*, Petrie had told them. And as he drove away from the quiet cul-de-sac, Black gave no thought to the woman he had just left, nor to the fact that he was planning to make her a widow.

Marlene sat in the café, one foot tapping relentlessly against the metal stem of the table. She was all out of gear and needed a fix so badly that her mind was beginning to play tricks on her. The boss had been in and out again, but was it him? Or someone who just reminded her of McAlpin? The man she had seen had no thick beard or long hair straggling over his collar. It *was* him, though, she knew it was, just as she was certain that the man who had been talking to him that day was the dead man in the photograph.

Twenty thousand pounds. She licked her lips as though she could already taste the drugs she craved. One phone call. That was all she needed to make. And a policeman she needed to talk to. *Lorimer*, that was the name she had overheard when the boss had been speaking to Harry. It was a name she knew. He'd got a result after those murders around Blythswood Square, hadn't he? Murders of girls who'd been Marlene's friends. Aye, that was who she'd call, Marlene thought as her foot suddenly stopped jiggling in mid air.

'This caller says she wants to talk to Lorimer,' the liaison officer in the CID room said, holding the telephone handset away from her ear.

'It's Alistair Wilson who's SIO on the case,' DC Lennox replied. 'Why does she want Lorimer?'

'Says she knows him.'

'Okay.' Lennox shrugged. 'Put her through to his office. But record every word. You know the routine, right?'

The woman nodded. They'd been inundated with stupid calls after the latest press release had mentioned the amount of that reward. Not one had been worthwhile, though they had all been investigated, taking up more of the force's precious resources. This agitated woman was different, though. She knew Lorimer from somewhere, needed to speak to him. They would record her call, try to put a trace on it if possible and take it from there.

In his office along the corridor, the detective superintendent picked up the ringing telephone.

'Putting you through now, ma'am,' the liaison officer said.

'Lorimer.'

'I know about that dead man,' a woman's breathy voice told him. 'Charles Gilmartin. I seen him the day he was supposed to have died, didn't I?'

'Who am I speaking to?'

There was a lengthy pause during which Lorimer wondered if the line was about to be cut, and then, 'Marlene. Marlene McAdam,' she said. 'I was a friend of Tracey-Anne Geddes.'

'Ah.' Lorimer let the word stretch out as he remembered the murdered prostitute. 'What can I do for you, Marlene?'

''S what I can do for you, Mr Lorimer,' the woman said slyly. 'See, I know something. That twenty grand. That's right, innit?' she added.

'If anything you tell us leads to an arrest and a conviction ...'

'Look, I gotta go. Can you meet me?'

There was a note of urgency in the woman's voice now, as though something or someone had disturbed her.

Lorimer glanced at the clock. It was already past five in the afternoon and he still had calls to make. 'Six thirty? Where shall I see you?'

There was another pause as though the woman had not yet decided on a meeting place.

'Where they found Tracey-Anne, okay?'

'But ... ' Lorimer heard the click and frowned. Why would she have chosen a place with such macabre associations? The cobbled lanes that ran between the backs of office buildings had been the regular haunts of street workers once. He gave a sigh. It was not a place that he wanted to revisit, but at least it was broad daylight at this time of the year. Marlene McAdam would be waiting for him. With news about Charles Gilmartin, she had said. Meantime, there would be officers checking on the woman to see if there was anything in her own background that could give a clue as to what links she may have had with the impresario.

The security engineer removed his headphones and frowned. Who the hell was Marlene McAdam? And what, if anything, did she have to do with their cause?

He lifted the red mobile from his jacket pocket and pressed one of the keys. Petrie would know if she mattered or not, wouldn't he?

Minutes later, Malcolm Black nodded as he listened to the voice of their leader. McAlpin was on the run and this woman was one of his employees. Black had made it his business to know about each and every one of the group's members, even down to Number Two's human trafficking enterprise. But until now he had not made any link between McAlpin's shady business and

Charles Gilmartin, the man whose photograph had been in all the newspapers.

Still, it was too good an opportunity to miss, Petrie had told him. *Get Lorimer,* Black had been ordered. And even as he started up the engine of his van, Malcolm Black was forming an idea of just how he might dispose of the detective superintendent for good.

CHAPTER FIFTY-ONE

'We need to get away,' Shereen told her, swinging the girl's arm up and down.

Asa grinned as she held Shereen's hand. It had not been so bad after all. The nurses had all been nice and it hadn't taken much time for them to release her from the heavy plaster cast. Now her arm felt much better, lighter of course, though the muscles were still weak.

The sun was shining as they entered the supermarket, a pair of chrome barriers swinging open before them. *Food,* Shereen had told her, *something for the journey.* And Asa had understood. They were going away now, on another bus, Shereen had explained, her hands making the shapes of turning wheels. Far from Glasgow to another city where Shereen had friends who would look after her.

'Asa, that's right,' the receptionist said, consulting the case notes in front of her. 'Left here about ten minutes ago.' Every hospital in the city had been instructed to call the police should a Nigerian girl called Asa turn up, but it was the Southern General that she had chosen.

The receptionist glanced at the clock on the wall as the voice of the police officer asked her more questions.

'Well we've got CCTV cameras everywhere, so we can track where they went,' she replied.

A small smile of satisfaction appeared on the woman's face as she listened to the police officer from Stewart Street. It was a bit of a thrill being able to help trace a missing girl. The hospital receptionist couldn't wait till her late shift was over to drive home and tell her husband all about it.

'Think we've found Asa.' Kirsty Wilson stood at the doorway of Lorimer's office.

'Where?'

'Southern General. She had her plaster off and she was spotted with another woman leaving the hospital and going across the road into Lidl.'

'Well, what are you waiting for?'

'You want me to go and find her?' Kirsty gasped.

'Alert the Govan office. Tell them to send a squad car. And you and Lennox get over there as quick as you can.'

'I thought you would ... ?'

'Other fish to fry.' Lorimer grinned. 'Just bring them back safely. Okay?'

There was no point in taking the Lexus up into town and the evening was fine, so Lorimer set off from Stewart Street on foot, his mind still on the Nigerian girl and her Jamaican-born companion. By the time he returned to the division they might both be back, ready to speak to him, a thought that gave him a sense of relief. If these women could tell him more about McAlpin's trafficking schemes, then Glasgow could soon be well rid of the scourge that had been so rightly attacked by the press. That the Commonwealth Games should have been a catalyst for an increase in what was little more than sex slavery appalled the tall man who strode through the familiar streets. The city was full of people intent on having a good time; a group of Japanese tourists stood reading the menu outside one of the bistros near the Theatre Royal, the tables spilling on to the pavement all taken. Then, as Lorimer strode further uphill towards his destination, he saw a sleek gold-coloured coach, a crowd of passengers waiting patiently as the driver took more and yet more luggage from the cavernous hold. Glasgow was the place to be, he told himself. The Games were like a magnet drawing folk from every part of the globe, the fluttering banners welcoming the Commonwealth for what promised to be an exceptional occasion. But how many of the people he passed by were looking for something more, something illicit?

Lorimer's face hardened as he thought about Drummond's latest visit. It was rare that any communication came in the form of a telephone call, and never by electronic mail, he suddenly realised, pausing mid stride to check his watch. For once the sandy-haired man with the cultured voice had seemed troubled. The Nigerians knew nothing about McAlpin's involvement with the Games other than the fact that he sometimes attended meetings over in the Albion Street headquarters. Had they got it all wrong? Lorimer had suggested. Perhaps McAlpin wasn't part of the terrorist cell after all? He remembered how Drummond had shaken his head. No, he'd said, the intelligence was good; McAlpin was definitely one of the men they sought. His lucrative human trafficking was something entirely separate.

Blythswood Square Gardens were silent tonight, the gates shut fast against any possible intruders, and the detective superintendent walked swiftly by, hardly glancing at the starlings twittering in the treetops. It was now six twenty-seven and he had agreed to meet this woman, Marlene, at six thirty.

His feet took him across the road where so much had happened during that terrible case and into the mouth of the lane. Images from the past seemed to flicker and die as he stepped on to the cobbles.

She was waiting halfway along, past the huge dumper bins next to a shallow doorway. Slight and pale, Marlene McAdam had the look of all junkies, thin to the point of emaciation, hair dragged back from a face that was all angles like a Modigliani painting.

'Thanks for coming to see me.' Lorimer smiled as he drew closer, a friendly hand extended for her to shake.

'I needed to speak to you,' the woman said, licking her bloodless lips.

'Well here I am,' he said. 'Though it's not the sort of place I'd have chosen to meet,' he added, waving a hand around the place.

Marlene shrugged, her eyes darting from side to side as though afraid to meet the cool blue gaze that regarded her thoughtfully.

''S quiet, though, in't it?' She shrugged again. 'Didnae want tae come doon tae Stewart Street,' she added. 'Never know who's watching you.'

The woman glanced behind her, the reflex action revealing just how nervous she really was.

What was it Marlene McAdam wanted to tell him? And who was she afraid of?

She turned back, and her entire body seemed to freeze.

The sudden look of terror in her eyes was not directed at Lorimer, but beyond him.

He turned, hearing the sudden noise of the vehicle screaming towards them. Seeing its headlights as it careered along the narrow lane.

A glimpse of a man's face, covered by a scarf...

The woman screamed as Lorimer grabbed her round the waist,

two bodies locked together, thudding against the doorway, his head striking the edge of something hard and sharp.

The blue van caught his elbow a glancing blow as it sped past and Lorimer cried out in pain. Then, releasing the woman from his grip, he began to run after the mad driver who had almost mown them down, cursing as the vehicle turned a corner, missing the chance to see its number plate.

But it was too late: the van had screeched away past the end of the square and was gone.

Lorimer limped back along the lane, his eyes on the figure slumped against the wall, one hand fumbling for his mobile to put out a call for assistance.

'Are you all right?' He looked at her ashen face, the eyes staring at him.

'He tried to kill us!' the woman whispered, her voice hoarse with shock.

It was an automatic reflex to turn and look at the lane where moments before a bright blue van had been deliberately driven at him. Or, he wondered, had it been aiming for the woman who was now whimpering by his side?

'Come on,' he said, one arm around her thin shoulders, leading her out of the lane. 'I think we both need a drink.'

Let others find the crazy driver, he thought, though the description he had given the officer on the other end of the line was minimal and there was little chance of locating him now. What he needed were answers to why on earth it had happened, and he hoped that Marlene McAdam would be able to provide them.

Asa pointed at the packs of ham in the chiller cabinet and turned to Shereen.

'Okay, some of those too, we can make up sandwiches,' she said, smiling at the girl as they made their way slowly along the supermarket aisle, the older woman pushing a trolley that contained a few essentials for their journey.

'Don't turn around, keep walking,' a familiar voice behind her said, the sound making her freeze with horror. She felt the point of a knife against her back, pressing into her flesh, and knew a moment of despair.

How had he found them? Her thoughts whirled as she tried to think what she must have done wrong.

'Just keep walking,' the big man repeated. 'Right to the exit, okay? Leave the trolley here.' Another jab made her want to cry out, Asa's terrified eyes boring into her own.

Shereen let go of the shopping and stumbled along the last aisle, past the checkout towards the automatic doors.

'Take the girl's hand ... that's good, no fuss now.' The man's voice was low and menacing as Shereen moved slowly along. It was like a nightmare in which her feet seemed unable to progress, fear turning her to stone.

She looked around in bewilderment. Why did nobody seem to notice what was happening to them? The girl at the checkout was putting items from the conveyor belt into a waiting trolley, the other shoppers intent on packing their goods into bags and boxes on a shelf to her right, oblivious to the drama being enacted under their very noses.

The door opened with a whoosh, then they were out on the concrete where the trolleys were stacked. A big black cab rolled up, its side door sliding open, a gaping maw intent on swallowing them whole.

Then, before the big man could push her further, Shereen saw the policewoman coming across the car park.

'Run, Asa, run!' she screamed, letting go of the girl's hand and giving her a shove.

'Get in!'

Shereen felt his hands on her, lifting her bodily into the taxi, then she fell to the floor as the vehicle began to gather speed, the door sliding shut beside them. Her head hurt where she had fallen, but her beating heart felt something other than fear.

Asa had escaped!

Shereen knew a final moment of triumph even as the foot pressed her flailing arm on to the floor of the cab.

She'd saved the girl from this monster.

Above her she saw the fire in the man's eyes.

And his terrible rage as his hand rose above her.

Police Constable Kirsty Wilson's bulky young frame was not built for speed, and she was no match for the African girl, who was flying across Govan Road, heedless of the traffic around her squealing to a halt. Too many of Mum's cakes, she thought to herself as she panted behind the fleeing figure, the taller shape of DC Lennox overtaking her. He'd get the girl. Surely he would?

Asa jumped on to the island of concrete that was raised up from the road.

All around her horns were blaring, lights flashing as she stood mesmerised by the noise and the nearness of the cars and lorries.

The girl looked back across the road to the car park outside the shop, but Shereen had gone. And so had the man. The one who had hurt her and kept her in that terrible place.

She raised her head to the unforgiving sky, seeing the clouds moving along the heavens. Then, putting her hands to her mouth, she uttered the wailing, ululating cry that had sounded out death and despair all down the countless ages.

Kirsty watched as the young detective wrapped his jacket around the girl's shoulders and led her through the halted traffic. She was so little, not more than a child, she realised, looking at the Nigerian girl as she came closer.

'Asa?'

The girl turned huge black eyes to Kirsty, and the policewoman could see that they were full of tears.

'It's okay, Asa, you're safe now,' she soothed, patting the girl's arm as they led her to the waiting car.

'*Safe?*' Asa whispered, looking at Kirsty in amazement. Then, swaying for a moment as though she might faint, the Nigerian girl turned her face against Lennox's shoulder and began to sob.

CHAPTER FIFTY-TWO

The Universal Bar was probably not the best choice, dark and gloomy inside in contrast to the brightness of the evening outside, but it was the nearest place that Lorimer could think of and their passage down Sauchiehall Lane had kept them away from any prying eyes.

'Feeling better?'

The woman nodded, her fingers clutching the glass of whisky that Lorimer had ordered. *Doubles*, he'd demanded of the barman, noticing how his own hands shook a little as he drew out his wallet.

'Know who that was, by any chance?' He asked the question softly, though in truth their words were muffled by the beat from a rap number coming from overhead speakers.

She shook her head, eyes fixed on his own in a manner that let him believe that Marlene was telling him the truth. He'd seen liars enough to know the difference. Any flicker from those pale eyes or a look to one side might have made him doubt her.

'Okay, let's talk about Charles Gilmartin, shall we?'

Was it his imagination, or was there a sudden lessening of tension in those bony shoulders?

'I seen him.' Marlene leaned in closer so that he caught a whiff of her perfume, something sharp and sweet. 'I seen him come intae the studio where I work. Skin Art,' she added.

'When was this?' Lorimer asked quietly.

'Same day he's meant tae have carked it,' she told him. 'See that reward ...?' Her face looked up to his, naked hope in her eyes.

'Let's come to that a bit later,' Lorimer said. 'If what you tell me leads to an arrest and a conviction, then you will be given the sum that was mentioned. No tax to pay, either.'

He smiled thinly as she gave a sigh and drank off the rest of her whisky.

'Right, the man comes intae the studio and our Harry – that's my boss, by the way – he tells me tae keep oot o' the way. Your man Gilmartin goes intae the back room where the big man's waiting. The owner of the place,' Marlene explained, seeing the frown appear between the policeman's eyes. 'Mr McAlpin.'

Lorimer clutched his glass a little tighter, swallowing hard, willing himself not to react to the name.

'How long did they spend in that room, Marlene?'

'Oh, I cannae right remember ... em, let's see. Ah wis doin' a butterfly fur a lassie. Wan mair tae join the ithers oan her back, like. Takes more'n half an hour for that kindae thing. Maybe nearer fifty minutes. Anyway, I wis still at the last wee bit when they baith came oot. McAlpin wis shakin' the man's hand like he wis richt please aboot somethin'.'

Lorimer nodded, trying to imagine the impresario in the run-down tattoo studio by the Clyde. *It isn't like Terry's,* he remembered Kirsty telling him. Stuart Wrigley's place was a palace compared to that other dump, the girl had said.

'And did you hear them say anything?'

Marlene frowned. 'Had the machine on, remember, no' sae

easy tae overhear stuff. But I did hear the older man telling McAlpin something before he went out the door.'

There was a pause as the woman seemed to be trying to collect her thoughts.

'*They'll come in with our lot.* Aye, that's whit he said.'

'And did you know what that meant?'

Marlene looked crestfallen. 'Naw,' she said at last. 'Does that mean ah cannae have the reward?'

Lorimer laid a hand on top of the woman's skinny fingers.

'You may well have told me enough to help convict somebody,' he whispered. 'And that reward will be yours if it happens, I promise.

She gave him a tremulous smile. 'Oh, and by the way, there's something else,' she said, eyes glinting. 'Ah seen him since then. The boss man, ah mean, no the wan that got killed.'

'When was this?' Lorimer sat up a little straighter.

'Yesterday? Day before? Cannae mind. Sorry. Not always on the ball, my wee brain, is it?' She tapped the side of her head ruefully. 'Onywye, it's the big man, like ah says. He comes in tae see Harry late on wan efternoon.' She paused. 'Naw, wasnae yesterday. Day afore?' She shook her head and sighed.

'He goes intae the back shop, like, stays in fur aboot three quarters of an hour then comes oot again.' She grinned at Lorimer. ''N guess what? Harry's just shaved aff the hale o' Mr McAlpin's beard and given him a buzz cut, hasn't he? Had tae sweep up a' his curly hair aff the flair, didn't I?'

Lorimer sat back, taking in this new information, already mentally passing it on to the investigating officers who were out looking for the fugitive.

CHAPTER FIFTY-THREE

The boy looked around to see if there was anybody else on the patch of waste ground, but he was quite alone. The big black car sat slightly to one side, the ground sloping away under its wheels. It had a long open doorway like that minibus with sliding doors for wheelchairs he'd seen when old Mr Thomson along the street was taken away to the day centre. Only this was a kind of taxi, he saw as he drew nearer. And the driver was slumped across the steering wheel. Funny place to choose for a nap, the boy thought, the driver's still form emboldening him to creep forward for a closer look.

In a few moments the boy had tiptoed up to the door.

He peered in, shading his eyes with one hand against the setting sun streaming in from the west.

There was something on the floor. He squinted, his brain suggesting that someone had left a big bag of rags in the back. Whatever it was must be smelly for all these flies to be buzzing on top of it.

Then the boy spotted the shoe. And something else, something he didn't want to acknowledge.

He blinked, trying to clear his vision, but the thing was still there and wouldn't go away; a dark red puddle that glistened under the sun's rays.

He began to back away, a small whimpering sound coming from his throat.

Then he turned and ran across the beaten earth, screaming for his mammy, desperate to find someone, anyone who would take away the sight of all that blood.

'Shereen Swanson was knifed to death by person or persons unknown,' Lorimer told the assembled officers. 'The taxi driver, Richard Bryce, sustained one slash to his throat.' He looked around at each of them in turn. 'He would have died immediately. It was an injury inflicted by someone big and strong who knew how to slit another person's throat. Maybe someone ex-military.'

As he spoke, Lorimer had a vision of a big red-headed man, the one who had felled him to the ground in Cathkin. He himself might have been a victim that night, like the unfortunate taxi driver, had McAlpin not been in such a tearing hurry to escape.

The SOCOs called to the country park had taken traces from Lorimer's clothes. McAlpin might have escaped that night, but at least they had his DNA profile on record, something that might well prove a match with samples taken from the two victims of the taxi murders.

The detective superintendent's head was beginning to swim. Everywhere he went McAlpin seemed to emerge like some latter-day bogeyman. MI6 wanted to question him about being in a terrorist cell here in Glasgow. So far he had eluded them. That he was wanted for murder was in no doubt, the two young Nigerian girls lying in the mortuary having died because of his fiendish trafficking business. And now there was a link with Charles Gilmartin. It could only be to do with the influx of Africans into the country. Was that why Vivien had been so adamant that the theatre project was to stop? Did she know a lot more about this other business than she was willing to admit? And – Lorimer blinked against the throbbing pain in his head – was Charles Gilmartin's involvement with McAlpin the reason he was poisoned?

'Sir?'

A voice seemed to come from far away, and Lorimer felt arms supporting him as he was helped into a chair.

'Think you should go home, sir,' DI Grant said. 'He's maybe concussed,' she said, turning to the men and women who were now crowded around their senior officer. 'Who's got the doc's number?'

Maggie pulled the curtains, then glanced down at her husband's sleeping form. His face, even in repose, looked strained and there were deep lines etched between his eyebrows and creases beside his eyelids. Laughter lines, but when had he last laughed? She bit her lip. Ever since the night of that school reunion back in April, he had been working long hours. Some days they hardly spoke, Maggie already in bed by the time he returned home. It was little wonder that so many senior officers' marriages ended in failure, she thought, slipping into bed beside him. They were luckier than most, perhaps, without the added strain of children to accommodate into their busy lives. And she had her special friends, other women to spend an evening with at the theatre or a favourite author's book launch.

It was a pity about Mull, she thought with a sigh, but there was something going on behind the scenes of Glasgow 2014 that was so secret that she suspected there might be some sort of terrorist threat.

Maggie's mind went back to their last holiday. Hadn't it been cut short on the day before Bill had been due to return to work?

That explosion outside Drymen, she remembered, and her husband giving out a reassuring message to the media. Had that all been some sort of camouflage? And had Detective Superintendent Lorimer become involved in a highly secure investigation into something much more dangerous than the usual crimes washed up on Glasgow's shores?

Suddenly her eyes flew open. That security alarm man from Folkfirst! How had he known that Mrs Lorimer was a school teacher? Was he some sort of surveillance man under her husband's authority? Or – and a cold shiver went down Maggie's spine at the thought – had he visited this house for some more sinister reason?

'Mags?' Lorimer whispered. 'Are you awake, love?'

Maggie curled on to her side, snuggling her body against her husband's.

'Yes. How d'you feel?'

'Still a bit drowsy. But I'm okay. How about you?'

Maggie thought for a moment. 'Can I run something past you?'

'Fire away.'

'You know that alarm company, Folkfirst?'

'Yeah, we use them at work.'

'Well, someone came to test the system. Didn't know you'd asked them to ... '

Lorimer sat up, propping himself on his good elbow.

'I didn't.'

'Oh, but he said ... '

'When was this?' Lorimer was fully awake now.

'Yesterday. Just about teatime. Arrived in a blue van.'

'What sort of blue?'

'Bright blue. Rangers blue.'

'Any lettering on the side?'

'No, come to think of it . . .'

'Whereabouts did he go in the house?'

'Well, everywhere, I suppose. The doors are alarmed upstairs as well as downstairs . . .'

'And did he check the telephones?'

'I'm not sure.' Maggie frowned. 'But there was something funny,' she said slowly. 'He seemed to know that I was a teacher. But I hadn't said anything that might have made him—'

She stopped abruptly as Lorimer put his finger to his lips. She watched as he got out of bed and walked slowly towards the hall. Her curiosity fully aroused, she followed him and watched him unscrew part of the telephone handset. As he turned silently towards her, he held out his hand. There in the centre of his palm was a small metallic object. And as she met her husband's eyes, Maggie Lorimer knew exactly what that object must be.

'Drummond? Lorimer here. Listen, there's been a development. Someone tried to run me down this evening.'

'Are you okay? Did they injure you badly?'

'No, they didn't, thank God. Just got a bit of a sore head, that's all. But I think my home and office may be bugged.'

'What about this conversation?' Drummond's tone was sharp.

'No, it's okay. This mobile hasn't been out of my sight since you gave it to me. You'll have been told the latest news about McAlpin, yes?'

'Two knifed to death,' Drummond replied, and Lorimer could hear the grimness in the MI6 man's voice.

'Yes. I was working on that earlier tonight,' he said, mentally crossing his fingers and hoping that Drummond would not receive any intelligence about the fact that the detective superintendent had collapsed in the office.

'Right,' Drummond said crisply. 'Now here's what's going to happen ... '

Lorimer sat in the rocking chair nursing a large mug of cocoa, Maggie having flatly refused to allow him any more whisky.

'The doctor said it wouldn't be a good idea,' she'd protested when he'd picked up the bottle of Laphroaig.

Now he was waiting for two men to arrive, men who would bring their technical expertise to bear inside his home, clearing it of any devices that might have been planted by the men who had wanted to kill him.

Asa sat on the edge of the bed, staring at the door. It was locked, but that was to keep her safe, she'd been told. Had that word taken on a new meaning? the girl wondered, hearing the click as a key had turned to shut her inside. A young Nigerian woman, Jeanette, had stayed with her all evening, her gentle voice explaining in Yoruba that Asa was going to be taken to a place of safety. The police would want to speak to her tomorrow, but meantime Dr Jones would take care of her.

Was she going to a hospital? Asa had wanted to know, but a smile and a shake of the head had been all the reply Jeanette would give.

And Shereen? Asa had whispered the Jamaican woman's name, fearful of the answer.

Nobody had answered. Nobody had needed to. Asa could see the words in their eyes. Shereen was dead and she would never be enfolded into her warm bosom again.

CHAPTER FIFTY-FOUR

July 2014

'What's this?' Gayle held out the little red mobile, watching her boyfriend's face intently.

'Where did you get that?' Cameron snatched it from her, but not before he felt the angry flush warming his cheeks: the sign of a guilty conscience?

'Who are all these people? Numbers of your old girlfriends?' Her voice wavered even as he heard her efforts to sound flippant.

'Is that what you thought?' He burst out laughing and the sense of relief on his face made Gayle feel suddenly ashamed.

'Come here, you silly cow!' Cameron held out his arms and the young woman allowed herself to be enfolded into his embrace. 'Silly girl! It's nothing like that,' he murmured into her hair. 'Just something we're working on at the uni. Bit hush-hush, though, so I'm not allowed to discuss it.'

'Something political?'

'You could say,' Cameron agreed, looking at his reflection in the bedroom mirror as he held the girl closer. The sense of shock at her discovery was wearing off now and he congratulated himself on his ability to fabricate a ready story.

'Oh, I've got something to show you.' She extricated herself from his grasp and pulled an envelope from her handbag.

'Look! We got them! For both of us. Isn't it great!'

Cameron Gregson looked at the pair of tickets being waved in the air by the excited girl. He had been told that he was to accompany the two Australians to Parkhead, but the leader had been a bit vague about what was to happen afterwards.

He had a sudden vision of holding Gayle's hand as the bomb exploded, smoke obliterating the sight of all those people thronged around the stadium.

'Cam? Aren't you pleased?' Her voice sounded peeved.

'Course I am. Can hardly believe it,' he muttered. 'Well done you.'

And as he listened to his girlfriend's chatter about what she wanted to wear and what they would do afterwards, Cameron Gregson experienced a feeling that was like an icy hand closing around his heart.

The old man opened the door and staggered backwards as McAlpin thrust him aside.

'What're you doin' here? What the hell ...'

Worsley's mouth opened as he saw the bloodstained shirt under McAlpin's jacket.

'Need to get rid of this. Find some new clothes.'

'What if I pick up stuff at yours?'

'Don't be so bloody stupid!' McAlpin snarled. 'Place'll be crawling with coppers. Get out and buy me some things, okay? And use cash.'

'What's happened?' Worsley looked the big man up and down as he pulled off the shirt and flung it on to the floor.

'Never you mind. But I need to lie low for a while, so don't let anyone know you've got a lodger, hear what I'm saying?'

Worsley nodded. They had three weeks until the day when he detonated the bomb that would blow up Parkhead Stadium. It had been one of his more intricate jobs. The *sgian dubh* had been a stroke of genius, McAlpin had agreed. The old Aussie would never know that he was carrying in part of a device that would allow him to set off the bomb. It would be like a ticking clock, except there was no crude machinery within the heft of the dagger, only the smallest components, arranged carefully to match the design that was visible to any prying eyes.

But with the big man here in his home and a meeting maybe scheduled for tomorrow morning with the rest of the group, Rob Worsley began to wonder whether he would see his beautiful scheme come to fruition after all. McAlpin was a liability at the best of times. And now, with the evidence of blood on his hands, the ex-weightlifter could easily ruin everything they had planned.

'Sleepy?'

Maggie shook her head. Lorimer looked much better after a decent night's sleep, and although he had agreed to work from home, whatever had taken place here during the day had not sapped his strength.

'The bugs have all gone,' he told her with a grin. 'And that's all I'm saying for now, okay?'

She responded with a half-smile. There was still a feeling that her home had been violated just as effectively as if a burglar had come in and trashed the place. Maggie had an urge to spring-clean the whole house, to rid it of whatever presence had tainted it. She'd given a good description of Mr Black to the police officers and could only hope that he would be apprehended. But to what end? There had been no explanation given for their home being bugged and her husband remained as tight-lipped as ever.

Sitting back in the armchair, she picked up an unread newspaper and flicked through it, only stopping when she came to the page that included theatre reviews.

'Here, look at this,' she exclaimed, opening the paper wide and turning it so that Lorimer could see. 'It's that play we went to see, remember? The one in the West End that Charles Gilmartin was involved with.'

'Yes?' Lorimer was frowning. 'That was years ago, love. Can't even remember what it was about.'

Maggie took back the newspaper and sat for a few minutes scanning the column.

'"Crime drama revamped",' she read aloud. '"New look for old plot ..."'

She bent closer to the page, her mouth opening in a moment of astonishment, then looked up at her husband.

'What?'

'The play.' Maggie had put the paper down on her lap, and Lorimer saw the colour drain from her face.

'What's wrong?'

'It's what they said about the plot ...' Maggie whispered. 'It's ... oh God, she *could* have done it ...'

She handed over the paper wordlessly.

Lorimer looked at a black-and-white photograph of two well-known actors, and then at the critical review of the play. There was nothing there to produce the sort of shock his wife seemed to be experiencing. That was, until he reached a description of the crime and its risible plot.

The hackneyed plot device was only redeemed by the excellent acting from one of our best young actors ... he read. Then, as the article continued, he suddenly remembered the play from all those years before, and how he had scoffed at its weaknesses.

'"The hackneyed plot device"! Don't you remember?' urged Maggie. 'The murderer turned up the heating to change the supposed time of death!'

Lorimer swallowed hard, her words drilling into his brain.

'She could have done it,' Maggie repeated, looking straight into her husband's blue eyes. 'Ask Rosie.'

Lorimer sat stunned by the simplicity of the idea. Had Vivien Gilmartin really poisoned her own husband? Could she have committed the deed then turned up the heating in the flat so high that it obscured the time of death the doctor had given hours later?

Worst of all, had they been harbouring a murderer in their home?

CHAPTER FIFTY-FIVE

Rosie Fergusson stripped off her gloves and threw them into the waste bucket with a sigh. The wounds on the woman's body were extensive and the report she would now write up would be one that she would certainly keep from her sensitive husband, who was squeamish about that sort of thing. Solly had never been happy to look at a crime scene where brutality was in evidence, and this one would turn his stomach for certain. The taxi driver had been luckier in one respect: whoever had slit his throat (and the police seemed to have a good idea of the person they sought) had killed him instantly. Not so with the big Jamaican woman, despite the number of knife wounds to her abdomen and chest, though the one that had cut through the pericardium must have been fatal. She had put up some sort of fight, defence wounds showing on the inside of one of her arms. The other still bore the imprint of her attacker's boot.

Lorimer had called her last night, asking about the flat where the impresario's body had been found back in April. Yes, she had told him. It was possible. Why? Had they new evidence to show that someone had tampered with the heating? But the detective superintendent had been non-committal, changing the subject to Abby and asking how Solly's latest book was progressing. It was odd, Rosie thought. But then she was not always conversant with the details of every case they worked on together. She shrugged as she untied her apron. He would tell her in due course, she thought. Meantime, there was that report to write up and a husband and daughter waiting at home.

'We need to bring her in,' Lorimer told Alistair Wilson.

He saw his colleague nodding gravely. Wilson had listened as he'd related the conversation with Maggie the previous evening. The germ of what had been only an idea was growing into more of a certainty now that Lorimer was telling it to the man who was SIO in the investigation into Charles Gilmartin's murder.

'And there may be a motive that we could never have guessed,' Lorimer murmured, half to himself. 'We need to find out a lot more about that Nigerian theatre company and just how Charles and Vivien had planned on bringing them over to the UK.'

'Right,' Wilson agreed, rising from his chair. 'I'll make that a priority. And put out an international call for help in finding Mrs Gilmartin.'

'And, when we bring her in, I'd like to be the one to interview her.' Lorimer said. Wilson would be there, all right, as SIO, but there were questions his superior officer needed to ask.

The other man nodded. 'See what I can do,' he said.

Once Wilson had left the room, Lorimer sat staring at the wall, though it was not the array of maps and charts he could see, but the image of a fox-haired woman with green eyes smiling up at him.

'Plans have changed,' Petrie told them.

'You're cancelling the whole thing?' Worsley tutted his disapproval.

'On the contrary. We go ahead as originally intended. And eliminate Number Six.'

'May as well call him Gregson,' Malcolm Black growled. 'Everyone else knows his name now.'

'You're the reason for our change of plan!' Petrie stormed at him. 'You were supposed to take care of that detective, and now, not only have you failed to eliminate him, we've lost contact with all of his sources!'

Black scowled back at the leader. 'Not my fault,' he grumbled. 'Spooks must have done a sweep of his place, then checked Stewart Street.'

'Well that's you effectively on their radar now,' Petrie argued. 'We should just deselect you and be done with it!'

'And who's going to clean up after the attack, eh? You still need me for that, don't forget,' Black told him. His job at Folkfirst might have ceased to exist, but Black had installed systems in several other areas, notably the stadium itself. They would be in constant contact through the communication channels he had set up through a bogus company, as well as their dedicated cell phones.

'Just keep yourself out of sight, okay? And what did you do with the vehicle?'

Black gave a short laugh. 'Burned out over in a dump near Lennoxtown,' he replied. 'Don't worry about me. I can take good care of myself.' He turned to smile at the others, a look of supreme confidence on his handsome face.

'The need to deploy officers to do further background checks on every member of the Games personnel is of paramount importance,' Lorimer told the woman sitting next to him. 'I am sure that there is somebody inside the organisation itself. Someone who knows one of the terrorists.'

Joyce Roger, the Deputy Chief Constable of Police Scotland, heaved a sigh. 'It'll blow a hole in the budget,' she admitted.

'But you can't put a price on human lives,' Lorimer finished for her.

'No, our responsibility is to the public. *And* to the members of our royal family,' she added with a twist to her mouth.

'Right,' she said at last. 'How long will it take?'

Lorimer raised his eyebrows. It was nearing the end of the first week of Maggie's school holidays, and there were just over two weeks until the Games began. 'Before July the twenty-third,' he replied, mentally adding a fervent hope that this enormous undertaking would indeed be concluded before the date of the opening ceremony.

It had not been as difficult as he had expected. Finding someone who had gone through passport control at several major airports and checked into a French hotel was easier now that so much was carried out online. Now, standing here at arrivals at Glasgow International Airport, Lorimer felt more nervous than he had on their first date.

Vivien Fox had turned up twenty minutes late, just when young William Lorimer had given up all hope of the zany redhead keeping to their arrangement. He recalled almost nothing of that first teenage date, just a faint memory of her green eyes laughing at him, the way they always had.

Now he was waiting for her again, but this time they would not be leaving hand in hand but accompanied by other officers, who were waiting outside in a white car emblazoned with the Police Scotland sign.

Several passengers had moved through the area already, their luggage showing the London Heathrow tags. Vivien would have been escorted from the Bordeaux flight through security and on to the plane waiting to take her to Glasgow.

And suddenly there she was, a uniformed flight officer by her side, walking smartly through the crowds and turning heads as if she were some VIP used to special attention.

'Mrs Gilmartin.' Lorimer reached out a hand and took the woman's arm.

'Oh, William.' She gave a small laugh. 'Do we really need to be so formal?'

But the laughter died on her lips as she looked up at the expression on the tall policeman's face.

The interview room smelled of her perfume for days afterwards, but that evening, Lorimer could only concentrate on the way she was affecting his other senses.

'We have your prints on the glass phials that were recovered from my garden,' he told her, trying to keep his tone as neutral as possible. 'And the shopkeeper who sold you the ginger wine has identified you from a photograph. So you may as well tell me exactly what happened.'

Vivien Gilmartin stared at him, her gaze unfathomable. She had barely acknowledged the prescence of Alistair Wilson, sitting to one side.

'What made you do it?' Lorimer asked, looking straight into the green eyes that had bewitched him so long ago.

For a long moment the woman seemed to consider the question. Then she gave a long sigh and sat back in the chair, her whole body seeming to register an air of defeat.

'It was the right thing to do,' she said simply.

'I have to ask you for all of the details,' Lorimer said, a note of apology in his voice. 'For the tape,' he added, nodding at the recording device that sat to one side of the table in the interview room.

'Oh, the details!' Vivien raised her eyes to heaven. 'What is it they say? The devil is in the detail?'

When Lorimer did not answer, she leaned forward towards him. 'I tried so hard to get everything right, you know,' she told him, as if this was an argument in her favour. 'The ginger wine masked the taste of the other substances. He didn't feel a thing.' She shrugged as though she had done something worthy of his approbation. 'And burying them in your garden, well, I loved the irony of that!'

'Why did you kill your husband?' Lorimer repeated patiently.

'Lots of reasons,' she sneered. 'Because he was a bastard, put me through years of hell, refusing to cast me in any of his damned plays, though if I have the money to pay for a decent brief, they'll tell a jury that I did it to stop him bringing all those poor girls across from Nigeria!'

'Please will you explain this, Mrs Gilmartin?' Wilson asked smoothly.

'For the damned tape!' she snapped, throwing a glance at the older detective. 'Oh, all right. Charles was a very greedy man, that's something you have to understand about him.' She turned back to Lorimer, eyes widening as though she could still persuade him to believe her. 'It wasn't just fame and prestige that he coveted, oh no, he had to have money and more money, even when his poor old mother died and left him a fortune. Set up this theatrical scheme to bring a troupe of actors over from Africa. Nigeria, to be precise. But of course there were always going to be youngsters involved, assistants paid for this, gophers paid for that. Rubbish, of course!' She shook her head, making her long gold earrings swing from side to side. 'Charles and that horrible man with the tattoos had an arrangement that he would supply young girls for the sex trade just in time for the Commonwealth Games.' She gave him a look of disgust. 'They're not all coming over here to watch a whole lot of men running round a race track, you know.'

'If you were aware of this, why didn't you inform the police?'

Viven Gilmartin looked down and began to pick at her finger-nails.

'Surely it would have been easier to leave your husband, ask for a divorce, tell the authorities what you knew?' His voice was low and soft, a reasonable man asking a reasonable question.

There was no answer, as the woman across the table continued to examine her perfectly manicured hands.

'You wanted money too, didn't you, Foxy?' he whispered.

Vivien's head shot up at the old nickname.

'You knew all about the plan to traffic young Nigerian girls into Glasgow, didn't you? It was to have been another lucrative money-spinner. But that wasn't enough for you, was it?'

Her mouth remained tightly closed, though the look in her eyes told him his guess was correct.

'You see, I think that when you found out the extent of the the-atre costs, all you could see was that huge hole blown in your husband's fortune,' he continued, watching the green eyes glaring at him malevolently, like some cornered beast. 'I think you wanted the fame and the fortune too,' he continued. 'Only fame had eluded you. Not because Charles Gilmartin had thwarted you in your career, but for the simple reason that you weren't good enough.'

'I . . .'

'You see, we've spoken to the management of several theatre companies, and they all say the same thing. You never made the grade, did you?'

Suddenly the woman's eyes filled with tears and her expression hardened.

'You could have divorced Gilmartin, but his fortune was tied up with the African scheme, wasn't it? You wouldn't see a penny of it. Unless you killed him before he could transfer the money. You see, we checked that too,' he went on. 'Had you waited any longer, your husband would have risked all his capital on this ... venture, shall we call it? And you didn't want that to happen, did you?'

The woman opposite shook her head.

'Speak for the tape, please,' he ordered in a firm tone.

'No, I bloody well didn't!' she yelled, the mask of respectability falling from her lovely face.

Lorimer felt a pang of sorrow for the girl he had once known who had become this snarling, spitting wretch.

'But I had you fooled for a while, didn't I?' she sneered. 'Thought I was the poor grieving widow. Acted that part well enough, eh?'

Her eyes narrowed. 'Not so sure about that little wife of yours, though.'

He could see a light from the kitchen as he closed the door behind him. There had been more questions, some of them yielding answers about the man he knew as Kenneth Gordon McAlpin, answers that were being investigated in several parts of the city even as the detective superintendent made his weary way back home.

'Maggie.'

She turned from the kitchen sink, a silent question in her eyes.

Lorimer heaved a sigh as he took her into his arms.

'She's admitted it. Everything. How she did it, why ... the way

367

she planned it all down to the last detail. The school reunion, luring me in so she would be above any suspicion.'

He drew back to look into Maggie's eyes.

'You didn't fall for her act, did you, my darling?'

'I never thought she was a killer,' Maggie said at last. 'But there was something ... the way she was so possessive of you ... I thought it was just jealousy on my part,' she confessed.

'It was more than that,' Lorimer whispered. 'The thing they call a woman's intuition.' He laughed softly. 'That magical sixth sense we men lack at times. Ever think of changing careers, Mrs Lorimer?' he added admiringly. 'The police could use someone like you.'

Later, as he slept by her side, Maggie gazed at her husband. The lines were still there and the strain across his brow. Would it always be like this? The endless search for clues leading to an arrest and hopefully a conviction? Or would this troubled man find peace somewhere? They had talked well into the night, Lorimer going over what had been said in the interview room, berating himself for his lack of insight, Maggie consoling him as best she could. Now he slept, but there was always tomorrow and the next day and the next, demands made upon him that would carve the signs of care deeper and deeper into the face of the man she loved.

'She beguiled you,' Maggie said quietly. 'Perhaps she wasn't such a bad actress after all.'

CHAPTER FIFTY-SIX

It was not unusual in her job to have to meet the police, but today was different, Gayle Finnegan realised. She had arranged a rota for all the staff to be interviewed, discreetly, as instructed, and in just over fifteen minutes it would be her turn to face the plain-clothes officers who had infiltrated the building on Albion Street. Routine, her line manager had said, but there had been a hint of anxiety on the other woman's face.

'Ms Finnegan?' A tall young woman with cropped black hair stood smiling at Gayle. Her summer frock was Cath Kidston, Gayle realised, looking at the floral dress and the open-toed sandals. If this was how the police dressed nowadays for work, then perhaps the interview wouldn't be too bad after all, she told herself, sitting down in the chair that the woman had pulled out for her.

'Just a few routine questions. Gayle, isn't it? My name's Kate.'

The handshake was warm, like the policewoman's smile, and Gayle Finnegan nodded, relaxing into the chair, ready to answer whatever questions were necessary to complete this security check.

There had been the usual things: home, hobbies, people she mixed with, then her relationship with Cam.

'Anything unusual happen to you lately, Gayle? Anything odd?' The woman smiled. 'Silly wee things, even they can be significant.'

The girl thought immediately of the red mobile phone covered in numbered stickers. But that wouldn't be of any interest to them, would it?

'Gayle?' Kate, the nice police officer, was looking at her intently. 'What is it? Something that bothered you?' Her voice was kind, understanding. And at that moment, Gayle felt that Kate was just the sort of person she could confide in.

She began to tell the officer about the discovery in their bedroom, how she had worried herself sick that Cam had another woman. Or other women. But he'd said it was to do with university stuff. He was always late home these days; the dissertation seemed to cause him to stay in the university library for hours on end.

And had anything else changed? Kate had asked, and Gayle found herself confiding about how worried she was whenever her boyfriend had those terrible dreams, and yet they had never been happier together, no more fighting about how he thought the Games were a load of rubbish. Yes. He'd changed his mind about that quite suddenly, she'd agreed.

The two Aussies had been extra nice to him tonight, Cameron thought, as he sauntered through the streets of Glasgow's Merchant City, heedless of the people around him, blind to the giant green G of Glasgow 2014 on every corner. Peter had insisted on picking up the bill for dinner, too. They'd wheedled it out of him, guessing that their tour guide was still a student, telling him how much they appreciated his services, even hinting that there would be a welcome any time he cared to venture Down Under.

It was different now, he decided. They were real people, not an abstract concept. And he bit his lip as he considered how he was going to prevent Peter and Joanne MacGregor from being part of the catastrophe that was planned for the opening ceremony. He had to do it somehow, extricate himself from the plot to which he had so readily agreed all those months ago. As his feet took him towards Gayle's flat, a place he regarded these days almost as home, Cameron Gregson never noticed the two men slipping out of a parked car and following him.

Lorimer and two of Drummond's men were waiting in the kitchenette, hidden from sight, as Cameron Gregson turned his key in the door of Gayle Finnegan's flat. The girl had been taken for further questioning, her face stricken with anguish as Kate and another colleague had helped her into a waiting car.

Gregson's professor had been helpful when Lorimer had telephoned him, concerned that his postgraduate student had failed to make contact for several weeks. The final draft of his dissertation ought to have been submitted by now. What was its subject? Lorimer had asked, and the professor had told him, unable to see the expression on the detective superintendent's face when he had revealed that the young man had been writing about the persecution of Clan MacGregor and its effect on Scotland's destiny.

Drummond's eyes had lit up when the detective superintendent had relayed that particular nugget of information.

'It fits,' he'd said. 'Everything his girlfriend told us points to Gregson being part of a conspiracy. How he asked her for inside information about the Games, his seeming change of heart. She's been well and truly conned by this man,' Drummond had declared. 'And if we can access that mobile phone, then we may just be able to find the other members of the cell.'

There were officers positioned outside the flat too, waiting to apprehend Gregson in case he made a run for it. But there was no need.

'Cameron Gregson?'

'Who the ...?' The young man's face paled and he began to back away, bumping into a chair then sinking into it as though his legs had given way.

'We need to ask you some questions,' Lorimer said, bending over Gregson, pinning him with his blue glare.

'Let's begin with a certain red mobile phone that we believe is in your possession ...'

CHAPTER FIFTY-SEVEN

'I swear I never seen him!' Harry Temperland spread his skinny fingers in a pleading gesture.

'That's not what Marlene McAdam tells us,' Lorimer replied, one eyebrow raised in a sceptical gesture.

The ageing tattoo artist's head sank, his grey hair falling in straggles across the edge of the table. Lorimer waited. The man's demeanour spoke of defeat already, and it simply required patience to bring out all the information he needed.

'Said he'd kill me if I spoke to youse. Always banging on about a singing bird.' He raised watery eyes to the detective superintendent. 'Know what that means?'

Lorimer nodded. To sing like a bird was to tell on your mates, and in some criminal quarters that carried a heavy penalty.

There was a sigh, then Temperland pulled the chair a little closer to the table, his feet shuffling on the linoleum floor.

'Met up with him some years back. We were doing a re-enactment up at Bannockburn. Took a shine to me, or so I thought at the time,' he said darkly. 'Then one day he appears at the studio. Talked about buying the place. Seemed to know an awful lot more about me and the business than I had let on.' He glanced up at the detective. 'Debts were crippling me.' He shrugged. 'Had a dealer who wasn't prepared to give me any more credit, so I'd remortgaged it.' He licked his lips, then stretched out a hand to take the plastic beaker of water that he'd been given earlier. A couple of sips and he was ready to continue.

'Bought me out and kept me on as manager. Paid me properly too, I'll give him that,' he said grudgingly. 'Wanted me to do all these tattoos for him, special things, Pictish mostly. Things that had meanings.' His pale eyes looked beyond Lorimer for a moment as though he were imagining a time in pre-history when the swirling designs had been created.

'Aye, and he wanted me to have a particular design tattooed on that black girl.' He nodded, still avoiding Lorimer's stare. 'Said he'd be bringing in more nearer the time of the Games. Then Gilmartin arrived.' He took another sip of water.

'Seemed a nice man,' Temperland mused. 'Would never have thought he'd have had dealings with someone like McAlpin. Specially not in *that* line o' business.' He sighed again. 'They'd met on the set of some film or other. Don't know which one.' He looked up at Lorimer. 'Does it matter?'

The detective shook his head. Let him just carry on talking, he thought.

'Anyway, seems they cooked up this scheme between them. Gilmartin supplied the cash, McAlpin did the rest.' He shrugged. 'Never knew much about how they got the girls over here, but I did know that Gilmartin was planning to bring more over from Nigeria with a theatrical group. Then he died.' He looked at Lorimer again.

'I saw him that afternoon.' He nodded. 'Like Marlene said. McAlpin seemed happy enough afterwards. Nothing that would suggest he was about to do the man any harm. I mean, why would he? Kill the goose that laid the golden eggs?'

374

'Where is he now, Harry?' Lorimer spoke so quietly that for a moment the tattoo artist seemed not to have heard him.

'Never knew much about his private life. Never seen him with a woman in tow.' He shook his head. 'If he isn't at his house or that flat where he kept his girls, then I don't know where he'd be.' He looked straight at Lorimer. 'Really I don't,' he added.

'We can safely assume that McAlpin was dropped from the cell and that these five remaining numbers are used for contact purposes,' Drummond told him.

They were walking together in Kelvingrove Park, along a path that lay directly in front of Solly and Rosie's house. Lorimer glanced upwards at the bay windows shining in the afternoon sun. He had kept so much of this case from his friends, and from Maggie, the need for absolute security precluding even those whom he knew he could trust.

'What we don't want is for any of them to go to ground, especially Petrie. He's a slippery customer, good at covering his tracks, never in the same place twice,' Drummond said, matching Lorimer stride for stride as they walked downhill towards the river.

'Having Gregson's mobile will enable us to pinpoint their location easily enough, though.' He exchanged a grin with the detective superintendent. 'We expect to have them all in custody by the end of today,' he added.

Lorimer did not reply. It was a strange thing to be part of such an important case and yet not to be in at the capture of these men. That would be carried out by MI6 operatives with the utmost discretion and without any assistance from Police Scotland. They had done their bit and Lorimer must be satisfied with that.

'I wanted to ask you something.' Drummond stopped and

turned to the tall man by his side. 'Wondered if you had thought any more about my proposal?'

'Joining MI6?' Lorimer smiled. 'I'm flattered that you'd want me,' he said.

Drummond looked at him shrewdly. 'You are exactly the sort of man we want, Lorimer. But I'm guessing you've made your decision. Am I right?'

'Yes.' Lorimer looked back at the man and nodded. 'I've already got the best job in the world,' he said. 'And I wouldn't want to change that for anything.'

'That's the leader's call.' Rob Worsley picked up the red mobile telephone and looked across the room at McAlpin.

'Don't tell him I'm here,' the big man hissed.

Worsley glared back at him, the phone already pressed to his ear. 'Number Four,' he said. Then, with a puzzled look, he took the mobile away and looked at it. 'Died on me. Bloody battery must've gone,' he said. 'He'll not be happy with that.'

The explosives expert chewed his fingernail. None of them would be happy if they'd seen him last night, showing McAlpin his handiwork. Showing off after one too many whiskies, he thought guiltily. He'd allowed his pride to take over as he'd explained how the device worked, demonstrating the technical intricacies while thinking that a big bear like McAlpin was incapable of that sort of delicate work, no matter how interested he seemed to be.

'Are you expecting a meeting, then?' McAlpin asked.

Worsley shrugged. 'Yeah, sometime this morning. Never know where, though, do we? They'll begin to wonder where I am when I don't turn up,' he said, gnawing his lip anxiously.

A knock at the door made both men turn in alarm, exchanging worried looks.

'Answer it, I'll be in the kitchen,' McAlpin commanded.

The young woman at the door smiled sweetly, holding out a collecting tin for the Sick Children's Hospital. 'Care to help?' she asked, looking up at the white-haired man on the doorstep.

'Just a wee minute,' Worsley replied. 'Need to find some change.' He'd turned to go back inside, ready to rummage in the pocket of a jacket that was hanging on the back of a chair, when he felt the gun in his back.

'Turn around slowly and don't make a sound,' the young woman said quietly, her tone suddenly different. 'There's a car waiting outside. Walk slowly towards it and get into the back, understand?'

Worsley nodded, his head spinning. The explosives were all in the back room, McAlpin in the kitchen. He cursed himself. McAlpin! It had to be him they were looking for, and now the big man had screwed the entire operation!

For a moment he thought about making a run for it as the door opened wider, then, as two fit-looking men strolled towards him, one on either side, Rob Worsley knew it was time to admit defeat.

As he was bundled into the car, he caught sight of a woman in the front passenger seat, holding up her hand to catch the men's attention as she listened to the mobile phone pressed against her ear.

'It's Drummond,' the female officer said, looking up at the men now on either side of their prisoner. 'There's an unidentified package in the Emirates Stadium. We've to pass this one over and get our backsides across there now!'

'What about the house?'

'Later,' she said shortly. 'Get a move on.'

McAlpin stood motionless, watching and listening through the crack in the kitchen door, sweat trickling between his shoulder blades. They'd be back to clear out this place in no time. He waited until he heard the sound of the car drive off from the kerb, then let out a long sigh, unaware that he had been holding his breath. Worsley's kit was in the back room. But was there time to retrieve it?

The big man crept through the flat and turned the key in the door. The room was in darkness, a blackout blind keeping it safe from prying eyes, but he did not dare turn on a light in case one of them was lurking out there still.

He bent down and felt under the spare bed, fingers touching a long metal box that contained enough explosives to blow up the entire Commonwealth Games village and the stadiums around it. He pulled it gently, unsure just how volatile its contents might be.

If they'd got Worsley then had they managed to locate the others? His bull head rose as he listened, but there was no sound to make him suppose that there was anyone else in the flat.

Rising to his feet, he slipped out of the room and looked around. The rucksack he had made Worsley buy was lying behind the settee, still in its plastic carrier bag. It was a matter of a few minutes to stuff his new clothes into it, the metal box snugly wrapped inside. Then, with only a backward glance at the empty room, the big man closed the door behind him and began to stride down the street towards the nearest bus stop.

Kenneth Gordon McAlpin would be heading out to Glasgow Airport to finish this job, one that other terrorists had failed to complete years before; and not before time either.

Detective Superintendent Lorimer's eyebrows rose in surprise at the sound of Drummond's voice. He hadn't expected to hear from the MI6 man again so soon.

'We've got them,' he said shortly. 'Thank God! All of them except McAlpin.'

Lorimer could hear the strain in the man's voice. They were only days away from the opening ceremony.

'You'd better get your officers out there now. Their explosives man told us he was harbouring McAlpin. False alarm out at the Emirates Stadium held us up,' he grumbled. 'By the time we searched Worsley's place there was no sign of McAlpin. But he can't be far away. *And* he's carrying the makings of the bomb they were about to use.'

Lorimer opened his mouth to thank him, but the call had already been ended. Now it was a matter for the police to apprehend this fugitive, a man who was not only a dangerous killer but was also suspected of carrying some lethal explosives on his person.

In a matter of minutes he had alerted several units, emergency services and firearms amongst them, plus their own anti-explosives team. Every train station, bus depot and airport was on alert through the British Transport Police, and many eyes were watching screens linked to the hundreds of CCTV cameras in and around the city. Thanks to Marlene McAdam, they also had a photofit of McAlpin's current appearance: a big thickset man with a mere fuzz of ginger on his newly shaven head, the tattoos more than likely hidden from sight.

Lorimer recalled the night on the Cathkin Braes when McAlpin had felled him to the ground. His fingers curled into fists as he thought about where the man would go. Would he have an alias of some sort by now? More than likely these groups were well prepared, with false names on a variety of passports.

His mind worked furiously, trying to put himself into McAlpin's shoes.

If he were trying to make an escape armed with a box of highly dangerous explosives, where would he go to inflict maximum damage? The thought was no sooner in his head than he had grabbed his jacket and was heading for the car park.

'Drummond, I think I know where he could be heading,' he said, the security service's mobile pressed to his ear as he hurried towards the Lexus. 'Can you meet me there?'

He was probably going to be booked for speeding, though that was the last thing on his mind as the Lexus raced along the outside lane towards Glasgow Airport. There would be no time to park anywhere properly. Barely enough time for Drummond to alert the Transport Police about their intentions. And the detective superintendent knew that it might be only a matter of minutes before they intercepted their quarry.

The bus rolled to a halt beside the concrete island, its door sighing open to allow the passengers to climb down and wait for the driver to take their luggage from the hold. Only a few moved away from the crowd, those with backpacks or briefcases, who headed towards the entrance of the airport. Destinations awaited them all, places where the sun shone more brightly or where home beckoned after time spent in Bonny Scotland. The mood was subdued, the passengers in that nowhere time between bus and plane, a feeling of patience building up for the procedures of passport control and body searches that were part of travelling in a world where terrorism held sway.

One, a tall, burly man with a black baseball cap emblazoned with the Glasgow 2014 logo, took a pair of sunglasses from his pocket and put them on, hardly breaking his stride. He had broken away from his fellow passengers and now he was crossing the last strip of tarmac that separated him from the entrance to the airport.

Once inside, he would merge in with the crowd, set down his rucksack beside a line of waiting passengers and saunter back out again into the sunshine. As the door to the airport grew closer, his fingers inched towards his pocket, feeling the bulge of the hidden device that would detonate the bomb.

A silver Lexus screeched to a halt yards from the man hurrying towards the door marked *Departures*. McAlpin caught sight of a familiar figure running towards him, followed closely by a sandy-haired man who was looking straight at him.

He hesitated for a moment, then stopped, raising the backpack in both hands.

'Come on then,' he sneered, waving the bag above his head. 'One more step and I'll blow your brains out!'

The tall man continued to walk towards him as though unconcerned for his own safety, the other retreating, waving people back.

'Hand it over, McAlpin. There's been enough bloodshed already,' Lorimer said.

The big man shook his head and grinned. 'Take you with me, won't I?' He laughed out loud. 'Well here you are. Catch!'

The backpack flew through the air, a dark shape against the pale blue sky, and for a moment both men seemed to freeze as they watched its rise and descent.

Then, as McAlpin continued to look up, Lorimer rushed at the man, grabbing his legs in a well-timed rugby tackle.

As the two men crashed to the ground, Lorimer was aware of the sound of running feet. Then other hands reached down, Drummond and the transport officers intent on containing the man who was groaning in a heap on the ground.

As they hauled McAlpin to his feet, Lorimer did not notice the dark baseball cap rolling away from him, its logo turning and turning until it came to rest, the green G winking in the summer sunshine.

He looked at Drummond, who was standing guard beside the backpack containing the explosives, a question in his eyes.

'The area's been evacuated,' the MI6 man told him.

Drummond turned to acknowledge the man in khaki uniform who had appeared by their side. 'Right, Sergeant. It's all yours,' he said, taking a few steps aside, allowing the soldier to examine the backpack.

'I reckon he hadn't the brains to set this thing off,' the sergeant told the detective superintendent. 'At least, let's hope not.'

Drummond raised his eyebrows and grinned, then sketched a salute of farewell as he made to follow the officer from the bomb squad who was carrying the backpack away.

Lorimer stood there for a long moment, a solitary figure gazing at the airport buildings, trying not to imagine the smoke and rubble that could have been there instead.

CHAPTER FIFTY-EIGHT

23 July 2014

'Pity it didn't work out the way we'd hoped,' Peter MacGregor sighed. 'Wonder what happened to the boy?'

'A girl will be behind it somewhere, I bet you,' Joanne replied, giving her husband's arm a squeeze. 'Handsome young fella like that. Anyway, we got tickets, just not so close to the royal box as he promised.'

'What annoys me most is not having my dirk,' Peter grumbled, indicating the top of his kilt stocking where the *sgian dubh* should have been inserted.

'Probably wouldn't have got it past security,' replied Joanne. 'My, but they sure are careful, aren't they? Never expected the military to search everyone's baggage and put us through those X-ray machines. Like going through the airport all over again. Anyway, here we are,' she said excitedly, gazing round at the ranks of people above and below them, the stadium filled to capacity for the opening ceremony of the Glasgow Commonwealth Games. The excitement was almost tangible as the crowd gave an appreciative roar, then everyone got to their feet.

'Is that ... ?' Joanne's eyes turned to a familiar figure entering the front row below them.

'Sure is, darling.' Peter grinned, clapping and cheering with the rest of the enormous crowd. Then, as a band struck up the first notes of the National Anthem, the sound of cheering was replaced by a wave of voices singing.

Joanne felt her husband's fingers entwine with her own and tears misted the woman's eyes as she watched the royal figure standing motionless and dignified below them.

Asa pressed her face to the window of the Land Rover, ignoring the man and woman who had come all the way to bring her safely home. A holiday, they'd said, the Nigerian officer interpreting their words for the girl. *We would like to see the animals and the birds in your country*, they had explained. And so she had been content to travel with Bill and Maggie, her two new friends, plus the lady from the embassy who was there acting as a translator.

The dust from the red earth blew up in twin clouds either side of the vehicle as they trundled over the pitted track, scrubby trees showing where elephants had been, branches split and broken as they foraged for food. Sometimes the Scottish woman would exclaim at the sight of a baboon running for cover as the Land Rover came too close; often the man was looking skywards, binoculars trained on some hawk or other, things that Asa had taken for granted all her young life but that seemed to be a new treat for these white people.

Looking up, Asa stared at the sky above her, an African sky, wider than the ocean they had crossed. And it seemed to the girl that the blue heavens were holding out their mighty hands, enfolding her in a blessing: the promise of sun, rain and starlight.

The vehicle turned at last into a flat clearing surrounded by a cluster of simple whitewashed houses, their roofs made from sheets of corrugated metal. Beyond them, past fields of tall green maize, she caught a glimpse of the thatched huts where her grandparents had been born.

A young girl, her hair braided tightly to her head, appeared from behind one of the buildings, then waved and yelled as the Land Rover came to a stop. In response to her cry, people began to emerge from the houses, until there was a small crowd of men, women and children running along the path towards them, their clothes bright splashes of colour against the dusty ground.

Asa stepped out, her legs weary after so much sitting.

Everything seemed so much smaller than she remembered. The few houses were as nothing compared to the city where she had been, the twittering weaver birds simply part of the landscape after the noises of traffic and shouting people.

'You're home now, Asa,' Maggie said, and the girl turned, hearing her voice. *Home*, the woman had said.

Asa smiled. She had learned only a few words of English, but as she walked towards the village and the welcoming faces of her African friends, she knew that this was one word she would never forget.

EPILOGUE

Daylight dazzles in its fading
a yellow sky above dry yellow bush,
tawny, like the lions
coming to feed at the waterhole.
A tree full of twittering weavers
stands out starkly
in this African gloaming.
Then, like a gauzy veil
the blue deepens
and the first star sparks.
The horizon spreads its burning fire
Like a sudden wind – though it is windless.
Water reflects back a vision
of ink-black trees
drowned in molten lava.
Then frogs and crickets chorus
louder and persistent
as the veil thickens into darkness.

ACKNOWLEDGEMENTS

It never fails to astonish me how willingly so many people give of their time and expertise to assist me in researching my work. Without them the novels would lack those authentic touches that I believe bring my stories to life. I have many people to acknowledge, experts in their own fields, letting me share the secrets of their professions. Several Scottish police officers must be thanked, including those in the anti terrorist squad at Stewart Street; DC Mairi Milne, whose words of wisdom keep me on the right track, and DI Bob Frew, who never minds my sporadic emails coming out of the blue; Dr Marjorie Turner, friend and consultant forensic pathologist without whose aid Rosie would be standing waving a scalpel in the air and not knowing what to do with it; Baillie Liz Cameron for introducing me to the right people; Jim Doyle of Glasgow City Council for sending me the extensive information about child trafficking; David Grevemberg's team at the Glasgow 2014 offices, especially Janette Harkess and Matthew Williams; David Robertson for being so willing to assist me in forensic matters; my friend Kate MacDougall for pointing me in the right direction about child protection; Stuart Wrigley of Terry's Tattoo Studio for being so willing to teach me all about the art of tattooing and even allowing himself to slip between the pages of the story as himself; Dr Fiona Wylie for the sound information about toxins and their effects; Professor Jim Fraser for his wonderful suggestions about explosive devices. And there are others whose support is invaluable to me: my great editor Jade Chandler, who is continually helpful; David Shelley (who seems happy to have me as his longest-standing author); my agent, the one and only Jenny Brown, who understands all the stresses and strains that are part of being a writer; Moira, without whom my diary would be a shambles, and the rest of the LB team, who do so much work; my family, who accept me despite the awful things I do to people between the pages of books, especially my husband, Donnie, who is the best roadie this crime-writing lady could ever wish for.